Under a Greek Spell

Simone Hubbard

Copyright © 2019 Simone Hubbard

The moral right of the author has been asserted.

Apart from any fair dealing for the purposes of research or private study,
or criticism or review, as permitted under the Copyright, Designs and Patents
Act 1988, this publication may only be reproduced, stored or transmitted, in
any form or by any means, with the prior permission in writing of the
publishers, or in the case of reprographic reproduction in accordance with
the terms of licences issued by the Copyright Licensing Agency. Enquiries
concerning reproduction outside those terms should be sent to the publishers.

This is a work of fiction. Names, characters, businesses, places, events
and incidents are either the products of the author's imagination
or used in a fictitious manner. Any resemblance to actual persons,
living or dead, or actual events is purely coincidental.

Matador
9 Priory Business Park,
Wistow Road, Kibworth Beauchamp,
Leicestershire. LE8 0RX
Tel: 0116 279 2299
Email: books@troubador.co.uk
Web: www.troubador.co.uk/matador
Twitter: @matadorbooks

ISBN 978 1789017 328

British Library Cataloguing in Publication Data.
A catalogue record for this book is available from the British Library.

Printed on FSC accredited paper
Printed and bound in Great Britain by 4edge Limited
Typeset in 11pt Minion Pro by Troubador Publishing Ltd, Leicester, UK

Matador is an imprint of Troubador Publishing Ltd

*In loving memory of my husband Martin Hubbard
who passed away shortly after I started writing this book.*

Prologue

Pamela

It's not very often that I can say this, but I was rendered speechless two hours ago.

My daughters Helen and Stephanie, and my hubby Michael, have organised this wonderful surprise birthday party for me at our local golf club. I didn't have a clue. I've no idea how they kept it a surprise. Thinking back, in the last few weeks, there *have* been a couple of conversations that ended abruptly when I entered the room.

My friends from work are here too. I'm a part-time nurse in the A & E department of our local hospital. I really can't imagine how they've kept it a secret. They can't even do the Secret Santa without revealing who's bought what for who.

I'd hoped to be retiring at sixty. That pipe dream went out of the window with all the hullabaloo of the banking crisis. Michael is in the same boat. Luckily, we didn't have all our eggs in one basket, so to speak, and we can retire together in a couple of years' time and travel the world.

Because I love travelling so much, Helen's arranged a wonderful Greek islands cruise on a clipper ship, which sets sail on 15 May. It's a present from everyone for my sixtieth birthday and for our fortieth wedding anniversary, which will be in the summer. I think they've all had enough of me rattling on about Greek islands, Greek mythology, Greek gods – in fact, anything using the G-word. Michael and I have been to a few of the islands over the years but there are so many more to see. The clipper ship cruise is perfect as it covers a good number of islands, especially the smaller ones that don't have an airport. A few months ago, Helen asked me to book a couple of weeks off work. I thought she was going to send us on one of her freebie trips. I'd no idea she was planning such an extravagant holiday. She's thirty-three now and has worked in the travel industry since leaving school. She's senior management at a local travel agent, so she was able to pull some strings. It's a perk of her job, to which she's very dedicated. She threw herself into her work after her best friend died of cancer. It was her way of dealing with it.

I do think her boss, Daniel, takes advantage of her at times. He's always changing his mind at the last minute about one thing or another, which often results in Helen cancelling personal commitments and letting down her friends and family. She's always at the office early and never finishes on time. A career is all well and good, but, as I keep subtly reminding her, if she wants children she's got to recognise that she's not getting any younger. A good starting point would be a stable relationship, but Helen seems to be struggling to find 'the one'. There's no sign of her latest boyfriend today. Michael and I still haven't met him and they've been seeing each other for a while now.

Then there's Stephanie. She's a couple of years younger than Helen. She'd been married five years when she broached the shall-we-start-a-family topic with her husband. Richard decided that he didn't want kids and walked out on her in January.

Of course, Michael thinks I should mind my own business, but, at this rate, we'll be grandparents to sperm-bank grandchildren, like Sally at work. That's all we heard about for months. She'd suddenly come out with the most bizarre statements, such as 'Just think, the baby could have blue blood,' or 'The baby might turn out to be a talented musician.' We switched off in the end, what with all the different outcomes this grandchild of hers could have.

No party, of course, would be complete without some family members and, as the saying goes, you can choose your friends but you can't choose your family. My older sister Angela and I are like chalk and cheese. When we reached our forties, we agreed to disagree and move on. She's got an amazing memory, which is a pain in the neck most of the time. Talk about how elephants never forget – she must have been one in a former life. I can't imagine how Tim, her husband, has put up with her for almost forty-five years. But his repertoire of replies speaks for itself: 'Yes, dear', 'Whatever you say, dear', 'Of course, dear...'

Angela does, however, have two very adorable grandchildren, Jack and Lily. Jack's five and absolutely full of mischief. Lily's three and angelic looking, with blue eyes and curly blonde hair. She's a little bit tamer than Jack but I'm sure she'll come out of her shell when she starts preschool in September. They're running around at the moment, chasing each other and popping balloons. Every time one bursts, Lily runs crying to her Uncle Tom. He's Angela's son and he's with his latest girlfriend, Skye.

I had trouble remembering her name until Angela sniped, 'It's not difficult, Pamela. If she married Tom, she'd be "Skye Bridge."' That made me laugh, but Angela wasn't for seeing the funny side. She didn't find it particularly funny, either, when I discovered that there's a Tom Uglys Bridge in Sydney and Snapchatted it to her.

At the moment, Skye is flailing her arms about trying to keep the children away from her cream dress. Angela informs me that there's no way on God's earth that Tom will have children. He absolutely hates them with a passion. So it looks like he and Skye are well suited. It's such a shame. Just think, they could have Brooklyn and Sydney Bridge to complete the set.

It looks like Tom's trying to coerce Jack and Lily to play over near his sister Amy, their mum, and Angela's eldest child. She's here with her husband. It doesn't look like they've slept for months. I'm surmising that the last time they slept properly was when Jack and Lily had a sleepover at Angela's. It took Angela and Tim a week to get over that. Angela said that Michael and I could have them next time, 'Being as though you have no grandchildren.'

Our neighbours from either side of us are here and were in on the secret too. One of the most staggering things is that neither side let the cat out of the bag despite me seeing them nearly every day and telling them that I was having a low-key birthday with just close family.

Ron, our neighbour on the right, helped Michael and the girls decorate the golf club with banners and balloons yesterday. Meanwhile, Jen, Ron's wife, was putting the finishing touches on the cake. They'd booked me into a beauty salon for some serious pampering to get me out of the way. I was there for almost three hours.

Stephanie was assigned the task of organising the cake; she somehow found out that Jen is a fantastic baker. I've told Jen loads of times to get herself on *Bake Off*. The cake has been given centre stage and has had more photos taken of it than I have. I've heard Stephanie trying to take credit for the golfing theme idea too. It's a putting green, with '60' piped on it in the shape of little golf balls and, underneath that, a couple of golf clubs crossed over. I can't imagine how Jen's been able to contain herself. She's certainly enjoying the attention her masterpiece is receiving, although I did hear someone say that Ron helped her make it.

I'm just shocked and absolutely delighted that so many friends and family are here. Good job I've made an effort with a pretty 'spring collection' dress and make-up. That's probably why they said we were going to the posh hotel down the road – so I didn't turn up in my jeans. I bought the dress with Steph, who's a sales assistant at Debenhams. I remember thinking she was being very particular as she made me buy matching shoes and handbag.

I did also think it was a bit strange when Michael wanted to pop to the golf club to drop some things off en route to the meal, especially when he insisted I go in with him. I thought I'd be polite and see who was about. I was speechless when he opened the door. I thought, 'What's everyone doing here?' I've been in a whirlwind ever since.

* * *

Ooh, the lights have been dimmed. Helen and Steph are standing at the door, holding the cake, which is now alight with candles.

'Hush everyone! After three,' Helen shouts. 'One, two, three! Happy birthday to you, happy birthday to you, happy birthday dear Pamela … Pam … Mum … Aunty Pamelaaaa, happy birthday to you!'

Helen and Stephanie are whispering, 'Make a wish, Mum.' I take a deep breath, close my eyes and blow out my candles, nearly setting fire to myself in the process. A little voice in my head is saying, 'Be careful what you wish for, Pamela.' But it's too late. I've made my wish and now there's no going back…

Chapter 1

Stephanie

Oh, excitement, I've got a text! My phone's just pinged to let me know that someone in the world wants to tell me something. My heart does a little flutter. It's probably just one of those silly messages about making a compensation claim, but you never know. I put the washing up on hold and peel off my bright yellow rubber gloves to see who wants me. I'm willing to take the risk that I could ultimately be disappointed, and that my time would be better spent sticking with the washing up instead of being hoodwinked into looking at a text. I open my phone and it's a text off my sister, Helen. I press the little message box to open it.

> Hi, how does 10 nights
> in the Caribbean sound?
> Flying on 18 May xx

Oh my God, is she serious? When I was moaning about having two weeks off work with nowhere to go, I didn't think Helen was even listening, let alone planning something as elaborate as this. Within seconds, I'm speed-dialling her number. I'm fit to burst –

1

a holiday, and not just any old holiday, but one to the Caribbean, where I've always wanted to go.

She answers within one ring. 'Hi, Steph! Thought you'd be straight on the phone with that invitation. What do you think?' Helen sounds very pleased with herself.

'How the hell have you managed to wangle this? The Caribbean – that's amazing! Where exactly are we going?' My head whirs with the excitement of it all. A few minutes ago I was doing the washing up and now I'm being whisked off to the Caribbean.

'I've wangled it, as you so nicely put it, by working some very long hours. When you said you'd got time booked off work and nowhere to go, I had a light-bulb moment. You've been through so much lately that I thought I'd treat you to a cruise round the Caribbean. Cruising is a new line that we're adding next year. I volunteered to try it out and do the review.'

Suddenly, I don't feel so good. I sit down. My head's spinning and I already feel seasick just at the mention of the word 'cruise'. 'Sorry, Helen, did you just say cruuuuuuuuz?'

The word resonates round in my head. Cruise, she said cruise. I can't believe she's said cruise. Surely she remembers my boat dramas from childhood? She can't seriously think that I could or would willingly go on a bloody cruise.

'Yes, Steph, a cruise. Isn't it wonderful? A different island every day, starting in Barbados, with two nights in a five-star hotel on the south coast. Then visiting St Lucia, St Martin, Tortola, St Thomas, Curaçao, Grenada and then back to Barbados for another two nights on the west coast before we head home.' Helen reels the amazing itinerary off in her professional work-voice. The place names trip off her tongue like the well-travelled professional she is. 'And we'll be flying business class. That will be an amazing experience for you... Stephanie, are you still there?'

'Yes, I'm here. I'm really sorry, Helen, I don't do boats and I can't possibly go on a cruise with you. I've never got over that time when our boat was put under arrest by the Spanish military and we were all disembarked in Bilbao at gunpoint. It's scarred me for life. Then there was the time I woke up alone in our cabin. I was found wandering round the corridors by a member of staff. I was searching frantically for Mum, Dad and you. I thought you'd all left me. Oh, and the time I lost Barney, my little blue bear, on yet another holiday. I had to be carried off the boat, crying hysterically, by Dad. And did I mention my awful seasickness? It takes me a week to walk in a straight line again. I'm sorry, Helen, but me and boats are a no go. I'm sure I drowned on the *Titanic* in a previous life.'

'Right, Steph, if you've quite finished. I know you've had more than your fair share of grievances on boats. I was there, remember? But look on the bright side: we didn't get shot, you didn't fall overboard, you can have an injection for seasickness and Barney turned up eight months later in one of Dad's shoes! You need to face your fears, not run away from them. So what about some holiday-clothes shopping?'

There's no arguing with Helen. I'm going on a cruise, whether I like it or not. I suppose I can take some seasickness tablets the minute I get on the boat. Let's face it, the Caribbean Sea should be pretty calm. Hopefully we won't get so drunk that I topple overboard. Barney can stay at home. I don't even know where he is. I'm assuming he's with all the other bears in the spare room… Note to self, check where Barney is.

'We could go tomorrow. I'm rostered off,' I reply, feeling defeated but slightly excited again at the chance of seeing some sun.

I need to be realistic. There's no way I could afford to go away on this scale, and it's just the tonic I need after the last few months. Not to mention that it's been the most miserable, wet winter and spring ever. Everyone's talking about getting away for a week in the sun and here I am, being ungrateful about a free cruise around the Caribbean with my sister. Get a bloody grip, woman. I constantly moaned to Richard, my soon to be ex-husband, about travelling abroad more. But the first opportunity that comes my way, I get into a right state. Be positive, Stephanie, embrace all opportunities. In fact, remember your New Year's mantra: go with the flow, go where the wind takes you. I just didn't expect the wind to take me that far and on a bloody cruise.

'Sorry, no, I can't do tomorrow. James is coming over tonight and is hopefully stopping. I don't want to push him out of the door, if you get my drift.' Helen's voice has changed into its James mode. I bristle at the mention of his name.

'Have you got this arrangement in writing, Helen? Going on past form, he'll cancel and you'll be spending another evening on your own,' I retort, and immediately regret it.

He's let Helen down so many times. I've never even met the guy and I could happily throttle him or hit him over the head with his trumpet or whatever it is that he plays in his jazz band. He works at the same travel agency as Helen. I don't think it helps that she's a senior manager and James is junior to her. It's always at the back of my mind that he's using her to get promoted. But when I've half mentioned this idea to Helen, she dismisses it as ridiculous. I've lost count of the 'Yes, but this' and 'Yes, but that' excuses that she has at the ready for every time he lets her down. They say love is blind, and in Helen's case it most definitely is.

'Yes, he's just texted,' she answers in a dreamy voice.

'Right, back to shopping.' I try and reel her out of her trance. 'What about Sunday? Can you pick me up at 11? We can have brunch at Kouros cafe where we've been wanting to try.'

'Yes, Sunday works for me. We can also check out the photos from Mum's party and choose some for an album that I'm doing for her.'

'It was a fab party, wasn't it? She loved it. Her face, though, when she first came in the room! I hope you've got a good photo of that.'

'I most certainly have, and many others. Listen, I'll have to dash and get this meal started. Otherwise, James will get here and the food will still be cooking. I'm already peckish, anyway.'

'Well, there's a first for everything. You're feeling peckish? You must be sickening for something. Couldn't you have James as a starter, if you get my drift? On second thoughts, let's not go there. See you Sunday. Let's say 10.30 – we'd better set off earlier as the shops shut early.'

'Yes, I suppose 10.30 would be better. Isn't your keep-fit class tonight?'

'Yes, I've just had my tea and was washing up when you texted me. By the time you have your meal, I'll have eaten, thrown myself round a hall and be ready to eat again.'

'Right, Steph, I really must get some food prepared. I'll see you Sunday. Enjoy your day off tomorrow.'

'And you. I hope James appreciates your efforts.'

'Yep, me too. Bye.'

I wish I could get enthusiastic about James but I can't. He didn't even come to Mum's surprise birthday bash. He was working, apparently, but he could have swapped days off like I had to. As the song says, that don't impress me much.

Anyway, I've got a fitness class to attend. The last few months of comfort eating have caught up with me. Now I've got a very good incentive to go – I need to get bikini-ready. Well, maybe tankini-and-kaftan-ready.

Chapter 2

Stephanie

'Earth to Helen, earth to Helen, come in, are you receiving me?'

She's very quiet this morning and has hardly said two words on the way here. We're having brunch at the new Greek cafe we wanted to try before hitting town for our shopping spree. Helen seems to be on another planet. I haven't mentioned James but I know he'll be at the bottom of this absenteeism.

'Sorry, did you just say something, Steph?' She glances up from the rabbit rocket, as I call it, that she's been pushing round her plate for the last ten minutes.

'I was just saying it seems very quiet in here today, a bit like you. What's up with you? I'm all excited about our holiday, even though it involves a boat, and you're limper than that lettuce. Let me have one guess – could it be something to do with James, by any chance?'

'Oh, don't, Steph. You're always putting a downer on him.'

I tut and take a deep breath in and out while I contemplate a tactful answer. 'That's because he's always doing something to let *you* down. What happened the other night?'

There's a big sigh as the lettuce is nudged round the plate yet again. 'He didn't show up,' she replies eventually, lifting her head and looking forlorn.

'What do you mean, he didn't show up? I thought he was almost on his way when he texted you.'

'I know. I texted him two hours later to say I was hungry and could he give me an ETA. He replied, "Really, really sorry. Just finished. I've let you down again." I rang him straight away but it just went to voicemail.'

'I bet it bloody well did! He's stringing you along, Helen. I keep telling you he's not interested.'

'Yes, but why not? When we're together, we have a really good time. He cooks dinner, we have plenty to talk about, he plays his trumpet and sings to me, he's amazing in…'

'Whoa, I don't need to know the rest, thank you. I bet your neighbours love him blasting out tunes on his trumpet.'

'No one's said anything.'

'No, I'm not surprised they haven't confronted you about the music man, knowing how you'll react. You'd be telling them where you'd stick that trumpet. Which makes me understand even less why you let him walk all over you. If I or any of your friends let you down like this, you'd soon put us in our place. But James gets away with it.'

'He did leave this on my desk at work with a note to apologise.' Helen pulls out a necklace from under her top.

Admittedly, it's very nice. But I'm not impressed by him trying to buy her affection. 'It's lovely, Helen, but that's not the point.'

'Yes, but he's got a lot on his plate with work and playing in the band…' Helen's off again, the defence for the accused.

'Yes, Helen, we've all got a lot on our plates. What gives James special dispensation? In fact, don't even answer that. I can't bear listening to another load of excuses for him. Let's pay for this food and get on with some retail therapy before I say something that I might later regret in court – like, I'm going to kill him.'

Chapter 3

Helen

We've been in the clothes department of Debenhams for about half an hour now. Steph works for the company but in another store. She's planning to use her staff discount card and she's having a field day. She shot off the minute we arrived, like a kid in a sweetshop. I'm just wandering around, picking things up and putting them back.

My head isn't in shopping mode. It's in why-has-James-let-me-down-again mode. I keep going over it, picking over conversations, wondering if I've missed some vital signs. But no, there's nothing; it's a complete mystery. I've still not heard anything from him since the other night. Steph and my closest friends have all told me that I'm not to text him under any circumstances. I'm naturally ignoring this advice and have just written him a text while Steph's been running around the store like a woman possessed. She's heading back in my direction, grinning like a Cheshire cat. I just about manage to press send and slip my phone into my bag. If she catches me texting him, she'll confiscate my phone and delete his number.

'Oh, there you are. Thought I'd lost you. What do you think of this? Is it a bit too long? Thought I could wear it with these…'

She shows me a nice long summer dress. But, oh my God, the heels on those shoes.

'Bloody hell, Stephanie, are you trying to end up in casualty? You'll do yourself a mischief in them.'

'Hmm, I suppose you're right. I just don't want you towering over me.'

'I'd hardly say that me being two inches taller means I'll be towering over you. What about lower heels and a shorter dress?'

'I really like this dress. I could always have it taken up, I suppose. I know someone who'll do it,' she answers cheerily. 'Listen, I've got loads of stuff to try on. The assistant's put it to one side for me. Can you come and give me your opinion? You're much better at putting outfits together than I am. Speaking of which, where are the things you're trying on?'

'I'm fine, I've got plenty of holiday clothes,' I answer half-heartedly.

'Oh, Helen, I wish you'd snap out of this trance that you're in. This just isn't like you. You'd normally have loads of outfits for me to swoon over by now.'

'I know, I'm sorry. Maybe we can pop into Michaela's Boutique after we've sorted you out. Right, lead the way. Let's see these clothes.'

Steph's got so many things to try on that we have to split them into batches. I sit on a faux leather cube outside the curtain and she bobs out to show me tops, skirts, trousers, dresses, tankinis, and swimsuits.

I'm so glad I've persuaded her to come away with me. The last year has been awful for her. She wanted to start a family and Richard kept stalling, saying, 'I'm not ready to settle down yet'. He then walked out in January admitting that he didn't want kids, which left Steph in bits. He's living with his best mate and it looks like the next step will be divorce. They've had some counselling but neither of them wants to compromise.

She's now immersed herself in going to the gym and to the various classes that are included in her membership. She has a brilliant circle of friends, and they go out all the time, leaving their husbands or partners babysitting. Sometimes they'll go out for the day and take the kids. She's a natural with them and she'd make a brilliant mum. Our own mum is disappointed that neither of us has any kids yet. She's desperate to become a grandmother. She used to always be dropping hints in front of me and Steph, but she's gone very quiet since Richard left. The situation is made worse by her sister Angela, who already has her grandkids Jack and Lily. I can tell Mum is envious of her sister because we haven't yet produced grandchildren for her to spoil.

While Steph is trying on the entire stock of clothes in the shop, I've got the store radio to amuse me. In-store offers are being announced in between Steph's outfit appearances. There are some knives on offer in the basement. I hope Steph's not heard that. She'll be down there like a shot and then she'll pay James a visit, shouting, 'Keep away from my sister or I'll set my dad on you!'

The adverts finish and a song comes on that sums up my feelings – 'Only Love Can Hurt Like This'. Two sales assistants are chatting away. My ears prick up when I hear the name 'James' mentioned. It follows me everywhere I go. I'm trying to earwig but my train of thought is broken by a rather pathetic-sounding whimper.

'Helen, are you there? Can you help me?' Steph's voice is muffled and she sounds a little distressed.

'What's up, sis?' I whip the curtain back. I'm confronted with Steph, who I can't actually see because she's disappeared into the long dress.

'I'm stuck in the dress. I think you'll have to cut me out,' she whimpers.

'Oh, don't be such a drama queen. I'm sure we'll wiggle you out somehow.' I can't help laughing uncontrollably.

'It's not bloody well funny, Helen! Mum's friend ended up in casualty after getting trapped in a dress and falling over.'

'Well, it just goes to show you why we need risk assessments for everything. Now, stay still. Is there a zip somewhere?' I'm still snorting with laughter.

'Yes, at the back. And stop laughing, it's not funny.'

'Not to you, Steph, but you can't see yourself. In fact, I'll just take a photo and then you'll see why I'm laughing.' I quickly pull my phone out of my bag and take a photo of Steph. This could be one for Facebook later.

'Don't you bloody well dare take a photo of me like this! Just get me out!'

'Okay, I'll try. Breathe in and I'll unzip you… It's coming. Stop wriggling about, you silly moo.' Now Steph's laughing too and I can't keep hold of the zip. 'Why are you laughing? I can't unzip the dress.'

'It's what you just said – "It's coming". I was just thinking that people are going to wonder what's going on in here!'

Right on cue, one of the assistants asks, 'Are you two all right in there?' at which point we both collapse into fits of hysterical laughter, barely able to answer 'Yes, we're fine, thanks!'

Chapter 4

Stephanie

It takes about ten minutes to get me out of the dress. We figure it out eventually, and finally queue up at the tills with all my purchases. I'm just glad I've got a staff discount card.

'Yes, please!' shouts a rather dishy assistant.

I glance at his name badge. My brain can't quite compute that his name is James. Un-bloody-believable. I've just got Helen laughing for the first time in I don't know how long and now we're being served by a gorgeous guy called James, who I want instantly to dislike.

'So, how are you two ladies today?' he asks in the most seductive voice I've ever heard. He's got an Irish accent that has made my knees go weak.

'Oh, we're great, thanks. Are you new here?' I can't believe this sex-on-legs guy with the voice of an angel is working at the store down the road from mine. Why on earth isn't he at our place? The hours would fly by.

'Oh, yes, I've just moved over from Ireland – you can probably tell from the accent,' he replies. He starts to scan my things through and packs them neatly in a bag. 'Are you going on holiday, ladies, or are you expecting a heatwave here?'

Before I can answer, Helen has got in on the act. She's already whispered in my ear that the guy is drop-dead gorgeous. 'Actually, I'm taking my sister on a Caribbean cruise.'

'Oh, fab. I went on a cruise around the Caribbean a few years ago. It was amazing. You'll love it,' he replies.

I get in quick before Helen starts taking over. 'I'm a bit apprehensive, if I'm honest. I get seasick for a start.'

'Oh, don't let that worry you. I'm the same. That ferry crossing from Ireland always makes me ill, but I was fine on the calm Caribbean Sea. Just think about all those exotic places you'll get to see. So, now, that will be £169.69.' Helen bursts into laughter, and James understandably looks puzzled. 'Was it something I said?' he asks, completely oblivious to the 69-69 bit that's obviously tickled Helen.

'No, it's my crazy sister's sense of humour. Just ignore her.'

'Would you like one of our store cards to receive ten per cent off your purchase today?'

'Well, actually I have this.' I hand over my staff card.

James looks a bit flustered, 'I'm so sorry. You should have said you worked here before I started prattling on about discounts and, well, everything else.'

'I actually work at the store up the road. You were just doing your job. I'll probably see you when we get back and we can exchange tales of the high seas.'

'Yes, that would be good. Enjoy your trip,' he says, smiling and giving us a cheeky wink.

I can't turn round quickly enough. I must be as red as a beetroot by now. 'Think I'm ready for a coffee, Helen, and a sit down. My legs have gone to jelly.'

'I'm with you there. He was absolutely gorgeous. Shame about his name, but then everywhere I turn these days there's a James. While you were having your dress drama, the two dressing-room assistants were talking about a James who, I think, works here. It's got to be him. All I caught was, "Oh, it must have been awful for him". Then you started whimpering for help to get you out of that bloody dress so I missed the rest of the story.'

'Oh, sooo sorry to have a crisis while you were earwigging sales-assistant gossip. Come on, lets grab a coffee here.'

Our coffee revives us. Helen is finally in high spirits and ready to hit her favourite, Michaela's Boutique. It's a bit fancy for my liking, and expensive, but she can easily afford it on her wages.

We stroll in and sink into the carpets. The boutique just oozes panache, with its chandeliers and beautiful vases of fresh flowers. Helen is in her element as she chats to Michaela about the latest must have items. Helen selects some classy separates and a couple of exquisite dresses while I examine the price tags, saying '*How* much?' every two minutes.

I don't think I'd pay these ridiculous amounts even if I won the lottery. I mean, £200 for a dress – it's just insane. And that's a cheap dress in here. Helen keeps reminding me about quality and I keep reminding Helen that fashions change before quality has time to matter. She just tuts and shakes her head. I think Michaela gets the measure of me and subtlety tells Helen and I all about her next venture which will be a mid-price clothes shop with home interior items.

'Right,' Helen declares, 'I'm going to try these on. Are you coming with me or are you going to continue your embarrasing "How Much" campaign?'

'No, I'll come with you. Might as well enjoy the luxurious changing rooms even if I'm just sitting outside.'

'Come on, Steph. I did offer to buy you that top you liked, but you refused on principle.'

'Too right. It's twice the price it should be. Anyway, I'm sorted with what I've bought.'

Helen disappears into the huge fitting room, leaving me to flop into the luxurious dark plum chaise longue in the seating area. I'd love to put my feet up but I'd soon be falling asleep to the relaxing music gliding through the sound system. Not like my place, where there's an advert every five minutes. What was it? Oh, yes, the offer on knives…

My thoughts are pulled back to the present when Helen appears, wearing the first of the dresses. She seems perplexed. From the front the dress looks fantastic but then she turns round and I understand why she's flummoxed. There's no way the two halves of material at the back are ever going to join up.

I can't resist a little snigger, as I attempt to zip the dress up. 'No, Helen, it's definitely not going to fasten. Do you want me to get you the next size up?'

'Absolutely not. I'm a size 10, end of. They've obviously cut it wrong.'

The dressing-room assistant offers her opinion. 'Quite a few clients have bought the next size up for this particular dress. It's from the French Oui, Oui collection. It seems French women are differently proportioned to us.'

Very tactfully put. So, basically, French woman are slim and we're fat, it's a fact, get over it. I wish I knew their secret – munching on croissants and cheese all the time – but they're never in a million years going to share it with us.

Helen doesn't back down in front of the assistant. She turns round and marches back into the changing room. My phone instantly pings to let me know I've got a text.

> Maybe you could bring me another 10 just in case and a 12 but I'm NOT a 12!!

I text her back.

> Whatever lol

We finally make it to the tills. After Helen's slow start, she's made a phenomenal comeback. The dress (in size 12 – she says she's cutting the tag out as soon as she gets home), some shoes to match and a clutch bag. She's also treated herself to a couple of other dresses, a nice pale green semi-formal one and something for work. I can't really remember; it's all a blur.

Michaela is folding all the items neatly into tissue paper as if she has all the time in the world. And wouldn't you just know it she's also going on a cruise blah blah blah, then she hits Helen with the total price like it's a couple of pounds. I don't even hear what she says past the six hundred bit, but Helen gets out her store card, calm as you like, and doesn't flicker an eyelid.

We finally leave the shop with Helen's purchases in some very posh bags, alongside my five-pence plastic carrier bags. Maybe one day I might treat myself to one extravagant purchase, just for the posh bag.

We chat on the way back about what trips we'd like to do on the cruise. I quite fancy anything that involves relaxing on a beach. The last few months have taken their toll on me. The counselling we had got Richard and me nowhere; our differences are irreconcilable. It all boils down to the fact that I want kids and he doesn't, and neither of us will back down. I had an appointment with a solicitor this week and she's going to put the wheels in motion for a divorce.

We pull up outside my two-bedroom townhouse. It will have to be sold. Neither Richard nor I can afford to buy the other out. It breaks my heart, thinking about all the work we've done on it to make it our home. I've still got photos of us scattered about the place, but Richard has already taken most of his clothes and belongings. I think a lot of his stuff ended up back at his parents' place. His mate's flat, where he's living, is tiny. Helen wanted me to shred all his clothes like they do in the movies, but he got to them before I had the chance.

Helen and I have now done the compulsory chatting-for-ten-minutes-while-the-engine's-running thing and she finally decides that she'd better make tracks. I get out of her little red sporty car and she pulls away. I wave her off and walk wearily to my door. My first job is going to be collapsing on the sofa with a cup of tea. Maybe later I'll start putting those photos away.

Chapter 5

Helen

I've been out of the office so far this week, reviewing hotels in the Cotswolds, one of my favourite parts of the country. I love all those pretty cottages in quaint villages, surrounded by beautiful countryside. I've got the added bonus that I stay with my friend Jill when I'm in the area so we can have a good catch-up.

When I arrived at the office this morning, it was immediately apparent that there's an atmosphere here that you could cut with a knife. I try to keep out of office politics so I've shut myself in my own office. Every now and again, I glance up and observe what's happening through the glass. Everyone's been going in and out of Daniel's office. He's the managing director of Loving Luxury Travel. I just heard raised voices and doors slamming; now, I've been summoned into the office for a 'chat'.

I normally breeze in but today I'm apprehensive. I knock on his door before walking in and sitting down.

He's obviously not in the mood for chit-chat and cuts straight to the chase. 'You've probably noticed, Helen, that there have been a few staff members in my office today – in fact, all week. Perhaps I should have consulted with you sooner but I didn't want to bother you in the Cotswolds. As you know, we're expanding into villa rentals in Florida. They needed someone to go over immediately and help set up over the next few weeks. I've sent James. This means I've had to change what everyone else is doing at short notice. Someone has to go to Mykonos to review our hotels there and to inspect three potential small and friendly hotels for next year's brochure…'

I'm not really listening. I'm stuck on the words 'I've sent James to Florida'. Why hadn't James even mentioned it to me? No bloody wonder he didn't turn up for that meal and hasn't returned my calls and texts. He really does take the biscuit.

'So, unfortunately, Helen, it will have to be you. It's time-critical.'

My attention is suddenly back in the room. Daniel annoyingly flicks his pen on and off on the desk. He's staring at me and I haven't got a clue what will have to be me. 'Sorry, Daniel, what exactly will have to be me?'

'Mykonos. I've simply got no one else who can go and, to be perfectly honest, I prefer you for the job anyway. There's something not quite tallying between the feedback James gives me and the reviews that customers send in.' He twirls his pen in his fingers. It's so distracting. One day I'll flip, grab the pen off him and launch it across the room.

'There's just one problem with all this, Daniel. I'm doing the Caribbean cruise review and I can't be in two places at once.'

'Yes, I know, but there are other Caribbean cruises that you can review later and they're not as time-critical as Mykonos.'

'I'm really annoyed about this, Daniel. I'd rather hoped that I'd be considered to oversee the Florida villa project myself and now you've sent James instead, who's been here five minutes.'

'Helen, I'd hardly call a year "five minutes". He was actually reluctant to go but he already had a valid visa. In any case, this is just some initial work. I'll consider sending you on any future visits.' I've still got my sulky face on so Daniel changes tack. 'Helen, I'm sorry, but you were in the Cotswolds and I was also thinking about what you said about taking your sister on holiday. This way, she can go with you. You'll be working for two or three days at the most. I've already checked availability for flights and altered the reservation to a twin room.'

'What about Sharon? Can't she go?'

'Sharon's on her booked annual leave, so, no, she can't go. And before you suggest Pippa, she'll be at her sister's wedding. So, as I said, you're my only option and I'd prefer you to go as you're more experienced than the others. You'll be stopping at the Mykonos Boutique Blue Hotel, which is absolutely amazing. I went there myself three years ago and I can guarantee that you and your sister will both love it.'

'Great, I'm sure my sister will be over the moon,' I retort sarcastically. 'And James? Where's he at this precise moment in time?' I'm immediately cross with myself for asking about James.

'Flying over the Atlantic, as we speak,' Daniel replies in a matter-of-fact tone.

My mouth drops open but Daniel doesn't notice. He's already reeling off what needs to be done in Mykonos.

I eventually leave his office with my itinerary, feeling close to tears. But I absolutely refuse to break down in front of Daniel or the others, who are watching me like hawks. I think they know I'm seeing James, so I'm probably a hot topic of conversation around here. My stomach is churning in turmoil as I return to my office.

On a positive note, Steph will probably be quite relieved when I tell her there's no boat involved in our holiday now. I might as well ring her straight away. I prepare to leave a message on her voicemail, hoping she'll be busy. But of course she answers on the second ring, sounding bright and cheerful.

'Hi, Helen! Before I forget, those photos from Mum's party are brilliant. I want a couple of copies. You'd make a fantastic party planner if you ever fancied a change of career. Speaking of which, aren't you at work today?'

'Yes, I am at work, worse luck, and it hasn't been a good day. Daniel has sent James to Florida to get that villa project off the ground – you know, the one I was telling you about that I fancied.'

'Er, sorry, Helen, are we talking about *James* James?'

'Yes, the very same James, who is, apparently, as we speak, forty thousand feet above the Atlantic Ocean.'

'I assume you knew about it, you being his girlfriend and all that?'

'No, Steph, he never even mentioned it. I'm lost for words. I feel like I've been kicked in the stomach. Anyway, the thing is, because of all this I've now got to go to Mykonos instead of James and that means we can't go on our cruise. You can come to Mykonos, though, if you want, or change your holidays and we'll do the cruise in a few weeks' time. What do you think?'

'You know what I think of James. You're better off without him.'

'Steph, I don't want a lecture about this now. I'm struggling enough as it is. I mean, what do you think about coming with me to Mykonos? It will be three days' work at the most and then we can relax at the Boutique Blue Hotel. It actually looks amazing.'

'Yes, all right, I'll go to Mykonos. Which is where, exactly? It sounds a bit Greek.'

'Yes, it's in Greece. Hang on, I'll read our brochure blurb. It says, "Welcome to Greece's famous cosmopolitan island, a whitewashed paradise in the heart of the Cyclades…"'

'Oh, Helen, not the Cyclades! I'm sure Richard mentioned going there next week with his mate.'

'Can you remember which island they're going to? There's quite a few.'

'No, I can't remember. I wasn't really listening to him. I was pissed off that he's suddenly okay about going abroad with his mate when he wouldn't go with me, especially since he's always saying he's skint.'

'Right, I've Googled it. There's Serifos, Kythnos, Antiparos, Sifnos, Paros, Naxos, Santorini... There's loads, Steph, and I can't pronounce half of them. You'll have to ask him.'

'I'm not bloody well asking him. I know it's not Mykonos and that's the main thing. Unbelievable! I'd now rather be going on a cruise around the Caribbean than to the same part of the world as bloody Richard and his mate.'

'Oh, I'm sorry, Steph. It's not quite going to plan, is it? On the plus side, we might be able to meet up with Mum and Dad. I'm sure their cruise goes to Mykonos. In fact, I think it's where Dad wants to sneak off to for a crafty game of golf.'

'Well, I'm sure the Cyclades are big enough for me and Richard not to bump into each other. I can't change my holiday days at work at such short notice, anyway. So, Mykonos here we come.'

'Thanks, Steph, you're a star. I'll make it up to you.'

'Too damn right you will. I'll never live this down at work. From a Caribbean cruise to a Greek island! And I've just bought two weeks' worth of travel sickness tablets.'

'Right, well, I'd better get on with writing up these reviews. I'll ring you in a couple of days to let you know what time I'll pick you up. Luckily, we're still flying on the same day but at nine in the morning.'

'Oh, I like how you've dropped that in. I assume it's a two-hour check-in, which means I need to be up at six. Could be worse, I suppose. I'd better get reading up on Mykonos. I've never been to any of the Greek islands.'

'No, me neither, so that'll be another box ticked on my extensive list of places to go. See you on Monday – bright and breezy.'

'You're ever the optimist!'

Steph clicks off the line. I feel a bit better because she took the rather major itinerary change in her stride. Her holiday clothes will be fine for Mykonos, although I must text her later to pack a jacket or something for the evening; the blurb says it'll still be cool at this time of year. That bloody Richard, though, what a cheek. All those holidays that I've found for him and Steph that he refused to go on and now he's flouncing off to the Cyclades with his mate. It just doesn't make any sense.

I half-heartedly finish my Cotswold reviews and shut my computer down. I'm still reeling from the news about James and feeling pretty pissed off at him. He's another one – a complete mystery. I feel like getting his trumpet – which he's left at my house – and launching it through one of his windows. I decide instead to send him a message.

> Hi another message to
> add to the others that
> you haven't replied to.
> Just had a meeting
> with Daniel. He tells me
> you're on your way to
> Florida and I'm going
> to Mykonos. Is this
> why you've been
> avoiding me?

For the first time ever, I leave the office early. Daniel and the others are gobsmacked.

Chapter 6

Stephanie

Thank goodness for that. The tannoy finally announces that we can board our flight after four very long hours of waiting. 'All passengers for Flight GA121, please make your way to Gate 22.'

'At long bloody last,' Helen huffs. At one point, I thought she was going to spontaneously combust. 'I can't believe we've been delayed for so long just because some idiot's dropped a wallet down the loo and blocked it. I hope nobody's wandered off to a bar and got drunk. That'll be the next bloody thing; we'll be unloading someone's luggage.'

'Please, Helen, don't even think it. Look on the bright side, we'll be there for sunset.'

'I suppose,' she mutters. 'But this delay's put me behind. Um, maybe you could do the observations at the Boutique Blue? It'll be a doddle. It's one of our platinum hotels. It consistently scores highly on TripAdvisor and on its own in-house surveys. It's just a straightforward tick sheet. I'll show you when we're airborne. Then tomorrow I can get on and visit the hotel that's getting the bad reviews and give them an action plan. Then the day after I'll visit the family-run hotels.'

'Oh, Helen, that means I'll be on my own for two whole days.'

'I'm sorry, Steph, but what can I do? It's not my bloody fault that Daniel's taken leave of his senses and dropped me in it.'

Another announcement comes on the tannoy. 'Can all passengers with wheelchairs and buggies, please make your way to the boarding gate.'

Helen rolls her eyes. It's all tedious stuff to her. She's never off planes. She taps away furiously on her laptop, rearranging her schedule. I'd love to be a fly on the wall at her family-run-hotel inspections. Helen doesn't do family-run. She does grand and posh.

She reckons I'll be able to relax at our hotel and take these day-to-day observations in my stride. I'm glad she's only busy during the day and will be coming back to our hotel at night. I'm not too worried about keeping myself entertained during the day, but I'd feel like a right idiot sitting on my own at night. Of course, Helen's used to sitting on her own. It's an occupational hazard for her. 'You get used to it,' she told me once. 'I don't even give it a second thought.'

The tannoy starts up again. 'We now invite passengers seated in Rows 1 to 10 to please make their way to the boarding gate.'

That's us. Helen finishes tapping on her laptop and at long last closes it. Ordinarily, these seats would mean we were in first class, but I don't think such a thing exists on this flight. Even so, Helen's spotted a couple of celebs. She's got an extensive knowledge of who's who, but I haven't got a clue unless they're in *Coronation Street*.

'They're from *Real Housewives of Cheshire*,' she says, shaking her head. 'It's a TV series.'

'Sorry, Helen, I don't watch it.'

'You don't need to watch it, you just need to flick through a normal magazine every now and again instead of that nonsense,' she snipes.

I'm not going to start arguing with her. My 'nonsense magazine' is *Healthy*, and sometimes there *are* celebs in it so Helen can bugger off. In fact, Alesha Dixon's in this month's issue. 'Right, let's get on this plane. I need to sleep,' I say, changing the subject.

'Steph, you can sleep when we get there. I want to go through this itinerary with you.'

'I need to rest my eyes for at least thirty minutes while they finish boarding and go through the safety stuff and then I'll be all fresh for your instructions. I hardly slept last night, fretting about getting up so early.'

'Okay, I suppose thirty minutes won't make any difference, and I need to finish a couple of things first anyway.'

We arrive at the entrance to the plane and the flight attendant indicates that we need to turn left. As I thought, there's no difference between that and turning right. Maybe one day I'll get to travel first class. Helen lets me sit in the window seat; I'm 5A and she's 5B. The one good thing about being up at the front is that the seat configuration is two, four, two, so there's no one next to Helen to annoy her. She already looks like an angry cat thrashing its tail, ready to lash out at the next unsuspecting victim.

I pop my bag under the seat in front of me, fasten my seatbelt and quickly read the safety card. I don't think I'd be much use in an emergency. I never willingly put myself on an emergency exit. I'd be pulling the door lever the wrong way or worse still the lever would come off in my hand.

Helen settles into her seat with her laptop already out so that she can do more work before we go. Helen is the definition of a workaholic.

For some reason, I can only ever get to sleep at this point of the journey. Once I'm airborne, it's a no go. 'Wake me up in a bit, Helen.'

'I'll wake you, don't worry. I want to show you the questionnaire and a couple of other things.'

I take my specs off, pop them in the seat pocket and close my eyes. I hear the pilot making an announcement in the background and then I drift off. I'm dreaming about Richard. It starts off okay, we're happy, and then I'm suddenly holding a baby girl and trying to persuade Richard to take her. He turns round and walks off, leaving me shouting his name in frustration. The baby starts crying. I slowly come round and realise I've been dreaming. There's a baby crying a few seats away. I can feel the plane moving. We're taxiing along the runway.

'Oh my God, Helen, why didn't you wake me? We're here.' I peer out of the window. 'Oh heck, it's a bit grey.' Not that I can see much without my specs.

'Yes, it's grey,' she confirms, sighing.

The plane has stopped, seemingly far away from the airport terminal. I look out of the window to see if I can spot a transfer bus. Everyone seems very restrained; no one undoes their seatbelt. People never take any notice of that please-remain-seated nonsense once the plane has landed and stopped. Maybe they've tightened up on it like they have with security. What a bloody nightmare that was. I was almost naked by the time I managed to get through the X-ray machine without it bleeping.

The plane's engines suddenly roar into life and there's an almighty feeling of power beneath us as we're pulled slightly backwards by the force. The plane accelerates down the runway, gathering speed and momentum, and then, moments later, we leave the ground.

My head is all over the place and I'm completely disorientated. 'Helen, what the hell is happening?' I shriek.

'Here, you silly moo, put on your bloody glasses. We're just taking off. It's grey because we're still in Manchester.' She finds my state of confusion very amusing. She can't stop sniggering.

'So I've only been asleep for a few minutes? I was having a bloody awful dream about Richard.'

'Well, actually, we've been waiting for a second take-off slot for an hour. One of the passengers didn't board and they had to offload their luggage – just like I predicted! And, by the way, you've been snoring. It was very embarrassing.' She shakes her head disapprovingly.

'Ooh err, sorreee! Not that you snore, of course.'

'Not like that,' she retorts, all high and mighty.

'Well, I'll be the judge of that when we get to the hotel. Oh, and thanks for asking about my dream! Don't worry about me!'

'I'm sorry, Steph. What happened in the dream?'

'Oh, Richard was being a prat. He walked away from me and a baby. It's probably my brain telling me to get the hint. Anyway, I don't want to talk about Richard. I need a rest from the subject. What's our ETA now?'

'About six, their time. I reckon we'll be at the hotel at about seven thirty – not too bad considering we've been up since six. Think I'll have a nap myself when I've gone through this work with you.'

'I need to eat something first, Helen, I'm starving.'

'Flipping heck, Steph, you just ate at the airport.'

'That was after we checked in three hours ago. You know what I'm like if my blood sugar levels start dipping.'

'Oh yes, I know. We don't want a Steph-style blood sugar dip at forty thousand feet. Let's swap places so I can have a snooze while you have something to eat. Wake me up to discuss this pile of rubbish ... sorry, I mean work.'

I don't need to ask if Helen's eating. She seems to exist on thin air. I wish my appetite were like hers, i.e. non-existent. We swap over and Helen sets out her stall with a neck cushion, eye mask and earplugs. Bless her, she's got everything in that bag of hers.

I notice that *Healthy*, which I'd popped into my seat pocket for a bit of light reading, has found its way into Helen's seat pocket. It's open at 'Twenty things every woman should achieve before she's forty'. I'm thirty-one and Helen's thirty-three and I don't think either of us could lay claim to more than five of them. But we've got a few years to chip away at them, after all.

Most are pretty boring, but Number 2 is quite interesting: 'Have hot sex with someone you work with or someone unsuitably young; the embarrassment should (hopefully) ensure you will never do it again.' Well, just the thought of having sex with anyone fills me with horror at the moment. In fact, the whole dating scene has put me off for life. My friend Debbie persuaded me to join an online dating website a few weeks ago. I've already bailed out of two dates by feigning a migraine before I fell asleep with boredom. I'm cancelling my membership as soon as I can. I've had enough of daily recommendations and ridiculous profiles. Yesterday it was Shabi69 from Jerusalem who doesn't have a profession so he needs a woman with whom he can live. Well, Shabi, that woman won't be me. I've also had enough of Bob who sends me a message every day asking to meet up. I was put off by the numerous tattoos in his profile photo. I don't mind the odd tasteful tattoo, but Bob is clearly hooked.

I could make a start with Number 1: 'Dye your hair every conceivable colour – red, black, blonde, pink.' Okay, forget that idea, I can just picture the look on the store manager's face if I turn up with pink hair.

Helen can claim to have travelled the world, which is the first half of Number 18. But then it goes on to say '… and settle in your favourite place.' I'm not sure she'll ever settle down. She's a career woman through and through, married to the job. She threw herself into her work after her best friend died. I think that's why she subconsciously chooses boyfriends who don't want commitment. That suits her because she's scared of getting close to someone and then losing them.

Thank goodness, the trolley's finally appeared. I get Helen a tapas selection, which is right up her street, with various nibbles to pick at just in case she does finally get peckish. I, on the other hand, have chosen the largest offering on the menu – the bacon ciabatta. I pay the flight attendant with a note and she says she'll have to come back later with my change. Yeah, right, heard that one before. But I'm too hungry to start hunting in my purse for change.

The bacon ciabatta goes down a treat with an aptly named cocktail – On the Beach. It's sadly minus the sex, along with the fancy umbrella and glacé cherry, but, surprisingly, it tastes okay. I'm just about to wake Helen to pass her a can of Mojito when I come across the film *Shirley Valentine* on the in-flight movie channel. It brings back bittersweet memories. My friends from work bought me the DVD as a joke when I got married. In the accompanying card, they'd written, 'To the new Mrs Valentine – don't morph into Shirley! lol xx'

Flipping heck, I didn't even make it to unhappily married middle-age. Richard, on the other hand, was already refusing to go on what he called the 'fancy' holidays that Helen found for us. He also looked forward to his steak night just like Joe in the film. Admittedly Richard was a bit more adventurous washing his steak down with a glass of red wine unlike Joe who preferred a can of beer. Oh yes, I remember this bit – Shirley talking to the wall. At least I'm not doing that … yet.

'Stephanieee, wake up! They're getting ready for landing! You were meant to be waking *me* up to go through this lot, remember?' Helen waves her file at me.

'Oops. I must have dozed off. I was watching *Shirley Valentine*.' I look at the screen. The film seems to have been replaced with information about the time and how many feet we're at. So useful to know. 'Anyway,' I retort, 'you've been asleep for the whole journey.'

'That's not the point. I left you awake and in charge of waking me up when you'd eaten. Now we'll have to go through this lot after dinner.'

'Okay, whatever,' I huff.

Just what I need, a stroppy sister. She can be a right pain in the neck at times. She'll be in strop for at least an hour. She was just the same when we were growing up. If something just slightly upset Helen's little world, we all knew about it. She'd win a slamming doors competition hands down. Good job she's belted into her seat by the window or who knows what door she'd take out her strop on.

The plane descends quickly, the seat belt signs are on and our flight attendant has done her final checks, which include handing over my change. She sits down and belts herself in next to her rather dishy colleague, who must have been at the back of the plane all this time. Now, if he'd been up at this end, I would definitely not have dozed off. He's the second dishy guy I've noticed recently. Maybe my senses are awakening, like I'm coming out of hibernation or something.

The lights in the cabin have been dimmed and my ears are popping like mad. Long gone are the days when they handed out a sweet to suck. I can just about make out the sea below us if I crane past Helen.

The plane touches down reasonably smoothly and slows quickly. As it taxis down the runway, there's a spontaneous round of applause, and, you know what, I join in. It's worth it just to see Helen roll her eyes and shake her head.

'Well, for all we know, the pilot might have manoeuvred us through a storm,' I say.

Helen's not rising to the bait. She's busy putting her travel accessories away and inspecting her tapas meal and Mojito in a can. As for me, I'm happy that I'm here and looking forward to some relaxation, lots of good food and plenty to drink.

The captain comes on the speaker. 'Good evening, ladies and gentlemen. Welcome to Mykonos, where the local time is 6.15 p.m. and the temperature is a pleasant twenty degrees Celsius. I'd like to thank you for travelling with us today. Once again, I apologise for the delays and the unexpected air pocket that we hit and I wish you a pleasant stay on the beautiful island of Mykonos.'

I can't resist a sneaky look at Helen, who seems to be avoiding eye contact with me for some strange reason.

Chapter 7

Helen

I wake early after a reasonable night's sleep – well, as good a sleep as you can get sharing a bed with a maniac sister. I was in a deep sleep when she whacked me and scared me to death by shouting out 'Stop!' and something about a roller coaster. I made it quite clear to the manager last night that the beds were to be sorted out today. My booking request definitely said a twin room.

I'm not one for lying about in bed and I've got a busy schedule, so I get up and make my way to the rather plush bathroom. We have a feature washbasin each that looks like a carved-out rock; each of them has streamlined chrome taps. There's a freestanding bath and a large shower cubicle that is nearly as big as my bathroom at home. I opt for a quick shower, using the hotel's complimentary Wild Olive accessories. They're apparently a locally sourced brand, which is really commendable.

I find my new dress relatively uncreased at the top of my suitcase and pop it on. I'll have to unpack the rest later.

Steph still hasn't stirred so I make her a cup of tea and deposit it by her bed. I tell her that I'm going for breakfast and that I'll see her later. I think she heard me but I can't really be sure if her grunt is for me or not.

I make my way to the buffet restaurant for breakfast. I'm greeted promptly and politely by Elena. She asks me whether I'd like to eat inside or outside. I request a table inside. When I'm working, I try and stay as cool as possible and avoid the sun and heat at all costs. It just makes me feel tired and uncomfortable.

The waitress, Katerina, takes my drink order and I make my way to the food on the buffet table. I pile lots of different fruits on to my plate and add a blob of zero-fat yogurt for good measure. I get back to the table and my pot of tea is waiting. It's no wonder James enjoys coming here – the views of the Aegean Sea are amazing from this restaurant, and the hotel itself, apart from the bed mix-up, is spot on.

I've just started checking my itinerary for the day when an email pings on my phone.

Helen,
Please can you go to the Royal Blue Hotel sometime today and ask why the pool bar isn't open? Guests are complaining – quite rightly so – about it. They're getting told it's too early in the season and this is NOT ACCEPTABLE. I've emailed the hotel already telling them to expect a visit. The manager is Selena Lexou.
Also, two more bad reviews for the Mykonos Gold.
Regards,
Daniel
Managing Director
Loving Luxury Travel

For goodness sake, doesn't he ever sleep? It's only seven in the morning at home and he's already at it. I haven't even had any breakfast yet. Bloody typical. I quickly reply.

Hi Daniel,

I'll make the Royal Blue my first visit as it's just down the road and I'll visit the Mykonos Gold this afternoon to assess the situation from a customer's point of view.

Regards,

Helen

Manager

Loving Luxury Travel

I finish my delicious breakfast and close my laptop. Elena wishes me a pleasant day as I leave the restaurant. Hopefully she'll be as pleasant to Steph and get lots of ticks in the 'met expectations' section. Poor Steph, I don't think she appreciated me going through the questionnaire and accompanying paraphernalia last night. Her default response of 'What a load of shit,' was repeated on several occasions. She didn't even notice a rather dishy waiter who I could have sworn was looking in our direction most of the night.

My heels click-clack on the highly glossed marble floor as I leave the hotel. The porter asks if I need a taxi. I have to reluctantly reply that I don't. Not even I can take a taxi to a hotel just down the road, although walking there isn't going to be the easiest task in these heels.

I walk as gracefully as I can, wobbling and cursing all the way to the Royal Blue Hotel. The automatic doors open and my fun day begins. I click-clack across another marble floor and approach the reception.

Eventually, a girl glances up and raises half a smile. 'How can I help?' she asks in a reasonably pleasant manner.

I look at her name badge. 'Good morning, Elysse.' I use her name deliberately because I know that will immediately put her on her guard. Half smiles and eventually looking up to acknowledge a waiting customer are not going to win any awards in my book. She would definitely have heard my heels approaching over this floor. 'I have a meeting with Selena Lexou.' I hand over one of my business cards.

I can see that she immediately recognises our company logo. 'Please take a seat. I will let her know you are here,' she replies a lot more enthusiastically. She even manages a full smile, which means the muscles of her mouth are fully functional.

While I wait, I observe the staff. Elysse has already tipped off as many of her colleagues as she can about my arrival and everyone suddenly seems busy. My phone pinged with a text alert on the way here; so as there's no immediate sign of Selena I have a quick look at it. Oh, very interesting. It's from James.

> Hi sorry for not
> telling you about Florida
> or replying sooner. Spot of
> bother with my phone. Hope
> you're not too mad about
> going to Mykonos but Daniel
> insisted on me coming to
> Florida as I had a visa.
> If you visit the Royal Blue:
> the manager is a bit
> high-maintenance. xx

'Spot of bother with my phone', my arse. I'm just about to send a reply when a woman heads my way. She's quite tall, especially in her heels, with dark hair in a neat bun. She's very slim. I reckon she's a similar age to me.

'*Kalimera*. I am Selena,' she says, extending her perfectly French-manicured hand for a firm handshake and smiling to reveal whitened teeth.

'Good morning. I'm Helen Collins. You should have received an email from our office regarding my visit.'

'Indeed I have, although I assumed it would be James whom I'd be meeting. Is he following on behind?'

'No, he's gone to our office in Florida to get our new villa rentals up and running,' I reply in a calm and matter-of-fact way. I don't want to have an emotional breakdown so early in the day, especially after that text. 'High maintenance' – I bet she bloody well is!

'Oh, I see, he never mentioned it,' she replies in a slightly less confident voice.

And why would she expect him to mention it? I manage to keep my composure. 'Well, it was a last-minute thing, which is why I'm here.' I'm not sure she actually registers my reply. 'In fact, he's just sent me text, which is most strange because it must be three in the morning in Florida. Maybe he's got jet lag and can't sleep.' I wonder if he's been panicking since I told him I've been sent to Mykonos instead of him. That would explain the warning about Selena being high maintenance. He's covering his own back, no doubt.

'How can I help, then?' she asks. I could be wrong but I'm sure her eyes are watering.

'I'll tell you what, why don't you give me a grand tour of the hotel and then we'll have a chat over coffee in the restaurant?' I feel like I could do with something a bit stronger but it's a bit early yet to hit the cocktails.

She leads the way and I seize the opportunity to get some background information. 'So, Selena, how long have you been the manager here?'

'I was promoted eight months ago. Our previous manager moved to another hotel, which created the opportunity for me here. James came out to help with the interviews. I was offered the job and was delighted to take it. James was very...'

Selena is obviously struggling to find the words for 'Very good at two-timing his English girlfriend' so I offer up 'Supportive'.

'Yes, supportive, and he is always available if I have any issues – work-related, of course,' she adds quickly.

Everything appears to be running smoothly and Selena is acknowledging the guests as we walk along, which is at least a good sign.

'Now, the main reason I'm here, Selena, is to find out why the pool bar isn't open at night. We've had reports back from customers saying they've been told it's too early in the season.'

'I spoke to James about this last week. I explained that there are hardly any guests using that particular bar and he suggested just opening the lobby bar until the end of May to save on staff costs. So this is what I have done.'

We come to a halt.

'James isn't authorised to make that kind of decision. He should have referred the matter to our managing director, Daniel.'

'I think you'll find that James did speak with Daniel and was told to use his … er, sorry, I cannot think of the English word.'

There's a word that springs to mind, but I'll give Daniel the benefit of the doubt. 'Initiative?'

'That is the exact word, but I cannot pronounce it. So James used his…' Selena prompts me for the word.

'Initiative.'

'… like he did many times on hotel visits.'

Now I'm curious. I can't help myself. 'And what other initiatives has James taken?'

She suddenly looks flustered and realises that she's dropped herself in it. 'Oh, oh, I cannot think of an example just like that.'

I notice she's twirling a familiar looking necklace nervously round her finger. 'That's a pretty necklace.'

'Yes, it was a gift for my birthday from, er...'

'In fact, it looks very similar to this one!' I yank mine out from under my dress. She looks like she's been hit with something rather heavy. I continue calmly. 'I'll be typing up a report on my morning's findings later. For now, I'm going to walk round the hotel on my own and speak to some guests.'

She appears to be quite worried by this parting shot of mine and quickly says Saint James of Manchester has never done any of this, that he gives them a clean sheet regardless and they just have a chat. Well, that explains everything. I suspect it's more than a chat but I'm not even going there. I ignore what she's said and extend my hand to her. She reluctantly shakes it and slumps into the nearest chair.

James has almost definitely been two-timing me with Selena. I'm not going to let her see how upset I am. I turn round and make my way over to the rather pleasant-looking pool area. The guests seem to be relaxed and the atmosphere is calm. I have a chat with a few of the guests. Their feedback is good, apart from the problem of the pool bar being closed at night. I reassure them that this issue is being addressed. They also tell me how good Selena is at her job. I'd dearly love to tell them that she's good at other things too, but I bite my tongue.

I find Selena back in her office, looking rather forlorn.

'Right, I'm done. I'll send an email to Daniel telling him that he authorised the bar closure with James. You might as well put this in the rubbish bin – it seems to have broken.' Before she can reply, I drop my necklace on to her desk and walk away triumphantly.

Inwardly, I'm shaking and furious beyond words.

Chapter 8

Stephanie

My goodness, what a wonderful night's sleep! I must make a note on Helen's questionnaire that this is the most comfortable bed in the world. I've slept like a log apart from a dream during which I nearly gave poor Helen a heart attack. I don't think she was impressed with my antics. I blame the memory of the plane's motion for me dreaming that I was on a roller coaster. I was with a gorgeous guy and a pop song was playing. It's a song that I keep hearing – 'Black Magic'. We've been doing Zumba to it recently and it's stuck in my head. It was also playing in the restaurant last night, but Helen drowned it out by droning on about that questionnaire.

The dream was like a James Bond film. After the roller coaster, we were suddenly on a speedboat, with the wind blowing in my hair and the spray from the sea splashing up on to my face. Then we were on a motorbike and driving ridiculously fast through narrow streets. I was very impressed with myself: Stephanie Valentine, the new Bond girl.

Anyway, I need to open the curtains. I'm desperate to see the sun and the view. I haven't seen anything yet as it was dark by the time we finally arrived last night. Thank goodness we were still in time for some dinner. I know we're near the sea because last night at the restaurant we could see it under the spotlights, and we could hear it too.

I peel the covers off the bed and make my way to the curtains, and... Shit, ouch, ouch, what the hell was that? One of Helen's bloody stiletto shoes. Why can't she put things away? I sit back on the bed, holding my poor toe, which throbs with pain. As the pain subsides, I attempt once again to draw the curtains back and look at the view.

The sun is definitely there, shining brightly and dazzling my eyes. The sky is a cloudless blue, and the sea view... Er, the view, well, it isn't of the sea.

Now, if I were paying for this holiday and for a sea view, which of course I'm not, I'd expect to actually be able to see the sea. But there's a pool and a garden that both look really nice. I can also see one of the restaurants, where they're serving breakfast. We've even got our own little Jacuzzi, and there are sun-loungers on our terrace.

Maybe it's just that we're in a different room to the one Helen expected. She wasn't exactly doing cartwheels when she clocked the double bed last night, but we needed food and sleep and the staff assured us that the bed problem would be sorted out today. The original booking was for a double room, which was a bit odd. Helen's boss changed it to a double with twin beds but communication seems to have broken down. We did, however, enjoy the champagne that was in the room. Another mystery – Helen says she didn't ask for it.

I'll finish my tea on the balcony. I slide back the balcony doors and realise it's already baking. I like to think that I enjoy the sun and heat but the balcony is so hot that I go back in after five minutes to have a nice refreshing shower.

I'm going to wear my new dress that Helen treated me to yesterday at the airport. Ridiculously expensive, in my book, but

I fell in love with it and Helen insisted on buying it for me. It's an all-over blue design in a bandeau style. The ruched bandeau means there's no need for a bra so I feel rather liberated.

I'm also going to attempt wearing some contact lenses. I've worn lenses a few times over the years but I hated the daily cleaning regime. I was chatting to a colleague a few weeks ago and she recommended daily disposable lenses. I went along to the local optician, tried out a trial pack and now here I am with a month's worth. I peer down at the mirror and my hair immediately flops into my eyes. I find a bobble to tie back my hair. The optician offered to mark the boxes with 'left' and 'right' as my prescription is different for each eye. I insisted there was no need… Now, what was it? I'm sure the left is the weaker one. I carefully peel the backing off the weaker prescription lens first and gently coax it from the compartment. It's a right faff. I finally manage to get the lens into my eye, which waters profusely for a few seconds. I dab my eye with some tissue and then repeat the same palaver for the second eye. I'm not sure this contact lens malarkey is for me but, at £40 for a month, I'll have to give them a chance.

I quickly glance at myself in the mirror before leaving the room to make sure my dress isn't tucked into my knickers – one of my previous embarrassing moments. I was about to walk out of the toilets at a hotel once when a very kind lady stopped me and pointed out my huge faux pas.

I make my way down to the buffet restaurant and wait dutifully at the post to be seated. I've got my questionnaire from Helen tucked into my magazine so that I can tick off the points as I go along. It's even worse than the rubbish we have at work but that's what happens in the service industry – everyone is judged. I blame the Americans with all that 'Have a nice day' nonsense.

A staff member approaches me. She's smiling, which is a good start, and she has a name badge on. I need to remember her name, which is… Oh my God, I can't see her name! It's blurry – I must have mixed up my contact lenses. I have to think quickly; I need her name for my tick sheet.

'Morning, madam. Table for one?'

'Yes, please,' I nod.

'Inside or outside?'

'Oh, outside, please. I'd like to make the most of this wonderful sunshine.'

'Are you from England? Having no summer again!' she laughs.

I feel like pointing out that having no summer isn't actually that funny, but I refrain. 'Yes, can you tell?' I reply instead, holding out my very pale arms.

'Smoking or non-smoking?'

'Non-smoking, thank you.'

We head outside and the warm air hits us nicely after the air-conditioned indoor restaurant.

'Is this table okay for you?' She points to a table by the pool.

'Yes, great, thank you.'

She pulls the chair out ready for me to sit down. 'Is this your first visit to the restaurant?'

I smile and nod. She explains that most things are on the buffet but if I want anything more specific, like eggs Benedict, I can order it from my waiter, who will also take my drink order. I think her name badge says 'El' something.

'Thank you. Er, sorry, how do you pronounce your name?'

'El-ena,' she replies, smiling and unfazed. She turns away to greet some new guests.

I sneak the questionnaire out of the magazine and promptly put it back as an absolutely gorgeous waiter approaches.

'*Kalimera.* Did you have a good night's sleep?'

'Oh, wonderful, thank you. The best ever until I...' I stop myself because if I tell him about whacking Helen he'll think I'm bonkers.

'Until you … woke up?'

'Ha ha,' I chuckle. 'Yes, something like that.'

'Is this your first time to the magical island of Mykonos?'

'Yes, it is, and it's actually the first time I've visited anywhere in Greece.'

'Well, I am sure you will like it very much. Be sure to visit our beautiful town and the rest of the island. Many of our guests never leave the hotel grounds, which is a great shame. Now, would you like some tea or coffee?'

'Oh, English breakfast tea, please. I can't face coffee until at least ten thirty.'

'Would you like milk?'

I can't help gazing into his deep brown eyes for a second or two and then I realise that he's waiting for my answer. 'Oh, yes, sorry, definitely milk, thank you.'

I'm so distracted by the gorgeous waiter's eyes – in fact, everything about him – that I completely forget to look at his name, and now he's gone. I've had enough of this sheet already. I'll fill it in later.

He's back quickly with my pot of tea. 'One pot of English breakfast tea. Enjoy your breakfast.'

'I will, thank you. Oh, sorry, have you got the milk?'

'I am most sorry. I have forgotten it. I will bring it now.'

'Oh, no worries. The tea needs to brew first anyway.' I can't help gazing into his eyes again for a bit longer than I need to. I'm mesmerised by his looks, and his Greek accent makes him sound so sexy. He leaves me simmering. I can see I'm going to be coming down earlier and having a very long breakfast if this guy's going to be about.

I'm suddenly aware that there's an insect flying about. It looks big and menacing. I don't do insects. I was chased by wasps as a child, and they won, so I panic at the sight of anything that can fly or buzz. I watch it intently as it hovers around some flowers.

I arm myself with my magazine, ready to protect myself. Oh no, it's coming my way. My heart is racing. I instinctively shriek and attempt to waft it away with the magazine. I throw my hand in the air and…

'Aargh! Oh my God! What on earth?' I'm suddenly wet. I've been doused with a jug of cold milk. It's in my hair and all over the table and my lovely new dress. People at the surrounding tables stop eating and gawp at me to see what I'm making a fuss about. I can hear sniggering.

The poor waiter was just behind me bringing the milk and now I've created a scene. 'I'm so sorry! A large insect freaked me out.'

'Oh yes it was a carpenter bee. It has gone now. Please, here.' The waiter hands me a napkin and I laugh. The shock of the cold milk shower has reduced me to laughter.

'When I said I wanted milk, I didn't mean that I wanted to be wearing the stuff,' I reply, feeling rather shy. I glance down and notice that the cold milk has caused a reaction in my nipples. They've very kindly put in an appearance, enjoying the freedom of having no bra to keep them under control. The waiter notices them as well and politely averts his eyes. 'Oh dear, I think I'd better get changed and send my dress to the laundry.'

'No problem. I will bring you a fresh pot of tea and some more…' he pauses, trying very hard not to laugh, '… milk? And please tell the laundry that the restaurant will pay for the cleaning.'

'There's no need. It wasn't your fault. Maybe next time there's an insect flying about I'll think twice before I start wafting magazines in the air.'

'Please, I insist.'

'Okay, very well. I'm starving so I'll be back in a jiffy.'

'Would you like some toast bringing with your tea? Then it will be here when you come back?'

'Oh, that'll be great, thanks.'

I scurry back to our room. I can't tell Helen about this latest calamity of mine. She'd be rolling her eyes in disbelief. And that waiter – he's knocked me for six and got me in a right tizzy. My heart is all a flutter and there's a funny feeling in my stomach … That could be hunger, though.

I change quickly into a clean dress, with a bikini top underneath as added security. I'm taking no chances. With my luck, lightning might strike twice. I also swap my contact lenses round.

I get back to my table and there's a pot of tea, a jug of milk and some toast waiting for me. As I eat, I try to discreetly watch the milk waiter; I'm fascinated by him. He seems really charming, he's got a lovely manner with the guests and his smile is, well, it's making my heart flutter again, which it hasn't done in a very long time.

It seems to be taking me ages to finish my pot of tea and toast. I don't feel that hungry any more so I'll leave the buffet for now and try it tomorrow.

'Would you like some more tea?' The milk waiter breaks into my thoughts, which were mostly about him.

'No, I'm fine. I'm going to relax and read my magazine.'

'Well, you have a good day. I am hoping no more insects will be bothering you.'

'Yes, thanks, I hope so too!'

I could quite happily sit there for a while longer and watch the waiter but I'm guessing that at some point the breakfast service will finish and I'll look a bit strange. I didn't see a name badge so I'm still none the wiser. Oh well, for now he's the 'gorgeous milk waiter'.

I reluctantly leave and set off to check out the sunbed situation. There's no sign of a free one in the garden or on the beach so I track down the guy who's in charge of the sunbeds.

'Oh, hi there, er…' I peer down at his name badge. Manolis. 'I can't find a free sunbed and I thought there was meant to be one for every guest.' I feel like I have some authority with my questionnaire, and he's caught slightly off guard by my knowledge of sunbed allocation.

'Yes, there is, but I think guests from the hotel next door have been taking advantage of our more deluxe beds. There are some cabanas available on the beach, if you are interested. They are forty euros a day,' he says, somehow keeping a straight face.

'Forty euros a day?' I screech. 'They should be free when all the beds have gone.'

I can tell I've touched a nerve because he comes up with a suggestion rather than just sending me on my way. 'I can ask the supervisor's permission to waive the fee, if you like,' he offers.

I now go off the idea of being in a cabana all on my own when I could just lie on the sunbed on my balcony. I make a hasty retreat, muttering that I'll be back first thing in the morning to claim my sunbed. Helen won't be impressed with all this.

I find a table in the lunch and dinner restaurant, the one overlooking the beautiful blue sea that's sparkling in the sun, and I make a start on this ridiculous questionnaire.

Breakfast buffet

Meeter/greeter
Were you greeted by a member of staff within five minutes?
Yes/No/Don't know/Comment
X

Was the member of staff wearing a name badge?
Yes/No/Don't know/Comment
X Elena

Did the member of staff offer a choice between inside and outside dining?
Yes/No/Don't know/Comment
X

Did the member of staff offer a choice between smoking and non-smoking seating?
Yes/No/Don't know/Comment
X

Was the member of staff friendly and professional?
Yes/No/Don't know/Comment
X

Was the buffet system explained?
Yes/No/Don't know/Comment
X

Waiters and waitresses
Were you asked in a timely manner for your choice of drink?
Yes/No/Don't know/Comment
X

Was the member of staff wearing a name badge?
Yes/No/Don't know/Comment
X He was the drop-dead gorgeous one.

Was your drink served in a timely manner?
Yes/No/Don't know/Comment
X A very timely manner lol.

Flipping heck, I've had enough of this. I want to get on a sunbed and start reading my big pile of books, which have used up a quarter of my suitcase allowance. I carefully return the questionnaire to its wallet and go back to our room, using the stairs for some exercise.

I take my dress off and throw it on to the bed. I pop the other dress, the wet one, into a laundry bag, tick the same-day option and write 'Milk spillage, please charge to restaurant' on the label.

I disappear into the bathroom to whack on some sun cream. Then I hear some faint knocking and a man shouting 'Hello!'

I quickly grab a bathrobe and peer round the door. There are a couple of guys in the corridor. They look quite alarmed, to match me being quite alarmed.

'Sorry. We knock and no one answer. You have "Make My Room Up" sign on your door.'

'Sorry, yes, I forgot to change it back. I was just in the bathroom putting on my sun cream.'

'We have come to sort out the bed. Housekeeping say it should be separate?'

'Yes, that's right, thank you. I'll go on the balcony and leave you to it.'

I scuttle out of their way, grabbing my book. When I open the balcony doors, I'm hit with a wall of heat. The sun is belting down and there's not much shade. It's a wonderful suntrap but there's no way that I can sit out here for more than ten minutes. I start reading my new book *In the Meantime* recommended by my friend Stella. She said it helped her move on with her life after her divorce. The back-cover blurb starts off promising enough: 'The windows of our hearts and minds are streaked with past hurts, memories and disappointments. The windows are so clouded by fear, self-doubt and inaccurate information that the light of love cannot shine through. What we must do is clean.' Um I'm starting to have second thoughts about this book. Cleaning isn't really my forte. 'We must mop and sweep...'

I glance up from the book and notice my milk waiter clearing the tables from breakfast over in the restaurant. I'm getting butterflies in my stomach again just thinking about him…

My thoughts are broken into by the sound of one of the men tapping on the balcony glass. He opens the door. 'We finish now.'

'Okay, thank you.'

It's definitely too hot on the balcony for me. I suppose I could wander around the town. I feel a bit nervous about venturing off on my own, but I'm sure I'll be fine. I need to learn to do things on my own again, and I've got a purpose – Helen needs some local information and photos for the brochure. I might as well make some inroads into that.

I step into the lovely air-conditioned room. As much as I like my dress, it doesn't go with my walking sandals so I quickly change into some shorts and a black T-shirt with pink hearts on it that says, 'Love Is in the Air'. I throw my sunglasses, sun cream, water and purse into my bag and set off on my first solo adventure.

Chapter 9

Stephanie

Right, I'm doing this the tourist way so I'm going to ask the reception staff for some information on the best way to get to town and also about any points of interest that are worthy of a visit that Helen might have missed.

The receptionist Nikos greets me with a warm smile and a pleasant, 'How can I help?' That will get a tick. But the questionnaire is having a rest until later – if and when I can be bothered with it. I explain my wish to explore the town and Nikos gets out a map from under the desk and unfolds it. It's so large that it takes over the whole desk. He very kindly starts with the really important information, like where the hotel actually is.

He explains that there's a complimentary shuttle bus that leaves the hotel on the hour, and town on the half hour. 'I am very sorry but actually you have just missed it. There is a local bus service, if you like, which will take about half an hour. Or I could call a taxi for you.'

'No, the bus will be fine.'

'Okay, so the buses are every half hour and they leave on the opposite side to the hotel track. They are one euro and fifty cents.'

Nikos circles places of interest on the map. I now know where the bus stops in town, where there are cafes if I fancy a drink or snack and also where the churches are; they seem to be in abundance. The harbour is self-explanatory, and there are some windmills as well.

'Oh yes, the windmills. My sister mentioned those. She wants some photos of them.'

'Your sister, she is not going with you?' Nikos asks, glancing around the reception area.

'Er, no, she's … working.'

'Oh, this is a shame. Anyway, after the windmills, there is the Little Venice area.'

I'm keeping quiet. I thought Venice was in Italy but I don't want to pull him up on minor details like where Venice is or isn't.

Nikos assumes correctly that I want to wander round the shops. 'There are shops all down this street, and this street. In fact, there are shops everywhere. It is easy to be lost but just ask the locals. Is there anything else that I can help you with?'

'No, this is great. Thanks.' I'm ready to set off with my map that I can no longer read as it's covered in Nikos's places-of-interest scribbles.

And so my adventure begins. Now, I turn right … no, left. It's obviously left or else I'd be walking off the edge of a cliff and free-falling down into the sea.

It's quite hot for me – at least twenty-five degrees, I reckon. It takes me only a couple of minutes to reach the bus stop. Luckily, there's a little bit of shade from a tree nearby so I stand under it. A coach goes by on the opposite side of the road; I watch it disappear. It's now eleven thirty and almost the hottest part of the day. I put my map to good use and wave it in front of me like a fan. I know some would argue this makes you hotter but all the same I'll carry on fanning… Now, I bet that's never been a *Carry On* film… My thoughts are interrupted by a little silver

Fiat that's shot past me and screeched to a halt at the side of the road. It's reversing, kicking up a load of dust that engulfs me and frightens me half to death.

The driver jumps out. 'Sorry, I did not mean to cover you with dust.'

The dust clears. Oh my God, it's the milk waiter!

'You want lift to town?' he asks in his broken English and his Greek accent, which I'm finding rather seductive.

'I'm fine, thanks. I'm waiting for the bus.'

'You know, bus for town is over there and it just went that way.' He's pointing in the opposite direction to which I'm planning on going. 'It go past here then turn round and go to town. The driver should have stop. Maybe the bus was full.'

'Oh,' is all I can say. I'm bloody hopeless. I've fallen at the first hurdle. Nikos did mention the other side of the road…

'Listen, it is a bit hot to be waiting for next bus. I live in town and drop you off. Please get in, it is no trouble.'

He's now got the door open and is gesturing me in. I'm really not sure about this. I scan the road to see if another bus is on the horizon, which course it isn't. 'Only if you're sure it isn't out of your way.'

'Please, I insist, it is no trouble.'

I hop in, shut the door and fasten my seat belt. The milk waiter jumps in beside me. I can feel something under my sandal and reach down to pick it up. It's a name badge. It says 'Costas Christopoulos'.

'Oops, sorry, this was under my sandal. I hope I've not damaged it.'

'I have been looking everywhere for that. It must have dropped down there this morning. I could not see it in the dark.'

'Gosh, you start work early then?'

'Yes, I was here at six thirty.' He fixes the badge on to his waistcoat.

There's still no sign of a bus as we set off. I now have my mother's words from when I was five reverberating around in my head: 'Never get into a stranger's car.' But surely he must be okay if he's a waiter at my hotel.

He breaks into my ridiculous thoughts. 'Do I detect an English accent?'

I nod and smile. He continues with all the other questions that I normally get from taxi drivers. It's like a comic script that they've made up for tourists.

'So, where in England do you live?'

'I live in a town called Chapel-en-le-Frith, not far from Manchester.' I always reply 'near Manchester' because no one has ever heard of Chapel-en-le-Frith and then I get 'Are you a Manchester City or Manchester United supporter?' Then there's the topic of our hideous weather and non-existent summers. Of course, he isn't a taxi driver and he's being very polite and making an effort so I join in the banter.

'What is your name?' he asks quite innocently, as you would.

Without thinking, I'm suddenly replying, 'Shirley Valentine.'

If he's a Costas, then I quite like the idea of being Shirley Valentine just for a laugh. I'm pretty sure 'Costas' was the name of the guy Shirley had a fling with in *Shirley Valentine*. I wish I'd not fallen asleep when I was watching it on the plane; I never even watched it properly when the girls from work bought it for me as a gift. We were too busy quaffing wine and chatting to be paying attention to some 80s film about a woman having a midlife crisis. But I might as well make the most of being a Valentine; I'll be back to Collins when the divorce goes through.

I smile, expecting him to suss me out. But he doesn't even take his eyes off the road. It's no bloody wonder. I reckon he's a couple of years younger than me and I was only six when *Shirley Valentine* came out. Well, this is another fine mess I've got myself into!

'So, Shirley, why you go to town? I thought you were relaxing today?'

Before I engage my brain, I reply, 'To buy a new dress.' The sun must be affecting me. The other dress will be okay once it's washed, and I've got others anyway, but I just can't help myself.

Costas is quick to reply. 'I know a shop to buy a dress just like yours.'

I'm sorry now because he's so lovely and is trying to help while I'm just taking advantage of him and winding him up. 'I'm not buying a dress, I'm sightseeing.' I catch his eye and he gets it.

'You English are so funny. I like your sense of humour. But I show you the town – it is where I grow up. I show you things that are not on map or guide.'

I giggle to myself. I'm sure he can show me plenty of things that aren't on the map or in the guide, but somehow I think he's got a totally innocent itinerary in his head. More's the pity.

'Okay, Costas, you can be my guide for the day. I'm all yours.'

I feel more at ease now. I wind my window down and the breeze blows through my hair as we whizz along. There are fields on either side of the road, with the odd goat here and there, and there are pretty spring flowers dotted about and a beautiful blue sky up above. Nearly every building is white and most have blue shutters. It's a sharp contrast to all our stone and brickwork houses at home. I did think the island would be greener, but the flowers provide colour, especially the dark pink and red bougainvillea plants that are cascading down most of the buildings. The whole place is intoxicating. I think back to this morning and the milk accident and wonder if this is fate…

Costas breaks into my train of thought. 'First I go home and change clothes and we leave car,' he says, smiling.

Okay, I'm panicking slightly again. But I don't have to go in with him, I can wait outside. After all, he's got to change.

I can hardly expect him to wander round dressed as a waiter all afternoon – although it would be quite amusing. I could spend the day clicking my fingers and saying 'Waiter!' at every opportunity.

We turn off the road on to a dusty single track with the sea on our left. The bushes scrape the side of the car and the odd insect falls in. I quickly wind up my window. I don't want another insect drama, especially with Costas next to me.

After a couple of minutes of bumping along on the track, we pull in at a small, quaint hotel. Just like most other buildings here, it's got whitewashed walls and blue shutters.

'Okay, Shirley, we here. Come meet my parents while I change. It is after ten thirty so my papa make you coffee.'

'Oh yes, thank you, that will be lovely.' I can't believe, after all the fiasco of this morning, that he remembers I like coffee after half ten.

We get out of the car and he shouts something in Greek. A couple appear at the door and he introduces us. 'Mama, Papa, this is Shirley, a guest from hotel who I show about town. Shirley, my parents, Stavros and Xena.'

They each extend a hand to be shaken and then Costas asks them to fix me up with a coffee. He says something to them in Greek. The only words that I can distinguish are 'Shirley Valentine' and 'Costas'. His mum smiles and shakes her head and shows me to a table with a view of the sea. I sit on a blue-painted wooden chair.

Stavros asks what kind of coffee I'd like and I try my luck with a request for a cappuccino.

'Oh, you just make his day,' laughs Xena. 'He can try out the new coffee machine.'

As I'm waiting, I can hear the machine shake into life in the bar. There's lots of screeching and swooshing and finally a banging noise.

Xena brings my coffee over and smiles. 'See, he even try his shapes.'

Stavros has shaken chocolate on the foam in the shape of a heart. Xena leaves me with the coffee and I soak up the lovely atmosphere.

The restaurant is in the style of a little *taverna*. There are vines growing everywhere, and olive and palm trees provide some welcome shade and dapple the light on to my table. The restaurant is built on wooden decking. There's an abundance of pretty flowers around: bright red geraniums and yellow and purple pansies are dotted about everywhere in terracotta and brightly coloured ceramic pots. My favourite is the bright pink bougainvillea bush cascading down one of the corner posts. A black and white cat is lying in the shade, without a care in the world. The hotel itself is situated on a golden sandy beach; there are a few people sunbathing under straw parasols. It's a bit of a mystery to me why Costas works at another hotel when he lives at one, but I'm sure he'll enlighten me.

Speak of the devil. He's heading my way looking even more irresistible than before. He's wearing a pair of jeans and a white T-shirt with sunglasses perched on his head. He shouts something in Greek to his parents and waves.

'So, Shirley, are you ready for your tour of town with the best expert guide? You better wear this, just in case.' He hands me a crash helmet and gestures towards a little orange moped with a shark motif on the back.

'No, Costas, I *don't* think so! I'll be terrified on the back of there.'

But he's already sitting on the contraption, ready to go. 'You have no need to worry. We not go far or fast, and this is better for town. You will be fine. Just hold on to me tightly.'

Now, there's an offer I can't refuse. I take off my hat, squash it into my bag and put on the rather awful helmet. I mount the moped awkwardly and thank goodness that I changed into shorts.

We set off along the track with the dust blowing up. The beautiful clear blue sea is on our left, and I can see a church and some white windmills in the distance. Pretty wildflowers are dotted along the track. After a couple of minutes, Costas stops by a weather-beaten guy who has just cast a fishing line into the ocean. I laugh to myself because he's wearing a sweater and I'm baking hot. I understand the first word of the conversation, which is *kalimera*, and after that I'm at a loss. As we set off again, Costas fills me in, although I can't hear much as he's facing forward. I glean 'family friend ... fishing for local restaurants,' from the conversation. There's now quite a strong cool breeze blowing. I wonder if maybe I do need a sweater after all.

We haven't travelled far before Costas stops again. This time, he gets off the moped and helps me off too. He chats to an elderly lady who's wearing an electric blue jogging suit with a navy canvas hat. Once again, I'm at loss after *kalimera*, but I can see that she's the town's answer to the problem of feeding stray cats. She's using a large bin lid as an improvised feeding tray. She puts it down and tips cat biscuits into it, along with some cat milk.

'You like cats?' Costas asks. He takes my hand and leads me behind the jogging-suit woman to show me some kittens playing in the shrubbery.

'Oh, they're adorable! I want to take them all home.'

'Me too,' he admits, 'but I would be in a big trouble.'

They're about five weeks old. They pounce on each other and roll around.

'I remember my sister once came across some kittens near my grandma's house. We sneaked Grandma's shopping basket out of the pantry and went to collect the kittens. We took them back to show her. She wasn't very amused and made us take them back. I've longed for a kitten ever since that day and I'm still waiting.'

'Maybe one day your wish will be granted and you will have a kitten like this one.' Costas picks up a white kitten with mottled brown markings and places it in my hands. It's an adorable little thing. He teases it with his finger and I wonder about putting it in my bag, under my hat, just as he whisks it away and reunites it with its playmates.

He leads me away from the moped, which he leaves with the old woman, and we wander over to a little church. I take a couple of photos on my phone and then I remember the camera that's in my bag. Helen wants some good-quality photos for her brochure; this scene will make a picture-perfect image, with whitewashed walls, terracotta roofs, the deep blue sea and the sky behind. I retrieve the camera out of my bag and take a few shots. I used to love taking photos, and this is a good reason to get the camera clicking away again.

It's a simple little church with an archway and two Celtic crosses on either side of the door, which also has a little cross on it. Above the archway, there's another arch with two bells, one on top of the other. The ropes are tied off down by the side of the door. I wonder how many people have untied them and given the bells a ring. Costas opens the door and we step inside. It's slightly cooler in the little church, which is a welcome relief. There are no rows of pews, just a couple of long wooden benches at the sides. On the back wall, there's a wooden panel and a silky white curtain.

'The confessional seat is behind the curtain, if you need to confess about anything, Shirley.'

'I'd need a full day, Costas. Maybe I'll make a list and come back another time,' I reply, laughing. I could start with lying about my name.

The Greek national flag is also there above the wooden panel, tied up next to a picture of Jesus. I'm drawn to a couple of memorial plaques, which I assume are written in Greek. Costas comes to the rescue.

'These plaques are in memory of my great-grandparents. My family has always come to this church. They take it in turn to attend the service every Sunday. Someone has to stay behind to look after the hotel. What about you – do you visit a church at home?'

'Only christenings, weddings and funerals, I'm afraid. What about you?'

'Yes, I come when I can. It is even harder now I work at the Boutique Blue, but there is service at night as well so that helps.'

I turn round and spot a mixed bouquet of roses and gypsophila in a vase by the altar that stops me dead in my tracks. It's exactly like my wedding bouquet. It knocks me for six. I feel like a knife has just been plunged into my stomach. I feel dizzy and my pulse is racing. I'm suddenly transported back to my wedding day, with all its fun and laughter. It seems surreal that my marriage is now coming to an end. I close my eyes and tears start falling down my cheeks.

'Shirley, are you all right?'

'Sorry, Costas. Ignore me, I'll be fine. It's just a difficult time for me at the moment. I've recently split up from my husband and it's all a bit painful, you know?' I reply in a whisper.

He smiles and wipes away my tears. 'Yes, I know, many memories, good and bad…' He takes my hand. 'Trust me, it will get better. Here, we both light a candle.'

I take a deep breath and manage to wipe away the rest of my tears with a tissue that I've thankfully located in my bag. Costas drops a coin into the little box and picks up a couple of long, thin, tapered candles. He passes one to me. There are already two candles burning, standing upright in sand in a circular tray perched on a brass stand.

'My grandparents light these this morning when they open church,' he explains.

I've watched people lighting candles before but never actually done it myself. I'm just going to follow Costas. He carefully lights his candle from one of the two lit by his grandparents earlier. This seems very poignant. He then bows his head, presumably to say a prayer.

I feel calmer now after my flower anguish. I light my candle from Costas's and pop it in the sand. I start to think about a prayer. Um, well, there's Mum and Dad. We've not heard from them yet so I hope they're enjoying their clipper ship cruise. Then there's Helen and her situation with James. I've got a sixth sense and I just don't think he's right for her. Then there's me. Neither Richard nor I are prepared to compromise over having a family. I honestly thought he'd come round to my way of thinking but with each day since he left in January that hope has diminished. I need to be realistic and move on with my life. A good starting point will be enjoying this holiday and, today, the company of Costas on our little adventure.

Costas still has his head bowed. He's obviously got a longer list than me. He's probably praying for world peace. He seems like a very caring person, one who looks out for others. I glance round the little church again and notice other things. The solid wooden pulpit to the side has a lace cloth hanging over it, with a picture of St George on a rearing horse, George with a spear pointed at a dragon's throat.

Costas has finished his prayer and resumes his tour-guide spiel. 'This is St George and the dragon. I believe he is the patron saint of England, as well as many other places. We have a St George church in the town which I will show you. Are you feeling better now?'

'Yes, I am, thank you. And thank you for showing me this beautiful church.'

Costas heads to the door. I feel quite humbled by this experience and I'm really pleased that I took him up on his offer of a guided tour. Otherwise, I would never have seen it from a local person's perspective.

'Right, Shirley, we carry on. I take you now to Little Venice.'

I'm slightly confused by this Venice thing. I don't want to sound like a complete idiot so I remain silent and follow Costas back to the scooter. He gives the cat lady a couple of euros. I pop on my helmet and climb on to the moped. We haven't gone much further when the track opens out into a car park. Dust is blowing up everywhere. Costas parks the moped next to a car that's absolutely covered in dust. Passers-by have written comments on it, which tickles me.

'Why you laugh?' Costas enquires.

'The message on this car: "Help! SOS! Also available in black. Wash me."'

'Oh, I see,' Costas replies, shaking his head and smiling. 'That English sense of humour again.'

There *are* comments in other languages, which I assume translate into the same thing. Other nationalities, it seems, also appreciate the joke.

'Anyway, Shirley, I bring you to see windmills not dirty cars.'

'Oh yes, the windmills. They do look charming and very rustic. I'll take some photos.'

It would be difficult to miss them. Five of them are standing neatly in a row. I get my camera out to capture the beautiful white cylindrical buildings. There are little windows dotted here and there and the roofs are thatched. The spokes of the windmills are wooden; they are framed beautifully by the clear deep blue sky behind them. As I walk round the side to see another aspect, the wind nearly knocks me off my feet.

'Oh yes, that is why they are here – the strong wind from the north,' Costas chips in, laughing at the wind blowing my hair all over the place. If I'd kept on my dress from this morning, it would have made a great Marilyn Monroe shot. 'They were built in sixteenth century to mill flour. These are *kato milli*, the lower mills.' He's taking his new role as a tour guide very seriously.

I take a photo from the windswept angle. Then Costas wants to take one of me on his phone, standing in front of a windmill. I resist, using my bad hair as an excuse, but Costas insists that it '*creates effect*'. Before I know it, he's taken a photo of me. A kind passer-by takes a photo of both of us; Costas carefully places his arm round my shoulder, which feels natural.

We wander back to the moped through the dusty car park. I'm enjoying the moped way of getting about, with the ease of parking just about anywhere and jumping on and off. I feel liberated. We'd still be trying to park here if we'd been in a car. There are several of them now circling the car park, adding more dust to the poor black wash-me car, and to me.

We leave the car park and manoeuvre down a narrow street, avoiding some tourists who clearly don't realise they're walking on a road. A small stretch of sand in a cove comes into sight, with some buildings backed by the sea in the distance. Costas says something; he obviously doesn't realise that I can't hear a thing. He's facing forward and talking to me through his helmet, and the wind is a force ten gale now that we've reached the waterfront. All I catch is 'Venice'. When we reach the water's edge, he stops. I can hear him better as he turns round.

'You want to take photo?'

He's pulled up alongside a small square white table and two white wooden chairs that are set on the concrete paving just off the water's edge. They remind me of *Shirley Valentine*. I seem to remember she asks for a table and a chair so she can drink her wine while watching the sunset. In any case, they look very typically Greek so I take a photo.

As I start putting my camera away he pipes up. 'You not take photo of Little Venice?' He points to the buildings backed by the sea.

'Oh yes, silly me, Little Venice.' That will teach me for not reading up on Mykonos or questioning Nikos. I flick the camera back on and capture Little Venice in all its glory, flanked by the crystal clear sea on one side and the cloudless deep blue sky behind. I've never been to the real Venice, but I remember a James Bond film with Roger Moore and a gondola chase that resulted in chaos. This, in turn, reminds me of my dream.

'Shirley, would you like to walk round the shops?'

'Yes, I wouldn't mind that. But I can always come back another day if it's not your cup of tea.'

'I'm sure we can find you a cup of tea.'

'No, sorry, Costas! I don't want a cup of tea. In England, "a cup of tea" can also mean something you're interested in. We can skip the shopping if there are other things you'd find more interesting to see.'

'Ah, I see! Very interesting. But no, the shops are fine. We will park the moped and have a walk.'

We come to a long row of parked up mopeds and scooters and he pulls into a space.

I clamber off the moped and unfasten my helmet, which Costas takes off me and hooks over the handlebars. Clearly, there's more trust here than in England. At home, they'd probably be on ebay in less than five minutes.

'So, Shirley, are you all right after scary ride?'

I smile back and mutter, 'Actually, it wasn't that bad.'

Before I can say another word, he gets hold of my hand and leads the way up a side street and away from the harbour.

I can't remember ever going on a shopping expedition instigated by a bloke before, so this is a new experience. Richard would do anything to get out of shopping. In the end, I just gave up. I used to envy all the couples wandering around on a Saturday and Sunday, holding hands and looking happy. Mind you, I've also witnessed some right arguments while I've been at work. Shopping does sometimes bring out the worst in people, especially at Christmas and the sales.

We make our way through the extremely narrow streets. I'm immediately intoxicated by the mix of colours against the background of white buildings everywhere. It's postcard perfect. I wonder if they've agreed at a town meeting that all walls have to be white, all paintwork blue. Every other colour comes from plants, pots and things for sale in the shops. I love it so much that I get out my camera to take some more snaps.

The first shop to catch my eye has bags of all shapes, sizes and colours hanging invitingly outside. Helen would absolutely love this shop. There's bags in blue, pink, red, orange, lilac, yellow, green, white and, of course, our old favourites, black and brown. Satchels, duffels, clutches, shoppers, totes, rucksacks … OMG, it's every bagaholic's dream.

Costas seems happy chatting away to the owner so I saunter to the shop next door. Another explosion of colour greets me. This time it's mini-guitars in red, orange, blue, pink and one in yellow that has eyes and a smile. There are some strange instruments here, ones that look a bit like guitars with long necks and rounded backs.

Costas appears and correctly interprets my curiosity. 'These are *bouzouki*.' He kindly proceeds to fill me in on their history, how they came to Greece and how they are used in a lot of the music that we hear in shops and restaurants. 'Here, I show you.' He lifts one off its hook and impressively plays a bit of a tune.

'Wow! That's really good.'

'Thank you. I play at my parents' hotel sometimes at night. I will have to play for you.'

'Yes, you must. I'd love that.'

He hooks the *bouzouki* back up and we carry on. As we mooch round, I marvel that there seems to be a shop for everything. There's a few brand names blending in nicely as well.

'Accessorize – this is one of my favourites.'

'I can show you a local shop where they make the jewellery right there.'

'Ooh, that sounds interesting. Lead the way.'

We carry on through the endless maze of shops and restaurants.

'Here we are.'

'Wow. I love the name.'

'Oh yes,' Costas laughs. '"*Amnēsia*" – it is Greek word meaning forgetfulness.'

We walk in. I certainly won't forget this shop in a hurry. My eyes widen at all the necklaces, earrings, bracelets and rings that are covering every inch of the shop. After looking around for a while, a necklace with a fine multicoloured string catches my eye. Its pendant is a flower with mauve, blue, turquoise, red, yellow and orange petals.

'I love this! I'm going to treat myself and get one for my sister too.'

The one I've chosen for Helen has a daisy pendant and will go with her new dresses. The sales assistant wraps them both in tissue paper and pops them in gorgeous little gift bags. Costas speaks to the shop owner and negotiates a better price, which is good because that means I can pay with the euros in my purse.

'Thank you for bringing me here, Costas. I could very well be coming back to buy some gifts. And thanks for your haggling.'

'Oh, it is no problem. They always do a better deal for a local person.'

We continue our exploring. We've not gone far when Costas pauses in an archway. 'And this is our outdoor cinema.'

Costas presents it like it's the best thing since sliced bread and I can't imagine anything more romantic than watching a movie with your loved one under a starlit sky, but this particular cinema doesn't give me that vibe. There are folding chairs lined up row after row and I'm sure it would make for the most uncomfortable, unromantic night ever.

'It doesn't look very comfortable, Costas.'

'When I show you where we watch film before you will see that this is luxury.'

'Really?' I'm unconvinced.

'Yes, really. Come, I show you.'

He leads me up a steep hill. Despite my weekly keep-fit classes, I'm soon panting and out of breath. 'Flipping heck, Costas, how much further is it?'

'Not far. You can have a rest here.' He points to a wooden swing seat that's attached to a wall with ropes. I can hear piano music, which is very soothing.

'That's thoughtful – a seat and someone playing a piano.'

'Yes, but there is music only when she practice. That is Pascale. She plays at many hotels in the area, including the Boutique Blue.' We listen for a couple of minutes while I get my breath back and then we carry on. 'It's just a few more steps...'

At last, we reach the top of the hill, where there's a spectacular rooftop view of the whole town. 'So, Shirley, here is our very own amphitheatre.'

'Wow, this is amazing!'

'Amazing, but rather uncomfortable, so we bring something to sit on.'

'Is it still used, then?'

'Yes, it is used for live performances such as plays or music and, for the health-conscious, there is yoga and pilates. Sometimes people get married here.'

'What a romantic place to get married.'

'Yes, I have been to a couple of weddings here. It is a most beautiful place to marry. Now, I do not want to upset you again talking about weddings. What do you think of walking back and going to a restaurant that I know for some lunch?'

'That sounds like a good idea... I'm sorry about what happened before at the church.'

'You have no need to be sorry, we all have emotion at some stage of our lives.' He looks into my eyes and for a few seconds I sense some sadness. Costas can tell I've picked up on it and quickly avoids any more questions. 'Now, let us go. At least it is all walking down hill.'

'Yes, thank goodness for that. I'm feeling rather hot.' In more ways than one!

Chapter 10

Helen

I walk back to our hotel, cursing my uncomfortable shoes. I contemplate finding Stephanie to tell her what's happened, but I can just *hear* her response, in her I-told-you-so voice: 'I've never trusted him … I mean, who doesn't return messages for days on end? Problems with his phone – yeah, right!'

Oh my goodness, how wrong could I be? The realisation is starting to dawn. I'm tempted to send him a message. 'Hi James, I've just met Selena. You two-timing weasel.' Maybe I'll send him one later after a drink or two.

I get back to our room just as housekeeping is leaving. They've separated the beds, so at least Steph can't clobber me again in her sleep, mad girl. It's just occurred to me – the double bed and the champagne. Maybe that was for Selena's benefit! I could finish off that text with 'P.S. Enjoyed the champagne.' My stomach churns in anguish. But I need to focus on getting my work done sooner rather than later so I can spend some time relaxing with Steph over the next two weeks.

My next stop is the Mykonos Gold, which will be downgraded to the Mykonos Bronze if it carries on the way it is. It's basically running the risk of losing its contract with our company, which would be a financial blow to the hotel. The last two reviews seem to be along the same lines; basically, it's a badly run hotel with a manager who treats complaints with indifference. I'm going to visit as a tourist, on the pretence of booking a room which requires me to change into something more causal, and also to take my overnight bag.

I quickly change my clothes and pop my laptop and note pad into my overnight bag. I take the lift back down to reception. There's no click-clacking this time. I've changed into my new jewelled flip-flops from Michaela's Boutique and I actually feel like I'm on holiday.

I do need a taxi this time; the porter sorts one out for me. Five minutes later, I'm on my way. I tell the taxi driver where I'm going. He raises an eyebrow and repeats the name of the hotel back as though to say 'Are you sure?'. Not a good sign.

We soon arrive at the Mykonos Gold, which actually looks quite smart. Once inside, however, I'm greeted by what can only be described as chaos. There's a handful of people complaining about a shuttle bus at the reception desk and only a couple of staff dealing with them – and not particularly well, by the sounds of it.

There are a couple of arrivals too. They're bewildered and probably considering asking for a transfer. I decide to discreetly video the fracas. The footage might be useful later. These are serious tactics; I feel like Alex Polizzi from *The Hotel Inspector*.

The discussion is getting more heated and voices are getting louder.

'Very well then, I want to speak to the person in charge.'

One of the reception staff replies quite rudely, 'He is unable to come to the desk.'

The spokesperson of the group is really fired up now. He retorts, 'Why? Has he lost the use of his legs?'

'No, he is out,' comes the sharp reply.

'So, who is in charge when the manager is out?'

'I am in charge and I have already told you I cannot do anything about the bus driver.'

The spokesperson is clearly at the end of his tether. He throws his arms up in disbelief. 'Right! I've had enough of this nonsense. What time will the manager be back?'

'At two.'

'Well, you tell him that I'll be back at two! This is an appalling way to treat your customers!'

The group are shaking their heads. I can hear one of them say, 'I warned you, John. It's bloody hard work. I was treated just the same yesterday when Karen slipped on the floor…'

I decide to defer my room enquiry and let them deal with the guests who need checking in. I'll come back at two o'clock for Part 2 of the shuttle-bus saga. That should be interesting.

I decide to have some lunch in the meantime. There are four restaurants to choose from. I don't want a huge meal so that rules out two of the restaurants straight away. I go outside in the direction of the pool, in pursuit of the pool bar. It seems rather quiet people-wise, but not noise-wise. There's some music blaring out, which isn't at all suitable. There are no staff members in sight and just one couple sitting at a table. I take a seat myself and wait … and wait … and wait. I glance round at the couple to see if they've even got a drink. They haven't, so I decide to go and find a staff member myself.

It doesn't take me long to find someone who doesn't seem to be doing an awful lot. 'Excuse me, is anyone serving at the pool bar? I'm wanting a drink and something to eat.'

'You can eat there if you want, but most people go to the restaurant near the beach. It's all the same menu.' He points me in the direction I should go. I'm not going to argue. I set off in hot pursuit of this other restaurant, which will hopefully include some staff able to serve me.

When I get there, I see that it looks like an authentic Greek *taverna* and there are people actually eating, which is a start. I wait a while. Eventually, a young waitress, whose name badge says 'Natassia', approaches me.

'Table for one, madam?' she asks, looking at me and then around the restaurant to see where she might seat me.

'Yes, please,' I reply.

'Follow me, please,' she says, not sounding like she's enjoying any part of her day. She sits me down, hands me a menu and disappears. No offer of a drink, no option of smoking or non-smoking and no mention of any menu specials. After five minutes, I've studied the menu and I'm ready to order some food. A drink would be nice as well. I discreetly try to catch someone's attention for the next five minutes. Then I resort to waving and saying in quite a loud voice, 'Excuse me!'

Natassia saunters over and opens her note pad. I ask her about specials, to which she says she'll go and find out. I fear she will go and never return so I hastily say it doesn't matter. I order a *spanakopita*, a Greek spinach pie. I also order a Mint Collins off the cocktail list. It's a working holiday, after all. It's quite apt as well, with my surname being Collins, and I love trying cocktails.

While I wait, I decide to do a little recce to the loos. I've brought along this clever machine that measures how clean things are. A few recent reviews have mentioned that the cleaning isn't up to standard here so this will be a good opportunity to try it out.

I retrieve the machine from my bag and get out one of the swabs that looks like a cotton bud. I rub it on the toilet door handle and then replace the swab in its tube. It feels like I'm on a top-secret mission. I have to now inject an enzyme into the tube, gently shake it, remove it and put it in the machine. Then I have to wait for fifteen seconds. Any reading up to a thousand is acceptable.

The machine whirs into action just as a woman comes into the toilets. 'Are you waiting?' she asks politely.

'Oh no, sorry, don't mind me. I'm just doing some cleanliness testing.'

'Really?' she laughs. 'Now this I must see, because this is surely one of the dirtiest hotels I've ever had the misfortune to stay in.'

We watch the machine together. It reaches one thousand in no time. It bleeps at every thousand mark and carries on and on and on, furiously bleeping away. One thousand, two thousand, three thousand, four thousand, five thousand, six thousand, seven thousand, eight thousand, nine thousand, ten thousand. And then ten thousand, nine hundred and eighty-two. It finally stops and flashes an alert in red. In other words, you're taking your life into your own hands by using these facilities. Not even in airport toilets did it go much past the one thousand mark.

'So, what does your machine tell you?' she asks, already knowing the answer.

'It says, "Houston, I think we have a problem." It's not good. I'm Helen, by the way, from Loving Luxury Travel. I'm doing our annual inspection.'

'Well, I never. We booked through your company and spoke to a lovely guy called James. We told him it was our wedding anniversary and that we wanted it to be special.'

My stomach churns again. He's already got a lot to answer for, and now he's apparently helped wreck this poor couple's anniversary.

'I'm Janette, by the way. Me and my other half have never seen anything like it. I've complained about our room twice. It's filthy. They seem to have a different idea of "clean" than I do. You can come and look if you like.'

After this experience with the loos, I don't doubt what she's saying. 'I'll tell you what. You write down your names and your room number on the back of my card and I'll get it sorted out.'

'Oh, thank you, Helen, we'd really appreciate it. But, to be honest, I think anything you say will fall on deaf ears.'

'Well, I'll try my best.'

I return to the restaurant and get my phone out to text Steph. My plan to spend the afternoon by the pool has evaporated along with my appetite. My Mint Collins has arrived so I have a sip… It's definitely minty; in fact, it would make a good mouth wash. Note to self: if ever on a night out and needing a breath freshener, order a Mint Collins.

Natassia appears shortly afterwards armed with my spinach pie and a little dish of mixed olives. She offers me some black pepper, which I accept. Off she goes to collect the biggest pepper mill I've ever seen in my life. I laugh to myself. She has to stand quite a way back to grind the huge monstrosity over the food. I've never been anywhere in Greece, so it's a whole new experience for me. At least the food tastes good. I even enjoy the olives, which I didn't think I liked.

I finish my food and decide to email Daniel about arranging an emergency meeting this afternoon with whoever's in charge here. If we schedule it for three o'clock, that will give me just over an hour to inspect a room and have a stroll round.

I have another battle to get someone's attention for the bill. I just leave some money when it finally arrives. I really can't be bothered waiting to pay on my card while they mess about getting the card machine. I need to get on and attempt to check in. As I'm leaving I can hear a couple complaining that their food is lukewarm. Natassia is dealing with the complaint but not particularly well, by the sounds of it.

I go back to the reception. Thankfully, it seems a bit calmer so I walk up to the desk. There's someone different on the desk this time. His name badge says 'Giannis', and he looks keen and ready to help.

'Hi, I'd like a room for the night,' I say.

'Okay, let me check our room availability. Is it just…' We're interrupted by the phone. 'Sorry, please excuse me for one minute.' He picks up the phone, rattles off something in Greek and seemingly tries to put the call through somewhere else. But no one answers. He resumes the call himself and spiels something else off. Then he ends the call and turns his attention back to me. 'I apologise. So, a room for tonight. Is it just for you?'

'Yes, just me. I'm stopping in Mykonos for a couple of days and my sister recommended this place.'

'Really? Does your sister—'

He's stopped in mid flow again but this time the interruption comes from a colleague who appears from the office behind him. I glance at his name badge and notice the word 'Manager' under his name. This is who I'm probably meeting at three. I can hardly wait. I wonder if Giannis was just about to say 'Really? Does your sister not like you very much?'

He answers the rather rude manager and starts again. 'You mentioned your sister. Has she visited the hotel recently?'

I feel guilty now and wish that I hadn't mentioned this fictitious visit. 'Oh, I'm not sure,' I answer vaguely so that we can move the conversation along and get me out of the hole that I've started digging.

'OK, we have this lovely—'

It's two o'clock and the shuttle-bus man from earlier is back. He's ringing the bell on the desk quite insistently. Our conversation is cut short again as we can't talk above the noise.

'Please excuse me for a moment,' says Giannis. He calmly walks over to the man. 'Yes, sir, how can I help?'

'I want to see the person in charge of this shambolic place that you call a hotel – immediately!'

I feel sorry for Giannis as he tries to pacify the angry man. Only the person in charge will do. Giannis disappears from sight to where I assume the manager is hiding. After a couple of minutes, he returns and tells the man that the manager is on his way.

'He'd better be,' is the reply. Quite frankly, even I'm scared.

Giannis comes back to me. 'I am very sorry about all the interruptions. This is your key card. Take the lift, which is down the corridor, and your room will be on the second floor. Turn right after you leave the lift. Do you need any help with luggage?'

'No, I'm fine, I only have this. I would like the Wi-Fi password, though.'

'Just log on to our site and use your surname and room number. There is Wi-Fi connection only in the reception and bar.'

'And it's rubbish, like everything else in this godforsaken place,' adds the man. He's still waiting.

'Thanks for the tip,' I reply, just as the manager finally appears.

This is a brilliant opportunity to watch his interaction. I devise an excuse so that I can hang about. 'I'll take a seat over there and sort out my emails,' I say to Giannis.

'Enjoy your stay, Miss Collins.'

Well, Giannis can certainly demonstrate good customer-service skills. Let's see how his manager does.

'Oh, so you do exist! I'm so glad you've given me some of your valuable time.'

'Of course I exist, Mr er...'

'Jenkins!'

'Yes, I apologise, Mr Jenkins. We do have many guests. My receptionist tells me you have a complaint about the shuttle bus.'

'Yes, indeed, the shuttle bus. This timetable says the last bus back from town leaves at ten thirty.'

'No, you are wrong, Mr Jenkins. The last bus back from town is at ten o'clock. That time is when it arrives here.'

'Yes, that's all well and good now but this information is misleading.'

'Well, it is looking very clear to me, Mr Jenkins.'

'Really? I didn't catch your name…'

'Michalis Pallis.'

'Well, Mr Pallis, there were eight of us waiting for that bus and we all thought the last bus was at ten thirty. So, it didn't look clear to us. Your driver left us stranded in town and he was very rude to us.'

'Well, you would not have been stranded. There are taxis and the bus service.'

'Mr Pallis, the last bus leaves at ten! We resorted to getting two taxis.'

'So, it is as I said, the problem is solved.'

'No, the problem isn't solved. There are eight of us who are now out of pocket. This information needs to be clearer.'

'Very well, Mr Jenkins, I will see to it that the information is made clearer and I will speak to the driver. I am very sorry you are out of pocket but there is nothing I can do about it.'

'Right, well, we'll see about that. I want the name and address of someone with whom I can take this further.'

'Very well. Here is a name and address. Enjoy the rest of your day, Mr Jenkins.'

Michalis retreats to his office and Mr Jenkins stomps off huffing and cursing under his breath. I pack up my laptop and finally go to find my room.

When I get there, I find the key card doesn't work. I try it a few times with no luck. 'For crying out loud!' I shout in frustration.

An elderly woman who is cleaning the room opposite mine hears me and lets me in to my room. She shakes her head, muttering, 'This happen all the time.'

At last, I'm in my room. It's mediocre but I don't need my machine to measure how clean it is. I can see with my own eyes the dust on top of the headboard, and the scene under the bed is just gross. There's at least one dead fly in among the dust and God knows what else. Unbelievably, there's also a condom packet. I pick it up as evidence. It's ribbed and dotted for maximum pleasure.

I resort to taking photos of the substandard cleaning. The bathroom reveals one of my biggest pet hates – hair in the shower plughole. I'm not touching it; it's disgusting beyond words. I just take a photo as proof. I type up my report and leave the room for my meeting.

Giannis is slightly confused when I arrive back at his desk for a meeting with his manager. But he rings through and, sure enough, the manager appears and beckons me into his office.

'I'm Michalis Pallis. I believe we have some urgent business to discuss. Is James joining us?'

I take a deep breath. 'No, James is not joining us. He's gone to our office in Florida.'

'Oh, this is a shame. Not permanently, I hope?'

'I wouldn't know.' I'm tempted to ask why it's a shame but think better of it. I'm guessing James turns a blind eye to all the issues in the hotel.

It's no great surprise that the office looks like a bomb's hit it, with papers piled high. There's a Chinese cat ornament rocking and waving to me from its perch on top of a filing cabinet. There's cat-related stuff dotted all around the office, including pictures on the walls and a rubber in the shape of a cat sitting on the desk. I half expect one to jump on my knee.

I can't resist. 'So, you like cats, then?'

He spends the next ten minutes telling me how his mother looks after the strays in town.

I'm seriously losing the will to live. 'So, Michalis, back to the matter at hand. There seems to be a trend of the hotel receiving bad reviews, which is bringing your scores down.'

'Really? I did not notice.'

'As the manager, Michalis, it's your job to notice. You should be looking at these reviews every day and addressing them.'

'Guests always complain about something. They are not happy unless they find fault.'

'They don't complain this much at our other hotels. What about Mr Jenkins? He had a valid point about that timetable. In fact, if you'd bothered to look at customer reviews in the past two weeks, you'd see that Mr Jenkins wasn't the first person to be stranded.'

'I keep saying this – they are not stranded. There is a perfectly good taxi service.'

'Right, that's enough. This incompetence stops right now. You have a compensation budget that you can use to recompense Mr Jenkins and the others. That timetable needs altering immediately. While I was being checked in, you rudely interrupted Giannis. That practice is to stop with immediate effect.'

'I did no such thing, I just ask question.'

'Yes, without acknowledging me! The customer! Maybe if I had long whiskers and miaowed, you might have taken notice?' I don't give him chance to answer. 'And another thing. The standard of cleanliness here is absolutely appalling. These are photos that I've just taken in the room I was checked into. I did a hygiene check in the restaurant toilets and that was off the scale. Oh, and I want the couple in Room 25 upgraded to the best room you've got and a complimentary bottle of champagne delivered to the room. And I want the room to be *clean*. Do I make myself clear?'

Michalis is shaking his head. 'This is so unnecessary. James never makes all this fuss. We get the nitty-gritty out of the way and then we hit the town...'

This is the final straw. I hand him my report. 'These are all the action points that I want sorting out before I go back to the

UK, which gives you nearly two weeks. Non-compliance will mean this hotel will lose its gold status, do I make myself clear?'

'Very clear.' He's about to say something else but changes his mind.

We part company. As I leave, Giannis is still looking confused and Mr Jenkins and the shuttle-bus party are heading back towards the desk. Part of me is tempted to hang around and listen in on how Michalis deals with the situation after my pep talk; another part of me is thinking I need a stiff drink. That part wins hands down.

Chapter 11

Stephanie

We twist and turn through the narrow streets. I wouldn't even know if we were on the same streets we've just come up. It's all a maze. Within a couple of minutes, we arrive at the end of a street that opens into a little square. There, in all its glory, is a Greek *taverna*. It's just like I'd imagined. A crude wooden structure, surrounded by lots of brightly-coloured plants, pots and painted tables and chairs, which are in the restaurant and also lining the wall in the square opposite.

Costas resumes his waiter's role. 'Does madam have a preference for a particular table?'

'Somewhere in the shade would be lovely. I need to acclimatise my pale skin.'

A woman greets us. Costas gestures towards a table that's nicely shaded. She seats us and returns with some menus.

'What would you like to drink?' Costas asks.

'Ooh, something nice and refreshing. I've worked up quite a thirst walking up to the amphitheatre.'

'I would recommend Afternoon Delight.'

I can feel my heart begin to race and I'm probably blushing like mad. 'And what's in one of those?' I'm half expecting him to suggest it's what we do later but, no, he hands me the cocktail menu and starts reeling off the ingredients.

'Now let me see if I remember … Bacardi, Southern Comfort, peach liqueur, cranberry juice and ginger ale.'

I check them off the menu. 'Well done. You've only missed this.' I point to one item.

'Oh yes, it is energy drink.'

'So, how do you know all about cocktails?'

'We love cocktails in Mykonos, and I have studied them for many years. I've even created some of my own.'

'Wow, a cocktail connoisseur.'

'I will make you one tonight at the hotel.'

'I'll look forward to it. Now, what do you suggest to eat? I'm starving.'

'I suggest we share a typical Greek meze, with things like *hummus*, *falafel*, *dolmades* and *fattoush*.'

'Sounds good to me. I've been to a handful of Greek restaurants at home so I've tried a few of those things.'

We place our order for some drinks and food. I can't help laughing at Costas who's ordered a boring coke. 'After all that, you've ordered a coke?'

'I do not mix driving and drinking.'

'No, but you do risk your passenger falling off the back.'

Costas laughs. 'I do love your sense of humour, and your eyes…'

'Why do you like my eyes so much?'

'They are so blue.'

'And yours are so brown…' I'm about to add that I find them very sexy but the waitress reappears with our drinks.

'Take a sip and tell me what you think of Afternoon Delight.'

'Mmm, it's delicious.' My phone bleeps with a message alert. 'Ooh, it's my mum with an update from her trip.' I hesitate to look at it because I don't want to seem rude but Costas waves his hands.

'Carry on, please, do not worry about me.'
'Okay. It says:

Having great time, just
stopped for lunch at
little taverna in Santorini,
amazing place, fallen in love
with all Greek islands so far.
Boat amazing we even have
on-deck whores. Your dad having
withdrawal symptoms from wolf.
The itinerary has changed because
of weather issues so can you book
him in for a game on Friday.
Hope u & Helen are
behaving ;)

'Wow, Shirley, your parents are very...'

'Technophobic, Costas, and bloody useless at texting. They're on a clipper ship cruise, where they all muck in, but not to that extent. She's obviously not read it before hitting that dangerous "send" button.'

'And your dad – what is "wolf"?'

'Golf, I suspect. He's itching to have a game. I think Helen's arranging something for when the boat docks here... Ooh, I think our food's here.' A huge platter of food is placed before us. 'Flipping heck, I'm not sure I'll eat all that.'

'Do not worry, I have a big appetite and this is my main meal of the day. Now, taste.' His hand heads towards my mouth with a black olive pinched between his fingers.

'I'm not sure about olives. I've tasted them before and didn't like them.'

'Yes, but not olives grown up the road.'

I reluctantly open my mouth and he puts the slimy olive in it, giving me no option other than to start chewing. It isn't actually that bad. In fact, I quite like it. He then tries his luck with a large green olive with a slightly tougher texture. I think I like it better. I'm glad the other diners are inside so they can't be put off by our seductive olive flirting. I now join in the spirit of things by putting them in his mouth. I find this feeding each other thing is a bit of a turn on.

After a few more sips of my Afternoon Delight, I start to feel relaxed and a bit giddy. It's a long time since I've enjoyed myself in a bloke's company. I feel like a teenager again, but without all the worry of not knowing how to kiss properly or how to have sex. Richard and I had a good sex life until the dreaded let's-start-a-family topic was brought up. It all went downhill from there. He must have thought I'd trick him and try to get pregnant on the sly.

'So, Shirley, do you like the food?'

'Yes, it's delicious, but I'm going to reek of garlic and onion.'

'Reek?'

'Smell.' I waft my hand in front of my face.

'Oh, I see. But only to other people – not me.' He winks cheekily and another wave of giddiness washes over me. 'Do you have plans for the rest of this afternoon?'

'Oh, I'm not sure. I was hoping to meet my sister back at the hotel. I thought she'd have texted me by now, though.'

'Was that your sister I saw you with last night?'

'Yes, it was. I didn't notice you.'

'No, I was working on the opposite side of the restaurant. I saw you come in and thought you were going to fall over, but your sister managed to keep you upright.'

'Oh, those silly shoes. Helen did warn me that I'd end up falling over, but who listens to their older sisters?'

'You looked like you were busy.'

'Oh, my goodness, that's another story...' My phone bleeps again. 'I'm really sorry, Costas. It's probably my mum with some spelling corrections! No, I'm wrong, it's from Helen.' I read it to myself just in case there's work stuff that affects Costas in it.

> Things not going to plan.
> Had to drop in at
> hotel down the road,
> will explain later.
> Mykonos Gold is
> awful so won't be
> back until at least 6.
> Really sorry.
> See you later. xx

'Oh dear, things aren't going her way ... which means I'm a free agent. I'd like to be back at the hotel by five thirty, so I've got a couple of hours.'

'What about little sunbathe on beach at my parents' hotel?' he enquires, looking hopeful.

'Yes, that would work, if you're sure you can spare the time. That would be a really nice way to finish the afternoon. I can fill you in about my sister Helen.'

Costas teaches me to ask for the bill in Greek: *To logariasmo, parakalo.*

'I'm paying for this, Costas, after the milk fiasco and all your time showing me around.'

'Shirley, it has been a pleasure sharing such good company, and the milk made me laugh. I have not laughed like that for a very long time.'

I suddenly detect some sadness in his voice that wasn't there before, so I quickly lighten the mood. 'Maybe you could teach me to say "I'm paying on my card".'

'We could be here all afternoon. Just leave your card there. The waitress will see and bring the machine out.'

Sure enough, she appears with a card machine and taps in the amount. I put in my pin. We wait a few seconds and then she looks embarrassed. 'I am sorry, it says the card is declined.'

'What? It can't be! I told the credit card company I was going away... Oh dear, I've just remembered something.'

'Shirley, what is it?' Costas asks, looking concerned.

'The credit card company must think my card's been stolen. I told them I was going on a Caribbean cruise. I've forgotten to update them...'

Costas is laughing. 'Caribbean cruise? You are a bit off course.'

'Ha ha. I'll explain it all later. But what about this bill? I've got roughly half so we could go Dutch.'

'Now we are talking about Holland? Is this a world cruise?' Costas is laughing even more.

'No, "going Dutch" means I'll pay half.'

'Shirley, you keep your money and I will pay. This is what I would like.'

'Okay, you win. I'll call the credit card company later and maybe you'll let me treat you another time when my card's unblocked.'

'Yes, I would like very much for us to have a meal together.'

We stroll back to the moped hand in hand, laughing about the bill and I tell him about our Caribbean cruise plans.

* * *

We arrive back at the hotel and everything is quiet. It looks like most of the guests are sunbathing in the garden area or on the beach. Costas's parents are busy in the little bar. They wave at us.

Costas pulls a couple of sunloungers together and fetches towels. 'What would you like to drink?'

'Oh, just water will be fine, thanks.' I don't want him thinking I'm a lush.

He's quickly back with water in a cooler jug and a couple of glasses with ice. 'I just change into swim shorts and be back in five minutes.'

'Don't worry about me. I'm wearing my bikini under my clothes so I'll just put my sun cream on while you change.'

'I can do cream for you,' he offers enthusiastically.

'Okay, if you insist. You can do my back.' Anything else and he'll turn me into a quivering wreck. I'll be wanting to do unmentionable things with him after having known him for only six hours.

'Okay, and you can do mine when I get changed.'

'It's a deal.'

I quickly take off my shorts and T-shirt and lie down on my stomach. He unfastens the clip on my bikini top to move the strap out of the way and glides his hands over my back, sending shivers of excitement all down my body. 'I will do your legs as well.'

'Okay,' I whimper.

'Is there anywhere else that needs cream?'

'No, I'm fine, thanks. I'll do the rest.'

He refastens the clip. 'All done.' That would be the understatement of the day. He leaves me smouldering and fantasising.

I catch sight of his dad in the little thatched-roof bar. I can see him shaking this and that, and I can hear a machine whirring away. It looks like he's preparing a couple of cocktails. They're both in tall glasses. One is dark and the other blue. He adds the finishing touches and places them on a tray. Costas has reappeared. He picks up the tray and heads in my direction looking ... how can I put it? ... heavenly.

'One Blue Lagoon for lady with intoxicating blue eyes, and a Cola Rolla for me – more cola than rolla!' he laughs, putting the drinks down on the little table in between the sunbeds.

'Are you trying to get me tipsy? Because you're doing a good job!' I try, unconvincingly, to sound like I'm objecting. Obviously, I'm enjoying every minute of my time with him.

He lies on the bed and looks over in my direction. 'I think it is my turn for some cream.'

Right. Deep breaths, I can do this. I squeeze some cream on to his back and glide my hands up and down his back, rubbing in the cream.

'You know, Shirley, you make fantastic massage.'

'Really? I'm glad you're enjoying it.'

'Yes, a bit too much,' comes the reply, and he promptly props himself on his side.

'We try these cocktails and see if my papa has learnt what I show him. *Yamas*.'

'Mmm, this is delicious. You taught him well.'

'Yep, mine is good as well. He is a good student. So, you were going to tell me about your sister and why she leave you on your own.'

'Oh yes. So, she works for a travel company and she was told last week that instead of reviewing a Caribbean cruise as she'd planned, she'd have to come here. She'll hopefully be done in a couple of days.' I don't want to say too much to Costas and blow Helen's cover, especially as I'm doing the Boutique Blue's observations.

'Oh, that is a pity. I will not have you all to myself.' He replies, looking quite crestfallen.

'I'm sure we'll sort something out. Besides, won't you be working?'

'Well, actually the Boutique Blue is very quiet at the moment. They ask for volunteers for unpaid leave so I put my name on the list. I have no mortgage and bills to pay, so I am keen for my fellow workers who do have commitments to have the work.'

'Gosh, I didn't realise things were so bad.'

'Yes, this is a very quiet May. Luckily, my parents are quite booked up so I can always help them and give my grandparents a break. Anyway, you are on holiday, not worrying about the Greek economy. What about a splash in the sea?'

'Or a swim?'

'You swim?' he says sounding surprised.

'Yes, Costas. England *is* an island. The sea that surrounds it may be freezing cold but we do have swimming baths. I'll have you know I'm a good swimmer.'

'Swimming baths,' he repeats, frowning.

'Race you to the sea!'

We run down to the water and straight into the rather cold sea. It momentarily takes my breath away. I was expecting it to be a bit warmer. We splash about like a couple of kids and finally adjust to the cold water enough for a swim.

After what seems like an age of splashing, swimming and floating about, Costas takes my hand to kiss the back of it and says, 'I will remember this day forever.'

I smile, blush and reply, 'Me too.'

We run back up to our sunloungers and dry off. I lie down, close my eyes and begin daydreaming again about Costas rubbing that cream all over my body...

'Shirley! Shirley, it's time to go.'

'Go. Go where? Where am I? Oh my God, I'm so sorry, I must have nodded off. What time is it?' I ask in a panic, suddenly remembering where I am and that Helen might be wondering what's happened to me.

'No panic, it has just gone five,' Costas replies. 'If okay with you, I take you to catch bus and then come home to change for work. I am not due back until six thirty.'

'Yes, that's great, whatever suits you. I've already taken up your whole day.'

'You have not taken up all my day. And, besides, you make my day happy.'

I pop my shorts and T-shirt back on over my still slightly damp bikini and stuff everything else into my bag. Costas has already put on his jeans while I was asleep. I do hope I haven't embarrassed myself by snoring or dribbling.

His mum is busy collecting towels and glasses and comes to give me a hug. 'It has been lovely to meet you, Shirley. I hope you will visit again.'

'Oh, I'm sure I will. I've had a lovely day. Thank you.'

'Right then, Shirley, back on the scary moped. I try to drive not too fast.'

We arrive in the chaotic main square. There are three buses parked up, with another bus trying to turn round in between cars, mopeds, trikes and people everywhere. Costas parks his moped and we make our way over to the buses.

'This is your bus. Just pay the driver. It is two euros. You get off where you wait this morning,' he says, laughing.

'Yes, I know. You'll not let me forget that in a hurry, will you?'

'No, but I am glad you missed the bus. Do you have plans for tomorrow?'

'My only plan was to relax by the hotel pool.'

'I could take you on a drive around the island, if you like. I could meet you here at midday?'

'Yes, that sounds like a plan. I'm sure you'll know all the off-the-beaten-track places to visit.'

'Oh, yes, I can definitely do off the beaten track,' he replies, mischievously raising his eyebrows. 'Oh, and Shirley, it is the hotel policy not to date the guests so I would appreciate that we keep this to ourselves.'

'No worries. But Helen will sniff out anything suspicious a mile off,' I declare laughing.

'Well, we better be careful,' he replies, winking and taking my hand to kiss it.

'Maybe I can have your number?'

'Of course.' He takes my phone, taps in his number and rings his with it. 'I can text you now,' he says smiling.

I get on the bus and hand over my two euros. I wave to Costas, who's now back on his moped. He waves back and the bus sets off. A couple of minutes later, my phone alerts me that I have a text. It's probably Helen back early. I open the message. It clearly isn't from Helen. It says:

I enjoy today. xx

My heart is all of a flutter. I text him back.

I enjoy today too
Glad I missed the bus
See you at dinner. xx

As we drive along, I daydream again, thinking about my lovely day with Costas. I've got distracted by my damp bikini bottoms, which seem to have got sand in them. They're beginning to get a bit uncomfortable and as I attempt to readjust them inconspicuously, I notice a woman in the seat opposite giving me a funny look. I offer an explanation. 'Sand – it gets everywhere!' She doesn't look very amused and looks out of the window instead.

What with all my fidgeting, I nearly miss my stop. Luckily, other people are getting off here so the bus is slowing down anyway. I follow the other guests down the track to the hotel and walk wearily into reception. Nikos immediately recognises me and comes running over.

'I am so sorry, I told you the wrong amount for bus journey! It is two euros. I just find out it has gone up last week,' he says, looking quite embarrassed.

'No problem, I sorted it.' I'm about to explain but think better of it.

'Did you manage to see the windmills and Little Venice?'

'Yes, I did. Thank you very much for all your help. In fact, what is the Greek for "Thank you"?' I enquire, thinking I can add it to my extensive vocabulary.

'*Efharisto*,' he replies.

'*Efharisto*,' I repeat.

'You say very well – a natural!' Nikos says kindly.

My plan is to find a sunbed and attempt to appear like I've been there all day, ready for when Helen gets back. As I approach the garden, I can see that there are now plenty of free loungers. I grab a towel and settle down on one. I might even get my bikini bottoms dry as I relax in the warm sunshine.

Just as I settle down, my phone bleeps into life with a text. I pull it out of my bag quickly feeling all excited that it might be Costas. But no, it's Richard.

> Hope you're OK.
> Just letting you know I've
> had a slight change of plan
> & I'm now island hopping
> around Greece. Phone
> signals not very good. x

My immediate reaction is to reply:

> Yes Richard I'm fine
> NO THANKS TO YOU
> Why is it that now we've

split up you're happy to
island-hop around Greece?
Anyway, having a great time
myself in Mykonos with a
gorgeous Greek waiter so
BOG OFF

Oh, sod it. I'll reply later or not at all. Just thinking about it is winding me up. I settle back down and do a bit of people-watching instead. A text from Helen distracts me from watching a woman who must have a fear of not getting an even tan.

I'm back where r u? x

I text back:

Sunbeds near the pool. x

I'm very tempted to add that I'm watching the funniest live show ever. The woman, who I guess to be in her early thirties, has adjusted her bikini now about fifty times. I never realised that you could make so many adjustments to such a small amount of material. She's no sooner lain down that she's tweaking here and tweaking there. I think she's trying to optimise the amount of sun that each part of flesh is absorbing. Then she stands up again, adjusts the bikini and moves her sunbed by an inch here and an inch there. I'm worn out just watching.

Within a couple of minutes Helen appears, looking like a dishevelled and harassed tourist.

'I need a drink,' she declares, throwing herself on to the lounger next to me. 'That was the worst hotel I've ever inspected.'

'Why, what's happened, Helen?' I try to sound concerned, but whatever it was that happened, it meant I could spend the day with Costas.

'I'll fill you in after I've ordered a drink. I thought we could try the buffet restaurant for tonight's meal, if that's okay with you?'

'Yes, that sounds good to me. I'm looking forward to it,' comes my reply. I'm trying not to sound too cheerful. I don't want Helen finding out my little secret and giving me a lecture about how he shouldn't be dating a hotel guest. Helen doesn't like breaking rules especially the ones she's probably written.

We both order a drink. Helen has a large G & T and I have an Island Delight off the extensive cocktail list, which sounds quite appropriate for my day. I nearly let it slip a couple of times about my Afternoon Delight cocktail and my day with Costas. I'm really going to struggle to keep my little secret. I pick my book up and find my place, oh yes… 'Perhaps it's because love rarely shows up in the places that we expect it to, or looks the way we expect it to look…' Blimey, that's a coincidence. I certainly wasn't expecting to fall for a Greek waiter.

'What's that you're reading?' Helen asks.

'It's called *In the Meantime*. Stella recommended it after she'd split with her hubby. You can borrow it when I've read it, if you want.'

'Why would I want to borrow it? I'm in a relationship.'

'Oh, yes, I forgot – James. Have you heard from him yet this week?'

'Yes, actually he sent me a text this morning saying he was having problems with his phone.'

'Problems with his phone… More like, problems with his memory. Have you sent him a thank you text for the champagne?' I can't resist winding Helen up and hearing what excuse she comes up with to protect James.

'No, I haven't. That could have been a mistake by the hotel.'

'Okay, fair play, we'll ask them.'

'Oh, that'll look good when they discover they've delivered an expensive bottle of champagne to the wrong room and we've drunk it. Anyway, have you done anything today apart from reading your book?'

Oh dear. I've hit the nail on the head about James so we're having an abrupt subject change. 'I've been out exploring, actually. I went into town and I've got some photos for your brochure.'

'Really? Let's have a gander then.'

I grab my camera and flick it on. Helen has a look through all my images.

'Wow, Steph, these photos are really good. I love this one. What a beautiful little church.'

'Yes, I even went in. There are no pews; it's all really sweet and simple. I lit a candle.'

'Oh my God. It's a wonder you didn't burn the place down, with your track record.'

'For goodness sake, Helen, are you ever going to let that drop? It was twenty years ago.'

'Ooh, don't get your knickers in a twist, I'm only joking. Anyway, I'm impressed that you've taken so many photos in a day. Daniel will love this lot for the brochure and the website. They're much better than James's efforts.'

'Well, let's face it, he's probably got much more important stuff on his agenda when he comes here.'

'Right, come on, let's get showered and changed. I don't want another ear-bashing session about James. We'll see what boyfriend material you find when you're ready for dating again.'

Usually Helen has the last word but today I just can't resist getting a little jibe in. 'Well, I hope for my sake they're nothing like James.'

* * *

The room now has two single beds. I dump my bag down and head straight to the shower while Helen tries out her dirt machine, as I call it.

'You'll never believe the reading I got at the hotel this afternoon!' I hear her shouting over the noise of the shower.

'What was it?' I shout back.

'Ten thousand, nine hundred and eighty-two!' comes the reply.

'How much?' I've stopped the shower because I can't have heard her correctly.

'Ten thousand, nine hundred and eighty-two. I couldn't believe it myself so I'm trying it in here to check it isn't faulty.'

I restart the shower and watch around the shower curtain as Helen takes a swab from the toilet flush button and inserts it into her machine.

'That's more like it. Thirty-eight. I think it's safe to say that this hotel is clean and this afternoon's place was filthy. No surprises there. I've given them until the day before we leave to clean up, otherwise they'll lose their gold status and their slot in next year's brochure.'

'Was it really that bad?' I enquire, freshly emerged from the shower and wrapped in lovely soft towels.

'Yep, worst I've ever seen. James will be getting a huge rollicking over it. I've seen another side to him today. A bone-bloody-idle side. The manager at that last hotel was absolutely bonkers. Why on earth James didn't pull him up I'll never know. And that Selena, at the hotel next door, looking all smug, thinking that James was coming along. I soon wiped the smile off her face when I told her he was in Florida.'

Thank goodness. It sounds like Helen's beginning to see what the real James is like. I wouldn't be surprised if the double bed and champagne thing is something that he always requests; the hotel must have just assumed it was him coming with a guest, maybe even that Selena woman at the hotel next door. Or, oh my God, the guy from this afternoon's place!

While Helen's in the shower, I'm going to attempt to read a bit more of my book. So far, I've only managed a few pages. Stella has put stars and lines all over the bits that she thought were relevant to her, which is the majority of it. The page I'm on is no exception. It's about the thirteen most common things we do in search of love... Flipping heck, what a minefield. But I'm okay, I'm not in search of love ... am I? My thoughts are disturbed by a knock on the door. Before I even manage to get to my feet, a woman is on her way in to the room.

'Housekeeping, evening service,' she announces.

'Oh, sorry, my sister's in the shower,' I reply, all flustered. What on earth is evening service? This is a new one to me. Thank goodness I've got a bathrobe on.

'No problem, madam. I come back when you go to dinner. I bring water and change your towels. I just change the sign on your door so you don't get disturbed again.'

'Okay, no problem, thank you.'

Right, where was I? Oh yes, my book. I skim through the next few points and reach the last two.

12. You don't express what you really feel because you believe it will hurt your partner's feelings.

Well, at least Richard and I were honest with each other. He could have given in and agreed to start a family and then regretted it and left me anyway. At least, this way, I'm still young enough to meet someone and hopefully fulfil my dream of having a family.

13. You choose to believe your partner's lies even when you know the truth. You act like you don't know what's going on when you do.

This is Helen. I don't think James is necessarily lying outright. I think it's that he's got different ideas about their relationship and that Helen hasn't made her thoughts about it clear to him. For him, it's casual, but I think Helen might finally be ready for a bit more commitment...

For goodness sake, there's another bloody knock on the door. I wait for it to open but it doesn't. There's another knock and a faint, muffled shout. 'Room service.'

I get up again and open the door.

'Evening, madam. You ordered some ice,' says the waiter.

'Ice – lovely, bring it in. My sister must have ordered it. Just pop it down.'

'Have a nice evening,' he says on his way out.

'Thank you, I'm sure we will,' I reply. I'm going to make use of the ice to have a Bacardi and coke out of the minibar while I start getting ready. I'm giving up on the book for today. All that love psychology is making my head hurt.

Helen has emerged from the shower. 'Has the ice arrived?' she asks, peering round the bathroom door.

'Yes, it's here, and the housekeeping evening service is coming back when we've gone to dinner.'

'Good stuff. Would you mind making me a G & T? Then let's go straight to the dining room, if that's okay with you.'

'No problem, I'm easy. Maybe we can sit outside. I think there's some entertainment on.' I'm not going to disclose my ulterior motive, which is that I want to swoon over Costas all night.

'Yes, that's fine with me. In fact, that means I can observe the outdoor restaurant staff so that'll be another area covered.'

She disappears back into the bathroom. 'By the way, how are you getting on with the questionnaire?' she shouts through to me.

'Oh, not bad. I'm sure I'll get in the swing of it by tomorrow. Like you said, everything is running very smoothly.' Good job she can't see me. She'd instantly know I'm being economical with the truth.

'Unlike this afternoon's Greek *Fawlty Towers* fiasco. You can put some music on, if you want, off my phone. There's all sorts on there.'

'Okay, will do.' Thank goodness she's not asked to see what I've done so far because I don't think she'd be very impressed with it.

I select random play and 'Girls Just Want to Have Fun' comes on. Helen appears from the bathroom with a towel tied neatly around her head.

'Oh my God, Steph, this takes me back to when we were teenagers! Do you remember standing in front of the mirror with our hairbrush microphones, singing along to our music and Dad yelling, "Will you turn that racket down? We'll have the neighbours complaining!"'

'Oh yes, I remember. They knocked on the wall once and he went mad. Then there was that "Saturday Night" song, when we did the actions and the light fittings in the lounge shook as we jumped around. We got the blame for the crack that appeared on the ceiling!' The thought of it makes us giggle together like teenagers again.

We carry on getting ready together, applying make-up and attempting to dry our hair with the rather pathetic bathroom hairdryer. Luckily, Helen's Glamour Jumbo Tong saves the day – apparently every girl should have one. She wants a wave in her straight blonde hair and gets herself in a right strop with it.

'Why can't my hair be wavy like yours?' she says in frustration.

'I don't know. Why can't I be a couple of inches taller like you?'

'Yes, that's all well and good but when I wear heels I tower above everyone.'

'Oh yes, those bloody shoes. Do you think you can put them away tonight? I stubbed my toe on them this morning. You're a bloody nightmare for leaving stuff out. Didn't you learn your lesson when Grandma tripped over one of your shoes and broke her wrist?'

'More like sprained her wrist, if I remember correctly.'

'Whatever. If you're wearing your dress, I'll wear my white cropped linen trousers with the blue and white striped top and those precarious wedges.'

'I did warn you about those wedges, but you wouldn't listen.'

'Yes, well, they're the only heels I've brought and I don't want you towering over me.'

Helen giggles. 'You look like you're going on a boat, with your white and blue stripes.'

'Oh, very bloody funny. If you cast your mind back a couple of weeks to when I was clothes-shopping for my holiday, you'll remember that I was going on a cruise and this outfit seemed very relevant.'

'Oops, sorry. Well, in any case, it flatters your figure. You look stunning.'

'Oh, thanks, sis. You look lovely too. Ooh, I nearly forgot. I bought you a little pressie in town.' I retrieve the gift bag and hand Helen the beautifully wrapped necklace. She carefully unwraps it.

'Steph, this is absolutely gorgeous! It goes perfectly with this dress. Funnily enough, the necklace James bought me for my birthday broke this morning.'

'How strange. I must have picked up on your vibes. Well, put it on. Let's see.' I fasten it for her. It complements her dress beautifully. 'And I treated myself as well.'

'Come on, open it. Let's see it.'

I carefully unwrap my necklace. I'm still delighted with it.

'Oh, that's pretty! Look at all those colours. We'll have to go back to the shop. I could do loads of gift shopping there.'

'Yes, me too. The best bit of all is it's called "*Amnēsia*".'

We chuckle and apply finishing touches to our make-up, spray on some perfume, choose our bags and then we're ready. For some reason, I'm quite nervous and have butterflies in my stomach. In fact, unusually, I don't actually feel that hungry. I remember my phone at the last minute and shove it in my bag.

We totter down to the restaurant where Elena is waiting to efficiently take us to our table. We go through the inside, outside, smoking, non-smoking options, which I can see Helen is impressed with, and then Elena leads us outside. Tonight's entertainment will include a couple of singers; Elena offers us a table just slightly away from the speakers, which seems like a good idea to us. She informs us that our waitress tonight is Elora.

A few minutes later, Elora arrives with a couple of interesting-looking cocktails. 'These are for you with the compliments of the restaurant manager, to make up for the incident this morning. This one is called Tomorrow We Sail – for you, madam. And for you, madam, a Cosmopolitan. Please enjoy and help yourselves to the buffet when you are ready. Let me know if you would like any wine or water.'

Elora is gone before Helen can quiz her, but I don't get off the hook that easily. 'What's this incident she's talking about?'

I need to act and look calm otherwise she'll pounce on me immediately. 'Oh, it was nothing,' I reply.

'It must have been something, Steph, otherwise they wouldn't have sent over two complimentary cocktails. Now, are you going to tell me or have I got to summon the manager over here and ask him instead?'

She's got that bossy-big-sister aura about her. I'm not going to be able to wriggle out of it so I offer her my watered-down explanation. 'Oh, I knocked a jug of milk out of a waiter's hands and it splashed on my new dress. There was no harm done.'

Of course, Helen's not entirely happy with my version of events. She digs a bit further. She's like a dog with a bone. 'It all sounds a bit odd to me. Your cocktail was quite apt, though. Maybe he spotted you in your sailor outfit. Anyway, if it was your fault, why have they sent us complimentary cocktails?'

'I don't know, Helen – good customer service?' I shrug my shoulders.

'Fair enough.' Ooh, that was close. She's finally let it drop. 'Now, shall we get some food? I'm feeling a bit peckish.'

We head towards the buffet. Costas catches my eye and winks as we go inside. I'm wondering what the hell Tomorrow We Sail is. I've never heard of it, and he's lucky that CID Helen Collins hasn't picked up on it either. Maybe it *is* just because I look like a sailor.

I'm back with my food from the buffet and I'm just about to start eating when I feel my phone vibrating. I quickly have a peep before Helen gets back with her rather boring-looking plate of steamed fish and vegetables.

Change of plan. Tomorrow
we go in boat if OK with u.
Meet outside church at 12.
Bring swimwear and towel.
I bring food. xx

I quickly text back, realising the Tomorrow We Sail cocktail was a cryptic clue. My head has registered the boat scenario and is wondering if I'll be able to go through with it. My heart overrules it, and I'm already tapping out a reply.

OK, sounds great. x

Helen makes me jump as she gets back to the table just as I'm putting my phone down.

'Have you heard from Mum and Dad at all today?' she enquires unsuspectingly.

'Oh yes, I forgot to tell you. They were having lunch at the harbour in Santorini. Oh, and there were a couple of Mum's infamous text message mix-ups. She reckons they help with "on-deck whores" and Dad's having withdrawal symptoms from "wolf", which turned out to be golf. Also, she asked if we can try and book them in for a round of golf on Friday.'

'Friday? I thought they were due here on Saturday?'

'Oh, that was the other thing she mentioned. The itinerary has changed because of weather issues.'

'Oh dear, I hope they're not encountering rough seas. That won't be pleasant on a clipper boat. Maybe we could fix up a spa day here if Mum doesn't fancy the golf – and if you're up for it?'

'Yes, that sounds like a plan,' I reply as enthusiastically as I can. I can't help thinking that I might want to spend time with Costas if things are still going well. 'Oh, I've just remembered. I also had a text off Richard this afternoon.'

'Oh yes? And what did he have to say for himself?'

'Apparently he's now island-hopping around Greece with his mate.'

'Oh, really? But he couldn't do anything that exciting with you?'

'Exactly. He's really annoyed me.'

'So you've replied, "Bully for you, Richard. Have a nice life. Now sod off and let me get on with mine."'

'I've not replied yet. I didn't want to wind myself up any more than I already was. He can wait until tomorrow. In fact, let's take some photos of us having a good time and post them on Facebook. See what Richard – and James, for that matter – think of that.'

'I wouldn't think it would make a jot of difference. The pair of them seem oblivious.'

'Yes, I think you're right. So let's not spoil our night talking about those two waste-of-space idiots.'

The atmosphere in the restaurant is very relaxed; on stage, a man and a woman are singing. The food is excellent. Helen decides that we'll have another drink, so she tries to catch someone's attention. Of course, the person whose attention she catches is Costas – un-bloody-believable. He's not even serving our area but Helen summons him over.

'Evening, ladies. I hope you are enjoying your evening. Would you like some more cocktails?'

Just hearing him speak gets me hot and bothered.

'Oh yes, thank you. The first two were very nice. Maybe we could try something new.' Helen amazingly manages to reply without passing comment on either the incident or the cocktail choice.

'Do you know which ones, or should I surprise you?'

I can see her weighing him up. I think he's won her over, judging by her fluttering eyelashes and her reply. 'We'll let you surprise us.' Helen smiles and ... gushes, I think the term is. I don't know what's come over her. As soon as he's gone, she turns to me. 'I don't know where I've been for the last fifteen years, Steph, but I wish I'd been to somewhere in Greece. Some of these Greek men are just so sexy. Take our waiter, Costas, for example. He's gorgeous. Those simmering dark brown eyes, his lovely olive skin, his dark hair, that sexy stubble, his...'

'Yes, Helen, I get the picture. But maybe you should think about someone a bit closer to your age? We don't want you to be accused of cradle snatching.'

That may have been a bit catty but Helen bounces back with a brilliant line. 'Actually, Steph, I think you'll find men prefer the more mature woman.' Before I can get another word in, she carries on. 'Anyway, I was actually thinking about you. I think he's got a soft spot for you.'

'And how have you reached that conclusion, Miss Marple?'

'Oh, just from the way he couldn't take his eyes off you when we were here last night. I have an amazing radar system, Steph. That's why I can do my job standing on my head with my eyes shut.'

'That's absolute nonsense. I hadn't even noticed him until you pointed him out. He's just doing his job, which is being nice.' I'm not sure how convincing I sound.

Helen gets the last word in as always. 'I'm just saying, he's very handsome and if we could clone him into a model that's about ten years older I might be interested.'

My ears suddenly prick up. 'Er, did you just say you might be interested?'

'I might have done. Why?'

'I thought you told me this afternoon that you're in a relationship.'

'Yes, I know, but maybe…'

Helen is saved by Costas, who's back with two fizzing cocktails adorned with fruit and umbrellas. He's looking very proud of himself. 'So, ladies, this is my very own personal recipes. The hotel has kindly allowed me to introduce my own selection of cocktails here. So now I would like to present the newest addition to the menu: Under a Greek Spell. I have heard that Prosecco is very popular with the ladies so I have make my own Prosecco-based cocktail.'

Helen smells and tastes it. She declares it's delicious.

'And what about you?' Costas looks me directly in the eyes.

I feel like the air is charged with electricity and that we're the only people here. Everyone else fades into the background. I take a sip and the bubbles seem to go straight to my head. I feel enchanted. 'Oh yes, thank you, it's magical…'

Costas seems happy. He returns to the bar, leaving me in my fantasy world.

'Steph, Steph, earth to Steph, are you having a dessert?' Helen waves her hand in front of my face.

I'm lost in the moment and half listening to the singers. 'No, I'm fine,' I reply in a dreamy voice.

'Oh my God, are you ill?'

'No, I'm just not hungry.'

'Well, this is a first! Are you sure you're all right?'

'Yes, I'm fine. It's probably the cocktails.'

'Oh yes. What was it? "It's magical, please whisk me away for a night of passion…"' Helen takes great delight in teasing me. I have to remain unfazed or else she'll be at it all night.

'You're just jealous because he fancies me and not you.'

'You know what, Steph? For once you're right. I *am* jealous and, if I were you, I'd bloody well make the most of it.'

'Okay, Dear Deidre, I'll bear your invaluable advice in mind. But for now, can we please enjoy the entertainment?'

'I'm just saying…'

'Yes, I know, and I appreciate that you're looking out for me, so thank you.' I'm not sharing my secret with Helen because the next thing she'll be doing is texting mum. Then they'll be looking at wedding venues and looking at wedding outfits. Oh my God the thought of it all makes me shudder.

The man who's been singing announces that the last song of the evening is 'For Shirley'. A couple of dancers appear on stage, as well as more singers and a couple of violinists. The noise in the restaurant dies down. The singers begin and the violinists and dancers join in the performance. Everyone in the restaurant seems to have stopped eating and become transfixed by the entertainment. I keep catching the chorus: 'I believe when I fall in love, with you it will be forever…' My heart is pounding like mad as I listen intently to the rest of the song.

The singing stops and there's silence for a few seconds. Then rapturous applause breaks out. The hairs on the back of my neck are standing on end. I search for Costas and spot him over at the bar. I know from the expression on his face that I'm Shirley and that he asked the performers to dedicate the song to me. I'm moved almost to tears, but I can't let myself go because Helen will be on to me.

She breaks into my train of thought. 'That was amazing! Lucky Shirley,' she says.

'Yes, lucky Shirley,' I reply. Lucky me!

We decide to call it a night. I tell Helen to go ahead. The singers are packing up; I want to know what that song was so I go up to the stage and ask one of the women. She tells me it was written by Stevie Wonder and that they've based their performance on a Josh Groban version. I thank her. At the same moment, I feel my phone vibrating in my bag with a message.

Hope you like song
Sweet dreams. x

I text back:

Loved it
See you tomorrow. x

As I walk through the restaurant, I hear the chorus of my earworm Little Mix song playing in the background, which makes me smile.

It suddenly seems very relevant. I do feel like I've been drinking a secret potion and I'm now Under a Greek Spell…

Chapter 12

Helen

I've had a much better night's sleep without Steph assaulting me. I'm going to be having breakfast at my first hotel of the day, but I need a hot drink before I leave. There's a nice selection of teas in the room, which I'm working my way through. This one's Lime and Ginger. That should help bring me round after the cocktails from last night. I collect my laptop and head to the balcony to enjoy the early morning peace and quiet. I love this time of day, before everyone else is up and about. The birds love it too. They're all singing, and one keeps hopping on to the balcony looking for stray crumbs.

Today I'm visiting three family-run hotels that have been put forward to be included in next year's brochure. There's only space for two so I'm going to mark them on a points system. I catch up on my emails and messages and remember that I never replied to James. I'm fed up with this ridiculous situation I'm in. I feel like something has changed in the last few days. I want a proper relationship. I want someone who wants to spend quality time with me, not snippets here and there. And certainly not someone who is more than likely two-timing me.

Hi James
Shame I got to hear
about Florida from Daniel
first. Must say I quite like
Mykonos - very laid back,
especially the Mykonos
Gold, soon to be Bronze!
See what you mean about
Selena. Expensive taste
in jewellery as well it seems.
Helen

Let's see what his reaction to that is, although I'm past caring. There's only a handful of guests having breakfast in the restaurant across the way. I can see Costas, the waiter from last night. He really is good-looking. I'm sure he likes Steph, but for all I know, he could be married with a family.

I go back inside and get ready. I'm wearing a nice light-grey trouser suit today with a plain white blouse and my Laura Ashley floral silk scarf to add some colour. Steph is still dead to the world. I close the door quietly as I leave but, quite honestly, I think Steph would sleep through a pop concert.

There's a guy on the reception desk who seems to be free, so I make a beeline for him. His name badge says 'Nikos'.

'*Kalimera*, madam. How can I help?' he asks.

'*Kalimera*. I want a taxi into town.'

'Unfortunately, the taxis are very busy this morning. Most of them will be at the airport waiting for two flights from the UK. If I call one now, it will probably be here in about half an hour. If you are just going to town, though, we have a shuttle bus leaving at ten o'clock, or, if you need to go now, I can recommend the local buses.'

'I suppose I could just take the bus. Where in town does it stop?'

'It ends at the square. You can't go any further.'

'Okay, thanks, you've been most helpful. Which way is the bus stop?'

'At the end of the road and then cross over. The stop is right opposite this road. Have a good day, madam.'

'Thanks, I will. You too.'

I make tracks for the bus, making a mental note to update my list and add the helpful Nikos. The staff here are friendly and they seem genuine, which is an added bonus.

I walk in the direction of the bus stop. It's still early and, thankfully, it isn't too hot yet. I've got reasonably sensible shoes on, for a change, so I can at least walk a few metres without being crippled. After a few minutes, a bus arrives. It doesn't look very roadworthy and I'll be surprised if it makes the journey into town. I get on and hand over my €20 note. The driver looks positively pained.

'You not have coins?' he asks, quite abruptly.

'No, I'm really sorry, I only have this.'

'Well, I will give you a lot of change or you can wait until we reach town and I change this at the kiosk.'

'Yes, that's fine, I'll wait.' I smile apologetically. I look for a seat but it's clearly standing room only. Cheeky sod, he should be letting me ride for nothing if I've got to stand.

We bump along and I admire the bits of countryside that I can see framed by the cloudless blue sky. As the bus halts at each stop, more people are getting on and not many are getting off. This must be rush hour. I'm getting quite squashed and now I can't see anything. After what seems like eternity, the bus slows and turns round. The driver waits for everyone to get off before he beckons me to follow him to the kiosk to change my note.

'Your €18 change.' He hands me the money. He's clearly not amused. Just in case I haven't got the message he adds, 'We prefer the exact money for the bus.'

'Okay, thanks, I'll remember that.' Well, he won't be winning a customer-service award any time soon, that's for sure.

I haven't got a clue where I'm going. I find the taxi rank but there are no taxis there, which is no surprise after what Nikos told me. I decide to have a wander and see if I can find the hotel myself. There's plenty of shops but nothing is open and there's no one about to ask. I carry on wandering down a narrow street. After a couple of minutes, I pick out a little church. I'm pretty sure it's the one that Steph took photos of yesterday. An elderly couple are unlocking the door. I approach them.

'Excuse me, do you speak English?'

'A little bit,' the woman replies. 'How can we help?'

'I'm trying to find the Hotel Niko. I have a meeting there in half an hour.'

'The Hotel Niko?' she laughs. 'This is my daughter's hotel. We go there in a few minutes to help her and her husband with the breakfast. You can walk there with us if you would like. It is only ten minutes walk from here.'

'Well, I might as well. I've got plenty of time.'

She beckons me into the church. 'My name is Eliana and my husband is Nikolaos.'

'I'm Helen.' I shake their hands.

'We just light candle and say prayers. Please take seat.'

I assume they're caretakers at the church. The old lady is tidying up some flowers. A tinge of sadness comes over me. The flowers are the same colours as Steph's wedding bouquet. It's such a shame that she and Richard couldn't work out their differences. Mind you, it's a pretty major difference. Mum and I thought Richard would come round, but, as each week goes by, it's looking more and more unlikely. And now he's well and truly wound Steph up with his Greek island-hopping trip. Honestly, it beggars belief.

Nikolaos removes the candles that have burnt out. I assume one is Steph's from yesterday. They now each light a candle and kneel to say a prayer. I feel quite humbled. When they finish I ask if I can light one.

'Of course. We will wait outside.'

I pop one of my euros in the box. I pick up a candle, light it and say a prayer. Top of my list is sorting out my relationship with James – well, more like my situation with James. I realise that this prayer could take quite a long time and I really need to get a move on. Maybe I'll come back another day.

Nikolaos and Eliana are waiting patiently outside talking to a woman who seems to be the town's answer to stray cats. She's probably Michalis's mother! At least I can smile about it all today. For some reason, I feel like a weight has been lifted off my shoulders. Everybody is so laid back here that I wonder if it's rubbing off on me.

As we walk along a narrow road, Eliana tells me about her family. She says they've always owned the hotel that I'm about to do my assessment on.

The Hotel Niko comes into view. It's small and well presented although it's not the sort of place that I'd normally stop in. I'll have to try to maintain an unbiased view. Eliana goes to find her daughter. I cast my eye around the hotel and get my first impressions, which are good. It's whitewashed, with blue shutters on the windows. The restaurant is perched just above the beach. Eliana returns with her daughter. She smiles as she approaches me.

'I'm Helen Collins. I'm here to discuss your hotel being included in our family-run hotels brochure next year.'

'My name is Xena. Welcome to our hotel. I am very pleased to meet you. You have already met my mother and father.'

'Yes, I gave up looking for a taxi and ended up wandering to the little church.'

'Oh yes, the taxis are in demand this morning at the airport. There is a London flight and a Manchester flight due. Most holiday people will be on the tour buses but some independent travellers need a taxi.'

'Well, it did me good to have a little stroll around the town. I was planning to start with breakfast and then I'll have a wander about, if that's okay with you?'

'Of course. Follow me.' Xena leads me to the restaurant and hands me a menu.

'This is a traditional Cycladic breakfast. There are many different local breads, pastries and buns. Our home-made bread of the day is Greek olive oil bread with olives and rosemary. We also have my sister-in-law's home-made fig preserve. Then we have a selection of cheese, including *kopanisti*, which is made on the island. There is some *louza*, which is dry salted pork. Also our home-made yogurt and honey, and fresh fruits of the season. If you would like, my husband will cook eggs, however you would like, and of course we have teas and coffee.'

'Gosh, what an amazing choice. I'll order an omelette and a pot of Earl Grey tea and I'll help myself to some of the rather tasty-looking buffet selection.'

Xena goes off to the kitchen with my order. She attends to other guests and then arrives back with my pot of tea. I help myself to the home-made yogurt and honey as well as some of the bread and the fig preserve. Everything is presented well and is protected from the flies and birds. The atmosphere in the restaurant is relaxing, and I can hear the sound of the sea in the background.

I help myself to the '*Kosmikós* Cocktails' menu, which is lying on the bar. The menu is pretty extensive; it includes some titles that are funny and some that are quite rude.

Xena arrives back with my omelette and notices me flicking through the menu. She goes rather red. 'I apologise. That is my son and nephew's cocktail menu, for their friends. It should be behind the bar. They think they are like Tom Cruise from the film *Cocktail*. I can bring you the one for guests, if you like?'

'Yes, that would be good. But you can leave this one with me.' I love learning about cocktails and this one is an eye-opener.

'Okay, I bring it over.' Xena scurries off in a fluster and leaves me with the hilarious menu.

I'm not sure how she'd react to someone asking her for a Slippery Nipple, especially this early in the day. As for some of the others, I think she'd faint. I'll make a note for future reference; you never know when you might fancy a Naked Waiter or a Titanic Uplift.

Xena returns with the normal drinks' menu and puts it discreetly on the table just as I'm scribbling in my pad the words 'Naked Waiter' and 'Titanic Uplift'. Poor woman, she probably thinks they've blown the whole brochure thing. I find it all quite amusing, and certainly better than yesterday's fiasco, when I needed to sample a menu of cocktails just to numb the memory of that awful place.

When I've finished my delicious breakfast, Xena clears my plate away. 'I have asked my son to show you around the hotel while I finish with the breakfast service, if that is okay with you?'

'Absolutely. I'll wait here and finish this tea.'

'I'll send him out. He has been helping with the cooking.'

After a couple of minutes, a person who I assume is Xena's son appears. My goodness, my day just got a whole lot better! Someone must have heard my request for an older version of Costas because he's *here*. He looks serious and sultry, with gorgeous deep brown, almost black, eyes. His black hair has that just-got-out-of-bed look. He's also got sexy designer stubble. Wow.

I stand up as he extends his hand to greet me. I'm sure I feel an electric charge as we shake hands.

'I am Costas. You must be Helen. Is James following on?'

Well that didn't take long. What should have been a pleasant experience has suddenly wound me up like a spring. I take a sharp intake of breath and bristle at the mention of that name. 'No, James is not following on. If you must know, he's getting a villa project off the ground in Florida. So I'm afraid you've got me instead.' My reply is rather snappy, which I instantly regret. After all, this guy isn't to know that he's just waved a red rag in front of a bull.

'Sorry. It has been James that I have seen in the past, that's all. I was also wanting to clear the air with him.'

'Really?'

'Yes, we had a disagreement last time he was here… Anyway, it can wait until I see him again. When you are ready, I will show you around.'

'After you,' I gesture.

'We have seventeen guest rooms…'

'Oh, I thought it said twenty in my information.'

'I was *just* about to say that there will be twenty by the time the hotels reopens next spring.'

'Is that guaranteed?' I ask a bit sarcastically.

'You have my word. If need be, I will come and finish them myself,' he replies, quite sternly.

Costas might be drop-dead gorgeous but, my God, he's a bit serious. I can't help myself. 'Oh, so you do up hotel rooms as well. A man of many talents…'

He unlocks the door of the first room. 'My family and I have done all the work throughout the hotel. I hope you like it. Each room is different. We try to mix modern with authentic Greek touches and the bathroom toiletries are made by my mother and grandmother.'

That's me told. Obviously, he *is* a man of many talents. The room is fairly basic but it has a modern look. The built-in wardrobe space is more than adequate. There's a nice big mirror and a chair to sit on for doing hair and make-up. It's clean and there's a good-sized bathroom, which has a modern shower, a toilet behind frosted glass and a double vanity unit that is very impressive for a small hotel. There's a small TV, a kettle and a little fridge.

'I like these toiletries. I've used them at the Boutique Blue, where I'm staying.'

'Yes, I introduced them when I worked there. They have been very popular.'

'Oh, so you're not there any more?'

'No, I have a new job. It will be...' he stops mid sentence and looks a bit upset, '...a new start.'

'Well, I hope it works out for you.' I decide to move the conversation on because this clearly isn't a topic he wants to talk about any further. Then again, he doesn't seem to be the chatty sort anyway. 'I assume you've somewhere to make the toiletries?'

'We have indeed. It is a workshop and we have the items on sale there as well. I'll show you, if you like, before you leave.'

'I'd love that. It sounds like I might need my purse.'

'Yes, I think you are right.' I'm not sure if I detect a slight chink of humour in his voice before he moves on. 'Now, please have a look at the view.' He opens the wooden shutters to reveal a small balcony with a view of the courtyard at the back. There's a water feature in the middle of it, lots of plants in brightly coloured ceramic pots and plants growing up and around a couple of informal seating areas. There are also some wicker tables and chairs. Part of the area is covered and a couple of olive trees provide shade as well.

'You've created a beautiful little oasis.'

'Thank you, but I cannot take much credit for it. It was my grandparents who did this. I *did* help a little with the heavy stuff.' For a minute I think he's going to smile but it doesn't quite happen. 'I will show you one of my favourite rooms.'

He opens a door to reveal one of the sea-facing rooms. It's similar to the first room in layout and decor but the view is spectacular. It overlooks some pretty gardens as well as the golden, sandy beach, and flows right down to the gorgeous blue sea.

'Wow, this is amazing! Who wouldn't want to wake up to that view? Or the courtyard? Or the gardens?'

'I am glad you like it. It is good to meet people who appreciate the love that has gone into it.'

There are also a couple of cabanas on the edge of the beach that I hadn't spotted from the restaurant. 'Those cabana's are a nice idea.'

'Yes they are my brother's contribution. He has an eye for detail.'

'Well you're clearly a very creative family.'

'Thank you, you are most kind,' he answers looking a bit awkward at receiving a compliment.

Costas goes on to show me the informal lounge area downstairs, which contains a bar. This area leads to the indoor restaurant, which has doors that open out on to a bijou terrace with a few tables and chairs. Finally, he shows me into the kitchen, where he introduces me to his father Stavros. He's just about finished making the breakfasts. Eliana is washing up and Nikolaos is drying the dishes and putting them away.

Stavros shakes my hand. 'Miss Collins, I am very pleased to meet you.' Like his son, he seems a bit familiar to me. I'm beginning to have this déjà vu feeling with everyone.

'Please, call me Helen. I'm pleased to meet you too, and thank you for the lovely breakfast.'

'You are very welcome. It was no trouble. Now, would you like to try a coffee from my new machine? And then we can all have a chat. My wife is very embarrassed about the cocktail menu. It is my son's fault.' He shoots a disapproving look at Costas, who shrugs and shakes his head.

'How was I meant to know that Miss Collins would look at it?'

Ooh, I need to deploy a distraction tactic immediately as I detect some father-and-son friction. 'I'd love a cappuccino. Please don't worry about the cocktail menu. I've made a note of a couple of them just in case I ever need some inspiration.' I raise my eyebrows and smile.

Stavros looks relieved. 'Please have a seat in the beach-bar restaurant and I will bring us all some coffee,' he suggests.

I follow Costas to the restaurant. I can usually read people quite well, but I haven't a clue about Costas. I don't know if me snapping about James has put him on his guard or whether it's something else. I decide to proceed with caution.

'So, you've had a disagreement with James. Nothing too serious, I hope?'

'As you would say in England, it is all water under the bridge.'

I try another tack for breaking the ice with the Mr Cool Costas. 'Do you know many of our English sayings?' That will throw him – a complete change of subject. I could be wrong but I'm sure the corners of his mouth are breaking into a little smile.

'I know a few,' comes the reply. 'I worked in Stratford-upon-Avon a few years ago.'

'Oh, that's a lovely part of the UK. I was reviewing hotels in the Cotswolds just last week. I always try to stop off in Stratford on my way home. Were you working in a hotel?'

'Yes, I did a hotel and management course and my placement was at the Stratford Hotel.'

'Well, fancy that. I bet our paths have crossed. My company has featured the Stratford for at least fifteen years.'

Our conversation is interrupted as Xena joins us. It's a relief, actually, as Costas still seems quite guarded.

'I hope you have liked the hotel, Miss Collins.'

'Oh yes, definitely. I love all your personal touches, especially the toiletries. Do the guests have a go at making anything?'

'Not at the moment, but maybe it is something we can think about in the future. It was something that James suggested to Costas.'

I'm once again suddenly jolted out of my idyll.

Costas, too, has flinched at the mention of James. 'Yes, I have to agree it was quite a good idea of his to involve the guests and to mention it in the brochure blurb.'

'He's full of good ideas,' I mutter under my breath.

'Oh, good, our coffee is here,' Xena says cheerfully. I think she's realised that mentioning James is causing tension.

Stavros joins us and I pull my file out. My head is whirring, trying to understand what's gone on between James and their son. But there's work to be done. We plough our way through all my boring paperwork, chatting about their expectations and my company's expectations, which are huge. There's loads of red tape to get through and, unsurprisingly, Costas doesn't fully appreciate all the stringent health and safety requirements. But I think they've understood what I've been saying, and Xena and Stavros have shown enthusiasm for the work involved.

'I think I've covered everything. I have a couple of other hotels to visit and I'll let you know in the next few days whether you've been successful or not. Does anyone have any questions?'

Stavros replies, 'No, I think you have covered everything...' He looks like he's going to say something else but he falters.

Xena sees this and comes to the rescue. 'We did not know if we should say, but the Hotel Giorgos is my brother's hotel. I am praying that you like both our hotels. With the economy as it is, we are really wanting to be in your brochure.'

'Well, thanks for being so honest. I hope you are both successful.'

'Thank you so much, Miss Collins.'

'No problem. It's been lovely to meet you.'

'Do you still want to see the workshop before you go?' Costas asks. He takes me by surprise; I thought he'd had enough of me.

'Yes, if you don't mind. I just need to book a taxi first.'

'We will ring for taxi, you go with Costas and have a look at the workshop,' Xena says.

I follow Costas, who is already halfway across the courtyard. He clearly doesn't want to engage in any small talk with me. He opens the door to the workshop and I'm hit by the fragrance of many different perfumes.

'So, here is our workshop. Today my grandmother is making some soap.'

'Hello again, Helen.'

'Hello, Eliana. Don't you ever stop?'

'Not very often, dear. My grandson is a slave driver,' she replies laughing.

'This is amazing! Look at all these beautiful products.'

'We use our own herbs in some of them, like this lavender bath melt.' Costas passes one for me to smell.

'Oh my goodness, that's divine!' I gasp at all the delightful colours and take in the mingled scents. This shop is every girl's dream. There are plates of bath melts stacked up to look like mouth-watering cakes – some have names like 'Pina Colada Bath Sundae' and 'Lime and Coconut Sundae'. Then there's soaps in their individual glass jars, also looking good enough to eat and sounding scrumptious too, with ingredients such as apricots, honey and almonds.

'You know, James was right to suggest opening this workshop up to your guests. It would be a fantastic selling point.'

Costas looks embarrassed. 'I apologise for what I said before. He is your colleague and it was not right for me to discuss personal matters with you. It was James who suggested putting the hotel forward to your company in the first place. Please ignore what I said.' He clears his throat and changes the subject. 'I did not know your company was starting villa rentals in Florida.'

'Yes, and I wanted to be the one to go there myself. But you know what? I'm glad I've come to Mykonos instead.'

'Really? And why is that?'

'I'm not sure. I can't put my finger on it. I suppose I feel at home here. It's weird. I've never felt like this before.'

The studio door opens behind us. It's Xena, come to announce that my taxi is on its way.

'Right, well, I'll buy a couple of these gift sets for my mum and sister. They'll love them.'

'I will sort those out for you,' Xena offers.

'I am going outside until your taxi arrives. There is only so much of this perfume smell that I can take in one day,' Costas exclaims, wafting his hand over his nose.

Xena takes my money and pops my purchases into a bag. She adds something else in there as well. 'And this a gift for you, Helen.'

'No, I couldn't possibly accept that.'

'Yes, you can. Now, please. I have no daughters to appreciate these lovely creations. You are also welcome to come back and make some soaps of your own. I can see you would love an afternoon here.'

'That would be really good. I think my sister would love it too.'

'Your sister – is she called Shirley?'

'No, she's Stephanie. Why?'

'Oh, nothing, it is just that someone called Shirley came here yesterday with my younger son and you remind me of her.'

'I think we do have someone stopping at the hotel called Shirley because there was a song dedicated to her last night in the restaurant.'

'Anyway, Helen, please come back with your sister. Eliana will help you make some soaps to take back to England.'

We walk back out into the bright sunshine. Nikolaos and Stavros appear from the kitchen to say goodbye. I've only been here for a couple of hours but I feel like I'm part of the family. They each give me a hug. As the taxi pulls up, Costas appears and opens the car door for me.

'It was nice to meet you, Helen.'

'Yes, likewise. I'll perhaps see you when I come back to make my soap.'

'I am afraid not. I was only here to help my parents with the visit today. Enjoy the rest of your time in Mykonos.'

'Oh, I will, thank you.'

As the taxi pulls away, I wave goodbye. I realise I feel disappointed that I won't see Costas again. For some reason, despite his cool and serious manner, I liked him very much.

Chapter 13

Stephanie

Unsurprisingly, the mix of cocktails last night helped me sleep soundly. I also had quite erotic dreams about Costas, so it's probably a good job that the beds have been separated. The room is still in darkness. I reach out for the cup of tea that Helen has left for me – ages ago, judging by its lukewarm temperature. I slowly peel myself away from the comfy bed and spot a note on my bedside table.

Hopefully will be back a bit earlier than yesterday. Will text when I'm on my way.
Helen. x

I can have a leisurely breakfast and maybe an hour by the pool, then meet Costas to go on this mysterious boat trip. I feel a bit reckless and nervous but my gut instinct tells me I'll be fine.

I do my usual faffing about what to wear for the day and decide eventually on shorts and a T-shirt over my bikini. I manage to get my contact lenses in a bit more easily this morning and don't look like I've been crying for hours. I shove everything that I'll need for the day into my bag. It's becoming quite cumbersome. I'm envious of those people who can trot about all day with one little bag and look like nothing they do is too much effort.

I amble through reception. There's quite a lot of people congregated with their suitcases, looking like they're going home. Elena is on duty again at the restaurant.

'Good morning. Would you like the same table as yesterday?' she asks in her bright cheery voice.

'Yes, that would be great, thanks.'

'I hope you are having a good holiday so far.'

'Yes, I'm loving it, thank you. It seems very quiet in here this morning.'

'Yes, today is a change-over day so we had lots of people for an early breakfast. Here is your table. Enjoy your breakfast.'

The person serving at this table is Costas. My heart flutters a little and my stomach decides to do a couple of somersaults. He pulls out my chair to seat me.

'*Kalimera*. Would you like English breakfast tea this morning, madam?' he asks, looking half-serious.

'That would be lovely. *Efharisto.*'

'You are quick learner. How would you like the milk?' He's grinning.

'Ha ha, very funny. In the jug will be fine. That's how we serve it in England, most of the time,' I reply sarcastically.

'Okay, so one English breakfast tea and milk in a jug.'

He disappears to sort out my tea order and I make my way to the buffet. I decide to keep breakfast simple and quick to allow it plenty of time to settle before the impending boat trip.

Costas returns with my pot of tea and places it on the table safely. 'One pot of tea and milk. Enjoy your breakfast,' he replies in a normal professional voice, and then he adds in hushed tones, 'I meet you at the church at noon.'

I decide to make some inroads into the questionnaire while I finish my tea. I add a few more ticks and comments. The trouble is, my comments about my waiter aren't really relevant to this questionnaire … or printable.

I check my watch. I've got plenty of time to relax by the pool while my breakfast digests. I reckon I'll stand a better chance this morning of bagging a sunbed as it's a change-over day; and if I get my skates on, I'll have time to make an impression on my book.

I fold my napkin neatly and pop it on the table. Costas is over like a shot to help me with my chair. 'See you in a bit,' he whispers.

'I'm going to relax by the pool for a while and then I'll meet you at noon,' I whisper back.

My bikini is already on under my clothes and I've got everything else I need in my bag. Manolis, the guy in charge of the sunbeds, comes across when he sees me approaching.

'Good morning. There is more choice today. Would you like sun or shade?'

'Oh, shade, please.' I don't want to get too hot and bothered this early.

He leads me to a sunbed that has shade from a tree and a parasol. 'Will this one be okay for you?' he asks.

'Perfect, thank you.' I set out my stall. Sun cream and sunglasses on, bottle of water on standby, book and phone out. All set.

I open my book at the bookmark and start reading. It all seems familiar. I skim to the bottom of the page, then the next page and the next. I carry on skimming until I reach the end of the chapter. There can be only one explanation for this. Helen has committed the heinous crime of moving my bookmark and wasting my valuable reading time. Why does she think this is funny?

I finally locate where I am. I was mid chapter, wasn't I? Oh yes, I was just here – you are separated or recently divorced... Oh no, I don't believe it!

Bridget the bloody Fidget is in my peripheral vision. She's doing the same routine as yesterday and I'm inevitably drawn into watching her. She's got a different bikini on today but it's exactly the same routine. Oh, good grief, she's turned round and it's not a bikini at all, it's a bloody thong. There's nowhere to go with that bit. She lies back down and goes through her motions again.

Right, that's it. I've had enough. If I can't concentrate on my book, I'll Google Mykonos instead and glean some information ahead of my boat trip. I was all clued up for my Caribbean cruise but I have no idea about Mykonos apart from what I learned yesterday from Costas. Halfway down the page I'm reading, I notice something about *Shirley Valentine*. There's a link to click. I skip through the plot highlights – Shirley is a bored Liverpudlian housewife, her friend wins a holiday to Mykonos, Shirley decides to go and leaves her husband a note and meals that she's prepared, her friend buggers off with a bloke off the flight, Shirley meets... Great, my suspicions are confirmed. She meets Costas, who invites her to travel around the nearby islands on his brother's boat. And, oh, bloody marvellous: they end up having steamy sex.

What an absolute noodle I am. Costas must have thought, 'Here's another one who thinks she's funny, I'll string her along.' That said, he is wearing a name badge that says 'Costas', so at least he's not lying about his name. Unlike me. I think I'd better confess all that before we go much further.

There's a link for the boat scene from *Shirley Valentine* so I click on it.

Manolis, who's laying out towels nearby, hears the orchestral music from my video clip. 'I like your music from orchestra,' he chimes in.

'Oh, sorry, I wasn't expecting the loud music. It's the *Shirley Valentine* boat scene.'

'I see,' he says, raising his eyebrows. 'I can borrow a boat if you fancy being Shirley Valentine for the day,' he adds scanning my face looking for a reply.

Oh my God. Now what have I got myself into? He looks old enough to be my dad. 'Nooo, I'm fine, thanks. I don't really like boats,' I reply in a rather panicky voice.

'Well, if you change your mind, you know where I am.'

'Yes, I'll bear it in mind.' He leaves me to finish watching the clip. Phew, thank goodness for that.

Costas is now kissing Shirley's stretch marks, which is one thing, thankfully, that I don't have to worry about. The clip finishes so I put my phone away and decide to have a dip in the pool, being as though Bridget the Fidget is still adjusting her bikini.

There's a guy at the poolside, stood next to some speakers, wearing shorts, a T-shirt and some jazzy trainers looking like he's about to start a keep-fit class. There's no one else around dressed for a keep-fit class and then I realise that there's a group of women in the pool facing him.

He sees me. 'Oh, fantastic, one more for the water aerobics!' he shouts enthusiastically. 'We're just about to start.'

Before I can make an excuse to escape, a woman pipes up. 'There's room here, lass, next to us.' I smile and join the group in the water. It's absolutely freezing.

'Oh my God, how cold is this water?'

'Aye, but nee bother, pet, you'll soon warm up when Maaartin gets goin', won't she, Sandra?'

'Aye, Maaartin will soon have your blood pumpin' round, lass. He gives us a right proper workout.' Both of the women start laughing.

'Aye, pity he bats for the other side, like. Such a waste! Look at those pecs, look at that body! And those tattoos. Ooh, he makes me go all funny. I'm Carol, by the way.'

'Hi Carol, I'm Steph,' I reply through chattering teeth.

'Morning, ladies. I'm Martin. Now, let's get everyone warmed up and get those hearts pumping.'

'My goodness, he's far too energetic for me this early in the morning,' I say.

'Aye, lass, this is nothin'. Wait until he starts his twerkin'. It will make your eyes water.'

He puts on the music and we're away. 'Big, big booty...'

'Okay, everyone, let's march on the spot and clap your hands above your heads. And stride to the left, one, two, three, four. And to the right, one, two, three four. And star jump, and it's eight, seven, six, five... Now march on the spot. Get ready for some lunges, eight, seven, six, five...'

Oh my God, I can't believe I've got roped into this. I'm going to be exhausted.

'And now for some twerking. I know it's not easy under water. Just imagine you're Jennifer Lopez.'

All I can say is, Martin isn't struggling to twerk his booty.

'Four strides to your right, ladies. And star jumps, eight, seven, six... And shake that booty!'

I'm absolutely useless. Carol and Sandra aren't much better, but they're too busy ogling Martin's expert booty action to worry about themselves. Fortunately, once we've got the booty song out of the way, that's the end of the twerking. The next bit requires us to go to the edge of the pool and sit on the edge. The only issue with this is the pool is slightly deeper where I am and I can't haul myself out of the water. Talk about embarrassment but Martin is swiftly to the rescue.

'On the count of three you jump and I'll pull.'

'Are you sure?' I ask 'I could just go over there.' I can't believe I've got into this predicament. Of course everyone else has realised and dispersed to water that was shallow enough.

'It's fine I do this every day,' he says bending down and getting hold of my arms.

'After three, one, two, three and jump.' With one little jump from me he manages to lift me on to the side. I'm relieved that he hasn't flipped over me and ended up in the pool – now that would rouse the people relaxing on their sunbeds.

'Okay ladies now let's work those legs! Push down in the water to the count of two and back. And that's eight, seven, six… And now as fast as you can. Come on, splash as fast as you can!'

This probably isn't the best activity for my contact lenses as the water splashes up into my face from the over enthusiastic woman who's next to me. Martin does some different variations with our legs then tells us to jump back in the water.

We carry on for about twenty minutes and then do a cool down before getting out of the pool.

'Thank you, ladies. I'm Martin, just in case you've forgotten. There's a list of my classes on the flyer up here at the front. Have a fab day.' He waves enthusiastically and we give him a round of applause and thank him.

I make my way over to the table and pick up a flyer.

'Hi there, I might as well make some attempt to keep fit while I'm here.'

'Here, take a couple. Leave one in the toilets or something,' he says, laughing and handing me another flyer.

'Great class, by the way, and thanks for pulling me out of the water.'

'Oh you're welcome. I should warn people I haven't seen before.'

'I'll probably come again and drag my sister along too.'

'Oh, fab, the more the merrier. I'll hopefully see you around, then.'

'More than likely. I'm Stephanie, by the way, I'd better dash –
I'm catching the bus into town.'

'Lovely to meet you, Stephanie. If you want to go into town,
I can give you a lift in about fifteen minutes.'

'Well, if you're sure. That would be very kind of you.'

'It's absolutely no problem. I'll meet you in the lobby.'

'Fab, I'll be there. I'll just quickly change into something dry.'

'Oh yes, I don't want a big wet patch on the seat. It's not my
car,' he laughs.

I hurry back to my sunbed grab my stuff and race back up
to my room; luckily, housekeeping has been and gone. I put
on my new bright green bikini and quickly put the other one
into the basin with a bit of the Wild Olive shower gel that's in
our toiletries basket. I scuttle out of the room and get to the
reception at the same time as Martin.

'Oh, great, you're here. Right, follow me.'

I follow Martin outside and start laughing when I realise
which car we're getting into. 'I can't believe this is your car! I saw
it parked up yesterday in town and it made me chuckle.'

'Oh, I know, it's a disgrace. It's my job to clean it. You've
shamed me into doing it this afternoon. Alexis will think it's his
birthday and Christmas all at once if he sees his car all nice and
clean. Right, hop in, if you dare – it's worse inside.'

'Oh my God, it's a skip on wheels.'

'I know, I know. I promise I'll clean it out this afternoon.
You've got my word.' We set off and Martin whacks the air-con
on full pelt. 'So, where in the UK are you from? I think I can
detect a Derbyshire accent.'

'Yes, you're right. And I think I can detect a Manchester
accent,' I reply.

'Yes, Manchester born and bred. Alexis loves this awful
Mancunian accent – the guy's insane. I assume you're on holiday
with your sister?'

'I am, but it's ended up as a bit of a working holiday for her. Hopefully, she'll be finished today and then we can enjoy this beautiful island.'

'Ooh, working holiday – that sounds interesting.'

'Well, it's not! She works for Loving Luxury Travel and she's looking for two new family-run hotels to add to their brochure next year. She's also inspecting the hotels that are already in the brochure.'

'Well, tell her to write a couple of lines about the fitness classes we're offering, then people can come prepared.'

'I will, and I'll also take some photos to go on the website. So, what brought you to Mykonos?'

'Well, I came here on holiday and happened to come across Alexis. He was a fitness instructor at the hotel where I was stopping. The rest is history! We fell in love, and two months later I was back here living with him. I work at various hotels and run my own classes in town.'

'Wow, that's amazing! Well done, you.'

'Yes, well, that's the abbreviated version! Let's just say we got there in the end. We're nearly in town – do you want dropping anywhere in particular?'

'Oh, where the bus stops will be just fine. I can find my way from there.' We arrive in the square, which is chaotic again.

'Well, Steph – here we are. I hope to see you soon at one of my classes and come along to take some photos.'

'Thanks, Martin, I will. Have fun cleaning the car.'

'Ha ha, very funny.' He drives off, waves out of the window and pips the horn, which makes everyone in the vicinity jump.

I weave my way in and out of cars, mopeds and people and make my way down one of the little streets towards the church. Everything is just like yesterday. The fisherman is poised on top of the rocks and the old woman is busy feeding her little entourage of cats and kittens. She acknowledges me as I pause to stroke and play with them. I root about in my bag for my purse so that I can put some euros in her little box.

'*Efharisto*,' she says.

I nod and smile, and then stroll over to the church. I've arrived a bit early so I decide to go in to light a candle. Just as Costas did yesterday, I pop a euro into the box and pick up one of the long thin candles. I light it from one of the three that are already there, and sit down on the bench.

I loved candles as a girl. That is, until one of them brought about a tragic end to Helen's beloved Barbie typewriter. She's convinced, to this day, that I sabotaged it deliberately because I was jealous of it, but it was a genuine accident. I mean, who could seriously be jealous of a blooming Barbie typewriter, for goodness sake? I was just having a little play on it while she was out of the room. I loved the way the bell rang when I returned the carriage. Anyway, I heard her coming back, so I left it, and looked busy doing something else. Now, I can't remember at this point why there was a candle burning on the table. I can only assume we'd had a power cut; candles for decorative purposes weren't the done thing in those days, and power cuts were. After about five minutes, we noticed a burning smell.

Helen leapt to her feet. 'Quick, get Mum! My typewriter's on fire!' she yelled hysterically.

Sure enough, there was a flame coming from the typewriter. I ran to find Mum. She came running in and whacked the flames with a tea towel until they went out. The typewriter's return carriage was a charred mess and a putrid smell filled the room. The blame was quickly apportioned to me, with the conclusive evidence being that I'd typed 'My name is Stephanie' on the piece of paper that was wound round the cartridge.

Mum was furious. 'Go to your room straight away, young lady, and don't come out until I tell you! In future, don't touch things that don't belong to you, do you understand? Now go before you get a smack as well.' So off I went, leaving poor Helen sobbing uncontrollably. Luckily, Dad must have been out, otherwise it would have definitely been a smack.

Helen's typewriter wasn't the only thing that I managed to wreck in our childhood. Actually, while I'm here, I'm going to sit in the confessional booth and get a few things off my chest. I know there isn't a priest on the other side but I'm sure the powers above can absolve me telepathically.

I open the door, sit down inside and clear my throat. 'Bless me, Father, er, I've never actually confessed before and, well, there's quite a lot of things that I need to mention. It's mainly childhood things, like Helen's typewriter that I set on fire, but not intentionally. Then there was her globe, which I was holding one minute and then it seemed to be in pieces the next... Maybe I threw it at her in a temper. Now, about her precious dolls' house that she hid on the top of her wardrobe, I might have "borrowed" some of its furniture for my own dolls' house but I still maintain to this day that she "borrowed" my dolls' house table. Oh, and her Monopoly – that's a game we have in England; there's probably a Greek version too, with places like the Acropolis in it. Anyway, it involves moving round a board with your chosen token. She always wanted to be the car, so I hid it and I "borrowed" some of the money, which was useless because I couldn't spend it in the shops. Anyway, Father, this is all childhood stuff, which I'm sure Helen's forgotten all about. But then when I was a teenager, let's say I "borrowed" lots of her things, mainly clothes, and they didn't look quite the same when I'd finished with them so I never gave them back. So, if you can forgive me for that as well, I'd be most grateful. Oh, and while I'm here, er, just one small thing. Well, it's a big thing, really. I seem to have told a little white lie about my name. I'm really called Stephanie but

I've told Costas, the waiter from the Boutique Blue, that I'm Shirley Valentine. I know I shouldn't have done it but it kind of just came out...'

'Is that you, Shirley?'

I jump out of my skin in fright and stumble out of the confessional. Costas is standing there.

'You frightened me half to death,' I reply in hushed tones. Not that anyone else is here. It's just what you do in church.

'Why are you in there?' he enquires, looking puzzled.

'Oh, you know, just chatting about this and that to an imaginary priest,' I reply, trying to look like it's the most normal thing in the world.

'Imaginary priest?' he asks, now looking completely baffled.

'A pretend priest, you know, like Father Christmas. I was just getting a few things off my chest, you know, talking out loud...' Before I can say another word, the door creaks open from the other side of the confessional booth and a priest steps out.

'Bless you, child, I am very sorry I have to leave. I suggest you say three Hail Marys in the morning and at sunset for a week and speak to your sister and to...' he pauses and smiles at Costas who he obviously knows, '... your friend.'

'So, this imaginary priest, what does he look like?' Costas is laughing and shaking his head.

'Oh, you know, a bit like that one but older.'

'Okay, well, if you have finish confession for today, I will light a candle then we can go.' He lights his candle and bows his head to pray.

I scurry out as quickly as I can. He's out a few minutes later, holding a cool bag. 'Think you could balance this on your knee for five minutes on the back of the moped?'

'I thought we were going on a boat?' I reply, trying to wind him up.

'We are going on boat but, as you see, there is no water here and no boats, so please when you ready I will take you to the boat.'

I laugh and hop on the back of the moped. Off we head to the harbour, down the narrow streets of the town. When we get there, Costas parks up near some of the smaller boats that are tied to the harbour wall.

'Your boat awaits, Miss Shirley. Let me help you.' He takes the cool bag off me and goes down the steps to a little boat. He puts the cool bag in the back. I follow him down the steps and he helps me in. The boat wobbles like mad, but he takes my hand and manages to get me safely on board. As he holds on to my arm, I can feel how strong he is.

'Costas, I think I'd better take my seasickness tablets.'

'If you look to the horizon, you will be fine.'

As Costas goes back up the steps to untie the boat, I giggle to myself. I'd been picturing the boat out of *Shirley Valentine*, from the video I watched earlier. It was quite big – well, big enough for Shirley and Costas to have a passionate sex scene. This boat is tiny and definitely not big enough for a romp. I can't decide if I'm relieved or disappointed. I'm out of practice, so at least now I can relax. He throws the rope back on board and leaps in. He starts the engine and away we go on our adventure.

Chapter 14

Helen

In the midst of my thoughts about James and my encounter with Costas is the dilemma that I can only pick two hotels out of three. In some ways, it would be better if I didn't know about Xena's brother. But I'm guessing James knows and, up to last week, they all probably thought it was a done deal. Now I've come along and put a spanner in the works. I'm really hoping that this next hotel doesn't come up to scratch.

When we arrive there, it looks deserted. The driver offers to wait while I go and investigate. I shout 'Hello' a couple of times. A girl finally appears. She hands me an envelope. Inside there's a note.

> Most sorie my wife has fallon of lader this morning and I take to hospitel. I think she brakes arm. My doorter Sofia can show you the rooms if you like and we can arange anover meeting.
> Regard,
> Antonis

'Do you speak English?' I ask Sofia, who I reckon to be about sixteen.

'A little,' she replies, very quietly.

'Okay, I'll ask the taxi driver to wait for me and you can show me a couple of your rooms. You wait here.'

I pop outside and ask the driver if he minds waiting for me. He explains that he has another job but is happy to arrange for someone else to come and meet me, which sounds like a good idea. I pay him and arrange for another taxi to collect me in half an hour, which will give me ample time to assess the hotel.

I venture back inside. Sofia is waiting. 'My name is Helen Collins. I just need to have a look at a couple of rooms and a little bit around the hotel, if that's okay?'

'Yes, this is fine. My father said you may ask to be shown round.' She retrieves a couple of room keys from the reception desk and leads me upstairs.

When she unlocks the first room, my impression is of the 1970s. There are orangey-brown bedspreads on two single beds. The room seems clean enough but it's sparsely furnished with just one little wooden chair and a table with a mirror. The bathroom is basic, with a shower curtain round the shower. The rail is a bit rusty and the curtain has a couple of mouldy marks on it.

'Okay, Sofia, I'll view the other room. Do you have any guests staying here at the moment?'

'No. Some will arrive on Saturday,' Sofia replies in her quiet voice.

'And how will your parents manage if your mum has broken her arm?'

'Maybe my grandparents will help,' she replies, shrugging her shoulders.

She opens the door to the second room, which is similar to the first room but with a green colour scheme. The bathroom is also similar to the first room and a little dated, to say the least.

'Now, Sofia, if you can just show me the dining room, then I'll be on my way.'

She leads me back down the stairs to the dining room, which isn't very exciting. The decor is unsurprisingly outdated and sparse. My prayers have been answered – there's absolutely nothing about the place that gives me any good vibes.

The whole place needs a major makeover to get anywhere near the standard that we would require. They obviously didn't understand the paperwork that the company sent through about our minimum expectations. Maybe in this day and age we should ask for a few photos before we agree to a visit. This is a massive waste of time and money.

I thank Sofia for her time and wish her mother well. I tell her that I'll be in touch by email in the next few days.

The new taxi driver is waiting outside as promised, sensibly positioned under the shade of a tree. I'm going to go straight to my last hotel and then maybe I can have a couple of hours to myself, or with Steph, if she's about. I need to eat somewhere so I may as well sample lunch at the next hotel and put them on their toes a bit. I show the driver the hotel name on my paperwork and he nods his head. We've only been going for a couple of minutes when he slows down.

'I am most sorry, there are goats everywhere,' he explains, gesturing at the road ahead.

'Don't worry, I've plenty of time. It's just part of life in the countryside. In England, we mainly have sheep and cows.'

'You live in the countryside in England?'

'No, I don't unfortunately, but I'm not far from cows, sheep and hills. I love it here, you know. There are no built-up areas and it's very peaceful and rustic.'

'Yes, I prefer it in the countryside. We go to Athens occasionally to visit family and I am always glad to be home, even if it does mean I have to wait for goats to move out of my way when I want to get somewhere,' he laughs.

'I'd love to visit Athens. Maybe I could go there next week for a couple of days with my sister.'

'Yes, you could easily do that. There are daily flights from Mykonos that are quite cheap, and it takes less than an hour.'

'I might just do that. Thanks.'

'You are very welcome. Ah, thank goodness, it looks like the goats have finally decided to move on.'

* * *

We've arrived back in Mykonos town and driven up quite a steep hill that has fantastic views of the town below. The taxi driver has pulled up.

'This is as far as I can go. You just walk straight ahead and the hotel is on your left. You will not miss it. The name is over the gate.'

'Thanks.' I hand over my money and turn to follow his directions.

The narrow concrete road is crazy paved in white edging and is dazzling in the bright sun. It's certainly very quiet in the streets. All I can hear is birdsong and four young children who are playing on some steps. I wander around a corner and, just as the taxi driver said, the Hotel Giorgos is right there, tucked away in among some beautiful gardens. The setting, if nothing else, already cheers me up. It's picture-postcard perfect. The building is pleasing to the eye, which is a great start. It's whitewashed, with blue shutters.

I walk through the pretty gardens and head to the hotel building. There's a familiar-looking guy behind the reception desk.

'*Kalimera*, madam. How nice to see you again. How can I help?'

'I'm Helen Collins and I have a meeting with the owners. I apologise for arriving early, but I thought I could have some lunch first.' I hand him my card. 'You'll have to forgive me – have we met before?'

He smiles. 'You forget me so soon. I am Nikos from the Boutique Blue.'

'Oh, yes, Nikos. I'm sorry, I didn't recognise you without your uniform on.' Oh my God, I can't believe I've just said that. I can feel myself blushing. 'How come you're here?' I ask, hoping he hasn't noticed my flushed face.

'This is my parents' hotel. I help out here when I can, after my shift at the Boutique Blue. I could make some suggestions for lunch and then come and join you?'

'Yes, that would be very kind, and maybe you could let your parents know I've arrived.'

'May I suggest we wait until after lunch? My father may burn the salad if he knows who you are. He is very nervous already – and that was when he was expecting James,' Nikos replies, laughing. 'Get to meet the real Mr and Mrs Papandreas, before you reduce them to quivering wrecks. So, no James then?'

I take a deep breath in. 'No, he's gone to Florida at short notice so I ended up coming here at the last minute.'

'Oh well, that is a shame. We always had a good laugh when James visited. Until he fell out with my cousin, of course.'

'Oh, really? What was that all about?' I seize my opportunity to get some more information.

'I believe it was over some woman, which does not really...'

'Nikos!' a voice calls from outside.

'It sounds like someone's looking for you,' I say.

'Please follow and meet my fiancée.' We pass through the colourful gardens. There's a swing seat out here on which I could just imagine myself gently swinging with a book in one hand and refreshing drink in the other...

'Helen, meet Selena, my fiancée,' says Nikos. 'Selena, this is Helen from...'

'… Loving Luxury Travel. Yes, we have already met,' Selena finishes his sentence, looking like a rabbit caught in headlights.

Nobody speaks for what is the longest few seconds of my life. Nikos can sense that there's an awkward atmosphere building and breaks the silence. 'I have just suggested having lunch with Helen. Perhaps you would like join us?'

'Yes, of course,' she replies still looking dazed.

I bet she bloody well does. She'll not want to risk leaving me with Nikos in case I spill the beans about her and James. Unsurprisingly, she is minus her necklace.

'Did you want me for something, Selena?' Nikos asks her.

'Sorry, want you?'

'Yes, you shouted for me.'

'Sorry, I have forgotten. Silly me! It will come back to me.'

Perhaps she was coming to tell Nikos what a two-timing trollop she is.

'Maybe you could bring us a drink each and ask Mama to throw together some typical Greek appetisers.'

'Of course. What would you like to drink, Miss Collins?' She practically spits the 'Miss' at me, the silly cow.

'Oh please, call me Helen. Surprise me with one of your cocktails – something to quench my thirst would be nice.'

'I have the perfect drink in mind. You take a seat,' she replies in a rather patronising tone.

The restaurant is by a small swimming pool. There are three couples having lunch and some Greek music playing on the sound system.

Selena arrives back with a tray of identical drinks. 'A Limoncello Collins for us all, a refreshing afternoon drink to cool us down.'

We all raise our glasses with a united '*Yamas!*'

I take a sip and it nearly knocks my head off.

'Is the drink all right, Miss Collins?' Selena asks, in a very concerned tone.

'Yes… It's a bit sharp, though.'

'Oh, I do apologise. I must have put a dash more lemon in yours.'

'Don't worry, I'm sure I'll manage. I'm used to bitter-tasting things,' I reply and look her directly in the eyes. If she wants to play games, I'll step up to the mark.

A woman appears with a huge tray of food.

'Mama, meet Helen,' Nikos introduces me, seemingly unaware of my stand-off with Selena. 'She is a guest of the Boutique Blue, and I recommend here for some authentic Greek food.'

'*Xéro polí*, nice to meet you Helen. I hope you enjoy our food. There is Greek shrimp and mussels *saganaki*, crispy lamb meatballs, fried eggplant, home-made potato and garlic dip, fried *feta* with honey and sesame seeds and some home-made *tzatziki* and, of course, our home-made breads.'

'Thank you. I'm sure I will. This looks delicious. But goodness me, I'll be here for the rest of the afternoon and need to sleep after all this lot,' I say in a semi-joking protest.

'You not worry. I am starving, so I will eat loads,' Nikos exclaims, already piling food on to his plate. 'And I am sure Selena will eat something as well.' Nikos makes a gesture to invite Selena to eat.

To be perfectly honest, she looks like she exists on thin air, and that's rich coming from me. She tentatively puts a couple of things on her plate.

'So, you mentioned that James has gone to Florida. Is that hotel-connected?' Nikos asks, completely unaware of Selena's predicament. She's visibly holding her breath waiting for my answer.

'No, it's villa rentals,' I reply, watching Selena like a hawk.

'I do not remember him talking about villa rentals. Do you, Selena?'

'No, he has never mentioned Florida to me,' Selena replies, sounding on edge.

'Well, like I said, it all happened at the last minute. The

Americans wanted someone to go over as soon as possible and James was the only one who could go at such short notice.'

'It sounds like it was James to the rescue, then?' Nikos says, as if James has gone to fight a war.

'What was your reason for not going?' Selena asks, only just managing to sound impartial.

'It's a long story. In any case, I didn't have a visa and James did. So here I am, enjoying this wonderful Greek island and your hospitality.' I smile at Nikos and then at Selena. I can't resist raising my eyebrows, which is enough to unnerve her.

We slowly make our way through all the delicious food and manage to keep the conversation away from the subject of James. I'm enjoying Nikos's company but Selena is clearly on pins.

'Now, what about some Greek coffees to finish off?' Nikos suggests.

'Yes, that would be lovely. I've not tasted a Greek coffee yet,' I reply.

'Selena makes the best coffee in Mykonos.'

'Yes, okay, I will make the coffees,' she says reluctantly, before strutting off.

'I will ask my parents to join us while we have coffee. Then I can introduce you,' says Nikos.

'Yes, that sounds like a good idea. Break it to them gently.' As Nikos disappears, I check my phone. There's a message from my parents.

We're visiting Anti Paris
this morning and Paris
this afternoon. We're loving
everything about the
cruise so far. We've even had
a go at the helm. Hope all
OK with both of you. xx

There's no sign of Selena, Nikos or his parents, so I quickly type a reply.

> Paris? OMG Mum
> you've gone a bit
> off course. They won't
> leave you at the helm
> again. Lol. We're both OK.
> Steph survived yesterday
> without me. Don't think
> she even noticed that I
> wasn't there. I'm at
> my last hotel now so I can
> start enjoying myself from
> tomorrow. xx

Selena arrives back looking pleased with herself. '*Eliniko cafe*, which is Greek coffees. The others will join us in five minutes. They are just finishing the lunch service.'

'Thank you, Selena. So, is it your day off?' I try to sound polite but, quite frankly, I just want to slap her.

'Yes, and what a great day it has been so far.'

'Anything planned for later?' I ask, sipping the hideously strong Greek coffee.

'I had plans but they seem to have changed.' I suspect her original plan had been to spend the day with James.

'Have you heard from Daniel about opening the bar?'

'Yes, he replied and apologised for the mix-up. He had forgotten about James's email.'

'Good, at least that's one matter cleared up,' I reply, smiling through gritted teeth.

'I think you just had a message or something on your phone,' Selena points out. She's looking pleased with herself. I'm sure she's overdosed me on caffeine. I'll be on a caffeine buzz until the early hours.

'Oh, I didn't hear it. It's probably just my parents but I'll have a quick look.' I scrabble about in my bag and find the phone. I also inadvertently pull out the condom that I stuffed in there yesterday. Selena immediately clocks it.

'Oops! Be prepared, and all that.' I stuff it back in just as Nikos makes a timely reappearance with his parents.

'Helen, meet my parents, Giorgos and Katina.'

'Hello, and thank you very much for the delicious lunch. Apologies for not saying who I was – that was Nikos's idea.'

'Yes, we have just reprimand him,' Katina replies, wagging her finger at him.

We shake hands and they take a seat.

'Okay, I'll go through the company's side of things and then you can give me a tour.'

I explain our paperwork and Nikos, in turn, explains a few things to his parents in Greek. Selena looks bored to death but she's clearly still not ready to risk leaving me on my own with Nikos.

'Well, I think we've covered everything. I'll have a quick look round and then I'll get going.' I'm feeling a bit uncomfortable. A sharp twinge in my stomach makes me catch my breath.

'Are you all right?' Katina asks, seeing my obvious discomfort.

Selena can't help herself. 'It is probably all that garlic and strong coffee. We are all used to it, after all.'

'Yes, exactly,' I reply, noticing the smugness in her face.

'If you're all right, Helen, I am going to show you round the hotel,' Nikos announces, which immediately wipes the smug look off Selena's face. 'I have booked my two favourite women into the spa at the Boutique Blue Hotel for a treat. I know how disappointed you were, Selena, when your friend let you down today.'

'Yes, but, Nikos, I would prefer to stay here with you...'

'There is no need. I have already arranged it. Now, you go and be pampered. You deserve it.'

'Okay, if you insist,' she mutters.

'Yes, I insist, and I have a surprise for later. Now go or you will be late.' He gives Selena a kiss and, for a moment, she softens. But she's clearly not happy.

Well, it serves her right. How convenient to say that her 'friend' has let her down; more like James has let her down. Well, she can join the James-has-let-me-down-again club with me. She's got a gorgeous fiancé who clearly adores her, so goodness only knows why she's fallen for James anyway.

'Nice to meet you, Helen.' Katina shakes my hand. 'I hope you are okay after all that garlic.'

'I'm sure I'll be fine. I'll just take some of these indigestion tablets that I've found in the bottom of my bag. I'll soon be as right as rain.'

'Are you planning to visit the Royal Blue again?' Selena asks, looking quite worried.

Before I can reply, Nikos chimes in with, 'Maybe you could go to the show night next week?'

'That's a possibility. I could see if my sister would like to go too.'

'Aha!' Nikos exclaims. 'I wondered if that was your sister. You do look a bit alike. You, of course, are the younger sister,' he adds laughing. Selena looks like she's about to combust at Nikos's flirting.

Of course, I willingly play along. 'Oh, Nikos, you're too kind. No, Stephanie is my younger sister. I'm sure she'd love your show night, Selena. I can't wait. We may even see you later at our hotel after you've had your spa treatment.'

'Yes, maybe. I suppose we had better go.' Selena reluctantly leaves with Katina, and Giorgos announces that he's got some food to prepare.

'Right, Nikos, lead the way,' I say.

'Okay, follow me.' He leads me up the stairs, which gives me the ideal opportunity to admire his perfectly shaped bottom. He unlocks a door and swings it open. 'This is our honeymoon suite.'

'Wow, a four-poster bed!'

Nikos pushes the netting to one side. 'And not just any four-poster bed. Come and see.' He pats the bed.

I sit down. 'Oh my God, it's a waterbed!'

'Have you ever slept on one?' Nikos asks.

'No, I haven't.'

'Well, I can recommend it. Lie down and see what you think.'

'I can't do that, Nikos, I'm wearing shoes.'

'You can take them off.'

'Okay, if you insist.' I take my shoes off and lie on the bed. 'I'm not sure I'd get to sleep with the sound of the water sloshing about.'

'Yes, but remember this is the honeymoon suite,' he replies, raising his eyebrows.

I'm not really sure whether he's flirting with me or just being nice but he's making me feel a bit giddy. In any case, I must be at least fifteen years older than him. And he's engaged, even if it is to that stupid cow Selena, who's cheated on him with James. I decide to reel the giddiness in.

'So, Nikos, how long will it be until *you're* booking into a honeymoon suite?'

He sighs. 'We are meant to be getting married next year.'

'Why, is there some problem?' I have a feeling I already know what he's going to say.

Before he can answer, his phone rings. 'Sorry, it is Selena, I had better take the call.' He answers it and after a couple of minutes it sounds like they're having a bit of an argument. Nikos is shaking his head.

I pop my shoes back on and have a wander around the room. The wall behind the bed is made of rustically exposed stonework. There are modern prints of local scenes on the walls; one shows the famous windmills, but I reckon Steph's shot yesterday is better. There are also a couple of art deco mirrors and some lovely pottery pieces.

I have a look in the bathroom. There's a sunken bathtub that looks into the bedroom and, unsurprisingly, there's a basket of assorted Wild Olive bath melts and toiletries. I can't resist picking up the bath melts and having a sniff.

'That is the Rose Geranium Soufflé,' Nikos appears behind me. 'They are all made by my aunt and grandmother.'

'Yes, I was at the Hotel Niko this morning. I bought some gifts for my sister and my mum – that's what's in my bag downstairs. Xena has kindly invited Steph and me back to make some soap.'

'You will enjoy it. I am sorry about taking the call. I do not know what is wrong with Selena. She is on edge today, and this is before I tell her about my job interview for a promotion.'

'Surely she'll be pleased for you? And it will be more money, I assume?'

'Yes, but the job is on another island for the next five months. I fear we will drift apart. I planning to discuss it with her tonight at her favourite restaurant.'

'Life is never straightforward, Nikos, but you need to seize opportunities and follow your dreams.'

'You are right. Anyway, enough of my problems. Do you like the room?'

'It's stunning. I love the art deco mirrors and the pottery.'

'I am glad you like the pottery. Those are pieces that I made.'

'I'm impressed! I've always fancied myself at a potter's wheel.'

'Really? Follow me, then, and I will show you something that I think you will like.'

'I'm sure you will, Nikos. Oops, did I just say that out loud?'

'You did, Miss Collins, and let me remind you that I am engaged to be married,' he says, trying to sound serious.

'Sorry, Nikos, just ignore me. I think that drink's gone to my head.'

I follow Nikos back down the stairs, outside through the courtyard to the back of the hotel and to a building with deep pink bougainvillea growing by the door.

'Okay, Helen, close your eyes and on the count of three open them.'

'Flipping heck, Nikos, what on earth are you showing me?'

'Nothing bad. Now close your eyes.'

I decide it's better to do as he says, otherwise I'll be here all day wondering what's behind the door.

He opens the door and begins to count. 'One, two, three … open your eyes!'

I open my eyes and I'm greeted with a wall of pottery pieces. Bowls, plates, vases, plant pots and everything else you could think of, all in various bright coloured patterns. There's a section of pieces showing striking local scenes, with the typical white buildings framed by blue skies. My favourite pieces are the art deco designs. I pick up a coffee cup and admire it. It's simple with a deep green line on the rim of the cup and saucer, straight black lines drawn down at an angle and curved black lines crossing over them.

'This is my own design.'

'Wow, Nikos I love it.'

The showroom area has a glass partition, on the other side of which is a studio. Nikos opens the door. 'Come through. As you see, we have two throwing tables and wheels, various shelves for the different stages of production and an electric kiln. And here, the part we enjoy the most – stamping your own design on whatever you have made.'

'Who makes the pottery?'

'It is mostly Mama and myself, but my Aunt Xena likes to make things for the Hotel Niko.'

'Oh yes, I noticed all those wonderful pieces there. You're all very talented.'

'If you are not in a rush, you could make something now and come back to decorate it in a couple of days.'

'Well, if you've got time and don't mind, I'd love to.'

'Okay, pop this on.' Nikos hands me an apron. 'What would you like to make?'

'Ooh, what about three soap dishes for Mum, Steph and myself for the soaps from your Aunt Xena's place?'

'Excellent idea, and a good easy item for beginners. I will get some clay from the storage area.' Nikos slices three equal pieces off the block and brings them over. 'The first thing we need to do is to knead it, like bread, and then roll it into a ball.'

I start kneading. It's hard work. 'Gosh, Nikos, this takes some doing.'

'You will soon get the hang of it.' Nikos has done his piece and is repeating the process. Then he cuts it with some wire. 'See, we aim for no air bubbles. Like this.'

'I see. Well, I'd better knead harder then.'

Nikos starts on the third piece while I'm still messing about on my first. 'Now, Helen, cut your ball.' I slice through it with the wire. It looks fine to me – no air bubbles. 'Very good. Knead it back into a ball and then we will begin the fun part. I will show you how to throw the clay.' Nikos expertly throws the clay on to his wheel and wets his hands. 'First, I cup the clay in both hands, squeeze it and bring it to a tower shape. Now, I push the clay down and let excess water and clay slide away. This part is done a couple of times to help centre the clay.'

I watch Nikos intently as he slides his hands up and down the spinning clay, wetting his hands from time to time. He makes it look extremely easy, and very sensual.

'Now, I open the piece. I have to make a hole in the exact centre otherwise it will wobble.' He makes a hole with his finger.

'And now I make the hole bigger and shape the dish. We need to make holes in the base so that the water drains away to prevent your soap going mushy. Now, we pinch the wall to get our desired thickness.'

I don't know about the soap going mushy – he's making *me* feel mushy watching him skilfully manipulating the wet clay with his hands. Within minutes, it's finished.

'Last, we tidy the edges and then you have your very own soap dish. Now, it's your turn. You might want to take off your scarf so it doesn't get dipped in wet clay.'

We swap places. I sit at the wheel and Nikos sits behind me. 'This is exciting! But I hope you're prepared for clay to fly everywhere, Nikos.'

'It will not fly everywhere because I am going to help you. Okay, now throw your clay as hard as you can.' I throw my piece of clay on to the wheel. It seems to land quite centrally. 'That is good. Now, I start the wheel. We need to wet our hands.' I dip my hands into the bowl of water that's sitting beside us, and Nikos wets his. 'Now, put your hands on the clay and shape it up into a cone. You need to press your arms into your legs and push your legs against here for your strength.'

'Yep, got that.' I start shaping the wet clay.

Nikos clasps his hands over mine. 'Let the clay slide between your fingers and bring the clay upwards.'

Oh my God, this is getting really weird. It's extremely sensual … well, for me, at any rate. My heart is pounding in my chest. Within seconds, we have our cone.

'Wet your hands again and press your thumb into the middle, but keep your hands firmly on the outside as you press down. Now, we bring it back up and stretch the clay out to our desired shape.' He clasps his hands over mine again as we pull the piece back up and shape it. 'And finally, I will trim the base and now you, Helen, have your first soap dish.'

'Thank you, Nikos! I'll look forward to coming back to decorate it.'

'Yes, and now you can try throwing the third one on your own.'

'Okay, here goes.' I throw the clay on the wheel and start off quite well. I tease the clay up and down. Gosh, Nikos made it look so easy. It doesn't seem to be quite as compliant for me. I press my thumb into the cone. Within seconds, the clay has spun off the wheel and splattered on the studio glass partition. 'Oh no!' I shriek with laughter. 'What a mess!'

'Oh dear, Helen, this is not good. Either the clay was not centred or your thumb did not go in the middle.'

We're both in fits of laughter at the sight of my first disastrous attempt at throwing, and we're unable to speak as we gasp for breath. We're that engrossed in laughter that we don't notice a rather angry Selena standing in the open doorway. She starts shouting at Nikos in Greek. I haven't got a clue what she's saying but she's absolutely furious.

Nikos is calm and is trying to pacify her, to no avail. As he approaches her, she grabs a piece of pottery and hurls it at him. Luckily, he ducks and it hits the wall behind him, smashing into bits. I've heard of Greek plate-smashing, but I don't think it's supposed to be quite like this.

Nikos shouts at her and throws his arms up in disbelief.

Selena turns and screams at me hysterically, 'I might have known you would do this! Well, here, have this! He is all yours!' With that, she pulls off her engagement ring, hurls it at me and storms out, with Nikos in hot pursuit.

I can just hear Steph later when I tell her about these shenanigans. 'Well, Helen, that's another fine mess you've got yourself into.'

I'm contemplating my next move when Katina comes rushing in. 'Helen, are you all right? I hear Selena shouting at Nikos. Oh my goodness, what happened to that plate?'

'I'm afraid Selena threw it at Nikos. Luckily, he ducked. Then she threw this at me.' I hand over the ring.

Katina shakes her head and starts crying. 'But why? Why is she so angry with you and Nikos?'

'I'm afraid you'll have to ask her, Katina. We were just laughing about my rubbish pottery-throwing when she came in. I think she has issues beyond Nikos and myself, but we have added fuel to her fire. Anyway, I'd better be making tracks. Give my regards to Giorgos and Nikos. I'll type up my report and email it to Daniel.'

Katina starts crying again. 'Oh, I cannot believe that this happen today. Whatever must you think of us?'

'Please, Katina, don't worry about what has happened. It won't be reflected in my report. You have a lovely hotel. I hope Nikos resolves his differences with Selena, and maybe I can come back next week when it's calmer to decorate my pottery. But maybe not that one!' I point to my throwing disaster. 'That's what we were laughing about – I don't think I'm a natural at making pottery.'

Katina takes my hands in hers. 'Thank you for being so understanding. Please do come back and I will help you decorate your pieces.'

'I'd love to – I need something to put my soaps in!'

I leave Katina sweeping up the broken pieces of plate. As I walk through the courtyard, I can still hear Selena screaming at Nikos.

Chapter 15

Stephanie

As the harbour slowly disappears out of view, I take some photos of the town and one of Costas with his hair flapping round his face while he steers the boat, which is bouncing gently over the waves. The boat gives quite a jolt from time to time when we hit a wave and water splashes up and back, but it's fun. I'm sure I won't be saying that tomorrow when my back is shot to pieces and I can't walk. As Costas predicted, as soon as we're out of the protection of the harbour, it starts to feel chilly in the wind. I drag my towel out of my bag and wrap myself in it.

We've not been going long when he suddenly slows the boat down in the middle of the sea. A silly thought hits me – he's going to chuck me overboard! I can just imagine the news headlines: 'British Woman Missing, last seen boarding a fishing boat...' And any interviews with my mum. 'I've no idea what was going through Stephanie's mind. I brought her up to know better than to get into a boat with a stranger. Didn't I Michael?' Poor Dad would be there nodding his head, replying, 'well maybe cars Pamela.' Then they'd have to end the interview as Mum and Dad argued over the finer details of boats and cars.

'Look over there.' Costas points into the sea, bringing my thoughts back. He turns the boat back towards where he's pointing and cuts the engine. 'Get your camera ready – there are some turtles. I will feed them and they will come to the boat.'

He throws some food scraps out into the sea and, sure enough, three or four massive turtles appear within seconds. It's amazing to watch. Other fish arrive to take advantage of the situation.

'We can come and swim with them one day, if you okay to jump into the sea.'

'I could jump in,' I answer in a non-committal way, not wanting to encourage him any further. 'I'm not sure I'd get back in the boat though.'

Costas grins. 'You leave it with me. Now we carry on.'

He starts the boat up, and off we go again, bouncing on the waves. A plush-looking hotel sits perched up above us on a hill. Costas steers the boat towards the edge of the small sandy bay below it and then he slows the boat and cuts the power. As we get to the shallow water, he jumps out and pushes the boat on to the beach. There are sunbeds and parasols on the stretch of beach in front of the hotel and a few people are on the beach and in the sea.

'Welcome to Shirley Valentine's beach. It is now a private beach belonging to this hotel but my friend, who is one of the managers, gave me permission to bring you here.'

'Wow! Thank you. It's lovely.'

'We used to come here as a family. My first memories are of watching the filming of *Shirley Valentine* from where the Grand Hotel is now. And now I am standing on the very same beach with Shirley Valentine herself. So, what would you like to do?'

This maybe wouldn't be the right time to confess that I'm not really Shirley Valentine; Costas has gone to so much trouble to bring me to my namesake beach. I survey the area, thinking that there doesn't actually look like there's much to do apart from swim and sunbathe.

He can see that I'm struggling, so he makes some suggestions. 'We can swim, snorkel, walk and explore, eat, sunbathe, go back to the town…'

'Sorry, Costas, you're right. It's beautiful here. Maybe I could try snorkelling, but you'll have to show me because I've never done it.'

'You live on an island and you not try snorkelling?' He looks astounded.

'No, Costas, I've never fancied snorkelling in the cold British seas.'

'Okay, well, of course, as you know from yesterday, it is quite cold here too. But we try it. Let's get the mask on you first.'

He reaches into a compartment in the boat and brings out a couple of masks. He gives one to me, spits into the viewing panel of the other one and then rinses it in the sea.

'Eww! That's gross! Why on earth are you doing that?'

'It will stop mist up,' he replies.

'Really?'

I'm not convinced, but he obviously knows what he's doing, whereas Little Miss Novice here doesn't. I spit into my mask, smear the visor and rinse it in the water. I then wiggle the mask over my head. The plastic really pulls on my hair.

'Actually, you better with wet hair,' Costas suggests, seeing me struggling.

I follow him into the sea. Just like yesterday, it's cold. I stop when the water reaches my knees.

'Come on, Shirley, the quicker you get in the better.'

'I'll be fine, just let me acclimatise slowly.'

'By the time you've acclimatised your way, it will be time to go home,' he says, splashing me. He comes over, picks me up and drops me in the deeper water while I squeal. 'Okay, you acclimatise now,' he says, laughing.

I splash him and he splashes me back. 'Stop!' I screech. 'I don't want water in my contact lenses.'

'You start it,' he replies in his defence.

'I think you started it, actually, by chucking me in the sea.'

'Okay, okay, you are right, I started it. Now, let me put mask on you.'

He stretches the straps over the back of my now wet hair and puts the mask over my face. It feels tight enough. I put the end bit of the air tube into my mouth in between my gums and teeth. Costas reminds me that I need to breathe through my mouth and not panic. He shows me a couple of signs to use, such as 'Okay', which is making a circle with my thumb and index finger, and 'Not okay', which is crossing my hands and shaking my head.

I submerge my head into the water and immediately start panicking as I fight for air. Costas gently pulls me up and reminds me that I need to breathe through my mouth. He calms me down and we try again. Amazingly, after a few minutes, I get used to it, so Costas swims off to lead the way.

I can immediately see fish darting about in their own little kingdom. Costas swims towards some rocks where there are dozens of fish. He taps my arm and points down to the ocean floor at a bright red starfish. There's also a lobster-like thing near it, with long antennae waving about in the water. I swim along a bit and spot a feathery creature waving in the motion of the sea. It looks quite pretty, and harmless, which is the main thing. Then a school of long pointed fish swim by. I don't like the look of them but thankfully they don't seem interested in me.

The sounds under water are incredible. Obviously, I can hear the water but, amazingly, I can also hear fish nibbling on the rocks. Costas taps me on the arm again and points to a yellow jellyfish with purple flecks, floating along like something from outer space. He indicates to me to follow him into the deeper water away from the rocks. I can feel the water get colder. Then I see why he's led me out. Some turtles are swimming about here. They're not bothered by us; in fact, they swim towards us, occasionally going up for air and then swimming back down. One swims really close to Costas. He touches its shell and then it swims over to me as if it's sensed that I want to touch it as well. I gently stroke its large shell. The feeling is awesome. I feel so humbled that these magnificent creatures have come to swim with us and let us touch them. There are a couple of smaller turtles with them as well, so it looks like they're trusting us with their young family. They swim around us for a while and then eventually swim off. Costas indicates that we're going back, and I give him the okay sign. We swim back to the shore and I remove my mask. My gums feel strange after having had the mouthpiece in place.

'That was incredible! It's like a different world down there. I can't believe those turtles swam up to us like that! Thank you so much for bringing me,' I say, slightly out of breath.

'It is my pleasure. I love to share it. I look forward to having children of my own to bring here one day,' he says, looking at some kids who are playing nearby. 'It is one of my favourite places...' He trails off as if he's got something else to add but can't find the right words.

'I'm sure you will, and that they'll love it. It's a beautiful place.'

'Yes, I'm sure you are right,' he replies, sounding positive again. 'Now, I think we should eat this food that my grandmother make. Let's sit under the trees for shade.'

He hands me a picnic blanket that he's brought and picks up the cool bag himself. We make our way over to the shade of the trees. I drop the blanket and wrap my towel round myself. I feel quite chilly now that I'm out of the water and in the breeze. Costas places the blanket on the sand and we unpack the food together, along with plastic plates and glasses.

'Your grandmother prepared all this lovely food for us? That was very kind of her.'

'Yes, she is very kind person. I will have to introduce you.'

'That would be good. Then I can thank her for all this.'

The food looks scrumptious. Costas scoops some gorgeous fresh *hummus* into a piece of bread and delivers it to my mouth. It tastes divine. The olives are even better than the ones from yesterday, and there's some *feta* and some sweet juicy tomatoes.

'Is this *tzatziki*?' I pick up a tub of dip.

'Yes, indeed, freshly made with cucumber, yogurt, mint, garlic and salt. I hope you like it. My grandmother make the best on the island.'

'It's very tasty – nothing like ours at home.'

'You make *tzatziki*?' Costas asks, looking surprised.

'No, I mean it's nothing like the stuff we buy in the supermarket.'

'Well, if you ask my grandmother for her secret recipe, you will be able to return home with an inside knowledge of how to make the most delicious *tzatziki*.'

'Yes, I'll be able to make some and invite Helen over to reminisce about our holiday in Mykonos.'

'Oh yes, your sister. What time do you meet her today?'

'Oh, I'll try and get back for about five again. And I can spend the day with her tomorrow,' I reply half-heartedly, because it means I won't be with Costas.

'If you like, I could take you both for a drive around the island tomorrow. Then I will still see you,' he offers.

'Yes, that could work, I suppose. She seems to like you. I'll suggest it to her at dinner tonight after a few drinks and see how the land lies.'

'You have not told her that I showed you about the town yesterday?'

'No, I wanted to keep it to myself. I didn't want a big sister's lecture on holiday romances. I had one of those when I was twelve. I got friendly with a boy and spent the journey home crying because I wouldn't get to see him again.'

'You never saw him again?'

'No, it was a seven-hour drive to a town in Cornwall.'

'Seven hours? This is a long way.'

'Yes, it would have been quicker to fly here and meet you.'

'And maybe we have a holiday romance?'

'What, then or now?' I ask, feeling my heart beating like mad.

'Both,' Costas replies, taking my hand and kissing the back of it. 'If I met you when I was twelve, I would send you a postcard every day. Written in Greek, of course,' he says laughing.

'Yeah, right, and I wouldn't have had a clue what it said.'

'It would say,' Costas clears his throat, 'I am missing you and counting the days to seeing you again.' Costas is laughing again.

'I think you'd write about two of those until the next plane-load of tourists arrived and then you'd forget all about me,' I reply in a serious voice.

'Maybe, maybe not, we will never know… Anyway, we will pack this lot up and walk down the beach if you like.'

'Sounds good to me.'

I decide, in my wisdom, to top up my sun cream, and Costas volunteers to do my back. It's not that I'm not grateful, but every time he glides his hands up and down my back it feels like an electric charge is running through my body. It's making me giddy.

'Maybe you could put some on my back, to stop it burning,' he says.

'How can a girl turn down such an offer?' I rub the cream in slowly and lose myself in the moment. He has a lovely toned brown body and it's sending me completely haywire.

We set off and stroll down the beach. We pick up shells, skim stones in the calm sea and chat. Despite the odd occasion when we don't understand each other, the conversation is nice and easy.

'Have you always worked at the Boutique Blue?'

'No. I have been very lucky and have travelled around many of the Greek islands and the mainland doing various jobs. It is very helpful when you grow up in a hotel to know many jobs. I can turn my hand to most things.'

'And which island was your favourite?'

'Oh, so many to chose. I prefer the greener parts of Greece and I like places with some mountains or hills. I worked in Crete last spring and early summer and walked through the Samariá Gorge before I came home. I really like the Peloponnese, and the Strofylia Forest. We have ten national parks in Greece and I have only been to five of them. How many national parks do you have in England?'

'I hate to admit it, Costas, but I don't really know. There's one near where I live, which is the Peak District, with hills and sheep as you'd expect, and pretty towns with tearooms. Then there's the Lake District, which speaks for itself, with lots of lakes, hills, sheep and more tearooms. Then there's a mountain in North Wales called Snowden, which is in Snowdonia. I visited there once on a school trip. Again, lots of hills, sheep, and of course rain.'

'So, seeing the great outdoors is not high on your list of things to do?' Costas says, laughing.

'Non-existent,' I reply, laughing too. 'But never say never, especially now I've rediscovered my passion for photography. Just think, all those photo opportunities.'

'Hills and mountains – you'd have to climb to get them.'

'Hmmm, I'll have to think about that.'

'Come on, we will go back and have a siesta. I have been up since six and I am back at work at six thirty.'

'You seem to work very long hours.'

'Well, it is usually about forty-two hours a week, but over two or three shifts a day. This week I'm on the early breakfast shift and the early evening shift.'

'I'm not sure I'd be any good at splitting my day like you.'

'Trust me, Shirley, you would soon adjust.'

There are a few more people on the beach. The sunbeds under the parasols are all taken, although a few people have moved theirs into the full sun and look like they're frying. People are reading books, newspapers and magazines. Some have got headphones plugged into devices and, by the sounds of it, quite a few are having their siesta already. God, I hope I don't snore like that.

We get back to the picnic blanket and lie down. Costas strokes my arm gently. I close my eyes. He's undeniably gorgeous, and seems to be a lovely person. He's easy to talk to and makes me laugh. So what if it's a holiday romance? I need to go with the flow and have some fun. The hypnotic sound of the sea is sending me into a trance-like state and I daydream, re-enacting the *Shirley Valentine* boat scene with Costas and me in the throes of passion…

I feel something tickling my face and ear. 'Shir-ley, hellooo, time to go.' Costas's sexy voice finally stirs me. He's tickling my face with a piece of grass and laughing. 'You sleep like cat.'

'I'm so sorry, Costas! It's all that food, wine and sun – it's knocked me for six. What time is it?'

'I don't know how you say in English.' He shows me his watch.

'I can't believe it's quarter past four already! Time flies when you're having fun.' I get up and we shake the blanket together.

'What is "knocked for six"?' he asks.

I try my best to explain as we pack our things away. Costas can speak good English, even if it is a bit disjointed, but we forget all the sayings that we take for granted. I'm not even sure myself about 'knocked for six' so I go with the cricket theme.

As we load the boat, I notice a large love heart drawn in the sand with my new name in the middle – I'll have to change it by deed poll at this rate. Costas puts his arms round me and whispers something in Greek in my ear. It sounds very romantic but I don't want to spoil the moment by asking for a translation. It probably won't sound as sexy in English. I respond by kissing him and he kisses me back. I needn't have worried about the long absence of kissing in my life: Costas is a natural and he's reduced me to a quivering wreck.

'My goodness, Shirley Valentine, I only whisper I hope you like my sand art.'

I laugh. 'I don't think it matters what you say, Costas, I just love hearing you speaking in Greek.'

'In that case, we will get on very well because I love hearing you speak in English. Please allow me.' He helps me into the boat. 'Okay, I push the boat in the water and hopefully jump in, otherwise you drive boat back,' he says, chuckling to himself. He pushes the boat out and pulls himself effortlessly on board. He starts the engine and off we go, skimming over the waves and getting wet all over again.

I wrap myself in my dry towel to warm up, and enjoy the wind blowing my hair about my face. As the harbour comes into sight and we start slowing down, I retrieve my phone out of my bag. I've had a message off Helen so I text her back.

C u by the pool
same place as
yesterday. xx

We seem to arrive at the harbour very quickly. Costas cuts the engine at just the right moment. He throws the rope up to the harbour wall, jumps on to the steps and has the rope securing the boat, seemingly effortlessly, in minutes.

'Welcome back to dry land. I hope you have enjoyed the trip,' he says, sounding very official while he helps me off the boat.

'I've really enjoyed it, thank you.'

We hop on to the moped and Costas weaves skilfully in between throngs of people as he takes us towards the square. I feel quite moped-savvy now. It's definitely the only way to get about these narrow alleyways.

He stops in the busy square. 'Don't forget to ask your sister if she would like drive round island tomorrow. I will pick you both up, in the car, of course.' He gazes at me with a hopeful face, giving me butterflies.

'I'll see, Costas, but she'll probably want to chill out tomorrow. It looks like the bus is here. I'll see you later and let you know what Helen says.'

As I start to turn, he catches my hand and pulls me gently back.

'I think you are forgetting something,' he says, wrapping his arms round me. 'Like a goodbye kiss.'

Oh my God, there's kissing and then there's Costas's kissing. My whole body is aroused. He seems to find some sort of switch that I didn't realise existed. I eventually break free, with my heart beating like mad and my head swirling with giddy passion. 'See you in a bit,' is all I can muster as I scurry off.

The bus is quite packed but I manage to get a window seat. Everyone seems to be tired and quiet after their day in town. As we set off, I contemplate what I'm going to say to Helen and whether or not I should just come clean. I'm already in enough of a pickle what with telling Costas that my name is Shirley Valentine. That's something I'll have to rectify, especially if Helen does agree to going on this drive around the island. She'll not find it remotely funny. I used to make up names to annoy her and her friends when we were kids. One of my favourites was telling her friends that I was Sabrina the teenage witch's English cousin. I told them I could put a spell on them to make them less ugly, which went down really well. I can remember her saying to her friends, 'Don't take any notice, she's just being stupid,' before marching off to report me to Mum.

As the bus starts climbing the hill, I glance down and notice the sheer drop. I suddenly don't feel so good about bagging a window seat. In an attempt to distract myself, I send a text to Costas.

Thanks for a
lovely day and
for taking me to
Shirley Valentine's
beach. C U later
:) Xx

It's now safe to look out of the window again and appreciate the sea sparkling in the late afternoon sun. The bus pulls into the town of Ornos. A few people get off and a handful get on. I assume the people getting on have been on the beach, which is lined with parasols.

The bus finally reaches the stop for the hotel. I walk wearily to the pool to find a sunbed. I lie down to catch my breath and absorb the impact of Costas's kiss and my afternoon with him. I'm half dozing, dreaming that we're running down a beach, splashing each other in the water. He's calling my name, but somehow, this time, it's my real name.

'Stephanieee! Stephanieee!'

Chapter 16

Helen

I've spotted Steph. I could be wrong, but I think she's catching flies.

'Stephanieeee!' No response. 'Stephanieeee!' I dip my fingers into a glass of water and flick her a couple of times with it, which seems to do the trick. I've stirred the sleeping lioness so I take a large step back.

'What the hell? Bloody hell, Helen! What are you trying to do? Give me a bloody heart attack? I was just having a lovely dream about… Anyway, what time is it?' she asks grumpily, stifling a yawn.

I think she's calmed down but you're never sure with Steph, especially when she's just woken up. 'Cocktail o'clock. I'm going to order while it's happy hour. Should I surprise you with something off the menu?'

'Yes, what-bloody-ever. I'll just dry myself off after someone flicked water all over me.'

'Flipping heck, Steph, it was only a couple of flicks of water. You'll soon dry off in the sun.'

I walk off before she can say anything else. I don't want another showdown – the one with Selena and Nikos was quite enough for one day. I can't wait to tell Steph about it.

I reach the pool bar just as my phone bleeps. It's an email.

Hi Helen,

Sorry to ask, but I need a massive favour from you. The interviews for the manager's assistant position at the Syros Boutique Blue Hotel, due to open in a couple of weeks, are taking place over the next couple of days.

Originally I was sending James to help with the interviews. Last week I lined up someone else so that you wouldn't have to go. Unfortunately, this person has had a family bereavement and can't go. I've therefore arranged for you to go instead. You're booked on to a flight that leaves tomorrow morning at 10.00 a.m. I'll email the necessary paperwork to you.

Again, please accept my apologies for the inconvenience. I realise that you were expecting to be finished today and spending some time with your sister.

I'll discuss some recourse with you on your return to show my appreciation for you both being inconvenienced.

As you are only going to be there for a couple of nights, I assume your sister will prefer to stay where she is, as the new hotel isn't open yet, but if she would like to travel with you I'm sure we can arrange something.

Regards,
Daniel
Managing Director
Loving Luxury Travel

I've now read the email five times and I still can't take it all in. I can't believe that I've got to stand in yet again. The planets must be in some strange alignment, that's all I can say. Steph's going to go mad unless she comes with me. But she's really not going to want to leave this five-star luxury for a hotel that isn't up and running yet. I'll break it to her gently over our cocktails. I send a reply to acknowledge the bloody email. I should just ignore it, as I officially finished my duties an hour ago.

Hi Daniel,

Can't say I'm jumping for joy at the prospect of spending another two days working while I'm meant to be on holiday, but I can see how you're fixed and I know you'll recompense Steph and me. Just on my way to break the news to her, so will let you know if she wants to join me.

Regards,

Helen

Manager

Loving Luxury Travel

I order a Strawberry Daiquiri for Steph, which sounds nice and refreshing, and a Limoncello Collins for me. I'm keen to try one that's not been made by Selena, with her extra dash of lemon. I make my way slowly back to the sunbeds pondering how I'll break this latest change of plan to Steph.

'A drink is on its way. How's your day been?' I'll get the small talk in first.

'Oh, you know. I just lazed on the beach mainly, and did a bit of swimming,' Steph replies in calmer tones.

'Well, that's what holidays are all about – lots of relaxation. Oh great, the drinks are here.'

'Strawberry Daiquiri? And the Limoncello Collins for you. Anything else, ladies?' asks the waiter.

'No, that's it for now. Thanks.'

'It's very considerate of them to name a whole bunch of cocktails after us. I had the Limoncello Collins at lunch at the

Hotel Giorgos. You'll never guess who made it.'

'Tom Cruise?' Steph replies.

'Yeah, right, he just popped in from his latest film shoot. No, it was Selena from the Royal Blue. It turns out she's engaged to Nikos – you know, who works here.'

'Whoa, you've lost me already. Why was Nikos from here, there?'

'Hotel Giorgos is his parents' hotel. He was there to help out and to meet James, who he thought was doing the reviews. Anyway, I didn't tell you the other day that when I first met Selena, she was wearing a necklace that was exactly the same as the one James gave me. After all her pouting about James this and James that, I yanked mine from round my neck and told her to put it in the bin. I couldn't believe it when Nikos introduced her to me as his fiancée.'

Steph has suddenly come to life and sat up on her sunbed. 'Oh my God, Helen! I bet her face was a picture.'

'Oh, indeed, but it gets better. We had lunch together and I swear she was trying to make me ill. She brought us all a Limoncello Collins and put extra lemon in mine, which made my hair stand on end. This one tastes nothing like the awful drink she made me. Then I think she told Katina – Nikos's mum – to put extra garlic in the food. Then she tried to finish me off with an extra-strong Greek coffee.'

'Are you sure you're not letting your imagination run wild?'

'Well, I'll tell you what I'm not imagining. Nikos arranged for her to come here with Katina for some beauty treatments. Understandably, she was really reluctant to leave Nikos with me, in case I told him about James, and even more so after *this* fell out of my bag in front of her.' I show Stephanie the condom, which she promptly takes off me to inspect.

'Ribbed and dotted for maximum pleasure. Wow, Helen, I'm impressed.'

'It's not mine,' I tut. 'I found it at that bloody awful hotel I went to yesterday, under a bed.'

'Lovely, and you've kept it because…?'

'I meant to show it to the manager as an example of poor cleaning standards. Anyway, back to the story. I'm pretty sure Nikos was flirting with me.'

'Oh, Helen, now you're being ridiculous. He must be at least fifteen years younger than you.'

'Well, thanks very much! Anyhow, some men prefer an older woman. I think the term is "cougar".'

'Okay, whatever. So let's hear your definition of flirting.'

'Well, I mentioned that I was here with you and he said he'd seen us and that you must be my older sister…' I can't resist a little snigger.

'The cheeky sod! Wait until I next see him. He must need his bloody eyes testing!'

'Ah, see, now who's getting her knickers in a twist? Anyway, the room he took me to was the honeymoon suite. It had a four-poster waterbed…'

'Oh my God, don't tell me you've been romping about on a waterbed all afternoon with a gorgeous Greek guy!'

'For crying out loud, Steph, of course I haven't.'

'Bloody hell, why on earth not? You could have tried that condom out.' Steph is sniggering.

'Well, Selena rang him, if you must know, and they started arguing. Anyway, at the end of the day, I didn't really want to take advantage of Nikos to get back at Selena and James.'

'Fair play. So, is that it?'

'Oh no, it gets much more interesting. I was admiring all the wonderful pottery…'

Steph bursts into laughter and her mouthful of drink is sprayed everywhere. 'Let me get this right. You're standing in a room with a gorgeous bloke and you're admiring pottery. Sis, you really need to get out more.'

'Oh, sod off. I'm not telling you the rest of the story if you're going to take the piss out of me.'

'Come on, Helen, you know I'm only joking. Please, pretty pleeeease, tell me the rest of this pitiful story.'

'Right, well, I'm admiring this pottery – art-deco-style if you must know – and Nikos tells me he's made it. I just happen to mention that I've always fancied having a go at a potter's wheel. So Nikos leads me to his very own pottery studio...'

'Whoa, now you're talking! Don't tell me you've had a steamy sex session on his potter's wheel...'

'Do you know what, Steph? You're not even remotely funny. It's not always about having sex, you know. Sometimes it's the sensuality of the moment. And it was a hot moment and pretty erotic without sex, actually. And, if you must know, Selena came storming in before anything happened – apart from my clay flying off the wheel.'

'Oh, right, so if Selena hadn't come marching in you'd still be there now would you, spinning round on his wheel?'

'Maybe. Who knows?' I reply wistfully. 'Anyway, she was furious and they started arguing. She threw a plate at him and her engagement ring at me, saying I could have it and was welcome to him.'

'Wow, I'm impressed. So, you're now engaged via a jealous ex-fiancée – congratulations. Where's the ring and when's the big day?'

'You are so not funny. I gave the ring to Katina, if you must know.'

And then Steph delivers the predicted line perfectly: 'Well, Helen, that's another fine mess you've got yourself into.'

'Yes, indeed, and there's more.'

'For fuck's sake, there can't be more. I'll need to lie down in a dark room after all this.'

Sod it, I'll have to take the bull by the horns. 'Daniel has emailed to ask me, or tell me, that I need to go to another hotel tomorrow and the day after to do some interviews.' I brace myself for her reply.

'Well, that's okay isn't it? Or is there a "but"?'

Steph has sussed me. 'The "but" is that the hotel is on another island. But you can come with me, if you want.' I say the last bit quickly and quietly to lessen the impact.

'Is your boss having some sort of laugh, Helen, at our expense? I hope you've told him to take a running jump.'

'Well, actually, no, I haven't. They'll compensate us for this – maybe with a nice weekend away or even another week here to make up for this one. Like I said, you can come with me. The only thing is that the hotel there isn't fully up and running yet because their season starts in two weeks' time.'

I'm expecting Steph to explode into another tirade, but she takes a sip of her cocktail and mutters, '*C'est la vie*. I'll be fine,' and lies back down.

My mouth opens and closes and no words come out. She must have knocked her head, or maybe it's sunstroke. Whatever it is, I'm leaving it well alone. 'I'll email Daniel then and tell him it's just one ticket?' I ask gingerly, for clarification.

'Yes, I'll stop here. No point in trailing off to another hotel when I've just got my bearings here.'

I email Daniel quickly before she changes her mind.

Hi Daniel,
Just one airline ticket. I'll await further information.
Helen,
Manager
Loving Luxury Travel

'Right, I've sent the reply to Daniel. He owes me big time.'

'Yes, he does. Oh, by the way, I've booked us into the other restaurant tonight, at half seven, for a change of scenery, if that's okay with you?'

'Absolutely fine with me. I need to visit it at some stage. Maybe Costas will be serving us. He's a bit of all right and I'm sure he fancies you. Could be a little holiday romance there...'

'Bloody hell, Helen, what's got into you? Are you on some sort of mission to marry me off before we get home? Have Mum and Dad bribed you with a load of money? I'm fine, thank you very much. I can sort my own love life out. You just concentrate on your impending engagement.'

'Flipping heck, Steph, I was only saying. No need to bite my head off. I'll sodding well not bother in future.'

I stomp off towards the pool and sit on the edge for a while. Steph went completely over the top with my comment about Costas. Hmm... I wonder if she's hiding something. It seems very odd that she's suddenly not bothered in the slightest that I'm leaving her for two days and a night.

I pluck up the courage to have a swim in the gorgeous but chilly pool. The hotel's idea of heated and mine are a few degrees different. I swim up and down for a bit and mull a few things over in my head. It's certainly been an interesting day, what with Costas this morning and my inherited fiancé Nikos this afternoon. And Selena with her little outburst – I wonder if Nikos picked up on what she said about me? She nearly dropped herself in it, the stupid cow.

My peaceful swim is shattered by a guy diving in and doing the front crawl like he's an Olympian. I bail out. When I get back to our sunbeds, Steph's phone is bleeping with messages.

'Gosh, Steph, you're busy.'

'Oh, you know what it's like, just trying to keep up to date with everyone.'

She looks positively guilty. I suppose it could be a fella, but she hasn't mentioned anyone to me. She reckons she's happy on her own at the moment.

We have our second two-for-one happy-hour cocktails before heading to our room to get changed. I can't wait to try the food in the main restaurant, and I can update Steph with the other events of the day over a drink or two. It'll be interesting if Costas the waiter is about. I could always stir things up a bit and see how Steph reacts to a bit of sisterly banter.

Chapter 17

Helen

I'm booked on a ten o'clock flight this morning. Before I leave, I'm enjoying a quick room-service breakfast on our balcony. The sun hasn't reached me yet so it's still a nice temperature here. I check my emails, messages, WhatsApp and Facebook; James still hasn't responded to the message I sent the other day. I wonder if Selena has mentioned my visit. Maybe's he's lying low. Or maybe he's been eaten by a shark.

I catch sight of Costas in the restaurant across the way. He seems like a nice guy. He obviously fancies Steph, judging by their flirting last night. I just need an older version – or even a younger version – for me. In my dreams! Mind you, I had both yesterday. The other Costas – sultry, serious, sexy. Then the gorgeous, carefree Nikos. Well, until Selena got the wrong end of the stick. He had to park the 'carefree' bit while he was ducking that plate. I wonder if he ever did manage to calm her down and take her out to her favourite restaurant. I'm guessing not.

My phone alarm alerts me that it's time to leave. I slip quietly back into the room so that I don't disturb Steph, and make her a cuppa from the remains of my pot. I leave it by her bed. I'm never sure that she actually drinks them, but I reckon that after all those cocktails last night she'll be a bit worse for wear and will drink anything when she wakes up.

I whisper to Steph that I'm leaving and apologise again. She mumbles something completely incomprehensible.

There's no sign of Nikos today but my taxi to the airport has been ordered and is already waiting. The driver doesn't seem interested in engaging in conversation so I start glancing through my interview notes. I'd love to ask one of those silly questions like 'If you could be an animal, what would you be and why?' I'd like to be something slinky and sexy with long legs. The animal that springs to mind is a giraffe, but is it slinky and sexy? A long neck would be useful, at a pop concert, say. On the other hand, it could be a hindrance. I'd always be hitting my head on something. I suppose I'd better just stick to the boring old script that I've been sent. 'Tell us why you think you're a suitable candidate for this job.'

These things always make me laugh. People who are good at blowing their own trumpet are always going to interview better. So, you give them the job and two months later you're left wondering what went wrong. James is a good example of this. He gave a brilliant interview. But I must have been wearing rose-coloured spectacles that day, anyway. I was dazzled by his good looks and taken in by his charm. My God, what on earth was I thinking?

The taxi driver breaks into my daydream. 'We arrive at the airport, Miss Collins.'

'Oh, right, thank you.' Gosh, that was quick.

He pulls up outside the terminal and comes round to open my door. He pops my suitcase on the pavement and then he's off quicker than I can say 'Here's a tip.' I assume my company has paid the fare directly.

It's reasonably quiet at the check-in desk, which isn't surprising for a domestic flight. I'm quickly checked in and through security. I walk into the small lounge. While I'm waiting, I Google the Syros Boutique Blue Hotel to have a peep at the website. It's still got artist's impressions up instead of photos; it wouldn't surprise me if Daniel asks me to take some while I'm there. There's also a link to meet the staff. I click on it. Oh dear, it's looking a bit sparse. There are just a couple of photos, one of the head chef, Jakub, who's from Poland, and one of the bar manager, Darius. Oh, this is interesting: he previously worked at the Mykonos Boutique Blue. I wonder if he can mix cocktails like Costas.

I need to text Steph. It will be a miracle, though, if she's up before midday after all those cocktails. It was quite amusing when Costas suggested she try his version of Sex on the Beach. I thought she was going to choke on the cherries from her Amour Smooch. I just get the message sent when the tannoy announces my flight. The first message is in Greek and then the English follows: 'All passengers for flight GA351, please go to Gate 2 for immediate boarding.'

That will be me, then. I gather up my things and join the queue. It's only short, and we all manage to fit into the shuttle bus that takes us the few feet to the plane. We're welcomed on board the small plane and directed to our seats. My seat is by a window. I get my laptop out and make a start with my recommendations for the two small hotels that I'm putting forward for our brochure. I'm sure Daniel will agree with me that they both fit our requirements perfectly.

The pilot announces that the doors are locked and cross-checked. I love that. I hope they cross-check other things, such as the fuel in the tank, that the engines are all in working order and that an experienced pilot is on board with a co-pilot. Pilots are one of those professional types that you'd prefer to be experienced, along with police officers, paramedics, dentists, doctors, surgeons and, of course, most importantly of all, hairdressers. I let Stephanie loose with my hair when we were teenagers; unsurprisingly, that year the school photo wasn't sent to relatives.

There are no TV monitors because the plane is so small. Instead, we're treated to a flight attendant performing a safety demonstration with an oxygen mask and a life jacket, and holding out a laminated emergency card for all to see. I'm reassured by now that I can handle any in-flight issues (not), but I'd have to remember to kick off my shoes immediately. I wouldn't want to be puncturing that escape chute with my heels. Imagine the headline in the news the next day: 'Woman's Stiletto Impedes Emergency Evacuation'.

We taxi down the runway, wait a few minutes and then take off. I retrieve Steph's magazine out of my handbag to flick through. I'm sure she won't notice it's missing when she finally wakes up. There are a couple of features that I've got my eye on. Now, what were they? Oh yes, twenty things a woman should achieve before she's forty.

I've already got a couple of boxes ticked. 'Number 3: own a little black dress that looks good at every party and makes you feel amazing.' I've got a few of those. 'Number 6: have shoes for every conceivable occasion.' I've definitely ticked this box – they have their own *room*.

'Number 2: have hot sex with someone you work with.' That would be James, although it's looking like the door on that chapter of my life is closed.

'Number 4: forgive your exes.' In my head, James is now an ex. So, unfortunately, I can't tick this box because James is not forgiven. He's a complete and utter waste of time and space, a womaniser and a selfish pig.

'Number 11: let passion be the driver of your profession.' I'm not sure about this one. Don't get me wrong, I love my job. But would I say I feel passionately about it? After this week, I'm not sure. Perhaps a career change could do me good. I feel like turning up at the Syros Boutique Blue and saying I've come for the interview.

I'm not sure about Number 1: die your hair every conceivable colour. Are they meaning different colours at the same time so you'd look like a human version of My Little Pony?

'Number 18: travel the world and settle in your favourite place.' Well, I've certainly travelled the world, and I love many places. But somewhere to settle down? I don't know. Well, I have been strangely drawn to Mykonos. I feel so at home here. Maybe I could look at buying a holiday villa on the island.

'Number 9: who you can turn to in a crisis?' Um, probably my parents or Steph…

I'm still pondering Number 9 when the plane seems to lose height and my ears start popping. I hope everything is okay with the plane. I wasn't expecting it to land this soon. My heart races slightly as an announcement is made in Greek. I glance round; no one seems to be looking panic-stricken, nor are they reaching for their life jackets. Then an announcement is made in English: 'Ladies and gentleman, we will shortly be landing in Athens. The captain has put on the seatbelt sign so please return to your seats and put them in an upright position.'

I could be wrong, but I thought she just said Athens and I'm meant to be going to Syros! Don't panic, Helen! There'll be a simple explanation. The flight attendant comes along to do her final checks and, meanwhile, what must be Athens looms below us. Before I've had a chance to even think about how long this detour's going to take, the plane has landed. It taxis down the runway and comes to a halt in the middle of the tarmac. A handful of people begin to gather their belongings, but everyone else stays put.

I press my call bell to ask one of the flight attendants what I'm meant to be doing. She explains very nicely that we're picking up some more passengers here in Athens and then we're continuing on to Syros.

I can't believe I didn't realise it wasn't a direct flight – that's so unlike me. I just checked in and went with the flow. I didn't pay any attention to my paperwork or to the flight boards. Oh well, these things happen. I chuckle to myself – that's on the list. 'Number 16: be able to say "Oh well" rather than "What if?"'

The new passengers are soon boarded. A woman who's probably in her late twenties sits next to me. She politely acknowledges me as she fastens her belt. She pulls some paperwork out of her bag; she obviously isn't going to pay any attention to the instructions on how to put on a life jacket or locate the exits. My attention is drawn to a letter she's reading. It's on our company-headed paper. The last thing I need is to chat to an interviewee – it might cloud my judgement in the interview – so I reach for Steph's magazine for another flick through.

Ooh, this article looks interesting: 'What Is Love?' Apparently it was the most searched question on the web last year, according to Google's annual Zeitgeist report. The article says, 'We ask an author, an artist, a psychologist, a vicar and a child what love means to them.' I have a quick scan over what they all have to say. The burning question at the end of all this is, of course, what does love mean to *you*, Helen Collins?

Well, let's see. I'm pretty sure it's not what I've experienced with James, or anyone else for that matter. I need to think about what I really want out of a relationship. I think I want shared interests and a solid commitment. And what interests do I have? Ever since losing my best friend to cancer, it's all been about work and the travel industry. I've been running away, too scared to get close to anyone for fear that I'll lose them. It's me who has the commitment issue, which is why I've been dating people like James in no-strings-attached relationships. At some stage, I also need to think seriously about whether I want to start a family. Steph's predicament has certainly made me think about the subject quite a lot lately.

My thoughts are pushed to one side as the captain announces that we're due to land. The woman next to me puts away her paperwork and takes out the safety card from her seat pocket. I feel like saying, 'It's a bit late to be worrying about that now you've missed the safety demonstration. Don't be expecting me to help you with your life jacket or your oxygen mask!'

Fortunately, the plane lands without incident and quickly taxis to the terminal. The flight attendant is making an announcement in Greek, but no one is taking any notice. They're engrossed in their mobile phones, which are all making various alert noises. Then comes the English translation: 'Ladies and gentlemen, please remain seated until the captain switches off the safety-belt sign.' She's only just finished speaking when the light goes out. Everyone immediately stands up, clutching their bags, checking their messages and listening to voicemails. We quickly disembark. From the lack of shorts and flip-flops, I assume the other passengers either live here or, like me, are on business.

There isn't a big queue for passport control, but the bags seem to take ages to arrive on the carousel. Finally, a handful of them appear. Of course, most of the passengers had only hand luggage, so they've all disappeared already. By the time I get through the barrier, everyone else has gone so it's easy to pick out the Syros Boutique Blue board. It takes me a couple of minutes to persuade the guy that I'm the last-minute substitute. He seems happy only when there's clearly no one else coming through the barrier from our flight. He leads me to a minibus and puts my suitcase in the hold. There's an empty seat at the back of the bus, which, it turns out, is next to my fellow passenger from the plane.

'Hello again. I'm Alexandra,' she says, in what sounds like a Greek accent.

'Hi Alexandra, I'm Helen. I noticed on the plane that you had a letter from Loving Luxury Travel. Are you going for an interview?'

'Yes, I am, but I think I am wasting my time. I only realise this morning who the new manager is. We work together before and things did not go well between us. Are you here for interview as well?'

'Actually, I'm here to do the interviews,' I reply.

'Oh, this is good news. At least, if I interview well, I may be considered for similar posts.'

'Maybe, but I'm afraid the manager is doing the interviewing with me,' I reply.

'Oh dear, I might as well catch the next plane home.'

'I'm sure you'll be fine. Like you said, the interview will be noted on your file.'

'Yes, it will no doubt be the worst interview on record.'

The hotel looms into view. 'Oh, look, I think we're here. Good luck with your interview. I'm sure you'll be fine.'

'I wish I share your optimism, but I will pray for a miracle over lunch.'

Chapter 18

Stephanie

There's a phone ringing annoyingly somewhere nearby. I wish it would just go away. Oh my God, my head's hurting. I realise after a few seconds that it's the hotel phone by my bed.

A weak husky 'Hello' is all I can muster.

'*Kalimera*. Shirley, is that you?' a voice asks in a hushed tone.

It takes me a couple of seconds to register my new alias, and that it's Costas on the phone. I clear my throat in an attempt to sound a bit more human. 'Yes, sorry, Costas, it's me. Is everything okay? Why are you ringing me on the room phone so early?'

'Shirley, it is not early. I already try your mobile and you not answer,' Costas replies, sounding quite amused.

'Oh, sorry. Maybe it's on silent. What time is it, anyway?'

'It is nine thirty and we need to leave at ten.'

'Oh my God, nine thirty! And the restaurant only serves breakfast until ten!' Then the next part of the conversation hits me. 'Why are we leaving at ten?'

'The boat trip to Delos. We agreed last night.'

'Boat trip to Delos…' Oh my life, what on earth have I agreed to now?

'Yes, remember? Delos is the island with the archaeological site. Listen, Shirley, I have to go. I will meet you at the bus stop just after ten. You can have a coffee and something to eat at my parents' hotel.'

'Okay. Thanks, Costas.' I put the receiver down and jump out of bed. Getting ready in less than half an hour is going to be a challenge, especially with a hangover. But here goes... I run into the bathroom and switch the shower on. I quickly brush my teeth and drink some water, and then stand under the shower. I half return to being human and finally remember what Costas said last night about this trip. We're going to an archaeological site without much shade – he mentioned sun cream, a hat and comfortable shoes.

Okay, shower time's over – too quickly – and I need to put in my contact lenses. After a couple of attempts, everything is blurred and I look like I've been crying, but hopefully that will subside.

Next challenge – sun cream. I reach for the face one first and squeeze it into the palm of my hand. I start smoothing it on my face. The gel glides on nicely at first and then it starts to get sticky. It wasn't like this yesterday. My fingers have got so sticky that I have to rinse them under the tap. Then I realise what I've done. I've just smothered my face in body wash. For goodness sake, this is all I need! I quickly splash water on my face, which works the wash into a nice lather. Oh, what a sight!

Get a grip, Stephanie! I locate the face sun cream, which, in my defence, has a blue top just like the body-wash bottle, and rub it into my extra-clean face. I then quickly rub the body sun cream on to my arms and legs.

I scurry into the bedroom. I feel just about brave enough to open the curtains so I can see what I'm doing. It's another beautiful sunny day, with a clear blue sky. The bright sunshine is actually hurting my eyes. I wonder if it ever gets tedious, opening the curtains to yet another glorious day? Anyway, it makes my decision about what to wear easy – it's got to be cropped jeans and a T-shirt.

My shoulder bag is still unpacked from yesterday, with all my day-out essentials and, most importantly, my camera. I check the time; I've literally got seconds to pop on some mascara, which, amazingly, I manage to do without stabbing the wand into my eye. I race down the stairs and out of the hotel. As I reach the bus stop, my phone pings with a message.

> Just waiting to board.
> Hope you're OK after all those cocktails. I really do think Costas fancies you, and that those cocktails were a message – Island Affair, Amour Smooch, Sex on the Beach... Yes pleeeeaaaassse
> P.S. He is gorgeous ;)
> Enjoy your day. XX

I didn't think it would be long before Helen picked up on things; she should have got a job with CID. I have a flashback to last night and remember her egging Costas on with those cocktails. I bet she was trying to get me drunk on purpose.

Costas appears a couple of minutes later and I hop in the car. '*Kalimera*, Shirley. Did I wake you up before?'

'*Kalimera*, Costas. Whatever gave you that idea?'

'Oh, just the way you could barely speak, and because it was nine thirty and there was still no sign of you in the restaurant.'

'Yes, well, I blame you and Helen and all those cocktails.'

'I think your sister suspects there is something going on between us,' he says, grinning.

'Judging by the text she's just sent me, I think she's definitely on the case. Anyway, she's away for a couple of days so we can please ourselves.'

'I am liking the sound of that. We have two nights to ourselves,' he says. 'Maybe we could start by having a meal in town tonight?'

'It sounds like I'm going on a date,' I reply, feeling quite giddy and excited at the prospect.

'And are you ready for a date?'

'Yes, Costas, I'm definitely ready for a date.'

'Good, then I will reserve a table for later.'

We arrive at the Hotel Niko. Costas makes a beeline for Xena and says something to her. She shakes her head, laughs and taps him lightly on the hand.

Then she shoos him away and approaches me. '*Kalimera*. My son says you might like a coffee – and maybe some croissants or toast?'

'Oh, that would be lovely if there's enough time.'

She glances at her watch. 'There is plenty of time. You relax and I will bring them over.'

She's back in no time with coffee that Stavros has made with his signature heart-shaped chocolate sprinkles. 'I believe you go to Delos for the day? So you enjoy.'

'Oh, thank you. I'm looking forward to it.' She's such a nice woman, and I'm getting good vibes from both his parents.

I pop to the loo while the coffee cools down. A mirror, with lovely bright mosaic glass flowers round it catches my eye. Now, why can't I find anything like that at home? I find my phone, eventually, in my bag and take a photo. Maybe I could recreate something similar. My phone's full of future projects that I'm going to get round to doing one of these days. I've always been quite creative, and this holiday is reigniting my passions in more ways than one.

As I make my way back to the table, Costas is approaching. He's changed his clothes and is carrying a tray loaded with croissants, toast, Greek coffee and water, looking like he's going to a photo shoot. 'This is how to drink coffee,' he declares.

'Really? I'll take your word for it. It doesn't seem worth the bother to me – one gulp and it's gone.'

'I just say, Greek coffee is best.' With that, he gulps it down in one mouthful. He washes it down with water while I have a bite of some toast. 'Okay. You ready?'

'Yes, I'll just finish this toast and coffee, and perhaps we can take the croissants with us.' I wrap a couple in the napkins and put them in the top of my bag.

'If you like, but my grandmama has packed enough food to feed the five thousand. Here she is now. She probably wants to make sure her grandson is in safe hands,' he says, chuckling to himself.

'Grandmama, this is Shirley. Shirley, this is Eliana, my amazing grandmama.'

'I am very pleased to meet you,' she says, offering her hand to shake.

'Likewise, and thank you so much for the picnic yesterday – and today.'

'Oh, it is no problem. I like to spoil my grandson. You know, you look very similar to Helen who came to the hotel yesterday,' she says, scrutinising me.

'Yes, Helen's my sister. She was telling me about...' I stop mid flow, as I realise that her tales from yesterday were about another hotel.

Eliana continues. 'This is strange! She told my daughter that she does not have a sister called Shirley.'

The moment has come when I must come clean and confess to my ridiculous name deception. I clear my throat. Some words tumble out of my mouth. 'Well, that's just typical of Helen, I can't imagine why she said that, maybe she misheard you…' I smile sweetly, let out a little giggle and shrug my shoulders.

Costas fortunately comes to the rescue before Eliana can question me further. 'Anyway, we really need to go and catch the ferry.'

'Oh yes, the reason I came out – please take these. There is two tickets to visit Delos with a guided tour. They were a gift from a guest and they are only valid until the end of the month.'

'Well, if you are sure, that is very kind.' Costas takes the tickets and gives her a hug. 'We will see you later.' He ushers me quickly to the moped. 'I apologise for my grand-mamma. She is so funny and always muddling things up, but she has a heart of gold.'

I feel really guilty now. Eliana certainly hasn't muddled up anything.

'Your bag can go in here.' He points to the moped seat and picks up my shoulder bag, making out that it's really heavy. He lifts up the seat and pushes the bag into the space under it.

'Well, that's my croissants nicely squashed, thank you, Costas,' I retort as I climb on to the moped.

He shrugs his shoulders and passes me the cool box, muttering, 'I do not know why you need croissants. We have sandwiches.'

'I always like to be prepared, Costas, that's all. You never know, we may get stranded over there and need some more food, even if it's just squashed croissants.' We both laugh.

He starts up the moped and we're off. Considering it's still quite early, there seems to be a lot of people mooching about the shops. When we turn on to the harbour front, we see that it's really busy with people crowded around the marble fish market that Costas showed me on our tour of the town. We park up in the harbour. 'It's very busy today,' I comment as I dismount.

'It is busy because cruise ship is here. We have this all summer now, with two or three ships a day. So it is good for business.' As we queue to board our boat, the *Margarita*, we see fish darting about in the clear water below, going about their daily business. Costas points to a couple and tells me their names but I don't really pay much attention. I'm more concerned about getting over to the island with my breakfast still inside me.

My last boat trip of a similar nature, with Richard, ended up with him trying to find a sick bag for me and only just making it back in time. Today, I'm prepared with a very handy brown paper Body Shop carrier that once held my purchases from the airport. I've also taken my seasickness tablet…

'Oh, shit,' I say out loud. 'Sorry, I mean, oh dear. I've forgotten to take my seasickness tablet.'

'You will be fine, Shirley, it is only a short trip,' Costas reassures me.

But I'm taking no chances. I rummage about in my bag to locate the tablets and my water bottle, and quickly take one. Fortunately, they're fast-acting so I should be okay.

The front of the queue begins to move and we start boarding. Costas asks if I want to sit on the deck, where it will feel cool once we get going, or downstairs. I opt for on deck so I can see the horizon, which Costas keeps reminding me helps with motion sickness. Despite this part of the boat being the most popular, we find a couple of seats.

A familiar face heads towards us. I realise it's Martin, the aqua aerobics guy from the hotel, with someone who I assume is his partner. 'Hi guys! Fancy seeing you two here. Are you on a hotel trip or something? I've just seen a couple of others from our hotel. Ooh, what's their names? The women from the North-East. They did aqua aerobics yesterday.'

'Carol and Sandra?' I offer. They're the only two guests whose names I know.

'That's it, Carol and Sandra.'

Costas looks a bit worried. 'We are not on hotel trip, Martin, and please do not say anything at work. You know how strict they are about staff seeing guests, if you know what I mean.'

'Yes, we know better than anyone, don't we, Alexis?'

'We certainly do,' Alexis replies.

'Anyway, Alexis, this is Stephanie. She's the reason you now have a clean car. And Stefanos, who, of course, you know already,' says Martin.

There's a couple of seconds of silence. And then Costas and I speak in unison. 'Stephanie!' 'Stefanos?' We look at each other.

Martin cottons on that he's put his foot in it. 'Oops, sorry, guys. Have I said the wrong thing?'

'Yes. I mean, no, my name *is* Stephanie. But I told Costas – I mean, Stefanos – that it was Shirley because … well, because my surname's Valentine.' I feel quite flustered but I'm also amused that I've been played at my own game. And I'm relieved that the cat's finally out of the bag.

'And I told Stephanie that I was Costas to wind her up, because I know she was not called Shirley,' Stefanos replies, laughing. 'Sorry, Stephanie, I checked your name on the breakfast list.'

'Well, you two jokers certainly know how to cause confusion! And I thought my life was complicated,' says Martin.

'But you were wearing a name badge that said "Costas".' I look at him, puzzled.

'Yes, it belongs to my brother.'

'And he's not wearing it because…?'

'He has left our hotel and when mine broke Elena gave me Costas's spare badge which they still had. Elena did not want to risk anyone seeing me with no badge. We lose marks on our inspections.'

'Oh, right, fair enough.' I pause while I absorb this new information. Then something else occurs to me. 'Hang on a minute, what about your parents? They've heard me call you Costas.'

He starts laughing again. 'I am sorry, they were in on it too. And my grandmama too. And she was trying hard this morning to try and trip you up with your own name.'

'Well, I guess we're even! I'll start again: my name's Stephanie or Steph.'

'Very pleased to meet you. My name is Stefanos.'

'And I'm still Martin and as far as I know this is still Alexis,' Martin adds for good measure. 'And you two are as mad as a box of frogs – so we'll all get on fine!'

There's no arguing with that. We're all soon engrossed in conversation, with me feeling relieved that I'm Stephanie again.

A couple of blokes on the harbour wall undo the ropes and throw them on board. The engines rev up, sending a horrible plume of diesel fumes into the air. The boat starts to edge away from the wall and soon it's moving at speed. I reach into my bag for my camera and take a couple of photos of the fast-disappearing Mykonos town. I start to put the camera away, but Martin insists that he takes some pictures of me and Stefanos. Then I take a couple of Martin and Alexis and then another passenger insists on taking a photo of all four of us. I love that holiday camaraderie, when fellow holidaymakers offer to take a photo of you.

Before I know it, the boat starts to slow down. It chugs towards the harbour wall and the ropes are thrown off to secure the boat to the posts. We all stand, ready to disembark.

We've each got a ticket that includes a guided tour so we make our way to our designated meeting place. There are soon about twenty of us there. I spot Carol and Sandra from our hotel. They see me and make their way over.

'We thought it was you, pet. We were just sayin', there's Stephanie with our gorgeous waiter Costas and the amazing Martin.'

'Er, nooo, Carol, that's what you said. I said it's none of our business.' Sandra doesn't sound amused but Carol carries on.

'Anyway, pet, how are you this morning? You were knockin' them back a bit last night.'

Sandra rolls her eyes in exasperation.

'Yes, I'm feeling better, thanks, after a couple of coffees.' I can feel my cheeks going bright red. I don't know why, as I don't have to answer to anyone. But I carry on with my justification. 'It was Stefanos – he kept sending me cocktails to try. I don't normally drink a lot.'

'Well, you seemed to be managing quite easily last night, pet. Anyway, I thought your name was Costas or have you got a twin?' She turns her attention to Stefanos.

'No, I am Stefanos. I just wear my brother's name badge because mine is broken. It has all got a bit complicated.'

'So, when we're back at the hotel are we to call you Costas or Stefanos?'

I pipe up and instantly regret opening my mouth. 'Well, actually, he's got a couple of days off so he's offered to take me sightseeing.'

'So we see. Is this a service you offer all hotel guests, Costas – I mean, Stefanos?' Carol is obviously keen to milk the situation as much as she can.

Sandra shakes her head. 'She just can't leave it alone. Is your sister not with you, pet?'

'Er, no, she's been called in to work at another hotel on another Greek island for a couple of days. Long story.'

'Oh, right. Well, if you want to join us later for dinner you're more than welcome, isn't she, Carol?'

'Oh yes, the more the merrier, especially if the waiter sends over cocktails for us to try.'

Martin and Alexis find this particularly funny. They're laughing at Stefanos's predicament.

Our tour guide clears her throat in readiness to speak. She doesn't look very impressed by our separate conversation, and our frivolity. 'Good morning, everyone. I'm your guide, Alissa, and I'll be taking you round the site today. Delos is an UNESCO World Heritage Site. Does anyone know which mythological god was born here?'

Stefanos half raises his hand.

'Yes, the gentleman at the back.'

'Apollo.'

'Yes, this is correct. In the ancient times, the myth of god Apollo, god of light, and goddess Artemis having been born here rendered the island sacred. So no mortals would ever be allowed to be born or die on this land. Even during the years of the Delian Alliance, women on the brink of childbirth and people close to dying would be carried to the island of Rineia. Please feel free to ask any questions as we go along. If you'd all like to follow me – and don't forget to drink plenty of water.'

I suddenly start to feel quite sick. It must be a delayed reaction from the boat. I pop my hand up in the air. 'Sorry – where are the toilets?'

'They are behind you. We will start the tour now so you will have to catch us up. We need to get going before the next group starts.' There isn't an ounce of compassion in her tone. I rush to the toilets, with Stefanos in hot pursuit.

'Are you all right, Stephanie?'

'I'm sorry. I feel really sick. It started when we were waiting to get off the boat. I thought it would pass.'

'It is no problem. I wait outside. Shout if you need anything.'

He's so kind, not like our tour guide. I splash some water over my face and that makes me feel a bit better. Whatever it was passes; maybe the seasickness tablet has kicked in. I rejoin Stefanos and we catch up with the group.

'Oh, good, the rest of our party has joined us,' Alissa snipes.

'Stupid cow,' I mutter under my breath.

'So, ladies and gentlemen, here we have the House of Dionysus, with a striking mosaic in the middle of the court that depicts the god Dionysus with open wings, riding a tiger that wears a necklace of vines and grapes. He was the Olympian god of wine, vegetation, pleasure, festivity, madness and wild frenzy. Does anyone have any questions?'

Martin and Alexis snigger and whisper that Dionysus is definitely their god. Alissa strains her neck in their direction; they promptly start snorting and sniggering even more.

Someone at the front asks a question that I can't hear. Alissa answers. 'Dionysus was the son of the god Zeus and Semele of Thebes. There is more information about Dionysus in the guidebook.'

Stefanos whispers, 'In other words, she does not know any more information so please do not ask any more questions.'

We stop at different points of interest and she tells us all about whatever it is that we're observing. It all looks pretty similar to me. Parts of broken walls and pillars, interspersed with sparse vegetation and the odd mosaic here and there. It's baking hot and Stefanos was right about needing a hat.

We've stopped at our next point of interest and Alissa has decided to encourage more audience participation. 'Now, does anyone know what these are?'

I'm about to say 'Seals,' but fortunately Stefanos beats me to it. 'The Terrace of the Lions,' he says.

Of course, it's the correct answer and that ruffles her feathers even more. That's not part of her very wooden script – someone knowing the answer. Her face is an absolute picture, and her praise is equally wooden. 'Yes, well done, that is exactly what they are. These are replicas of the surviving ones, which you can see at the end of the tour in the museum.'

'Um, it will be interesting to see if they look any more like lions than this lot, that's all I can say,' I mutter. 'You seem to know a lot about Delos,' I whisper to Stefanos.

'Yes, we studied it at school. I found the whole thing very boring then. It is funny how you change when you get older.'

Alissa has answered a couple more questions and is now continuing with her spiel. 'The Terrace of the Lions was dedicated to Apollo... Is that someone's phone *ringing*?'

That's a bit of a random thing to say. Then I hear a phone ringing that clearly no one is answering.

'Sounds like it's near us,' Martin says, looking in the direction of my bag.

Oh my God, it's *my* phone. 'Oops, sorry! It's mine. I'll switch it to silent,' I shout to an unimpressed Alissa.

I look at my phone and whisper to Stefanos, 'That's all I damn well need – a call from Richard.'

'Do you need to ring him back?'

'No, he can wait, like I've done for the last few months.' It's bloody typical of Richard. He always seems to ring me at the least convenient moment when my phone should be on silent, like at the dentist's.

As interesting as the tour is, I'm beginning to feel a bit tired. Without realising, I yawn out loud.

Alissa hears me and responds in a nice loud voice. 'That covers almost everything here, so we'll move on to the remains of the amphitheatre and the final points of interest on the tour.' She glares in my direction. If she had the power, I'd be turned into a statue that she could talk about on her next tour: 'And this, ladies and gentlemen, is a rather irritating tourist who annoyed me earlier!'

We trail off behind her and I yawn again. I'm brought out of my yawning spell, however, when Stefanos whispers in my ear, 'I hope you are not tired later.'

I nearly faint on the spot from his lips touching my ear. I take a deep breath in and muster up enough strength to reply. 'I'm sorry, it's just that after a late night and all this sun and walking, I can't help it. What's happening later, anyway?'

'I thought after the meal we could go to a bar, then the night club on Paradise Beach and then who knows?' he whispers in my ear again.

I don't think I can take much more, it's all too—

'Stephanie, Stephanie, can you hear me?'

I can hear a couple of male voices but I'm not quite sure where I am. One of them is saying, 'I know some first aid. Let me have a look at her.'

I slowly open my eyes and see Martin and Stefanos looking down at me. 'Hello, Stephanie, thank goodness you wake up,' says Stefanos.

I notice more concerned faces peering down at me, and an exasperated Alissa, who's clearly not impressed with me stealing the show. 'Oh, good. Dehydration, no doubt. I think your friends will give you some water and stay with you. I'll *try* and finish this tour, so, everyone, if you'd like to follow me, it looks like Stephanie is fine.' Alissa says all the right things, but her tone is questionable.

I smile as humbly as I can and attempt to say sorry, but she's already gone. The others all follow Alissa.

'Stephanie, does this happen a lot to you? It is lucky I catch you,' Stefanos asks.

'No, Stefanos, I've only ever fainted once before in my life, when I was five, at the hairdressers. Thank you for catching me.' I want to answer, 'Only when a gorgeous Greek sex god of a man is nearby,' but I think better of it.

'The pleasure was all mine. I will always catch you.' With that, he kisses me gently on the lips and helps me to my feet.

My heart soars off somewhere, and I need to sit down before I faint again.

'Come on, we will walk to the museum and sit where there is shade.'

We cut across the site and I perch myself on a seat in the shade. 'I'll send Richard a text while we wait for the others.'

Just noticed I've missed a call
from you. I'm in Mykonos
with Helen so if it's nothing
urgent you can ring me when
I'm back in a couple of weeks

'So you not ring him?'

'No, I'm not ringing him. If he desperately needs me, he'll ring back. I've spent the last few months trying to ring him and he's not been in the slightest bit interested. He can stew.'

'Is "stew" not something you eat?' Stefanos asks, looking concerned.

'Don't worry, I'm not going to eat him! It just means he can wait.'

'Do you not think you can make your marriage work again?'

'I don't think so. I want children and he doesn't. Even if he's suddenly changed his mind, I think it's too late as far as I'm concerned. Things have—'

Alissa reappears with the weary-looking group. 'So, ladies and gentlemen, I hope that you enjoy the tour. Now you can look round the museum and, of course, the gift shop, at your leisure.'

There's a quiet round of applause by way of appreciation before the group disperses. Martin and Alexis head in our direction.

'Well, Stephanie Valentine, I don't think you'll be on Alissa's Christmas card list,' Martin laughs.

'No, I think you're right. She took a dislike to me right from the start. I can't think why.'

'Actually, I think I know why,' says Stefanos.

We all turn to him and ask 'Why?' in unison.

'She was at my school. She wanted to go out with me and I refused. It was nearly twenty years ago and I have not seen her since I left school. I assume she move away to work or study.'

'Oh, great. An unbalanced tour guide who thinks I've stolen her childhood sweetheart.'

'I know how you feel, Steph,' Martin pipes up. 'Alexis was engaged to his girlfriend when I turned up in his life. I'm constantly looking over my shoulder.'

An image of a rather angry Greek girl chasing Alexis with a pile of plates to throw at him one by one flashes through my head. But I'm sure they don't all settle a score like Selena does.

We trundle round the museum. I still think the lions look like seals but I keep my thoughts to myself. We've got some time before the boat leaves so everyone disperses to have a drink or snack. Stefanos finds a wall for us to perch on to eat the sandwiches Eliana made for us.

'Did your brother move hotels for a promotion?' I ask as we eat.

'Not exactly. He move for personal reasons. His wife had an affair with another member of staff. Costas filed for divorce and decided he couldn't work with the guy. He just wanted a new start, but it did end up that he got a promotion with his new job. He also started seeing someone else but unfortunately they are not getting on very well.'

'So he's at a crossroads in his life?' Stefanos looks confused, and I realise he's not quite grasped my little metaphor. 'He needs to choose a direction to take,' I add for clarification.

'Yes, I see, crossroads. Well, my advice was to finish his relationship. But will he listen to his younger brother?' Stefanos laughs.

'Probably not! Just like I don't listen to any advice my sister gives me, and vice versa.' We laugh together.

People are starting to walk towards the jetty.

'Come on, we need to catch this boat,' Stefanos says.

We board the boat. Everyone looks weary after traipsing around the island for almost two hours and then visiting the museum. But we were wrong if we thought we'd have a rest. Greek music starts playing, and a guy hands out plastic cups and pours *ouzo* into them, which goes down well.

As we push back from the harbour wall, a few people get up to have a go at Greek dancing – well, their interpretation of it. It's funny watching people dance; even those with a good sense of rhythm need a cup of *ouzo* to loosen up.

Martin decides to get Sandra, Carol and myself up. 'Come on, ladies, you can practice your twerking, Greek-style!'

I'm reluctant but Stefanos is pulling me up. 'Come on, Stephanie, let me see this dance move. It might be useful for the beach club later.'

Alexis joins us. 'I can guarantee that no one can twerk better than Martin. He's a master at it.'

Alexis is right. No one can beat Martin's twerking. He seems to have sabotaged the Greek dancing; everyone is now attempting to twerk to Greek music, which is hilarious.

We're all in high spirits after Martin's antics as we come to dock in Mykonos. We're meeting Martin and Alexis later at a piano bar. Until then, Stefanos and I have opted to chill out for the rest of the afternoon back at his parents' hotel. This time, he'll be able to introduce me to them properly, as Stephanie Valentine.

Chapter 19

Helen

The minibus pulls up outside the hotel and everyone piles out. I recognise the bar manager immediately from his photo on the hotel's website.

He waits until we've all gathered round. 'Good morning and welcome to the Syros Boutique Blue Hotel. My name is Darius. The manager is just finishing a phone call and will join us shortly. Refreshments will be served in the bar before a buffet lunch. Interviews will commence at two o'clock. You are most welcome to relax in your rooms or in the hotel grounds until then. Oh, here is Costas now.'

We all turn round and my mouth drops open in disbelief. No, this isn't happening. It's Mr Serious himself. I quickly sneak behind the others to buy a few seconds in which to compose myself.

Costas welcomes everyone, introduces himself and ticks names off on his sheet while moving around the gathered group. When he reaches Alexandra, there's definitely some tension in the air. I'm wondering what on earth has gone on between them.

Finally, it's my turn. I extend my hand to be shaken.

'Oh, Miss Collins. Nice to meet you again,' he says. But I'm not convinced he means 'nice'. He seems a bit confused. He checks his list, moving up and down it with his pen, and then looks at me with a puzzled expression. 'I do not seem to have your name on the list.'

'Oh, sorry, I should have explained. I'm not here for the job. I'm here to interview the candidates with you,' I reply, smiling.

'Oh, I see,' is all he says. Then he says something in Greek to the group and Darius leads them away. We're now alone and he seems to be awkward. 'So, you are not here for any of the jobs?' he asks again looking a bit disappointed.

'No, I'm just here to do the interviews.'

'Is James following on?'

I bristle at the mention of bloody James yet again. 'No, James is NOT following on and, quite frankly, if I hear his bloody name again I'm going to scream.'

Costas is understandably taken aback by my outburst. He regains his composure. 'Sorry, but when they said someone was coming from Loving Luxury Travel, I just thought it would be, er...' He pauses and thinks how he's going to avoid the taboo name. '...Mr Hobbs. He speaks some Greek, which would help for the interviews.'

'Well, hooray for him, James can speak a bit of Greek.' I'm really mad now and in full strop mode. 'I'm really sorry to disappoint you, Mr Christopoulos, but you've got me instead. I suggest we discuss a few things before the interviews start rather than wasting time talking about my colleague.'

'Please call me Costas. My surname is a bit of a mouthful,' he says, sounding quite amused at my outburst.

I don't even answer him back. He's really annoyed me now, the sarcastic sod. I snatch my case and follow him into the hotel.

He shows me to a table in the bar area. 'If you would like to take a seat here, Miss Collins, Darius will bring a drink over for you.'

I reply with a reluctant 'Thank you,' and sit down.

He says something in Greek to Darius, who's making drinks for the others.

Costas takes the large tray of drinks through to the interviewees while Darius prepares a drink for me. He adds the finishing touches and brings it over. It's green. I take a sip. It's cool and refreshing, which is just what I need.

'This is very nice. What is it?' I enquire.

'Er, Green ... er, sorry, I do not know English word.' He does an impression.

I feel like we've started a game of charades. 'Er, animal, big, fire,' I try to guess. I'm trying hard not to laugh but he looks so funny.

He points to his mouth and says, 'Fire! Here, I show you.' He runs back to the bar and brings a menu over to the table. He points to an item: Green Dragon. 'Costas says, it like you.' He points to my dress and returns to the bar, oblivious to the insult.

Costas appears and sits down opposite me with his own drink. There's an awkward silence.

'Interesting choice of drink. It's nice and refreshing,' I comment, wondering what he'll have to say for himself.

'Yes, it is colour of your dress and fiery like you. Now, maybe we should get on with the job in hand.'

This is a great start to our two days of interviewing together. We flick through the CVs in silence. I notice that he's put on a pair of glasses; he now looks very sexy and serious at the same time.

I have a go at breaking the ice. 'Have any of the CVs stood out to you?' I enquire cautiously.

'Maybe these two,' he replies, giving me eye contact over his glasses as he passes them over. My heart does a somersault.

'Really?' I glower at him for some sort of explanation. They're the two that I immediately dismissed. Neither of these candidates seem to have much experience.

'You don't approve?' He peers at me over the top of his glasses again.

'Well, they do not seem to have as much experience as the others, for a start.'

'This is exactly why, Miss Collins, I would choose one of them. I can train them to my standard and they do not arrive with other ideas that I do not like.'

'Please call me Helen. Surely, if someone who has experience comes here, you can share best practices?'

'Okay, which candidates would you choose?'

'These are the ones that I will be interested in when we interview.' I hand the CVs over.

'No,' he says to the first one. 'Er, no,' to the second. 'Hmm, maybe,' to the third and 'Definitely not,' to the last one. He slaps them all back on the table.

Interestingly, the last one is Alexandra. So she was right to feel she's wasting her time. 'What's with the "Definitely not" candidate?' I ask with trepidation.

'I work with her before. We did not get on and then she left.'

'Oh, well, that will make for an interesting interview then,' I reply sarcastically.

'I think, Helen, I will ask Darius to show you to your room. I need to organise a few things and we are not achieving anything here. A buffet lunch will be served at twelve thirty. The interviews start at two o'clock in the room over there,' he points. 'Maybe we can meet up about fifteen minutes earlier. I will see you later.'

With that, he stands up and disappears to find Darius, who appears seconds later like a genie from a lamp. 'Okay, Miss Collins, follow me. I show you to your room.'

Darius leads the way with my suitcase. My shoes echo on the marble floor of the reception area. We arrive at the lift, he selects my floor number, which is the top one, and we step inside.

I seize the opportunity to get some feedback from Darius, who seems more than happy to be here. 'It's a lovely hotel,' I say.

'Oh, yes, it is most beautiful hotel, with pretty gardens and beach. I love it here,' he replies enthusiastically.

'And Costas, what sort of boss is he?'

The lift arrives and Darius leads the way with my case. 'Costas is a very caring boss. He take care of everyone. He always ask how we are, and everyone like and respect him. I came from last hotel with him. The staff cry when he left. Here is your room. Allow me.'

He opens the door and I step inside a room that is – how can I put it? – not quite finished. There are no curtains, the bed isn't made and pictures are leaning against the walls.

I turn to Darius for an explanation. 'What on earth is going on here?'

'The workmen are a bit behind. Costas wants to keep finished rooms clean, as housekeeping is busy, so you and interviewees are in the partly finished rooms,' he explains, smiling and obviously not seeing any issue.

'I see.' I survey the scene while Darius lifts my case on to one of the rather bare-looking beds.

'Okay, see you for lunch, Miss Collins. Someone will make up your bed later, and hopefully put up the curtains,' he says, before scarpering away.

I dread to think how many rooms are like this. I'm sure they're going to be almost full, with bookings from the week they open. At least it all seems finished downstairs.

Apart from the fact that the room is unfinished, the view from the balcony is incredible. The room overlooks the gardens and the pool, and then, beyond that, the beautiful blue sea and a little island.

I decide to unpack a couple of things that will crease and hang them up... Or I would hang them if there were any hangers. But why would there be any hangers in an unfinished room? Let's face it, you're lucky to get more than a handful in any hotel wardrobe.

I place the clothes flat on top of my suitcase, quickly freshen up and head back downstairs to grab some lunch.

I help myself to some rocket, tomatoes, cucumber and *feta* to make up a salad, and some olives, which I've now got a taste for. There are some glasses of fruit punch on the side so I pick up one of them and make my way to a table away from the others. It's a beautiful open-plan restaurant that overlooks the pool and the sea. I'd normally have my phone out but I can't be bothered checking messages today. Instead, I gaze at the sea sparkling under the clear blue skies.

'May I?' A voice interrupts my daydreaming. It's Costas. He's holding a plate of food and indicating that he'd like to sit down.

'Of course, be my guest,' I reply.

'So, what are your first impressions of the hotel?' he asks, sounding a bit happier than before.

'It's lovely. But I do have concerns about some of the rooms not being finished. I thought the hotel was fully booked for its opening week.'

Costas puts his knife and fork down on to his plate. He seems to be contemplating what to say next. I brace myself. 'Helen, you do not need to concern yourself over whether the hotel will be finished. Everything is on track. The workmen will be back the day after tomorrow to finish all the work, which will take only a few days. You have my word. I can do it myself if I need to.'

I suppose he has a point, as I saw at the Hotel Niko. 'Well, if you say so, Costas. Daniel won't be happy if guests arrive to rooms with no curtains on the windows. Now, if you'll excuse me, I'll have a little wander around the gardens before our meeting.'

'Indeed. Hopefully, you will find the gardens are to your satisfaction.'

'Yes, I'm sure they'll be fine.' You sarcastic sod!

This site has some beautiful established gardens. Our company bought the hotel and invested in its refurbishment and modernisation. We've added the pool, which has a little wooden bridge going over it, and the restaurant where I've been having lunch is an extension on to the existing indoor restaurant; it has the best of both worlds. I wander over to a seat in the garden and sit down to listen to the waves gently hitting the beach and the birds singing in the garden. There are some goats bleating to each other in the scrubland next to the garden. The air here is clean. I feel like I'm a million miles away from the seats I seek out in my lunch break in Manchester. There, I have to walk along a busy road with noisy traffic. There are horns beeping because someone has dared to get in someone's way and sirens blaring as emergency services dash from one incident to another. I haven't heard a single siren in either Mykonos or Syros. Just peace and quiet, which is music to my ears.

I glance at my watch and decide that I'd better make my way to my rendezvous point with Costas. He doesn't strike me as the kind of person who'd be impressed with poor timekeeping.

We arrive at the door together and he politely lets me go into the room first. There's a table set up with a jug of water and glasses and a chair for the interviewee. We take our respective seats next to each other and study the interview question sheets.

'I like this one as a starting question: "Tell me about yourself." It's a good one to put the candidate at ease,' I say.

'Yes, well I prefer "How do you handle stress and pressure?"'

'What? On a laid-back Greek island?'

'Yes, Helen, even on a laid-back Greek island there is stress and pressure,' comes the serious reply.

'Okay, I'll take your word for it. I think we'd better get on with interviewing the candidates or else we'll be arguing all afternoon.' I must admit, he does amuse me when he peers over those glasses or perches them on his head.

I go to the door to invite in the first candidate. Of course, it has to be Alexandra. This is going to be fun, not. Understandably, she's looking uneasy so I get in with my question first before Costas draws breath. 'Good afternoon, Alexandra. Tell us a bit about yourself.'

After a shaky start, she composes herself and tells us about her background, the different roles she's performed and why she likes the hotel industry.

Then it's Costas's turn to hit her with his question. 'Okay, Alexandra, that is good, all very positive. But now, can you describe a difficult work situation and how you overcame it?'

Well, talk about being able to cut the atmosphere with a knife. I think he's just sliced cleanly through this interview.

Alexandra blushes and stumbles through her answer. I don't even pay attention to it because I feel so sorry for her. I met Costas only yesterday, but one thing's for sure, you certainly wouldn't cross him. Unfortunately, poor Alexandra has apparently done just that and is now paying for it big time.

I try and rescue her with my next question, which takes us back to neutral ground. 'Tell us about your goals for the future.'

Unsurprisingly, she wants to be a manager of her own hotel. I already know she isn't going to be climbing her career ladder with any help from Costas.

His next question finishes her off. 'Why do you want this job?' he asks, peering over his glasses.

By the time she's finished, she's effectively talked herself out of it. She leaves the room, looking decidedly shaky.

'Well, Costas, I think we can safely say that even if we offered Alexandra the job she'd turn it down.'

'Good, I could not work with her again,' comes the calm answer.

'Yes, I think I got the gist. You take no prisoners.'

'Exactly. Now we have established that, I'll call in the next candidate.' With that, he pushes his chair back and goes over to the door to greet the next candidate, who just happens to be one of his favourites. Immediately, the mood lifts as he welcomes Markos into the room.

Costas starts with his favourite question: 'How do you handle stress and pressure?' I think this is a really difficult one but Markos demonstrates that he handles stress and pressure well by keeping calm and answering the question particularly well.

I feel that Markos is more than capable of answering one of the more complex questions so I hit him with 'Tell us about a time you felt a conventional approach would not be suitable. How did you adopt and manage a new approach? Which challenges did you face and how did you address them?'

I can hear Markos give what I'm sure is an excellent answer, but for some reason I'm daydreaming and answering my question in my own head.

My example is from when a new person started at our office; let's, for argument's sake, call him James. He was clearly not going to take seriously any instructions from me – what with me being a woman – although I was in a senior position. The new approach I adopted was to flirt with him. The new approach was managed outside office hours within a personal relationship. The challenge that I faced was the grief caused by my getting involved with such an idiot in the first place. I am going to address this situation with a text to say the whole thing was a huge mistake and we're finished. Not very creative or innovative but I'm past caring.

Costas fires off his next question: 'Describe a time you had to win over someone who was reluctant or unresponsive.'

Markos sets off with his reply. I've got the perfect answer to this one too. Well, there was this guy, let's call him James again. He was charming at first, spent time with me, took me out, seemed interested and then, all of a sudden … nothing. I sent texts that were unanswered, I rang him and the phone went to voicemail, I messaged him on social media, I even sent him a letter. What the hell was I thinking? I mean, who sends bloody letters in this day and age? Anyway, I clearly failed to win him over as he's now in Florida and didn't even bother to tell me he was going there. Oh and did I mention, he's probably had an affair. In fact, he's probably had affairs, plural, left, right and centre.

Markos answers the question calmly while Costas makes notes. I, on the other hand, can't make any notes because I haven't been listening. But I get the impression that Markos will be a favourite of Costas's; he seems to tick all the boxes. The interview concludes well and Markos leaves the room in better shape than Alexandra. So I'm a little surprised by Costas's less than enthusiastic feedback.

'He is definitely an improvement on Alexandra, but he is…' Costas stops in mid flow.

'He's what, Costas?' I ask, tapping my fingers on the table. I can't wait to hear this.

'He is … well, we'll just see the other candidates first, shall we?'

I scrape my chair back loudly and march over to the door for candidate number three: Stefani.

We have a little chat about my sister's name being Stephanie, which I can see is irritating Costas. I eke it out as long as I can to wind him up even further. He's now rapping his fingers on the desk and clearing his throat.

'If we could start, ladies,' he finally interjects.

I feel like we're on a panel of judges and Costas is our Simon Cowell: he says it like it is. He even has that Cowell look of 'I'm not amused and I'm going to press my buzzer any second now.'

I start with my good cop's question: 'Tell us about yourself.'

Costas leans back in his chair and shakes his head, immediately putting Stefani off. She's barely finished her sentence when he launches in with: 'What is your greatest strength?'

She responds well and tells us about her organisational skills, how she organises weddings at the hotel where she works now. She sounds perfect to me, but I suspect our in-house Simon Cowell doesn't approve of her.

Sure enough, when she leaves the room, he mutters, 'I am not looking for a bloody wedding planner.'

By the time we've interviewed the last candidate of the day, I'm exasperated with Costas. He's hard work, to say the least. So I'm completely thrown by his next comment.

'I have organised a barbecue for everyone this evening and you are welcome to come along if you would like.'

'Well, I suppose it saves me going into town on my own,' I reply, sounding like a stroppy teenager.

'Yes, well, I thought it would be the same for everyone. All today's interviewees will be there, and three of tomorrow's have arrived as well. I will leave it with you. The barbecue will be at seven thirty.' He excuses himself and leaves.

I'm now annoyed with myself for not sounding more appreciative. To improve my mood, I decide to relax on a sunbed and check my emails, texts and Facebook messages. I stop at the bar, where Darius is busy making a fruit punch for the barbecue later.

'Afternoon, Miss Collins. Would you like to try my fruit punch? Or you prefer something else?'

'Ooh, something refreshing would be nice. It's thirsty work doing interviews.'

'Okay, you go and relax and I bring you my thirst-quencher speciality.'

I find a sunbed under the shade of a tree. Darius comes over with my drink, which is adorned with fruit. He hovers in anticipation, to see if I like it.

'Yum, this is delicious! Dare I ask what this one's called?'

'Yes, it is Frosty Amour.'

'Oh, how apt,' I say, sarcastically.

'Sorry, I not understand. What is "apt"?'

'Oh, nothing, ignore me. It's lovely, very refreshing.'

'Yes, that is why I chose it for you,' he replies and disappears back to the bar.

Well, that'll teach me for assuming Costas was behind the drink choice. My goodness, am I thinking – or hoping – that he secretly likes me?

All this sun and fresh air has obviously got to me. I check through my messages and, as always, there's an email from Daniel. He wants an update on the day's events. I flick a quick reply back.

Afternoon Daniel,
Lovely hotel, all going to plan. Four candidates interviewed so far, the rest are tomorrow.
Regards,
Helen
Loving Luxury Travel

I can't be bothered going into the fiasco of the unfinished rooms. If Costas says they'll be done, I'll have to take him at his word. If I mention anything to Daniel, he'll probably suggest I stay and finish them myself. I check my texts next. I've got one from Mum and Dad.

WE ARE

That's it. WE ARE – what? Sinking? Is it an SOS? Or what about WE ARE sailing? They've had a bit to drink, they've burst into song and dropped the phone in the sea. The options are endless. Ah, here's the rest on the next text.

VISITING SYRIA DAY
AFTER NEXT COULD
MEET UP WITH U. WE
ARRIVE 8 A.M.

Now, I know the schedule has been altered slightly because of bad weather earlier in the week, but surely not by way of Syria. I assume predictive text has played a part in this latest techno blip, and they actually mean 'Syros'. In theory, I can meet them for lunch before I leave; my flight back isn't until the late afternoon, and they could enjoy some time sitting round the pool if they want. There are no guests at the Syros Boutique Blue yet, so I'm sure this will be okay.

Yes this could work, assume
you mean Syros not Syria - lol.
Could come to hotel and
relax by the pool, then we
could head into town for
lunch before I leave. xx

Finally, I have a look on Facebook as a last resort to see if James has sent me a message. All the usual suspects have been on, making comments about posts and sharing this and that. Florida is seven hours behind Greece so it's ten thirty in the morning there. He's had enough time to have seen my last message and responded either last night or this morning. I can see immediately that he hasn't; the little box is empty.

I then check my notifications. There's nothing on there, so he hasn't commented on any of my posts or the photos with Steph from last night. I click on his profile; I just can't resist it. Steph's already threatened to unfriend him on my Facebook to stop me 'stalking' him, as she calls it.

Any doubts as to whether he's been eaten by a shark or swept away by a hurricane or twister are dispelled immediately. The recent activity button says he's now friends with Tracey. My finger hovers over her name, ready to press and have a nosey at her profile. But I stop myself. What's the point? What's the bloody point?

I feel gutted and my stomach is churning again. He's managed to ignore at least five comments and attempts at communication from me, but he *has* been in touch with this new person, who looks stunning in her thumbnail photo.

I close my laptop and stare at the pool. The realisation has finally dawned. A movie that I saw a few months ago suddenly comes to mind: *He's Just Not That into You*. So, Helen, get a bloody grip and move on. On that positive note, I finish my aptly named Frosty Amour and head to my room to get changed.

Chapter 20

Stephanie

At long last, I'm ready. I've tried numerous outfits on, taken them off and then put them back on. I've finally decided to wear a knee-length flowery dress, and flat sandals so that I don't sink into the sand. I cram what I think I'll need into my little bag and do one final check of my make-up.

I'm meeting Stefanos at the end of the road. Even though he's officially on holiday, he's adamant that he won't come on to the hotel premises and risk being seen with me. He's offered to pick me up, promising that he'll be in the car. I send Helen a quick text while I'm waiting.

Visited Delos, archaeological
site today. It was tiring but
quite interesting
Met Sandra & Carol who
we were talking to last
night, oh and Costas aka
Stefanos...
Hope your getting on
OK with interviews. XX

Bang on cue, Sandra and Carol appear at the bus stop just as Stefanos pulls up in the car. We establish that we're all going into town so he offers them a lift.

I squeeze into the back of the tiny car with Sandra, while Stefanos has the pleasure of Carol chatting to him in the front. I can hear only snippets of the conversation because the windows are down, but she'll know his life story by the time we reach town. Sandra's shaking her head and muttering, 'She's unbelievable. Totally wasted in the NHS. She should work for MI5.'

We soon arrive at Stefanos's parents' hotel. That leads to another twenty questions from Carol, but Stefanos is totally unfazed.

'You join us at piano bar, ladies? It is a very popular bar in town,' he says.

'Thank you, pet, we'll see how we feel after our meal. But if we don't see you, you two enjoy yourselves,' says Sandra.

'Aye, and don't do anything I wouldn't do, pet,' Carol adds for good measure.

'Come on, woman, will you never learn?' Sandra ushers Carol away, leaving us giggling.

'Do you think they are a couple?' Stefanos asks me when they're out of earshot.

'No, they're both married. Helen and I talked to them last night. I can't remember that much, though, because someone sent over lots of suggestive cocktails and got me tipsy.'

'How terrible. You need to report them,' he replies, smirking.

'Yes, you're right, I'll do it first thing in the morning. Now, what was his name?'

'I think it was "Costas",' says Stefanos, laughing.

'Oh, yes, I remember now. Bloody Costas indeed.'

We stroll into town holding hands and chatting about our day. I can't believe how at ease Stefanos makes me feel. It's like I've known him forever. We weave in and out of the crowds of people and pushchairs, through the narrow streets, past all the colourful little boutique shops and eventually arrive at the harbour front and at the restaurant he's booked us into.

We're shown to our table outside, just in time to see the sun setting. The waiter brings the menu and we order some drinks. Stefanos explains what the different things are, and I decide on *kleftiko* – 'a typical Greek dish' – and he's trying the *moussaka* to see how it compares to his mum's.

My phone bleeps with a text.

> What school did you go to?
> Your previous text should be
> hope YOU'RE getting on OK
> with interviews!!!
> What do you mean – Costas
> aka Stefanos? Anyway
> glad you've done some
> sightseeing. Done 4
> interviews with Costas the
> manager here.He's hard work
> – makes Simon Cowell
> look like a pussycat lol. xx

'All okay with your sister?' Stefanos asks. 'I hope you tell her that I take care of you.'

'Well, not exactly. I just mentioned the sightseeing in Delos and about bumping into Carol and Sandra, but I didn't quite get round to explaining that I was actually with you, more that you just happened to be on the trip.'

'Okay, so you not mention the fainting?' He looks at me in an I-know-you-didn't way.

'Er, no, I forgot to mention that bit. I don't want her worrying about me. She's got enough on her plate by the sounds of it. I hope her boss realises how dedicated she is – changing all her plans at the last minute to come here and then to go to another island. Then there's her so-called boyfriend, who, in my opinion, is a complete waste of time. He doesn't even return her messages. All in all, she's having a shit time. Do you mind if I text her back? She must be really fed up.'

'Of course you text her. I too will send a message to my brother who is in a quandary.'

I quickly type my reply.

> Ha ha same school as you but I wasn't any good at English, didn't like the teacher, good at maths though. Teacher was dead fit always had my full attention. Got your work cut out there – maybe Mr Pussycat will be better after a couple of drinks. Good luck with that one ;) Costas the waiter is actually Stefanos And he's looking after me ;) xx

I pop my phone on the table as our drinks are delivered. I just about manage my first sip when the phone bleeps with a reply.

> Aren't you the funny one. I remember that maths teacher and your school report – Stephanie is a joy to teach. It was sooo funny, it had Mum and Dad scratching their heads for days. They thought

217

he'd mixed you up with the
other Stephanie. lol. Glad Costas
aka Stefanos is looking after you
I knew he liked you – my
suspicions were right –
enjoy & keep me updated
;) XX

'Cheeky mare.' I slip my phone back into my bag out of earshot. I don't want to spend the whole night texting Helen.

'Everything okay?'

'Yes, thanks. I've just mentioned that you're looking after me so she's not worrying about me but now she'll be wanting updates all night. So, what's happening with your brother?'

'Well, as I said earlier, he's divorced and not getting on very well with his latest girlfriend. My advice was to finish with her and just have some time on his own.'

'Sounds good to me. Is he going to do that?'

'Well, it looks like he's on his way now to finish with this girlfriend, which is good. Also, he mentioned earlier that he has met someone else but "It is complicated". I have no idea what he meant by that.'

'Nothing is ever easy, especially where love is concerned,' I reply with a sigh, thinking about our own predicament. Why couldn't Stefanos just work in a Greek restaurant in town?

'No, life is not easy.' Stefanos replies, looking deep in thought.

The waiter arrives and places our food down in front of us.

'Wow, this looks interesting.'

'Yes, it is all wrapped in parchment paper to keep the flavours and juices inside. It will be very tender.'

I unwrap the paper and steam wafts out. I slice into the very tender lamb. 'Mmm, it's delicious! I'll definitely have to try making this back at home.'

'Yes, we know how to cook lamb.'

'And is your *moussaka* up to your mum's standard?'

'Yes, but do not tell her,' he replies, laughing. 'She is very competitive and always likes to be the best.'

We chat and people-watch as dusk turns into a cooler night.

We could talk all night long but Stefanos has arranged to meet Martin and Alexis later. I attempt to ask for the bill in Greek after a brief refresher from Stefanos. The waiter must understand me because he arrives back with the bill and a rose for me.

'Oh, how romantic! And pink is my favourite colour.'

'I take it you like receiving a bunch of flowers, then?'

'Yes, definitely, which was something Richard just didn't understand. Anyway, don't let me start on a rant about Richard! Now, hand that bill over. I said I'd get the next meal after you paid for lunch yesterday.'

'Oh yes, did you manage to sort out your card?'

I roll my eyes. 'Eventually. It took me ten minutes to convince the fraud department that I'd had a last-minute change of plans from the Caribbean to Mykonos. I saw the funny side in the end.'

'Well, I hope you see the funny side of this bill – they have charged for that rose!'

'No way! They've never added it to the bill?'

Stefanos is laughing. 'I am afraid they have, but I am paying for the rose and the drinks at the piano bar.'

'Okay, sounds like a deal. Let's party, the drinks are on Stefanos!'

We meander over to the bar, which is tucked away in the narrow streets. It doesn't appear very big from the outside but, once we're inside, it stretches on from one room to another. It's busy, noisy and dark, but there are some colourful lights on the tables to brighten things up a bit. We make our way past the bar, the pianist and the singer, who's belting out 'American Pie'. We finally locate Martin and Alexis, who wave us over.

'You found us, then?' Martin shouts. 'There's a couple of seats here.'

'Oh, thanks,' I shout back. 'Flipping heck, it's a bit lively.'

A waiter brings Alexis and Martin's drinks and passes us a menu each to study.

'We've ordered a Slow Comfortable Screw,' Martin shouts.

'Really? Well, I'll try one too. If you can't beat them, join them – that's my motto!'

'And I will have This is the Night,' Stefanos whispers in my ear.

I feel like I'm about to pass out again as his lips touch my ear and my heart flutters. I can't say I've ever heard of this particular cocktail so I have a sneaky peep at the menu. Sure enough, it's there.

'You already decide what you order next?' Stefanos asks.

'I was thinking about a Screaming Orgasm – I've not had one of those for years,' I reply, trying to keep a straight face.

'I sure you will have one later. And remember, you need to pace yourself or I end up carrying you.'

'Okay, I'll pace myself. I'll just enjoy my Slow Comfortable Screw for now.'

Stefanos whispers, 'Maybe we try both later.'

'Um, definitely,' I reply as my heartbeat goes off the scale. Before I can say anything else the singer stops.

'So, ladies and gentlemen, that was my little reminder of home. We're just off for a quick break but any requests when we return will be gladly received.' There's a round of appreciative applause.

Our drinks arrive and we clash our glasses together with a loud, united '*Yamas!*'

I excuse myself to 'powder my nose'. Only Martin understands what I'm talking about, so I leave him to explain it to Stefanos and Alexis.

I quickly check my phone while I'm 'powdering my nose'. There's another message off Helen. I don't want to jump to conclusions but I think she's had a bit to drink. I'm not overly worried so I send a quick reply and rejoin the busy bar area.

I push my way through the crowd to get back to our table just as the American singer returns. She reminds me of Elizabeth, a work colleague of mine. Elizabeth is a lovely lady, with gorgeous long auburn hair, who also likes to sing. Maybe she's doing a spot of moonlighting; come to think of it, she does have rather a lot of time off work. Maybe her Manchester accent is a cover.

She announces the next song. 'Welcome back, ladies and gentlemen, we're going to kick off with Kylie Minogue's 'Can't Get You Out of my Head'. This song dedicated to Shirley Valentine. Come on, Shirley, it's time we had a sequel!'

Martin, Alexis, and Stefanos all gawp at me. I'm just about to say 'What?' when I realise that it's me the American woman is talking about.

'A huge round of applause for Shirley! Keep your requests coming in – we're here until it gets light.' The music starts and the audience join in with 'La-la-la, la-la-la-la-la'. Everyone claps and a couple of wolf whistles are audible.

I can feel my cheeks burning. Now look what's happened – a whole bar of people applauding Shirley Valentine. I'll be changing my name at this rate. At least Stefanos knows now. He obviously loves to join in with this in-joke, which I really appreciate.

The atmosphere in the bar is lively and we're all quite happy to stay there for another drink before we leave for the beach club. We order our next round of drinks. Stefanos has chosen the Trouser Rouser, which gives him another opportunity to whisper in my ear. I've never even heard of half these cocktails, but he reels off all the ingredients.

'You try.' He passes the glass to me and I take a sip.

'Mmm, very tasty. Maybe I'll try one at the Paradise Club.'

'Yes, we go after this drink. The taxi is booked for midnight and we have to walk back to the square.'

The piano bar is heaving; the singer is keeping everyone entertained. She's got us clapping and singing along to choruses of well-known songs. I can't believe that it's already nearly midnight. Stefanos soon taps his watch and points to the door, which means we need to leave for our taxi. We all finish our drinks and push our way through the very crowded bar.

I feel okay until we get outside and then the fresh air hits me. I'm a bit hazy. I can just about walk by clinging on to Stefanos, which he doesn't seem to mind. We make our way up to the square for the taxi, all singing and laughing along with loads of other revellers. The place has come alive.

The taxi ride to the beach goes by in a blur. Stefanos pays the driver. We all stumble out of the taxi and follow him to the club. The queue to get in seems to go on forever, but we're soon making our way inside and I can hear the thud, thud, thud of the music.

I'm unprepared for the scene that greets us when we finally get in and can see beyond the person in front. There are thousands of people dancing – well, when I say dancing, I mean gyrating – to music that's so loud I feel it vibrating through my chest.

I can't hear a word that Stefanos says so he catches my hand and leads me over to a bar. I feel like I'm the oldest person in this club and very overdressed. Most of the girls are dancing about in bikinis and the blokes are in shorts. Stefanos finally manages to order a drink. I assume when he shouts 'Sex on the Beach' down my ear that he's suggesting a drink rather than actually having sex on the beach, but, the way it looks in this club, nothing would surprise me.

We've lost Martin and Alexis. We push our way through to the dancing area. I can see the DJ in the distance, up on the podium, and there's a palm tree behind him lit up in bright pink. There are guys and girls up on the podium, spraying champagne on everyone below. The whole place is crazy. I watch it all in amazement.

Stefanos asks if I want to dance. I've given up trying to talk over the noise so I nod to agree and follow him. Martin and Alexis appear. They seem to be quite at ease with it all, and so does Stefanos. I follow their lead and do my own version of what everyone else is doing, something between dancing and gyrating. Nobody stares at me so it must be okay. Of course, it's an ideal opportunity for Martin to show off his twerking abilities and attempt to fine-tune ours, but we're nowhere near his standard. He's soon drawn a large crowd of onlookers and people eager to show off their booty.

The DJ gets everyone jumping up and down, singing, clapping, waving their arms in the air, screaming and having a great time. After my initial trepidation, the night is flying by and I can't believe it when I eventually see daylight breaking.

Stefanos suggests that we leave before the mass exodus for the taxis. We say our goodbyes to Martin and Alexis and some others whom we were dancing with, and make our way to the taxi rank. I struggle to walk in a straight line and talk any sense, but I've been worse and Stefanos isn't much better. I sober up slightly at the sight of the long queue for the taxi, but Stefanos reassures me that it will soon shorten.

'Are you coming back to the Boutique Blue with me, Stefanos? I've got a room to myself.' I ask in my slurred speech.

'I am not allowed, Stephanie,' he reminds me. 'But you can come back to my parents' hotel, if you like.'

'Um, I might take you up on that offer.'

Our taxi is next. We've got an English guy called Al. He asks where we're going and we both get in the back. Our attempts at kissing are thwarted by Al's erratic driving. I don't want to put my emergency dentist cover to the test. We arrive at the hotel at record speed after what feels like some sort of rally experience. He screeches to a halt, with clouds of dust billowing up into the cold morning air. Stefanos pays him but he's clearly not amused with Al's driving. I go into giggle mode – he looks so funny waving his arms and presumably swearing in Greek.

Al screeches off and kicks up more dust. Stefanos shouts, 'You crazy English driver!'

Stefanos tries to stop me from laughing so that we don't wake up anyone, but it's too late. His father appears at his bedroom window and has a loud whispering altercation with Stefanos, who I assume is apologising profusely. I'm now laughing uncontrollably while Stefanos keeps putting his finger to his lips and saying, 'Shush, shush.'

His father disappears from view and then returns with some bedding. He throws it out to us, points towards the cabanas and mutters something in Greek before shutting the window.

Stefanos turns to me very sheepishly. 'I am very sorry, my father is cross. He say we are not allowed in hotel to disturb the guests, so we go to sleep in the cabanas. I call taxi if you like, maybe the wonderful Al, to take you back to your hotel.'

'Stefanos, the cabana will be fine,' I reply, still slurring my words.

He leads me down the path, across the garden where the birds are now chirping merrily away, and over to a cabana on the beach. The sea is calmly lapping on to the shoreline. I feel the cold sand slipping unpleasantly through my sandals. Stefanos peels back the curtains of the cabana. I can hardly believe my eyes – it's the most luxurious cabana that I've ever seen. There's some matting on the ground so I can uncurl my sand-fearing toes for a start. There's an informal seating area and a double sleeping area, which is where I flop down. There are some pretty lights draped down from the ceiling, which Stefanos turns on, and a large candle in a storm lamp on the table.

'You like?' Stefanos asks.

'Very much. I never expected anything this posh behind the curtains.'

'It was my idea. I like the cabanas at the Boutique Blue, so I persuade my father to buy a couple. But these are much better, as you see. Now, you make yourself at home and I bring some coffee – or would you like a Screaming Orgasm?'

'No, I'll stick with the coffee, thanks. I've had enough to drink for one night. I'll have a Screaming Orgasm for breakfast,' I answer, smiling mischievously at Stefanos.

'Yes, me too,' he replies as he exits the cabana.

I decide to go and freshen up in the loo while Stefanos is making the coffee. I'm so nervous. I've suddenly got a load of what ifs going round my head. Oh my God, condoms... I used to have a couple of emergency ones in my little make-up bag. I empty the contents on to the side by the washbasin and spread them out – oh, thank goodness for that, they're still here. I shove everything back in and pop the condoms on the top just in case. I notice there's an expiry date on the edge of the packet, which is ... unreadable. Oops, they've been in here that long the expiry date has worn of. Never mind, I'm sure Stefanos will have the situation under control. Right, take a deep breath, Stephanie Valentine, you can do this.

I stagger back to the cabana and nervously open the curtain. Stefanos is back with the coffees. After all that build up – I can't help but giggle – he's fast asleep on the bed. I put a blanket over him and crawl under it. Oh well, tonight wasn't the night after all...

Chapter 21

Helen

My bed seems to be made, which is good news, and the window has been left open to air the room out. I need to get a move on, so I quickly strip off and step into the large glass shower. I immerse myself under the wonderful hot jets of water and reach for the shower gel – oh, for the love of God, there isn't any.

I open the shower door and step out on to the mat. I do a shower-mat-shuffle over the floor towards my wash bag to retrieve my own travel-sized shower gel and then shuffle back over and into the shower.

I don't suppose I can expect five-star treatment when they're not even open for business. I love showers that do what they're meant to do. A simple request in life, surely – hot and powerful and none of those clogged-up heads that end up spraying you in the eye.

I reluctantly turn off the shower and step on to the mat to grab a... Where are the towels? I can't believe I've stepped in the shower and not noticed there are no towels apart from the one I'm standing on. Un-bloody-believable. There's only one thing for it: I'll have to ring for some.

I do another shower-mat-shuffle into the bedroom and over to the phone. I've not quite pushed in the fourth digit to ring downstairs when the door to my room opens.

A male voice is speaking. 'Sorry, but I'm going to have to share with you tonight. I am just checking that housekeeping have—'

I turn round and grab the duvet to cover myself up, but it's too late. My bare bottom has already been on show.

'For crying out loud, Costas, are you trying to give me a heart attack? And what do you mean you'll have to share with me?'

'Er, sorry, I am not meaning sharing with you, I am meaning... Oh, it is not important.' He returns briefly to his phone call. 'I have got to go, I will see you later.' He suddenly realises that I'm on the phone too. 'Sorry, I interrupt. Are you speaking to someone?'

'No, I was actually ringing for a towel because there are none in the bathroom, which is the reason I'm naked.'

'Sorry! I will fetch a towel. I think I know where they are. I will be back in a minute.' He's tongue-tied and embarrassed, to say the least, and he's back very quickly with a whole stack of towels. 'I found the towels. Please use as many as you like. I will leave them here. I apologise again. I am sure Darius said this room.'

'Okay, thank you. I'm sure Darius didn't mean any harm. Mistakes happen.'

'You know, there is phone in the bathroom,' is his parting shot.

I can't resist shouting back, 'I'll remember that for next time!'

I retrieve a gorgeous new towel from the stack that he's thrown on to the bed and laugh to myself. Oh, what a sight for him – me bending over the telephone. Poor Costas! The look on his face! Talk about a rabbit in headlights. I've just got to text

Steph. She'll find it hilarious. Actually, I'd better text her later. I'm running out of time now.

I lightly touch up my make-up, which seems to have lasted quite well even in the steamy hot shower, fix my hair and look at the clothes I draped over my suitcase earlier. It's a lovely warm evening so I've chosen a flowery orange Monsoon dress to wear, which is summery and isn't too crumpled, and some low-heeled slingbacks. It makes a nice change to wear these things and actually have the weather to match. I arm myself with a little clutch bag that has just enough room for the essentials, and a pashmina just in case it cools off like it does on Mykonos.

By the time I get downstairs, the group is milling round the bar, enjoying the fruit punch that Darius was making earlier.

'Evening, Miss Collins. Please help yourself to a fruit punch. I believe you had a surprise visit from Costas? I think he mishear my numbers, or maybe I get them wrong. Either way, no harm done.' Darius gives me a cheeky wink.

'No harm done?' I retort. 'He's scarred for life! The look on his face was priceless. I just wish I could have taken a picture of him.'

'I think he just embarrassed. It is not every day you walk in a room and find a naked woman on phone.' Darius laughs, shaking his head, and goes down the bar to serve the others.

I get out my phone and see that I've had a text from Steph. Oh well, at least it looks like she's keeping busy. I wouldn't have put her down for going on a trip to an archaeological site, though – just when you think you know someone. She's seemed pretty glued to her sunbed to me, but at least she's taking an interest in the island and its culture. I can't imagine what possessed her to visit Delos, which entails a boat-crossing… Oh, hang on a minute, this is interesting… That's more like it. Sounds like I was right. But why 'Costas aka Stefanos'? And she's done that you're/

your thing that drives me mad. I send her a text back. I want to know more about the Costas/Stefanos comment.

Darius reappears at my end of the bar. 'Miss Collins, Costas send his apology. He has to go to town, I think to see his girlfriend. He ask if you supervise the interviewees until he get back.'

'Right. I see,' I reply, feeling deflated.

I'm not sure exactly what I see, if I'm honest. For some reason, my heart has just hit the floor. Why am I surprised that Costas has a girlfriend, and why am I so disappointed? What's wrong with me? I'm only here for a couple of days and I do actually have a boyfriend. Mind you, I think I'm clutching at straws when I use the term 'boyfriend'. Let's face it, a boyfriend would send me messages such as 'I'm missing you' or 'I can't wait to see you', whereas with James it's a complete communication blackout as far as I'm concerned. I bet he's communicated with that bloody Tracey woman, though. Aargh, here I go again. Stop it, Helen, pull yourself together. He's not a boyfriend. Send him the bloody we're-finished message and get on with your life.

My phone pings with Steph's reply. My suspicions were right about Costas, who seems to be actually called Stefanos. I wonder what that's all about? And so much for enjoying my evening with Costas, now that he's gone to his girlfriend's. I was looking forward to getting to know him a bit better. I send her a quick reply and slip my phone in my bag, otherwise I'll be texting her all night.

Darius clinks a glass a couple of times to get everyone's attention. 'I think everyone is here now, so please all follow me through to the restaurant.'

I follow everyone and sit down next to Alexandra, in one of two empty seats left by the others. I assume the second one was for Costas. I can't say that I'm particularly looking forward to this. It's slightly weird socialising with people whom you've interviewed for a job. And I don't want to have any preconceptions about the others before I even start, like Costas did with Alexandra.

Our first task is to help ourselves to food. The head chef, who has arrived to make sure things are in order for the hotel opening, has been busy barbecuing. 'Help yourselves. There is chickens, fish in seasons, beefs and lambs kebabs, corns on the cobs and some salads over there.' He sounds like Aleksandr Orlov, the meerkat. I want him to squeak and say 'Simples.'

When I sit down again, Alexandra smiles sweetly at me.

'Well, Alexandra, I did try my hardest for you. But Costas made his decision before you even got in the room. What on earth did you do to him?'

'It all happen just after his marriage break up. His wife had affair with a member of staff at the hotel, so he was not in a good place.'

'But that doesn't explain why he isn't speaking to *you*.'

'It is because I set his friend James up with my friend, who fancy him, and when Costas found out he went mad.'

'Why did Costas go mad?'

I'm confused, and on top of everything else, the room has started spinning round. The fruit punch must have more alcohol in it than I'd realised.

'It was because James have girlfriend in England. But it was too late. I try to call my friend and it went to voicemail. Costas said I knew James had girlfriend, but when I ask James he say he finish with this girlfriend. So I say, honestly, I did not know. Costas did not believe me so he not speak to me any more. We not able to work together so I leave… Ooh, ooh, he just walk in, and he is not looking in good mood.'

My goodness, she isn't wrong. He appears to be fuming over something. He heads our way with a plate of food and a beer.

'May I sit here?' he asks, pointing to the empty chair next to me in a rather polite tone, considering.

'Yes, of course. Are you okay? You seem a bit pissed off – sorry, I mean annoyed – about something.' Oh my God, what the hell is wrong with me, swearing and telling the truth?

'I am fine. It is complicated. Anyway, I have it sorted now.'

I'm not going to delve any deeper, but if Darius was right I assume that Costas has just had a row with his girlfriend over something. I can't actually believe the next sentence that comes out of my mouth. The fruit punch is obviously working its magic. 'So, Costas, why did you leave such a successful hotel and team in Mykonos?' For goodness sake, what's the matter with me? Alexandra's just told me his wife was having an affair with another staff member.

'Because I needed to get away and start again,' he replies, with pain etched all over his face.

'Oh, Costas, I'm sorry. I didn't mean to pry.'

'What is "pry"?' he asks.

'To be nosey.'

'Yes, I understand. You were not to know. I am sorry for before when I walk in your room,' he says.

'Oh, don't worry. No harm done. It's nothing you haven't seen before.' For God's sake, what the hell is wrong with me?

'Indeed, Helen, but the phone pose was a new one.' I catch his eyes and we hold a look that makes my heart do a double beat. 'Listen, I am sorry that I am not very good company. I have a couple of things to do so, if you will excuse me, I will be back shortly. In the meantime, you should know that Loving Luxury Travel is covering the bar bill; maybe you could keep everyone under control.'

'Of course, Costas, I'll keep everyone in order,' I reply, winking at him.

Clearly, whatever Darius is serving me is loosening me up. He's now delivered a Vodka Collins to me, insisting that I try all the Collins cocktails. 'This is the last one, Darius. Coshtas has left me in charge.' I'm not sure, but I think I'm slurring my words.

'Okay, Miss Collins, I will not bring you any more cocktails. Maybe you finish tomorrow.'

'Exactly, Darius, I finish tomorrow,' I reply, defiantly thumping my fist on the table. 'I'm on a mission to work through these cocktails and I've got tomorrow night, so I can pache myself.'

The group are all engaged in conversation so I text Steph about the hilarious towel fiasco. It seems to take me a while to type this short message but I get there in the end and press send.

Hey sis, you'll never guess
what happend earlier Cistas
come in my room with me
naked because there wernt
Any towles. lol. Xz

A voice from behind interrupts me.

'Do you mind if I join you?'

'No, be my... Oh my God, Nikos, what on earth are you doing here?' I stand up and we do the obligatory kiss on the cheek and hug before sitting down again.

'I have been sent to keep an eye on you.'

'Really? By who?'

'Costas. Anyway, never mind what I am doing here, what are you doing here?'

'I've been interviewing candidates for the job here with Costas.'

'Oh no! When Costas mentioned a "Helen" I never thought it would be you.'

'What do you mean "Oh no"?' I reply, laughing.

'Sorry. It is just that Costas can't interview me because he is my cousin. Loving Luxury Travel wanted an independent person to do it.'

'It's fine, Nikos, we're only engaged. That doesn't count.' We both start laughing.

'Oh yes, my new fiancée.' Nikos takes my hand and kisses the back of it.

'And how is your ex-fiancée?' I can't believe I've just said that. I need to get a zip fitted to my mouth.

'She is still sulking. She refused to reason with me yesterday and would not join me at her favourite restaurant last night. So I had to text her this morning to tell her I was coming here.'

'Maybe we should take a selfie and post it on Facebook – the newly engaged couple. She'd be over here like a shot.'

'More like she would be over here with a shotgun. You saw what her temper is like.'

'I certainly did. But at least I've now ticked off Greek plate-smashing on my list of things to do.'

'And what other things to do are on your list?'

I'm sure I'm not imagining that Nikos is flirting with me big time, which serves me right. I attempt an answer that will hopefully get me off the hook. 'Now, that would be telling, and a girl needs some secrets.' Before he can say anything else my phone pings. 'That's probably my sister. I can't see the screen very well in this light – I'll read it later.'

'I can try and read it if you like, although I am not too good at reading English,' Nikos offers.

'Okay, you read it.' I pass the phone over to Nikos.

'Well, first of all it says it's from your mum. Do you want me to carry on?'

'Sure, it will probably be an update about their cruise.'

'Okay, it says "I've had a little dick on deck and I'm a little bruised".' Nikos reads the text out quite loudly; the opening line has gripped everyone's attention. The whole table's gone silent and all eyes turn in Nikos's direction.

'This is not me, this is Helen's mum,' he clarifies. He continues in a slightly quieter voice. '"I haven't told your dad yet but, yes, it would be good to rest by the pool. Love, Mum."'

He shrugs his shoulders and shakes his head. He's clearly not sure that he's read the message right. He passes the phone to Markos.

'Yes, it says "little dick". I don't think size should matter though,' he says, blushing.

'Let me see,' I demand, my cheeks are now rather hot and flushed. The only trouble is that I can't see the text very well in the dim light and I think I need some reading glasses. Oh, poor Mum – what has she done?

Someone pipes up. 'It is a bit worrying that it's caused bruising.' Everyone starts laughing uncontrollably.

'I think this calls for a stiff drink,' Nikos announces. The whole table erupts again.

'Not for me. I'm going to ring Mum and see what on earth is going on,' I say.

'Come on, Helen, it sounds like she is enjoying herself, and I have not yet finished telling you my story,' Alexandra says between gasps of laughter.

'And I have drinking game to show you from Poland,' the chef pipes up.

So we all head to the bar. I get there before my legs, with a little help from Alexandra and Nikos, who get me on to a bar stool.

The head chef has got Darius to line up small bottles of *ouzo* for us all. 'Okay, we bang bottle on bar like this, then we put the top on nose like this and grip bottle in teeth and knock back. After three! One, two, three!'

After the quick demo, everyone bangs their bottle on the bar, puts their bottle tops on their noses and grips their bottles in their teeth before knocking back the *ouzo*. A rapturous round of applause indicates the completion of the game.

'I am going to try and call Selena before it gets too late to see if I can talk some sense into her,' Nikos tells me when the noise dies down.

'Well, good luck. I hope she answers.'

'Me too. I will probably be back for the next round anyway, since she has not replied to a single text or call since yesterday.'

As he disappears, I seize my opportunity to get the rest of her story from Alexandra. It all seems a huge coincidence that this guy was called James, especially after what's come to light with Selena. I want to establish if Alexandra's friend is, in fact, Selena. But then, surely Alexandra and Nikos would know each other. But if the friend isn't Selena and we're talking about the same James, that means... Suddenly, there's an alarm bell ringing in my head. Things are coming back to me.

'Alexandra, you were telling me about someone called James. Does he live in Mykonos?'

'No, he is working for Loving Luxury Travel, and he is very good-looking...'

I cut her off in mid flow. 'Hang on, Alexandra. Is this him?' I somehow locate a photo of him on my phone and pass it to her.

'Yes, Helen, this is James! You know him?'

'Well, I thought I knew him. He was my so-called boyfriend.'

'Oh, Helen, I not realise! I am so sorry. I would never have said anything if I knew!' Alexandra is beside herself.

'No worries,' I say numbly. 'I'd already decided he isn't worth another minute of my time. He's finished, and,' I raise my voice, 'I think that calls for another round of *ouzo* to celebrate!'

No one argues with that. The next lot of bottles are quickly lined up on the bar and we're ready for Round 2. One, two, three! I tip my head back and lose my balance. I'm falling backwards...

Chapter 22

Stephanie

'*Kalimera*, Stephanie!'

As I begin to stir, I'm aware it's light. I can hear the sea, and there are birds chirping away far too noisily for my liking. My brain processes information very slowly. *Kalimera* is 'Good morning' in Greek.

'Stephanie, *kalimera*!'

Oh, my goodness, there he goes again. Pleeeease, I need to sleep. I turn over and then it hits me like a ten-tonne truck. The voice is … ohhh myyy God … Stefanossss … I need to open my eyes pronto.

'Stefanos, where am I? What time is it? What's happened?'

'Stephanie, do not worry, calm down, nothing happen. I bring coffee last night and fall asleep while I was waiting for you and you fall asleep after me. Now it is nine thirty, and time for fresh coffee and breakfast, if you like. Then I take you back to hotel. I thought you might like to get changed into something else, and maybe we go to the beach later.'

'Yes, great, sounds like a plan,' I reply, with a rather big yawn.

'Would you like me to bring the coffee and breakfast out here, or you prefer to eat in the restaurant?'

'I think here would be better. I don't like eating breakfast in public in the previous night's outfit,' I reply, rather sheepishly. 'Not that it's a regular occurrence or anything,' I add quickly.

'Good choice. I think my father will still be cross with me, so I stay out of his way.'

I have a flashback from last night, when his father threw some bedding out of the window. I don't want to face him yet either.

Stefanos rolls back the curtain to reveal a beautiful sunny day, and goes off to get our breakfast.

My poor head is pounding and I desperately want to go back to sleep, but I need the loo. I drag myself off the bed. Luckily, I get to the toilet without bumping into anyone.

I peer into the mirror; the vision I'm greeted with, quite honestly, isn't the best look I've ever had. My mascara has rubbed off half an inch down from my eyes, and other bits of make-up are smudged here and there all over my face. Goodness only knows what Stefanos thought of it all. And I've been asleep with my contact lenses in, so my eyes are red.

I wet some tissues and start rubbing off what I can, helped by a bit of soap. I'll probably have an allergic reaction but I'll have to take that risk. It'll be bad enough arriving back at the hotel in last night's outfit without my face looking like I'm a cast member of *The Rocky Horror Show*. I can just picture it now. Sandra and Carol are bound to see me and I'll be the talk of the hotel.

I go back to the cabana. Guests are already claiming their sunloungers for the day. Meanwhile, I haven't even got back to the hotel after my night out. If Helen finds out, I'll never hear the end of it. That reminds me, she sent a bizarre message last night and I haven't heard from her today. I send her a quick text while I wait for Stefanos to return.

That will wind her up, me using 'your' incorrectly. She's so bloody nitpicky with grammar.

Stefanos arrives back with some fragrant coffee and croissants. We scoff them pretty quickly as we're both absolutely starving. I feel like I could eat a horse, but a cooked breakfast would suffice. The trouble is, the only place you can get a decent one of those is in England, and so croissants will have to do.

Stefanos breaks into my cooked-breakfast fantasy just as I take a sip of coffee, and I almost spit it out. 'I not bring you here for sex, Stephanie, you know. I don't do this every week like in the film.'

'Oh, Stefanos...'

Before I can finish speaking, we hear a male voice calling '*Geia*!' I suspect it's his dad, thankfully sounding a lot calmer. Stefanos goes out and I can hear a calm conversation between the two of them.

He comes back in, smiling. 'My father forgive me for last night, and he say we can use his boat again, if you like. Or we could just go to a quiet secluded beach and sleep.'

'I think the beach sounds like the best idea, Stefanos. I could do with some sleep, and a quiet beach sounds like just the ticket.'

'Right, give me fifteen minutes to shower and change, then we go.'

'Okay, see you in a minute. I'll just lie down here and have forty winks.'

'What is forty winks?'

'Oh, it's just an English term for a little sleep.'

'You English and your little sayings. I need a lesson.' He shakes his head and laughs.

I close my eyes as he leaves. He's back in what seems like five minutes, but he's changed and has wet hair so he's clearly had a shower, while I've had what feels like about five winks.

'Okay, I'll take you back to the hotel, Stephanie, in the car, then we come back here and go to a little beach on the moped.'

'Great. Sounds good to me.'

As we step out of the cabana, Xena gives us a cheery wave and a friendly '*Kalimera*' from up by the hotel. I wave and shout '*Kalimera*' back to her. It's clear she's not angry with me.

The car is baking hot, so Stefanos winds down the windows to let a breeze in as we get going. We drive along the coast road, following the beautiful blue sea, which is sparkling in the sunshine, and chat about the night before. The car crawls up the steep hillside. At one point, we have to stop for a bus coming round a hairpin bend. The car struggles to get going again to the point that I think I'll have to get out and push.

'No power,' Stefanos announces. 'We nearly go backwards!' He seems to find it amusing.

We finally arrive at my hotel and Stefanos decides to wait for me in the car, parked down the road and out of the way.

'I'll be as quick as I can,' I say as I leave. This usually means at least half an hour. I can't get sidetracked with chatting, so I put my head down as I enter the hotel grounds.

'You just gettin' back from last night, pet?'

I haven't noticed Carol and Sandra sitting on sunbeds with a coffee each. This is all I bloody well need, the third degree off Private Eye Carol.

Sandra's quick to chip in. 'You ignore her, pet. She's only jealous.'

'Eee, I'm not jealous, lass, I were just sayin', makin' polite conversation.'

'Aye, and just being nosey. It's got nothing to do with you whether she's been out all night, you're not her mother.'

I decide to escape while they're distracted by their little disagreement. 'Must dash, ladies. I'm on a tight schedule.'

I move quickly on, leaving poor Sandra fending off Carol's 'I was only being polite, and anyway...'

I arrive at my very tidy room, with not one but two un-slept-in beds. That will please housekeeping.

I throw my bag on the bed and jump straight in the shower with my toothbrush. I need to try and make a list of things that I need for the day in my head. Now, let's see, swimsuit or bikini? Defer decision until getting ready. Sunglasses, sun cream, towel. I can't think of anything else – my head hurts too much. I step out of the shower, quickly dry off and slap on some sun cream. Right, I think I'll go for the ease of a bikini, and, because we'll be going on the scooter, I decide to wear my nice light cropped cotton trousers along with a white top. I find a pair of Helen's sandals that she hasn't taken with her. They finish off the outfit nicely.

I snatch one of the hotel beach towels and stuff it into my beach bag along with all the other essentials. I'm ready to leave in a new all-time record of just twenty-five minutes. I'm about to open the door when there's a light knock on it, and a faint mumble that I can't understand. I look through the spy hole and all I can see is flowers.

I open the door and a man on the other side of a rather large bouquet says, 'Flowers for Mrs Valentine.'

'Yes, that's me,' I reply, flabbergasted.

'Please allow me to bring in your room.'

'Sorry, yes. They'll probably be okay on there,' I reply, pointing to the coffee table.

He puts down the gorgeous boxed bouquet and I notice an envelope on a stick.

'Have a good day, madam.'

'Yes, thank you...' My voice trails off as I reach for the envelope. The card inside reads:

We need to talk.
Richard x

Chapter 23

Helen

I'm not entirely sure where I am, apart from that I'm in a nice comfy bed. My mind's blank, my head's thumping and my tongue's stuck to the roof of my mouth. I can't move my body and I hear snoring. It must be Steph. I drift back off to sleep.

'*Kalimera*. I bring coffee to help wake you up.' I can hear these words, said in a man's voice, but my brain isn't co-operating at all. It must be Room Service.

I try to say 'Leave it there,' but I can't operate my mouth. My head is whirring. How can it be Room Service? I'm... I can't actually remember where I am.

I peek out from under the covers. There's daylight, which is painful to my eyes, so I pull the covers back over my face. I don't want light, I want darkness and more sleep.

'Don't think you're hiding under there for the whole day, either. We have work to do.' The man peels the cover from my face.

I try to shriek, but my mouth is as dry as a bone, and I'm reduced to a hoarse whisper. 'Oh my God, Costas, what on earth are you doing?'

'Bringing you coffee. I am surprised you have survived the night.'

'What do you mean, survived the night? I was all right …
wasn't I?'

'No, you were not all right,' comes the curt reply. 'You could
not walk or barely talk, so I carry you up here and put you in bed.
You do not worry – I see nothing that I not see already. I had no
choice, Helen, but to sleep in the other bed and make sure that
you…' His voice trails off. He's actually beginning to sound as
though he was slightly concerned about my welfare. 'Anyway,
you are fine. I will meet you in an hour, for the interviews.'

Before I can ask any more questions, he leaves. I inch myself
up to tackle the coffee that he's left by the bed. It dawns on me
that his comment about not seeing anything that he hadn't
already was because I'm still wearing my dress. I remember the
towel fiasco from yesterday and I want to laugh. But my head
hurts too much. And, oh shit, the bloody interviews! What on
earth was I thinking, knocking back cocktails, rum punch and
ouzo shots on a work night?

There's only one thing for it: a long shower. My legs are on
a different setting to the rest of me so I end up clinging on to
bits of furniture to make the journey to the bathroom. This time
I make sure the towels are in the bathroom with me – it just
makes life so much easier. The shower starts working its magic.
I embrace the hot water as it soothes my poor abused head. I
mean, what on earth was I thinking? What possessed me to get
into such a state?

I can't remember not being able to walk but then I can't
remember anything beyond Costas leaving me in charge of the
group and me promising to keep them in order. What must he
think of me now? Typical shameless English lager lout… Okay, I
wasn't drinking lager, and I don't think I was dancing on tables,
or fighting, but I'm not sure. I haven't got a bloody clue. I'll ask
Alexandra, she'll know. After all, we were sitting next to each
other for most of the night.

I step out of the shower and wrap myself up in a towel. I can hear my phone bleeping somewhere. I locate it in my handbag, which has been put neatly on my case, I assume by Costas. It's an email from Daniel, which can wait, and there's a message from Steph from last night, which I can't make sense of.

Blimey, Helen, you OK? You're standard of English has slipped, I'd give you a Grade U for grammar and spelling and A+ for turning things round so quickly with Costas or is Cistas someone else? lol. xx

What the hell is she going on about? It's her who can't get her grammar right, with that annoying 'your' and 'you're' thing that she does. She's even done it on here. And what's she going on about? Who's Cistas?

I'm just about to launch into a reply when it occurs to me to check my previous text to her. There's the evidence. But I didn't send that, did I? Oh my God, I must have done.

I'll have to reply to Steph in a bit, but, for now, I need to get dressed and make an attempt at putting on some make-up. Then I need to go to the restaurant for something to eat before the interviews start because I'm absolutely starving.

Getting dressed is a painful process as it requires movement, which my head can't handle. I do my best, given the circumstances. I only poke myself in the eye twice with the mascara wand but you'd never know as my eyes are bloodshot anyway. I gather up my work things and close the door as gently as I can.

I can't bear the thought of the lift so I walk very slowly down the stairs to the restaurant. Every step's a challenge, and I begin to think that food might not be a good idea. I make my way towards the coffee station instead.

Darius is heading in my direction. '*Kalimera*, Miss Collins. You look, how you say…?' He pauses, trying to choose some tactful words, '… not very well.'

'Darius, I feel not very well. I don't know what I was thinking.'

'Well, good job for you that Costas and Nikos catch you when you fall.'

'Fall!' I shriek. 'I don't remember falling! Or Nikos or Costas, for that matter.' Now he's mentioned Nikos, I get a tiny flashback. 'Oh yes, that was it, I was talking to Nikos and Alexandra, and we were all playing that *ouzo* game.'

'Oh yes, Alexandra,' Darius cuts in. 'She say sorry, she has gone for early flight and to give you this. She seem very upset about something.'

Darius takes a note from his pocket and hands it to me. Then he leaves, muttering something about getting me some toast.

> Hi Helen,
> I leave early to catch flight. I not sleep much last night. I so sorry if I upset you. I no I will not get the job but I not blame Costas. He is good man reelly.
> Alexandra. xx

Darius is back, with toast as promised.

'Darius, I don't understand this note. What happened last night?'

'I am not sure. You seem all right at first. You order drinks and play the drinking game with the others. I think you got upset and cry, but I am not sure. Then you fall backwards, but Costas and Nikos catch you and carry you to your room. For the rest, you will have to ask them. Now here is some toast to help you be better.'

'Thank you, Darius, I think I'll need a bit more than toast for that.'

Oh my God, I'm starting to panic now. Never in the whole of my life have I experienced anything like this. I literally have no memory from the point of Costas leaving me in charge. I can just about remember Nikos arriving and that's it.

One thing's for sure, I won't be asking Costas to fill me in. But I *am* surprised, in the light of my behaviour last night, that he was so nice this morning. I'm bracing myself for the interviews; I'm sure his Jekyll and Hyde character will reappear by then.

Bang on cue, Costas appears from behind me and makes me jump. He speaks in a tone that makes me think I'm not going to be let off the hook that easily. 'Helen, I am very surprised you made it down here. I will meet you in fifteen minutes to have chat about today's candidates.'

He really does remind me of a Greek version of Simon Cowell. Oh well, this should be interesting, if nothing else.

I muster enough strength to get to the coffee station for another coffee – not that I think it will help much. I've reluctantly eaten the toast that Darius brought over. If anything, I'm now feeling worse. I'm grateful there are only four more candidates to interview. We'll finish by lunch so that the interviewees can catch the early afternoon flight back to Athens. Maybe I can lie on a sunbed in the afternoon and sleep my hangover off.

I stumble into the room where Costas is waiting. He's flicking through the job applications. He has a Greek coffee in front of him, with the compulsory water by its side. 'Ah, you made it. I did not think you would be up to interviewing today after the state you were in last night.'

'I'm really sorry, Costas, I don't know what on earth happened. I've never been like that before. I can't remember a thing after you told me to keep an eye on everyone.'

'Well, I do not know what happen either. I got back and you were ... well ... I think the term is "pissed as a newt" ... and not keeping your eye on anything. These things happen; you were upset about something. Anyway, we'd better discuss today's candidates. Andreas, the first one, is due in fifteen minutes. Then we've got Nikos, my cousin, who I believe you have already met.'

'Yes, I had a meeting with Nikos and he introduced me to Selena, which was interesting to say the least.'

This has caught Costas's attention. 'Interesting because...?'

Oh no, I've done it again. Why can't I just keep my big mouth shut?

Costas can see that I'm hesitating and rescues me. 'Look, I know they have fallen out. Nikos filled me in last night. I also know that Selena plays with fire, so I am not surprised that she thought he was up to no good with you. My wife had an affair and she constantly accused me of doing the same.'

'I'm sorry to hear that, Costas.'

'Yes, well, so was I at the time, but I move here for a new start. Anyway, we are not here to talk about this. Will you be okay interviewing Nikos on your own?'

'Yes, I'll be fine.'

'Good. I suggest these questions for Nikos.' He lists them but I'm too weak to think or argue so I just nod in agreement and stifle a yawn. 'Listen, Helen, I know you probably just want to go to bed but I appreciate your help here.'

Despite the pain, I grin.

'What is so funny?' he asks in his serious voice.

'Nothing, Costas. It's just that, for a second there, I thought you were propositioning me.'

'What do you mean?'

'That you wanted to take me to bed.' I feel my cheeks flush. I can't imagine what on earth possessed me to say that.

To make matters worse, Costas peers over his glasses and looks very serious and very sexy at the same time. 'I already take you to bed, Helen, last night. But what about taking a few steps back and going into town tonight for some food? The candidates will leave with the rest of the staff and I do not like cooking very much.'

Now I'm confused, and speechless. Costas has somehow turned my silly comment round and asked me to dinner. I open my mouth and manage to reply quite sensibly. 'Er, yes, Costas, that sounds like a plan – if I'm up to eating, that is.'

'You will be fine. We do these interviews, I bring you hair of the dog and maybe you sleep by the pool this afternoon. Deal?'

'Worth a try, I suppose. I'm not too sure about the dog-hair bit but, hey ho, I'll try anything once.'

'I am not meaning actual dog hair, I mean…'

'Yes, I know. I'm joking.' We smile at each other. I'm not sure what's happened to Costas overnight, but he seems different today. Not that I'm complaining; I prefer him like this.

'So, Helen, I think I use this question today: "Tell me about a time when you have gone the extra mile for a customer".'

For some reason, the way he says it amuses me and I laugh again.

'Okay, what is funny now?' He shakes his head, but he does look mildly amused.

'It's just the way you say things. It makes me laugh. Sorry. I won't do it again, honest, and it's making my head hurt anyway. So don't make me laugh again.' I take a deep breath and put my serious face back on.

'You know, Helen, laughing suits you.'

Before I can answer him by suggesting he tries it himself sometime, the first candidate, Andreas, knocks on the door.

Costas waves him in. He must like Andreas because he nudges me for my favourite opening question.

'Hello, Andreas. Take a seat and tell us a bit about yourself.'

Andreas plunges enthusiastically into his answer but I don't really hear what he's saying. I seem to be lost between feeling ill and feeling confused. Costas seems different this morning, in a nice way.

Andreas must have finished the first question because Costas asks his question next. I hear bits of the answer, which involves taking a guest on a bus to a pharmacy for some medication for her husband. I drift off again. Quite honestly, I think that if I make it through these interviews without passing out or being sick, it will be a major achievement.

Costas nudges me for my next question. I glance down at my paperwork. 'So, Andreas, why do you want this job?' Andreas seems prepared with an answer.

All I can say is, it's a good job I'm not being interviewed because my mind would be blank. I'd probably give up at this point and say, 'You know what? I'm not sure why I want the job. My head hurts and I need to lie down.'

'I think Miss Collins has your next question, Andreas, when she's ready, from the creativity and innovation section.'

'Oh, sorry. Yes, the next question, er, oh yes. What decision have you put off the longest, and why?'

Andreas is very well prepared and fires back his answer, but I'm on a roll as well. What would I say to this? I think we should all do one of these interviews every five years. They make you stop and think. I know one decision that I've put off: drawing a line under the James thing and moving on. I still haven't sent him a message. I keep starting it in my head but that's it. Note to self: send the bloody message.

I've also been putting off a decision about a career change for quite a long time. When James started in the office, he was a nice distraction at first. I was fed up, but ended up staying to keep him entertained. When I get back home, I should look at some different options. Maybe I need a completely new start or…

Something is niggling at me about last night, and I've just had a flashback. I was talking to Alexandra about James. God, I wish I could remember what the hell she said. Alexandra holds the key…

'Well, that concludes our interview today, Andreas. Thank you for your time,' says Costas.

Andreas stands up and heads out of the room, looking quite pleased with himself.

'Well, he scored quite highly compared to yesterday's candidates. What are your feelings?'

'Er, yes, he seemed to tick quite a few boxes and he was very pleasant. I like him, but the final decision is yours. You'll be the one working with him.'

'Hmm, I think I will have to compromise at some point.'

'Anyway, let's see how Nikos fares. I'll get him.' I can't begin to imagine what Nikos is thinking of me right now, especially after what Darius said earlier. I go out into the corridor. 'Good morning, Nikos. Please come in and have a seat.'

'Morning, Helen,' he says as we re-enter the room. 'It is a pleasant surprise to see you doing the interview. I did wonder…'

'Yes, thank you, Nikos. We need to keep this on a professional level, please,' Costas interjects, to my surprise. 'As you know, Helen is going to ask the questions and I will observe. So, when you are ready, Helen…'

'Thank you, Costas. Okay, Nikos, tell me what's the worst communication situation that you've experienced?'

I could be wrong, but I'm sure Nikos is blushing. He answers after a very long pause. 'I am very sorry about what happen last night.' He looks in my direction.

'What do you mean? What happened last night? And what relevance has it got to the interview?'

'My worst communication situation was last night, with the text message on your phone.'

Costas quickly intervenes. 'I don't think we need concern ourselves about that in today's interview. Please move on to another question.'

What the hell is Nikos going on about? Why is he talking about a text message? I'll have to wait until we've finished this interview to even check my phone.

'Nikos, what is your greatest strength?'

He recovers his composure with this answer, which is that he is a good communicator. Oh yes, that's a bit ironic, considering the last time I saw him he was trying to communicate with Selena who hadn't spoken to him for twenty-four hours.

My greatest strength, when my head is functioning, would be my organisational skills. For example, I organised Mum's surprise sixtieth birthday party. Her face when she walked into the room was a picture. Mum … that's it! Suddenly I'm jolted into remembering last night. The text that Nikos referred to was from Mum. I can't remember it fully, but she'd probably got her predictive text on and was texting about… Oh my God, that was it: a little dick. God only knows what she was going on about. I need to alter that setting on her phone before she gets anything else muddled up.

Costas says my name, which snaps me out of my thought bubble. 'The next question, Miss Collins, when you're ready.'

'Yes, thank you. So, Nikos, where do you see yourself in five years' time?'

Nikos has his answer all ready. He sees himself as manager of his own hotel. My thoughts stop me in my tracks. I'll be forty in a few years; where do I want to be by then? I've always pictured myself being married with two kids so, with my biological clock ticking away, this goal needs addressing pretty quickly. But then, if I meet another idiot like James it just isn't going to happen. I need to meet someone and get to know them a bit before starting a family… Maybe a sperm bank is the answer… This thought is pretty scary to say the least, and too much for my poor little head this morning.

Nikos's interview comes to an end. Costas offers to fetch some coffee, and takes the opportunity to have a quick chat with Nikos. I get my phone out and look at Mum's text message. I'm struggling to read it so I borrow Costas's reading glasses, which he's left on the desk. There's a new text from her, which reads:

I'VE HAD A
LITTLE TRIP ON
DECK AND I'M A
LITTLE BRUISED.
I HAVEN'T TOLD
YOUR DAD YET.
IT WOULD BE GOOD
TO REST BY THE
POOL.
LOVE, MUM XX

Thank goodness! At least Mum isn't having a midlife crisis! Costas returns with the coffee, and looks amused because I'm wearing his glasses.

'Sorry, Costas. I was struggling to read a text off my mum.'

'No worries, it comes to us all. Speaking of texts, what was Nikos talking about? He seemed very embarrassed.'

I hand Costas my phone to show him the messages. He sees the funny side.

'You see, Costas, predictive text at its best and people who don't do technology – not a good combination.'

Just as the words leave my mouth, my phone pings with another text. I can see it's from Steph but before I can get my phone back from Costas, the message has scrolled across the top of the screen. Costas hands my phone back, looking somewhat embarrassed.

I hold the phone at arm's length to read the message.

Hi Helen, just checking
your OK after your
night with Cistas or was
it Costas in the end? lol
Xx

My face and neck flush with heat and I'm sure I've turned red. I put the phone back in my bag. I'll reply to bloody Steph later. She couldn't have timed that any worse if she'd tried. And she's done that bloody 'your' thing again – give me strength.

Costas very kindly turns the conversation to my parents' impending visit. 'So your parents will be here tomorrow? If you like, I can send a car to pick them up and organise some food for them from town. Or I could recommend somewhere for you all to eat.'

'That would be great. I think we'll eat in town. If you can arrange a lift, I'll text them with the details.'

'Tell them George will pick them up at nine at the port. He will have a sign with their names written on it. And I will write down the name of a fantastic restaurant, with views over the seafront, for your lunch.'

'Thank you, Costas. You're welcome to join us for lunch. It would be nice for you to meet my parents.'

'Thank you, that will be good. If you are sure, I will book the restaurant for an early lunch. Now we'd better get on with the final two candidates.'

Our next interviewee is Anna, who seems very confident. She starts off well with my favourite Tell-us-about-yourself question. She replies with a very polished answer.

Costas asks her the next question. 'Can you tell us about a situation in which you had to deal with an angry customer?'

Anna starts her answer, and in my head I start mine. Working in the travel business entails endless issues that can lead to angry customers. I could spend a whole day talking about them. One of my most memorable would have to be the ash cloud crisis in 2010, when we had to deal with hundreds of angry customers all at the same time. It was extremely stressful. We had customers stranded all around the world, trying to get home, and customers stuck in the UK, trying to go on holiday. What a complete nightmare. I didn't sleep properly for days. We were all in the office working flat out, ordering takeaways, going home exhausted and falling into bed for a few hours.

Then there was the liquid and gels scare, when suddenly everyone was greeted with a massive queue at the airport and given a little plastic bag for their cosmetics. There were a lot of upset and angry customers then, mainly ladies who had been forced to bin perfumes and moisturisers that went over the maximum allowance or were deemed suspicious. I lost a very expensive mascara to a bin myself, and nearly got arrested when I protested that I didn't turn into some wonder woman with special powers when I used it, like the woman in the advert. And the French and all their strikes are another favourite for upsetting customers. I mean, let's face it, they strike at the drop of a hat.

Suddenly, I hear my name. Anna's waiting for the next question and Costas chirps in with 'In your own time, Miss Collins.'

'Sorry, yes. So, Anna, how do you deal with stress?'

Anna's approach is a little bit different to mine. She exercises, does yoga and uses some breathing technique that I've never heard of. My very short answer to this would be to open a bottle of wine – but maybe not today. Ooh, I feel rough.

Costas asks the next question and I begin to feel really queasy. My nausea is accompanied by that feeling of going cold and clammy but somehow still sweating. Oh my God, I'm going to have to make a run for the toilet in the middle of an interview.

I cut in. 'I'm really sorry, I don't feel well. Please excuse meee...'

I fling my chair back and run out of the room. I head towards the nearest toilet and get there just in time. I throw up, and my legs immediately turn to jelly. I can't believe I've just done that! How utterly embarrassing! I can't imagine what on earth Costas and Anna must think.

I splash my face with some water, rinse out my mouth and perch myself on a chair. My pulse is racing and I'm shaking.

'Helen, are you in there?'

Oh my God, it's Costas. 'Yes, I'm here.'

He comes in, actually looking concerned. 'Look, there is only one more person to interview and I can do that on my own. Why don't you go and lie on a sunbed in the shade? I will bring you that hair of the dog. We can discuss all the interviews later, when you feel better.'

'Thanks, Costas, if you're sure. I feel really awful about all this. I was a teenager when I last felt this rough after a night on the booze.'

'Well, I think you have a lot of *ouzo* mixed with cocktails, so I am not surprised you are ill.'

Costas disappears and I make my way over to the sunloungers. I pull a chair under a large olive tree. It's pleasantly warm. I lie down, still feeling shaky. I close my eyes, and just minutes later I hear Darius.

'Costas send me with this drink for you, Miss Collins, to make you feel better. He said I can finish early so I am going home for a few days. It was nice to meet you, and I hope to see you again. You know, Costas is really kind man. He is ... how you say? His bark is worse than his bite.'

'Thank you, Darius, I'll bear that in mind. It was nice to meet you too. Have a nice few days off and, who knows, maybe I'll come back and visit you when the hotel's open.'

Darius shakes my hand and leaves me with my 'hair of dog' concoction, which tastes quite pleasant. I drink it all. Suddenly, I feel extremely tired and can't resist the urge to close my eyes and drift off.

I'm not sure how long I've been drifting in and out of sleep when I feel my dress being pulled and hear some strange noises. But I don't really care; they'll go away. I drift off again. Now something is licking my face. This instantly wakes me up. To my horror, there are a couple of goats eating my lovely dress. I scream, but, frankly, they don't seem that bothered.

'For pity's sake, look at the state of my dress! Get off, you stupid bloody animals! Shoo!' I get up but they just stand there, completely unfazed by my flailing arms, clapping hands and shouting.

Costas needs to know about this. I march off to the interview room. The door's open and the room's empty. He must have finished the last interview. I find him in the bar and restaurant, where he's talking to Nikos.

'Sorry to interrupt, but look at the state of my bloody dress! It's ruined! How the hell have those goddamn goats got in? You can't have goats wandering round chewing the guests' belongings! The guests will have a field day on TripAdvisor: "Eaten alive by goats"!!'

'I am very sorry, Helen, but they must have escape and got through the fence. I will sort it out before we open,' says Costas.

'Well, make sure you do. It's just not acceptable. I mean, people don't expect to come to a five-star hotel to be eaten alive by...' I'm mid rant when I feel the earth beneath my feet tremble. Everything around us shakes violently. 'Oh my God, Costas! What's happening? What is it?'

There's a sudden horrendous, deafening noise, which I feel vibrating through my chest. Costas and Nikos are shouting something at me. Before I register what they're saying, they lurch forward and push me down to the floor. And then everything is black.

Chapter 24

Stephanie

A tear rolls down my cheek. Once again, Richard's timing is crap. The situation doesn't seem real, because the writing on the card isn't his, and that makes me feel angry. All those times when he could have sent flowers but he didn't see the need. And now, when I've lost all hope, he does this. He's suddenly interested in talking again – or, more likely, his flatmate wants him out and he can't bear the thought of going back to his parents. Well, I'm sorry, Richard, I've moved on. I pick up my bag and close the door quietly behind me.

Miraculously, I manage to leave the hotel without bumping into Carol or Sandra so I'm still in good time, although Stefanos didn't seem too bothered about me getting back particularly quickly. I like his laid-back approach. That seems to be everyone's way on the island.

That being said, he's seen me approaching and is running towards me, looking agitated. 'Oh, thank goodness you are back. I was just about to ring you.'

'Why, Stefanos, whatever's the matter?' I can tell immediately that he isn't fooling about. He looks deadly serious.

'I just have call from my mama. She was so upset, I hardly understand what she was telling me. She said a newsflash came

257

on to say there has been an earthquake in Syros – and my brother is at the Syros Boutique Blue. We have both try to ring him but there is no answer. Then Aunt Katina rang to say she can't get hold of my cousin, who has gone there for interview.'

'Oh my God, Stefanos, I think that's where Helen's gone! I'd better try and ring her.' My hands are shaking and I struggle to find Helen's number even though it's in my favourites. Her phone clicks on to voicemail almost immediately and I leave a garbled message. Stefano's phone is ringing again; there's a frantic exchange between him and a woman. It sounds a bit like he's arguing with her. I send Helen a text, which is really hard to do because my hands are shaking so much.

Stefanos finishes his call and looks quite irritated. 'I assume your sister did not answer.'

'No, she hasn't, so I've sent her a text. I'm really worried, Stefanos, and I can't even remember properly where she said she was going. I was just happy…' I break down at this point because when Helen was telling me her plans, I was looking forward to spending time with Stefanos and wasn't paying any attention to what she was saying.

Stefanos puts his arms round me. 'Look, do not worry, we will find out where she is. Can you remember anything?'

'I know it was the name of an island, followed by "Boutique Blue".'

'Okay, well, that narrows it down to about ten hotels. What about ringing her boss?'

'Well, I can ring her office. I've got that number in my contacts.'

Luckily, whoever answers the phone in Helen's office is able to put me straight through to Daniel. He confirms that she's at the Syros Boutique Blue Hotel, which makes me feel sick to my stomach. I relay the earthquake information to Daniel and he promises to ring the hotel immediately and get back to me.

'What did he say?' Stefanos asks. He's looking a bit calmer now.

'It is the Syros Boutique Blue and he's going to try ringing the hotel and then he'll let me know.'

'Well, that was Nikos's fiancée that I was speaking to. She has already been trying and there is no answer, even on the emergency phone line. The other problem is that the hotel is a bit isolated and, with people assuming it is closed, they might not raise the alarm. My mama says everything looks quite frantic on the news. I suggest we go over there on the next ferry, which gives us an hour to pack an overnight bag and get to the harbour. Is that okay with you?'

'Yes, anything is worth a try. I'll go back to my room now and pack an overnight bag.' I feel better now that we're doing something, rather than just trying to get through on phones.

'Okay, I will go and fill up with petrol and meet you back here in fifteen minutes. You will need your passport, and maybe some money would be useful. I will ask my father to pack some things for me and also to book us on the next ferry to save time.'

'Right. I'll see you in fifteen minutes. Let's hope Stavros can get us on that ferry.' This is a first for me, actually wanting to get on a boat.

I race to my room and arrive at the same time as the housekeeper. I ask her to wait for ten minutes. She seems to understand and retreats back outside, leaving the door wedged open.

My passport's the priority. It's in a safe at the bottom of the wardrobe. I get down on my hands and knees and key in the code. Nothing happens. Well, why would it, when I'm in such a rush? I remember Helen said something about the hash key; now, was it supposed to go before the code or after? I try it before the code and nothing happens. I try it after and again nothing happens.

'Oh, please, don't do this to me. For crying out loud, just bloody well open!' I shout in frustration at the stupid thing.

'Hello? Is everything all right?'

The housekeeper's back. She's probably wondering why neither occupant of this room has slept in the beds, and why someone is now trying to get into the safe while talking to herself.

'Oh, yes, sorry. I need my passport. My sister set the code and now I can't get in to it and I'm in a big rush.' I'm starting to panic. We simply don't have enough time to get a locksmith in.

'Oh, I see. Well, you press the star key first, then the code, then this key,' comes a calm reply. The housekeeper points to the hash key with her foot.

'Well, no wonder it wouldn't work! Helen never mentioned the star key,' I say, half laughing while I repeat the instruction to myself. 'Star key, two, five, one, two, hash key,' and, hey presto, the safe makes a funny little noise and the door opens. Thank goodness.

'Thank you! You've saved the day,' I say to the housekeeper. Of course, now I'm going to look really guilty, taking a passport and helping myself to the money that's in there as well.

'Now, how do I lock it?' There are a couple of bits of Helen's jewellery in there, which I'd better secure.

'Just the same, then the code will flash on the screen for a few seconds.' With that, she disappears, and, sure enough, the safe is locked.

I gather myself up off the floor, grab a bra and knickers and head to the bathroom to change out of my bikini. Then I tip the contents of my beach bag on to the bed. I throw in a change of underwear and some clothes, and I zip my passport and money into a pocket. I chuck my emergency make-up in a small zipped pouch for good measure, and race out of the room in a record time of twelve minutes. This gives me three minutes to get to the front of the hotel, where Stefanos will hopefully be waiting.

He pulls up just as I arrive and I jump in. 'Okay, fasten your seatbelt. We need to catch that ferry. Did Helen's office get back to you?' Before I can answer, Stefanos hits the accelerator and we screech off. This poor car is going to be pushed to its limit.

I haven't heard my phone ringing but I get it out to check. 'I've had a text from an unknown number.'

Sorry we've been unable
to contact the hotel
where Helen is. There
is no reply from our
other hotels on the island
or the reps. I'm really sorry
I don't know what else to
suggest but will let you
know if we contact anyone.
Please let me know if you
find anything else out
Regards, Daniel.

I can see a bus coming up the hill. Stefanos obviously notices it as well and accelerates as hard as he can. We get to the hairpin bend first, almost on two wheels. I daren't even look down at the sheer drop on my side. My stomach's churning and I'm anxious that we catch the next ferry. Bloody hell – the ferry! What am I thinking? I'd better take some seasickness tablets. Please let there be some tablets in my make-up bag! I start rummaging through my beach bag and finally find the little pouch, which has made its way to the bottom. I open it and, there on the top, are the two out-of-date condoms, which Stefanos immediately sees.

'I like to see a woman taking equal responsibility for these matters. By the way, I am sorry about last night. I must be getting old. How embarrassing to fall asleep! I was planning to make it up to you later, and now this has happened.'

'Oh, don't worry. I was too drunk and knackered. I'm glad you fell asleep because I'd like our first time to be special.' I can feel myself blushing.

Stefanos smiles and says, 'Me too.'

I push a tablet out of the blister pack, chew it and wash it down with my water, which I nearly end up wearing as we make our way, Wacky Races style, back down the winding road.

'You okay?' Stefanos enquires, taking his eyes momentarily and worryingly off the road.

'Yes, fine, thanks. I'm just self-medicating so I don't get seasick.'

'I keep saying you will be fine if you look at the horizon.'

'Well, on this occasion, Stefanos, I'd rather be safe than sorry.'

'Okay, you are right, I understand.'

We have reached town in record time. Stefanos weaves round a bus that's turning in the square and drives quite erratically down a narrow street, which is a car's width at a pinch. He hoots the horn to disperse the poor unsuspecting tourists, who are wandering about like tourists do. I just look ahead; I can't bear to make eye contact with anyone. This would be a good time to have my sunglasses on, but mine are somewhere in my black hole of a bag and as I'm unable to locate them at this crucial moment, I'll just have to carry on looking ahead. Perhaps I can imagine that we're filming a James Bond film. Thankfully, we get to the harbour, with people flailing their arms at us but luckily no casualties. I can see Stavros waiting for us. He's with a woman.

'Stephanie, I need to tell you something,' says Stefanos suddenly.

'That sounds a bit serious.'

'The woman standing there with Papa is Selena. She was my fiancée until she had an affair with my cousin Nikos three years ago.'

'Oh,' is the only word that comes out of my mouth.

'Yes – "oh". We have not really spoken since.'

'Well, this will be interesting.' I could let Stefanos in on my information about Selena and James, but this is not the right time.

'Well, interesting or not, Stephanie, there is no place in my life for her. I just want you to know that.'

'That's all I need to know.' I take a deep breath and get out of the car.

'Stephanie, this is Selena.' Stefanos sounds quite business-like. 'Selena, this is Stephanie. We are both going to Syros. Costas and Stephanie's sister are both at the hotel and we can't get hold of either of them.'

'Hello, Stephanie,' is all Selena says to me. She turns to Stefanos. 'Would you mind if I come with you?'

Stefanos looks at me for approval. 'I don't see why not,' is all I can say. I'm hardly likely to turn round and refuse, but I feel quite smug because he's asked me.

Stefanos has a chat to his father. Stavros hands him a bag and the tickets for the ferry before giving him a hug. He looks quite emotional; he's obviously really worried about Costas and Nikos. But Stefanos is doing a good job of reassuring him.

'Okay, we had better get in the queue for the ferry.' Stefanos puts his seat forward and beckons Selena to climb in the back. This offer doesn't go down well. She huffs and tuts, but Stefanos immediately reprimands her. I get the impression she's quite high maintenance. I can't imagine Stefanos and her together at all.

Stefanos drives to the barrier, where our passports are checked. The guard asks Stefanos some questions. There seems to be a lot of discussion. The guard then makes a phone call. We seem to be waiting forever. Thankfully, he finally hands back our passports and lets us through.

'What was all that about?'

'It is essential journeys only going to Syros. Some people do not know about earthquake and they want holiday people to stay here to await further news. I explain our situation so he had to get authorisation. They suggested that we speak to someone from the army personnel that are travelling over on this boat. They will be able to radio the emergency services in Syros and get someone over to the hotel.'

The situation now seems surreal. This just can't be happening! I must be having a nightmare. Oh no, not a panic attack! I feel like I'm being strangled. I can't breath. Poor Helen could be trapped or even worse... I break down sobbing. Stefanos puts his hand on my arm and tries to reassure me. 'Stephanie, try not to worry too much. We will soon be there.'

Chapter 25

Stephanie

It's taken an hour and a half to get to Syros but it feels more like ten hours. It was clear right from the start that Stefanos wasn't going to let Selena call the shots, so she went off in a sulk. I've been trying to ring my parents to no avail and have ended up texting them, which I didn't want to do.

As we approach the harbour, the realisation of why we're here hits me again like a brick wall. Only a few hours ago, this small Greek island was shaken by an earthquake. I try and stop my thoughts drifting any further than finding Helen, Costas and Nikos safe and well. Stefanos did manage to speak to some army personnel, and they took down the details of the hotel. That was a huge relief. At least someone should already be there.

We can see from the ferry that the port is really busy, with cars, trucks and people going in all directions. Various sirens are sounding continuously. There's an announcement made as we jostle along with the other passengers back to our respective vehicles. Stefanos tells me that they want the army personnel off first. Apparently, they've got a specific meeting point.

Selena is already waiting for us at the car. Stefanos gives her an update as she climbs reluctantly into the back. Wearing some sensible shoes instead of her ridiculous heels might have helped her. We're soon driving off the ferry. Stefanos pulls up to get out and speak to someone at the army meeting point.

He jumps back in the car. 'There is a search and rescue team at the hotel. They are radioing ahead to let someone know we are on our way.'

'And have they found Helen, Costas or Nikos?'

'I am sorry, Stephanie, they have no update. It is all quite a lot of chaos at the moment but at least they are there.'

'Yes, I suppose. I just want to get there as soon as possible but it looks like we're going to be stuck in this traffic for ages.' Nothing is moving.

'Well, hopefully I can find my way round the back streets, the way Costas took me when I visited.'

Sure enough, once we leave the port, we get moving. We're soon on a coastal road travelling out of town. Most of the smaller buildings we've seen so far seem to be okay, but we spot some emergency vehicles at bigger buildings. We pass one that looks like it's collapsed, and there's debris in the surrounding area. There are also people everywhere, looking dishevelled.

The airport comes into view. There doesn't seem to be much activity there. It could be that they have only a few flights a day and it's nothing to do with the earthquake. As the runway ends, we turn off the tarmac road and join a dusty track.

The hotel comes into view. It's still standing! As we pull into the car park, I notice that a couple of plant pots have smashed to the ground and there are a few other bits of debris scattered about as well. A couple of army vehicles are parked up but there's no sign of anyone. We can hear a noise that sounds like it's coming from the back of the hotel. We get out of the car and cautiously make our way towards the noise, with Selena stumbling on the debris in her silly shoes.

The noises get louder and we're greeted by the army personnel beavering away. One of them urges us to move away from the building. It's then that we notice its collapsed roof. The realisation that Helen, Costas or Nikos could be trapped beneath it hits us all at once.

'God help us,' Stefanos mutters and Selena breaks down sobbing. I stare at the roof in disbelief.

Someone who must be in charge comes over to update us; I brace myself. He explains what's going on in Greek, using a lot of hand gestures, which include pointing up at the sky and over to some scrubland.

Stefanos looks concerned and nods slowly, taking the information on board.

Selena shakes her head, mutters 'O Theós na has voithísei' and puts her hand to her mouth.

Finally, the guy hurries off and leaves Stefanos to explain things to me. 'Oh my God, Stefanos, what did he say?'

'He say that when they arrived they thought they could hear a faint muffled voice under the roof. They were not sure if it is was a man or a woman and have not heard anything since. They cannot confirm how many people are trapped in there. A dog is being sent to go in and look. It will let the team know if it finds a person and where the person is. They are securing the roof as much as possible in case it drops again. Then they will use some cutting tools and start the rescue. They have searched the hotel and there is no one there. So they assume Costas, Helen and Nikos are all under that roof. There is a helicopter on standby to take them to Athens if need be.'

'Oh, Stefanos, what if…?' I break down sobbing again.

Stefanos puts his arms round me to console me. 'Stephanie, we have to be positive and pray that they are all okay.'

'Yes, I know,' I sob, 'but it's so hard.' My sobs are interrupted by a phone ringing. 'That's Helen's ring tone.'

'It is Nikos's ring tone also,' Selena adds. 'It seems to be coming from that direction.' She points to the garden.

We begin to move towards the spot. But then the noise stops. I get out my phone to ring Helen's phone. Sure enough, it rings somewhere nearby. Of course, when the voicemail cuts in, the phone stops ringing. So I ring it again. My heart races. Maybe she's not in the building? Then I spot her phone on a table near a sunbed. A couple of goats are chewing the straps of her bag.

I clap my hands furiously and chase them away. 'Shoo, shoo! Go on!' I pick up Helen's phone to see who was ringing her. Unsurprisingly, there are some missed calls. Five from her work, ten from me. The last one, unbelievably, is from James. 'Bloody James Hobbs, you just couldn't write the script!'

'I wonder if he has heard about the earthquake?' Stefanos asks, completely unaware of the situation between James, Helen and Selena, who is looking decidedly uneasy.

Helen's phone pings with a new message, which scrolls across the top of the screen. 'Oh, speak of the devil, he's sent a message instead. I'll read it hot off the press.'

Selena suddenly looks even more worried. 'Maybe you should let your sister read her own message, Stephanie,' she says, in a rather panicky voice.

'Really, Selena? And how is she going to do that when she's trapped under a bloody roof?' Selena correctly realises it's a rhetorical question and remains silent. 'So, if you don't mind, I'll do what I bloody well like with my sister's phone until she says differently, and that includes reading this text.' Stefanos is smirking. 'Right, here goes: "Hi, tried to ring but no answer. I don't want to keep putting this off. I think it's only fair that we go our separate ways. You deserve to share your life with someone special and that sadly isn't me. Take care. James." I can't believe he's done that! What a complete and utter moron. Right, I'm texting him back on Helen's behalf.'

'Are you sure about this, Stephanie?' Stefanos asks cautiously. 'Absolutely positive. Helen is better off without him.' I furiously type my reply.

Hi loser, my sister is currently
unconscious under a collapsed
roof and unable to reply,
but what she'd like
to say is thank goodness that
****** ******* ******
is finally out of my life.
Yours, Stephanie.

'Send. How easy was that? Hopefully, she can now find someone who'll treat her properly. What do you think, Selena? You've gone very quiet all of a sudden. I believe you know James.'

'Well, of course I know James. He is the Loving Luxury Travel representative. I had no idea that your sister was Helen, who I met earlier this week.' She casually brushes her hair behind her ear. She thinks she's off the hook because there was no mention of her in James's text.

Then Stefanos interjects. 'And I had no idea that your sister was going out with James either. He is a nice guy, but he likes to party and play with fire. That is why my brother has fallen out with him.'

I seize my opportunity to find out what else Stefanos knows. 'Why has Costas fallen out with him exactly?'

Selena is now winding her hair nervously round her finger.

'Well, Costas knew that James had a girlfriend in the UK. Because of what happened to him, he is really against anyone having an affair. James had confided in Costas and told him he was meeting someone.'

'Who was this woman?' I ask, knowing that Selena's game is up.

'I do not know if it is my place to say anything.'

Selena is looking at the ground, hoping a fresh new fault line will appear and swallow her up. It's about time her affair with James was exposed. I'm determined to drop her in it for Helen and Nikos's sakes.

'Well, he's clearly finished with Helen, so I can't see why,' I reply.

'Okay, but please you have not heard this from me. It was a man. James was seeing another man. I think he is a manager at one of the hotels.'

'*O theé mou!*' Selena gasps as she flops on to a sunbed. She puts her head in her hands.

'Oh my God, this just goes from bad to worse! That thought *had* crossed my mind, but I just dismissed it. For now, I think it's information that Helen doesn't need to know. We'll just end this situation with the text from James.'

'Yes, I agree,' Stefanos nods.

Selena has gone very quiet. I decide to leave my campaign to expose her for the time being.

The army guy is striding towards us again. He gives us another update. Stefanos and Selena are listening intently. My stomach is in knots, I'm full of anguish and my mind is awash with hundreds of what ifs. Once again, the guy leaves and Stefanos fills me in.

'Okay, Stephanie, we need to go back to the collapsed roof. The dog has been under it and the team are pretty sure there are three people there. They heard the voice again and they think it's a woman speaking in English. They want you to see if you can make a positive ID, and to try and keep her awake and calm. They have secured the roof as much as possible, so now they will start the rescue. They want you to reassure her because it will be noisy with all the cutting equipment.'

'And what about Costas and Nikos?'

'They assume they are trapped with Helen. Maybe you will find out a bit more if she can hear you.'

Stefanos and I run over to the collapsed roof. Selena follows at her slower high-heeled pace. The army guy shows me where to stand and gives Stefanos some more instructions.

'He said there will be about ten minutes before the cutting starts. Also, there has already been one aftershock, so if we feel any tremors we need to move back into the garden immediately.'

'Okay. Well, here goes ... Helen, can you hear me?!'

We all listen intently for an answer, but there's silence.

Stefanos shouts, '*O Costas me akoús?*' Selena shouts the same to Nikos. But there's still nothing. 'Try again, Stephanie. We need to try and wake them up,' Stefanos urges.

'Helen, are you there? It's Stephanie!'

We listen for an answer and then Stefanos shouts out for Costas and Nikos again. Then one of the army men starts shouting. He beckons us over and says something to Stefanos.

'They are pretty sure they heard a woman's voice coming from this area. They want you to shout again.'

'Helen, are you there?!'

This time, we hear a muffled voice and relief washes over me. Helen's weak voice replies, 'Yes, I'm here.'

I immediately break down. 'Oh, Helen, we've been so worried! Are you hurt?'

'I'm not sure, I can't move,' comes the laboured reply.

'Well, don't try to move. Are Costas and Nikos there?'

'Yes, they are both here, but they've lost conscious ... ness.' I can tell that talking is hard for Helen, and it's going to be a battle to keep her awake.

'Listen, the rescue team are going to start cutting their way through. Don't panic at the noise. And you need to stay awake.'

'I'll try,' comes the weak reply.

The cutting starts; it sounds like the dentist on a bad day. There's absolutely no point in me trying to shout over the noise of the cutting equipment and I'd be really surprised if Helen could fall asleep, anyway, through the racket that they're making.

'Stephanie, is that you?' I spin round. Either I'm hallucinating, or Mum and Dad are heading in our direction.

'Oh my God, thank goodness you're here!' I throw my arms round them both. 'Did you get my message?'

'No, sweetheart, our phone network is down. The captain of our ship heard the news. He knew Helen was on this island because we told him our plan to visit her here. Anyway, the group we're with insisted that we come straight here, and the captain negotiated the rest. So, where's Helen?' Mum looks around.

I break down sobbing. Stefanos answers for me. 'Hello, I am Stefanos. I am afraid she is trapped under this roof with my brother Costas and my cousin Nikos.'

Mum and Dad look horrified. I quickly update them in-between sobs, with help from Stefanos.

Bang on cue, the helicopter arrives, which completely halts the conversation because it's absolutely deafening. When Stefanos said earlier that a helicopter was on its way, I pictured the sort of thing that you might see flying about anywhere. But this is a huge army helicopter, and it's sending debris flying everywhere and making the trees bend and shake like there's a hurricane. It hovers for a couple of minutes over the scrubland and then it comes to rest on the ground. Finally, the engine is switched off and the noise dies down.

'As I was saying, they are taking them to Athens when they've cut them free from this godforsaken roof.' As I speak, army personnel appear from the helicopter with stretchers and equipment.

'Athens?' Dad exclaims.

'Yes, I am afraid so,' Stefanos confirms. 'The hospital here is already full.'

The guy we've spoken to before comes over to give us the latest information; Stefanos translates. 'They are bringing Costas or Nikos out first. They will all have neck braces on as a precaution. Also, he says there is only room for two of us to go in the helicopter.'

Mum offers without a moment's hesitation. 'I'll go. My nursing skills may be useful.'

'Okay, that sounds like a good idea. Who else?'

Selena speaks up. 'Maybe I could go?'

Stefanos looks surprised. 'I thought you did not like helicopters?'

'No, but it is the least I can do. You can catch the ferry tomorrow and follow on. Then you will have your car.'

'Is that okay with everyone else?' Stefanos asks.

We all nod in agreement. I just want someone to be with Helen, and Mum is the best person out of us three. Nikos is Selena's fiancé, after all's said and done, and she obviously knows Costas as well.

The medical team are on their hands and knees, ready to crawl through the gap that's been cut in the roof. The first stretcher is pushed through.

The cutting noise has stopped so I shout out again to Helen. 'Helen? Mum and Dad are here! Can you hear me?'

'Yes, just about,' comes the muffled reply.

'Oh, thank goodness for that!' Mum sobs as Dad puts his arms around her. 'I'm here, sweetheart, with your dad. The medical team are coming to get you.'

'Yes, they're here now … putting a drip in my arm.'

'Has Costas or Nikos woken up yet?' Stefanos asks.

'Costas has been talking … to me on and off … and they're with Nikos now … he's responding. They're putting him on … a stretcher now.'

There's a huge sigh of relief from us all as we realise they're all alive. The next worry now is how injured they are.

A few minutes later, the medical team carefully push out Nikos. He's rigged up to a drip, covered in dust and there are a few bits of debris on him, along with some visible cuts. Selena and Stefanos rush over to him. She's crying. It looks like Nikos is conscious again; he's speaking as they take him over to the helicopter with Selena trying her best to keep up.

'What did he say?' I ask, wishing I could understand Greek.

'He say thank God someone came, he thought he was going to die. He hopes Costas and Helen are okay.' Stefanos looks pretty shaken up, and Mum and I burst into tears.

A second stretcher is now being pushed through the gap with some more equipment. We suspect that Costas will be next. Dad comforts Mum, and Stefanos comforts me.

'Everything will be fine, trust me,' he says.

'But we don't know that,' I answer in-between sobs.

'Stefanos is right, sweetheart, we have to be positive,' Mum says.

'Yes, I know, Mum, it's just such a shock. She shouldn't even be here. Sorry, Stefanos, I didn't mean that. Costas and Nikos don't deserve this either. It just seems so unfair – why did it have to be any of them?'

'Look, another stretcher is coming out.' Stefanos points to the opening.

The stretcher is finally pushed through, and we all rush over to see who it is. It's Helen. She's got a cut on her head and blood is trickling down her face. Like Nikos, she's covered in dust and debris.

I try my best to be brave but I'm fighting back tears. 'Helen, it's Steph, we're all here for you. Mum's going with you in a helicopter. She's always wanted to take a helicopter ride, haven't you, Mum?'

Mum chokes back her tears. 'I wasn't really thinking of a trip like this, though. I actually had somewhere like the Grand Canyon in mind. Anyway, plenty of time for that.'

Dad then says his little bit while fighting back tears. 'You're going to be all right, Helen. I know you're a tough cookie, and your mum will take care of you. Steph and I will see you in Athens.'

'She *is* going to be all right, isn't she?' I ask one of the medics, who is adjusting a drip.

He tries his best to reassure us. 'The main thing is that she has been awake. We take all the injured to the hospital in Athens, where they will be examined properly. I believe one of you will come with Helen? Come to the helicopter when you are ready.'

'Yes, it's me, I'll follow you now. Stephanie, I assume you're waiting here with Stefanos for his brother. Me and your dad will go with Helen now and see you at the helicopter before it leaves.'

'Okay, Mum. I don't think they'll be too long. See you in a few minutes.'

Helen looks awful and she's unconscious again. I just hope she can hear us, so she knows that she isn't alone. Mum and Dad follow the medics carrying her stretcher.

The rescue teams now get ready for the third stretcher, for Costas. As with Helen and Nikos, the team inside the rubble are on their hands and knees, coaxing the stretcher through the gap to the team outside.

It's finally pushed through and we see Costas. Like Helen and Nikos he's looking rather battered and bruised and covered in dust. Stefanos goes over to him, takes his hand and talks to him in-between his sobs. I can tell that he and Costas have a special bond, like I do with Helen. His big brother, my big sister.

We follow the medics carrying Costas to the helicopter. We're greeted by a hive of activity, as more seriously injured people arrive in army vehicles and local ambulances. The local hospital just can't cope with the demand so they're using the helicopter to its full capacity.

We follow Costas up the ramps at the back of the helicopter. It's huge; there are loads of casualties on board already. Mum is in a blue plastic apron and she's helping. She's even given Dad a job, to keep him occupied.

Costas is the last person they're taking on this flight. The officer in charge confirms that there are no other casualties in the building. They've been given clearance to leave in ten minutes.

I go over to Helen and take hold of her hand. Through my sobs, I tell her that I love her and that she must stay strong. I spot Selena with Nikos; she's stroking his forehead. Stefanos is with Costas and he has tears streaming down his face. Costas does seem to be responding to him, which is a good sign. The crew tell us we need to leave. The engines start up, making a deafening noise.

I give Mum a huge hug. Dad comes over to give her a hug too. 'You're so brave, Pam. I love you.'

'I love you too, Michael Collins. It's only Athens. We'll be there in half an hour and I'm sure you'll all catch me up by tomorrow. Now go, before they shut you in.' Typical Mum, putting a brave face on the situation.

We're ushered down the ramps and away from the helicopter. The helicopter blades rotate above us, making our hair blow in our faces. The doors shut, and seconds later the ground crew give the signal to take off. As the helicopter lifts into the air, we all look up and watch through our tears as it noisily disappears. I feel numb.

Over the noise, I can just about hear Stefanos saying, 'Come on, Stephanie, we need to get to Athens.'

Chapter 26

Helen

I've been in and out of consciousness since the earthquake. I'm in the hospital in Athens with Mum at my bedside. She's been running between Costas, Nikos and me, making sure we're all okay. Apparently, Selena is with Nikos; hopefully that means they've made up. Mum's told me that we've all escaped with minor cuts, bruises and concussion and that we've been really lucky.

When I woke up under the roof of the hotel, I was surrounded by complete darkness. I was terrified. I'd no idea how long I'd been unconscious. I knew where I was and I could feel an arm over my chest but I'd no idea if it was Costas or Nikos. I started shaking him and whimpering, 'Please wake up.' There was something stopping my legs from moving, and I didn't dare start struggling for fear that something else would collapse.

Costas finally stirred. It was his arm that was draped over my chest. 'Helen … are you … okay?' he asked, struggling for breath. The dust irritated his throat and made him cough.

'My legs … seem to be … trapped,' was all I managed to tell him.

'Mine too… You need … to stay awake.'

'I know … but it's so hard.'

Costas tried to wake Nikos by saying his name, but his voice was too weak. I think we both soon drifted off to sleep again.

I dreamt that I was in a massive whirlwind, trying to pull Costas towards me. I was screaming at the top of my voice for him to stay with me. Suddenly, the wind subsided and we dropped to the ground with a thud. Someone was shouting our names over and over again… I realised it wasn't a dream. I tried to respond but they couldn't hear me. Despite the effort I was putting in to speak, I was hardly making a sound.

The shouting woke Costas up. He whispered, 'You must stay awake, Helen… You must be strong… They have come to rescue us.'

The shouting also made Nikos stir. That was a huge relief, to hear him responding. Costas reassured him that help had arrived. Then we felt the ground shaking beneath us and heard a deep loud rumbling noise, which I could feel vibrating through my chest.

Costas whispered, 'Cover your heads. This is aftershock.'

We could hear glasses and bottles smashing as they fell off shelves. It was absolutely terrifying, but we seemed to be safe and cocooned under the roof. I drifted off again. Then I was woken by a dog barking and I could also hear someone shouting. I realised it was Stephanie; she was frantically shouting my name.

I put as much effort as I could into saying 'I'm here!'

Luckily, she heard my feeble reply. I was so glad she was there, but I felt too weak and tired to listen to her. I started drifting off again. I dreamt I was at the dentist. I could hear the sound of a drill. I spiralled down a dark tunnel, going faster and faster. Then I came to an abrupt halt. My dream was broken into by some people talking nearby. Their voices were getting closer.

I was so relieved when the medical team reached me. They started checking me out and put something in my arm. I was aware of a weight being lifted off my legs. Then I thought I could hear Mum, but I couldn't work out how. She was on a boat with Dad… I was really confused and the effort of thinking was too much.

My memory of the rescue is sketchy. I seemed to be in the helicopter one minute then at a hospital the next. I was being wheeled into the accident and emergency department. All I've wanted to do since is sleep.

'Helen, Helen, can you hear me?'

For goodness sake, of course I can hear you, I want to say, but I want to stay in my dream. I'm in a garden with Costas. It's so beautiful and there's so much vivid colour. I'm sure there are colours that I've never seen before. We're holding hands and talking. It's truly magical. We're about to kiss… Again, I hear my name.

'Helen, it's Steph. Are you going to wake up?'

Then I hear Mum. 'She's very sleepy, Stephanie. She's opened her eyes briefly a couple of times for me and that's been it.'

I fight my tiredness and mumble, 'I'm awake. I was dreaming that Costas was about to kiss me.'

'I knew it! She just needs a prince to kiss her and wake her up. Thank goodness you're okay, Helen. We've had a sleepless night worrying about you all. Anyway, I thought you and Costas didn't see eye to eye?'

'Um, maybe I was bit hasty… While we were trapped, he asked me … if I believed in love at first sight … and I need to tell him that I do.' That's all I manage to say before I drift off again, back to my dream about Costas.

Chapter 27

Stephanie

The hospital in Athens discharged Helen, Costas and Nikos after a couple of days. They were all extremely lucky to have been standing under the apex of the roof when the earthquake hit. Amazingly, there were no serious injuries or deaths from the earthquake. Its epicentre was out at sea, which may have helped dissipate its force.

Helen and I have taken up the offer of a room each at the Hotel Niko. This means Stefanos and I don't need to sneak about. Costas has also been recuperating here, which has given Helen the opportunity to get to know him a bit more. We've given our parents our room at the Boutique Blue. Mum's been enjoying Martin's water aerobics with Carol and Sandra, while Dad's been off golfing.

Today is our last full day here. There's going to be a party tonight here at the Hotel Niko for Nikolaos and Eliana's golden wedding anniversary. Nikolaos and Eliana have been sent off for the day to be pampered at the Boutique Blue and the rest of us are mucking in. Mum's been helping Xena in the kitchen with the food preparation. Giorgos has already delivered a wonderful cake that he's made for his parents. It's in the fridge, all covered up so we can't see it.

Costas and Helen are helping Stavros – or could that be hindering Stavros, judging by the number of times we've seen him shaking his head. Dad's helping Stefanos and me to blow up balloons, put up bunting and lights and set up the tables. The place is a hive of activity and everything seems to be falling into place. Dad's drifted off to the kitchen to see if he can help in there and Stefanos has gone to make us a well-deserved drink. It's thirsty work, especially in this heat.

I sit down and put my feet up in my favourite spot overlooking the beautiful bay to reflect on the last two extraordinary weeks. I didn't come to Mykonos to find love, but I definitely have found it. Stefanos and I hit it off immediately. My heart has been soaring from that very first minute. We just *get* each other. Our occasional language misunderstandings always end with us creased up with laughter.

I'm going home tomorrow, but Stefanos has made it clear that one way or another he wants us to stay together. The prospect of finding a job here is slim, though, especially as I don't yet speak Greek. I can't imagine Stefanos wanting to move from this idyllic place to the UK, but he has said he'll do whatever it takes for us to be together, even if that means being cold for the rest of his life. He says fate has brought us together and will lead us on a journey. His quick thinking and ability to stay calm last week will be something I'll always remember and be grateful for. I shudder to think what would have happened if we'd just assumed that someone would search the hotel without word from us.

Costas and Helen have also hit it off. She looks really happy today, like a weight has been lifted off her shoulders. They already look like a couple who have been married for years. They're so funny to watch, especially now, with Stavros trying to give them orders. It's clear they each want to do it their own way. They could be the Greek version of Basil, Sybil and Manuel from *Fawlty Towers*.

I confessed to Helen at the hospital – when she was able to stay awake for more than five minutes – about my text to James.

She laughed. 'Dumped by text? Hey, sign of the times. You answered it much better than I would have done.'

'Good, I'm glad you approve of my to-the-point answer.' I didn't bother filling her in on the rest of the story.

'Oh, definitely. I should have done it weeks ago. But you know what it's like – you hang on thinking something is better than nothing when it really isn't.'

'I know…'

Mum and Dad appeared then, leaving me to mull over my thoughts. I was beginning to think that even if Richard had agreed to have children, or had wanted them in the first place, it wouldn't have worked out between us. My time with Stefanos has made me realise that Richard and I were missing that special something.

Stefanos has reappeared with our drinks and my heart has just skipped a couple of beats. I'll never tire of that feeling.

'Sorry that took so long. Everyone wants a drink when I offer to make them.'

'You're just so good at it. Dare I ask what this one is called?'

'It is called Love in the Afternoon, and I think we should go back to our room and enjoy the drinks before a little siesta.'

I can see from the look on his face that he's got no intention of having a siesta. 'Oh, really Stefanos Christopoulos? And may I ask what you're drinking?'

'Bury Me Deep, Stephanie Valentine,' he whispers in my ear, making me shudder. 'A drink made exclusively with you in mind. Now, hurry up before anyone assigns us another job.'

We get up and scamper across the courtyard, giggling like a couple of teenagers without a care in the world.

Chapter 28

Helen

I went back to the Mykonos Gold yesterday. Thankfully, things had improved enough for it to retain its gold status, on the understanding that an action plan will be followed and reported on for the next two months. Michalis seemed a bit more receptive to my visit this time. I assume the realisation of things not meeting our company standard and him potentially losing his job played a major part.

I've also been back to the Hotel Giorgos with Mum and Steph to decorate a soap dish each. They didn't look too bad in the end. Of course Steph took great delight in asking me to regale my pottery throwing disaster and my subsequent accidental engagement with Nikos. There was still a bit of clay stuck on the glass partition which amused Steph even more. We also had a go at some soap making here at the Hotel Niko which involved making our own perfumes to go in them. We got rather carried away so everyone is going to have soap for Christmas and birthdays for the next year.

Costas and I had a romantic meal in town last night and then he took me to watch a film at the outdoor cinema at the Royal Blue Hotel. Selena arranged it. She seems to have had some sort of personality transplant. She was very helpful; she made sure two nice seats were saved for us and sent along a complimentary bottle of Prosecco. After the film, we found a quiet terrace and relaxed on a sofa looking at the stars and listening to the sea lapping on the shore.

Beneath Costas's serious, chiselled looks, there's a caring, deep-thinking man whom I'm rapidly falling for. When we were trapped under the roof, his main concern was for me and Nikos. I keep replaying the moment when Costas and Nikos ran towards me and pushed me to the ground as the earthquake struck. Just the thought makes me shudder.

We talked into the early hours about our past lives. We both share a fear of getting close to someone and losing them. My fear comes from losing my best friend to cancer and Costas's comes from his wife having had an affair.

'What if I come and live in Mykonos or Syros?' Before I know it, the thoughts that had been whirring round in my head have come out as a question.

'What about your job?' Costas asks sounding understandably surprised.

'Daniel owes me big time, and I've got an idea that he might just like anyway.'

'Well, Helen, you will make me a very happy man. I was dreading the thought of you going home and trying to have a long-distance relationship.'

'Me too. It's time for me to do something different. I've been throwing myself into work and now it's time to live a little. What better place to do that than on a Greek island with a gorgeous guy who cares about me?'

'Even one who goes out of his way to argue about suitable job candidates?'

'Oh yes, who was your favourite candidate after all that? I assume it was Nikos?'

'No, actually. After I got over the disappointment that you were not a candidate, the best person for the job was Alexandra.' My mouth drops open. Costas continues, 'I am going to recommend her for the job.'

I'm baffled. 'But I thought you two were arch-enemies. How on earth are you going to work with each other?'

'Helen, I was wrong about Alexandra. I know now that she was telling the truth. And anyway, I am going to resign from the Syros Boutique Blue.'

'Resign?' My eyes widen. 'And what are you going to do?'

'Do not worry. I have something in my sleeve.'

'I think you mean you have something *up* your sleeve.'

'Okay, you win! I will find out in the next few days about my idea.'

'Wow, it all sounds very exciting.'

'It *is* very exciting. Whatever I do, it will not be in Syros. It was foolish of me to go there and think that a new place would solve my problems. My problem was in my head and, in any case, I have now come to terms with my marriage break-up. So, I propose a toast.' Costas empties the remainder of the Prosecco into our glasses. 'To us!'

'To us,' I echo, as we chink our glasses together. I think my life might finally have turned round.

* * *

The party is in full swing and everyone is having a brilliant time. The weather is perfect. It's been warmer the last couple of nights. Nikolaos and Eliana are in their element with all their family and friends around them. There's no shortage of entertainment. Nikos, Costas and Stefanos have been playing some cute guitar-style instruments. Stephanie has informed me they're called *bouzouki*. We've had some Greek dancing, which was accompanied by our *bouzouki* players. And I'll be leaving Mykonos having not only seen an unofficial plate-smashing between Nikos and Selena, but also the official one that will happen later on.

It all seems to have fallen into place this week. Mum and Dad get on really well with Xena and Stavros. Selena is really making an effort with Nikos; her engagement ring is back on her finger. The last thing I wanted was to come between her and Nikos. And the James thing all seems surreal now. I feel like someone's clicked their fingers and snapped me out of some ridiculous spell. Maybe Nikos and Costas knocked some sense into me when I hit the ground.

'Hey, sis, you okay? You look lost in thought,' says Steph. She's come to stand beside me.

'I'm fine. I was just thinking how happy everyone looks. Who'd have thought we'd end our holiday like this? Actually, I'm glad that you're on your own. I'm nearly fit to burst with some news.'

'You're pregnant!'

'No, Stephanie, I don't think so!'

'What then?'

'I wanted to tell Mum, Dad and you together, but my news might affect you so I think I should tell you first.'

'Go on, then. It sounds intriguing.'

'Daniel has given me the go-ahead to do villa rentals here in Mykonos.'

'No way! That's brilliant, Helen! I'm so pleased for you. I'm assuming you have an ulterior motive concerning a certain Greek fella... But how does this affect me? Apart from the fact that you won't be in the UK any more.'

'Well, Steph, I was wondering if you'd like to be my very capable personal assistant?'

'Oh, Helen! I don't know what to say.'

'I was rather hoping that you'd say yes.'

'Of course I'm going to say yes! You've just made my dream come to life. I love you, sis.'

'And I love you. I'm sure Mum and Dad will give us their blessing.'

'Yes, and I'm sure these two will be over the moon.' Costas and Stefanos have finished their *bouzouki*-playing and have sauntered over.

'If I did not know any better, Stefanos, I would say these two are up to something,' says Costas.

'Yes, I think you are right. They have a look of mischief. Come on, tell us. What have you done?'

'*We've* not done anything, but Helen's got some really exciting news that affects us all.'

Costas and Stefanos look at me. In unison, they cry, 'You are pregnant!'

'No, for the love of God! Do I look pregnant or something? On second thoughts, don't answer that. Actually, I've been given the go-ahead from Daniel to start villa rentals here in Mykonos.'

'Congratulations, Helen, I am sure you will make it work, and I know you have just made my brother very happy,' Stefanos says, shaking my hand.

'You have indeed! Congratulations, Helen Collins, you are amazing. Come here.' Costas puts his arms round me and kisses my lips gently. He whispers, 'I am the happiest man alive.'

'Helen, please control him!' Stephanie protests, pretending to look embarrassed.

'You're only jealous,' I reply, laughing.

'I would have been a couple of weeks ago, but now I've hit the jackpot too. Anyway, I've got some news as well.'

Costas and Stefanos look at Stephanie in the same way they looked at me. 'You are pregnant!' they exclaim simultaneously.

'Er, no. Actually, I've also got a new job.' She looks very pleased with herself. 'I'm going to be Helen's personal assistant here in Mykonos.'

'That is great news, Stephanie! I guess this means Stefanos will not be playing out the Costas scene from *Shirley Valentine* after all.'

'Ha ha, big brother, you are not funny. Congratulations, Stephanie Valentine!'

Stefanos puts his arms round Stephanie and whispers something in her ear, which has her in fits of giggles. I love the way they are together, and it's brilliant to hear her laughing again.

Mum and Dad are making a beeline towards us. 'There's a lot of frivolity over here!'

'Hi Mum, hi Dad. We were just about to come over and tell you our news.'

Mum's eyes light up and she glances over to Dad, who gives her a don't-say-a-word-Pamela look.

Steph and I put her out of her misery as fast as we can with our 'No, Mum!'

Costas and Stefanos are grinning from ear to ear. Costas says, 'I think we had better help Papa in the bar, Stefanos, and leave our guests to chat. We will catch up with you all later.'

'So, go on, what's your news?' Mum asks when they've gone.

'I've been given the go-ahead from Daniel to set up Loving Luxury Travel villa rentals here on Mykonos.'

'Well done, Helen,' Dad says, putting his arms round me. 'We're really pleased for you, aren't we, Pam?'

Mum's a bit hesitant. 'Of course we are. It's just a bit unexpected… And, well, it's not exactly round the corner from us.'

'And there's something else,' Stephanie prompts me.

'Oh yes. My personal assistant is going to be Steph.'

'Oh my God! Both of you here!' That's it for poor Mum. She starts crying.

'Now, come on, Pamela, you've just been telling Xena and Stavros how lucky they are living here. This will give us the perfect excuse to come to this wonderful island as much as possible. We've been discussing having a holiday home somewhere in the sun for the past five years. This might just be the incentive we need to put our words into actions.' Good old Dad, he can always turn a negative into a positive.

'I suppose you're right,' Mum agrees, dabbing her eyes. 'It was just the shock of you both moving here at the same time.'

'Well, I'll be back here in a couple of weeks to look for some premises and get the ball rolling with various things. I'll also need to find somewhere to live, and learn some Greek. I'm sure Costas will help me with everything. I expect Steph will need to go home and work her notice.'

'Yes, work will be shocked when I hand in my notice. And I'll have to discuss selling the house and divorce proceedings with Richard.'

'Or you could discuss it now,' says Dad unexpectedly.

'I don't think we'd achieve much on the phone.'

'I'm not talking about the phone, Steph. Richard's just walked in. He's stood at the bar talking to Stefanos.'

Chapter 29

Stephanie

'Richard, what on earth are you doing here?'

'That's a nice way to welcome your husband who's just island-hopped to see you.'

'Let's get this right. You are my *estranged* husband. So why are you here? I'm coming home tomorrow. What couldn't wait until then?'

'I just needed to see you. I'll be away for work when you get back. And you never rang me back even after I'd sent you those flowers.'

'What flowers?' Stefanos chimes in.

This clearly ruffles Richard's feathers, which makes me giggle to myself. 'Is there somewhere a bit more private where we can talk?' Richard asks, raising his voice above the noise of the music.

'There is the office,' Stefanos suggests. He looks a bit worried.

'Are you sure?' I ask as I'm not particularly wanting to go anywhere with Richard.

'Of course I am sure. Follow me.' Stefanos unlocks the office door and gestures for Richard to go through. He whispers in my ear, 'Will you be okay?'

'I suppose so. I guess we need to talk.'

'I will be just out here if you need anything.'

'Thanks, Stefanos.' He shuts the door on his way out. 'So, what do you want to talk about? And why now, after all these months?'

'Look, Steph, I miss you. I've been stupid. I don't know why I'm so against having kids but if it's what you want, then I'm willing to give it a try.'

This immediately infuriates me. 'What, give it try and if you don't like it, you'll leave me with the baby? Or we give it to someone else? It's not like having a bloody dog, for Christ's sake. Oops, sorry! We've bitten off more than we can chew. Oh, I know, let's take it to the baby refuge! It's got to be something you really want, Richard, or else it's never going to work.'

'At least I'm making an effort.' He sounds agitated because I haven't thrown myself into his arms. He probably wants me to thank him for sending the flowers. Well, it's not happening.

'Oh? And haven't I made an effort over the last six months? I'm sorry, Richard, but even if you really wanted to start a family, I'm afraid my life's moved on.'

'What do you mean?'

'I've learned to see my life from a different prospective. I know things change after the first few months of a relationship, when all the excitement dies down, but I can see now that we were never quite in sync with one another.'

'Oh, come on, Steph, it would be boring if we were too alike. Please, at least think about it. We had our good times, and every relationship has its ups and downs.'

'If we'd had this conversation three weeks ago, Richard, I might have changed my mind. But I've got an opportunity to start a new life here and I'm going to take it.'

'Oh, please don't tell me you're going to shack up with that waiter like in that film … er, what was it called?'

'*Shirley Valentine*,' I answer.

'Yes, that one where she goes to some Greek island.'

'Ironically, Richard, it was Mykonos, and her husband even turned up to take her home. Actually, if you must know, I'm going to "shack up", as you so nicely put it, with my sister.'

'What, and wait on in some restaurant, with no prospects? What about your *career* with Debenhams?' Richard's never thought much of my career prospects at Debenhams, either.

'One thing I've learnt in the past two weeks, Richard, is that life is a privilege. We only get one chance. The things that are important are having enough money to put food on the table and pay the bills and, above all, to be happy. All the rest is stuff that we think we need. And for your information, I'm going to be working for Helen's new villa rental business.'

'I've heard it all now!' He laughs and shakes his head. 'You don't know the first thing about the travel industry, or about villas, and you don't even speak bloody Greek. How the hell are you two going to pull that off?'

'We'll manage, Richard. We've got contacts here and, yes, of course, we'll have to learn some Greek. Helen's boss has obviously got enough faith in her to get this venture off the ground, and so have I. She's brilliant at what she does. I can learn as I go along.'

'And what's with the Greek fella?'

'What Greek fella?'

'That guy who just let us in here. He looked worried when he realised who I was.'

'That was Stefanos.' I'm not going to play any games with Richard. He can make his own deductions. I'm not bothered any more about what he thinks.

'Oh yes, *Stefanos*. Someone mentioned a Facebook post showing you and *Stefanos* looking all cosy. It all makes sense now. I knew you wouldn't be staying here just for a lousy job with your sister.'

'Right, Richard, enough! I've made my decision and that's the end of it. I'll be back in the UK tomorrow and I'll be getting the ball rolling for a divorce straight away.'

'Right, well, whatever. And while you're at it, you'll need to clear the wardrobe in the spare room because I'm moving back in,' he replies smugly.

'You're what?'

'You heard me. When I get back from my work trip, I'm moving back in.'

'You can't do that. What about your mate's flat?'

'He's renting a different flat on the other side of town with his new girlfriend.'

'Oh, so now we're getting to the real reason you're here! You'll have to buy me out or the house will be on the market by the time you get back.'

'You know I can't buy you out. Do whatever you need to do. I'll see you in a week.'

'Fan-bloody-tastic! I can hardly wait.'

'Look on the bright side, Steph. Once you've worked your notice, you can come running back here to lover boy.'

'Bye, Richard! It's been such a pleasure ... not.'

'The feeling's mutual, Steph. Don't forget to clear that wardrobe.'

'Oh, sod off.'

'Don't worry, I'm going.'

He saunters out of the office without a care in the world and I break down sobbing. What an idiot! And to think I wanted to start a family with him!

A faint tap sounds on the door, and then Stefanos comes in. He immediately puts his arms round me. 'Are you all right?'

'Not really. Richard's ulterior motive was to try and patch it up between us because he's moving back into our house next week.'

'But you are still going ahead with your plan to come here?' Stefanos asks, wiping away my tears.

'Of course I am, but I'm going to struggle until the house is sold. Richard isn't going to be in a rush if I'm over here.'

'Listen, Stephanie, I am sure we can sort something out. One of the perks of having parents who own a hotel are rooms – and lots of them. Or there's even my room,' he says, winking. 'So, do not let this spoil your last night here as a tourist. Come and join the party. Martin and Alexis have arrived, which will really get the party started, and Nikolaos and Eliana are getting ready to cut their cake.'

'Okay. Has my make-up smudged?'

'Not enough for anyone else to notice. You look beautiful.'

Stefanos leads me out of the office and over to where Mum, Dad, Helen, Costas, Nikos and Selena are chatting to Martin and Alexis.

'Hi guys, you're not too late, then, after your classes?'

'No, we let them go five minutes early,' Martin laughs.

'And made them work twice as hard,' Alexis adds.

'Stephanie, are you all right?' Mum asks, sounding concerned.

'I'm fine. I'll fill you in later.' I don't want to tell her now and risk bursting into tears again.

Nikolaos and Eliana have made their way on to a little stage and are waiting for the chatter to settle down.

Helen whispers, 'Are you okay, sis?'

'I'll be okay. I'm sure it will all work itself out. There's no way back for Richard and me.'

Nikolaos clears his throat and begins to speak, in Greek, of course. My mind drifts; I try and imagine how our lives will be in fifty years' time. I suppose it's right what they say: you're better off not knowing. I didn't stand at the altar on my wedding day thinking I'd be filing for divorce six years later. I've no idea if it will all work out for Stefanos and myself, but I'm willing to take a chance. I feel at home here and it feels so right when I'm with him.

The sound of everyone laughing bursts my thought bubble. Stefanos whispers in my ear, 'I will tell you later what he has just said. It was a funny story about Grandmama's cooking skills when they first got married.'

Nikolaos has finished talking and Eliana is waving her finger at him humorously. Everyone is clapping. Giorgos and Xena have now joined them on the stage with the cake. It's still covered up. Giorgos is saying a few words. He's standing next to Nikolaos and I notice that there's a striking resemblance between father and son. Xena, too, looks very much like Eliana. Despite the Mediterranean sun, Eliana has retained her youthful looks; Xena is the same. I think Costas and Stefanos take after Stavros, with their strong dark Greek features. Stavros is busy pouring something fizzy into everyone's glasses for, I assume, a toast.

Costas whispers to our non-Greek group, 'This is a toast to Eliana and Nikolaos. Get ready to raise your glasses.'

We all hold up our glasses and duly toast to Eliana and Nikolaos.

Giorgos taps his glass with the cake knife and everyone goes quiet again. 'I would like to say a few words in English. We would all like to welcome Helen, Stephanie, Pamela and Michael to the party. We hope you have enjoyed your time on Mykonos. I will not dwell on what happened in Syros; thankfully, you all returned safely. We would also like to thank Helen for putting the Hotel Niko and the Hotel Giorgos forward for her company, and would like you all to know that they have both been recommended to be included in Loving Luxury Travel's family-hotels list from next May.'

Everyone claps. Helen looks relieved and happy.

'I will now hand you back to my father, who would like to say a few more words.'

'As you all know, Eliana and I have been married for fifty years. I met her here, when it was her mother and father's hotel, and we have worked together ever since. We have been thinking about this for a long time and have decided that now would be a good time to retire.'

There are gasps round the terrace, and lots of people are looking surprised. It looks like the only people who knew are

Xena, Stavros, Giorgos and Katina, and possibly Costas. He gives Helen a knowing look.

'Well, I never thought I would hear those words from Grandpapa,' Stefanos says, looking shocked.

'Or me,' Nikos agrees. 'But they are in their seventies, and they deserve some quality retirement time.'

'So now we can cut our cake that has been such a big secret,' Nikolaos says.

Xena and Giorgos carefully remove the cover that has been hiding it all day. And now we can see why. It's *two* amazing cakes. One for their golden wedding anniversary and one for their retirement. Everyone moves forward to admire the cakes and take some photos before Eliana and Nikolaos cut into them.

'And now we request that all guests join us in the Greek *zorba*!' Nikolaos shouts.

There's a huge round of applause and everyone gathers together as instructed. We place our arms on each others' shoulders. I have Stefanos on one side and Helen on the other. The music begins. Slowly, to begin with, and then we start picking up the pace. Our private lesson earlier with Stefanos and Costas is paying off because we actually know what to do. Everyone is happy and laughing. Martin and Alexis are trying their best to show off their twerking skills, and Nikolaos and Eliana are showing no signs of giving up as we go faster and faster, round and round the terrace. It seems to go on forever and then it suddenly finishes, leaving us all breathless.

We all cheer as slower music starts to play. We reach out to hold our respective loved ones in our arms. All of us are happy, under a Greek spell.

Epilogue

Pamela

It's hard to believe that it was my surprise sixtieth birthday party twelve months ago. I'm celebrating my birthday this year here in Mykonos, with Michael, Helen, Costas, Stephanie and Stefanos at the Hotel Niko. Xena, Stavros, Nikolaos, Eliana, Giorgos, Katina, Nikos and Selena are here too.

I couldn't have wished for better partners for Helen and Stephanie. I've never seen them looking happier. Costas and Stefanos are very caring, and they always put Helen and Stephanie first.

It was a bit stressful getting them moved over here, but they're here now and are building up a successful villa rental portfolio for Loving Luxury Travel. Their first clients will be arriving in the next few days for the start of the holiday season.

Michael and I were going to buy a villa ourselves, but that plan went awry. To help Stephanie, we gave her the money to buy out Richard. The house is on the market now and hopefully a sale is imminent. Helen has assured us that she'll always be able to find us a villa or hotel room on the island, so our villa idea has been put to one side for now.

Xena, Stavros, Costas and Stefanos have been busy getting the hotel ready for its first season with Loving Luxury Travel. Helen and Stephanie have been helping by giving the hotel some subtle modern touches. They've framed some of the photos that Stephanie took last year and used them as their theme. There's a beautiful canvas in the dining room, of the windmills. Steph's photography skills have come into their own. She has done all the photography for the villa rentals website and brochures.

Nikolaos and Eliana have been enjoying their retirement and have been to see us in the UK. They are busy here, too, with the soap workshop and the little pottery workshop at the Hotel Giorgos.

I'm having a go at making some pottery tomorrow with Helen and Steph. Eliana will be showing us what to do. I've always fancied having a go, especially after watching that film *Ghost*. After what happened to Helen, Costas and Nikos during the earthquake, we all realised that life can take unexpected turns and that we should make the most of the opportunities that come our way. Our new family saying is *carpe diem* – seize the day.

* * *

Ooh, the lights have been dimmed and Helen and Steph are stood at the door with a cake alight with candles.

'Hush, everyone! After three!' Helen shouts. 'One, two, three! Happy birthday to you, happy birthday to you, happy birthday, dear Pamela … Pam … Mum … Happy birthday to you!'

Steph and Helen are saying, 'Make a wish, Mum.' I take a deep breath in, close my eyes, blow out the candles and make my wish.

The little voice in my head tries to stop me, but it's too late. My wish has been made…

References

Healthy Magazine Issue No. 102 May/June 2013
Pages 26, 29, 179, 180, 181

Vanzant I (1997) In the Meantime. Simon and Schuster UK Ltd
Pages 49, 94, 97, 98, 126

Delos, Pages 193, 194, 195, ancient-greece.org

Thank you

Thank you to all my friends and family who have waited so patiently for the arrival of this novel. At times it's felt like the day would never arrive but with all your encouragement I've persevered and if you're reading this you've got my first novel in your hands.

Thank you Troubador and all the team who've helped me self publish my first novel. And to Chelsea Taylor for designing the cover.

Thank you to Dea Parkin and the team at Fiction Feedback who critiqued and edited the book.

Thank you to my parents Liz and Keith Cox for your support and love.

Thank you and much love to my husband Chris Pottage for listening to endless stories about my novel and writing in general and for the technical support when the computer is having a bad day. Thank you also to Lizzie and Sam for taking an interest in my novel.

Thank you Jen Cox, Sandra Hulme and Bridget Maddison for reading the early drafts and giving me the encouragement to carry on. Special thanks to Sandra for introducing me to punctuation!

Thank you to Carol Hibbs for going on holiday to Mykonos with me. Although I'd written a lot of the book before we went, actually visiting Mykonos enabled me to put some personal touches into the book.

Thank you to my Creative Writing Group especially Margaret Holbrook and Mark Henderson for your encouragement and advice.

Thank you to Anna Wickham, Debbie Rathbone, Sharon Wood and Jen Cox who I've consulted with on numerous occasions about various book conundrums.

Thank you to the 'Ladies who Lunch' who are the amazing colleagues that I worked alongside for almost 30 years, especially Helen Heery for holding the vision of a book signing.

Thank you Joanne Hibbert, Pippa McCartney and Dawn Hänsch for looking out for events and articles of interest in the literary world.

Thank you Martin Jensen for being the fabulous Aqua Aerobics instructor in my novel.

Thank you to Michaela from the lovely Itsy Bitsy shop in Chapel-en-le-Frith and the inspiration for Michaela's Boutique.

Thank you to Spiros and Karen from Kouros cafe in Chapel-en-le-Frith for checking my Greek phrases and spelling.

I'd like to mention my dear friend Jill Leyden who sadly passed away in 2015. I met Jill regularly for lunch and she gave me lots of encouragement to keep going with the book. She gave me a card with a little Greek boat on the front that hangs in my office as inspiration.

Thank you to the reader – I hope you enjoy it.

Afterword

I've always wanted to write a book. I loved writing short stories at school and I did attempt to write a book in the late 1990's but I ran out of steam. When I worked at the TSB I really enjoyed writing poems for my colleagues who were celebrating birthdays, getting married etc.

In January 2013 my husband Martin was diagnosed with cancer. After his chemotherapy treatment we went on a holiday to Paphos. It was during this holiday that I had some ideas for a book floating about in my head. With inspirations drawn from people watching especially the porter Nick, I was determined to commit to writing something and I downloaded Scrivener as soon as I got home and started writing.

During the early draft of the book I was picturing the hotel and surrounding area where Martin and I had stayed in Cyprus. As my character Stephanie was taking shape she decided to throw me a curved ball and the novel screeched to a halt. I was suddenly plunged in to my first rewrite with hundreds of words being deleted. That was my first harsh lesson in writing a book – using the delete button. It was also when the title *Under a Greek Spell* emerged as the story switched to Mykonos.

Unfortunately Martin's health deteriorated in late October and he sadly passed away in November 2013. My writing pretty much came to a standstill for nine months.

The story was revived by a girly holiday to Mykonos with my friend Carol. Although we couldn't afford to stop in a luxurious hotel where Stephanie and Helen would have stayed, we made sure we visited a couple of five star hotels for the purposes of research and sampled some cocktails. Visiting Mykonos also gave me the opportunity to wander around the town and soak up the ambience. I hope that my experiences in Mykonos come through in the book, although we never visited the beach club!

The whole process has been a rather steep learning curve (more a vertical line!). I have treated it as a hobby which has opened up many new doors and I hope any would be writers will be encouraged to give it a go.